MW01124985

***Discla***

***fiction.*** *Names, characters,*
*businesses, places, events and*
*incidents are either the products of*
*the author's imagination or used in*
*a fictitious manner. Any*
*resemblance to actual persons,*
*living or dead, or actual events is*
*purely coincidental.*

# Table of Contents

# Book 1 – Donuts, Delights & Murder

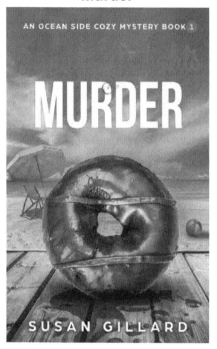

## Chapter 1

"Welcome to paradise," Ryan said, smiling at his wife.

"I'm not so sure about paradise yet," Heather said. "Once all our boxes are unpacked, and this new house starts to feel like a home, and once the chaos from opening a new shop abates, and when I can find time to relax a little on one of the beaches here, then I think it might become a paradise."

"Anywhere I am with you is paradise," he countered.

Heather answered with a kiss. Though there were still many things to do, the move already seemed to be agreeing with the Shepherd family. They had recently relocated from Hillside, Texas to Key West, Florida where Heather was going to open up a second Donut Delights.

She was certainly going to miss Hillside. It was the place where she had opened her first store, met the love of her life, adopted the daughter that made their family complete, and where she had caught her fair share of murderers with her sleuthing skills.

However, Key West was going to offer its own set of challenges and adventures, and she was eager to face them. As their flight had brought them closer to their new home and Heather saw the clear waters and sunny beaches, she couldn't help but become excited (and hoped that she packed sunscreen.) The move had finally felt real.

As she saw the boxes from their move scattered throughout their new house, the reality set in even more. This was their new home.

As they had traveled to the house, she had enjoyed seeing all the pastel-colored Conch style houses that were so different from her Texas neighborhood. Her house was directly on the beach, but no house on the island was really too far away from the sandy shore. The reason that she had chosen this house instead of one of the beachfront properties was also for the happiest of reasons. They had moved into a three-family house because their best friends had decided to follow them to Key West.

"Tell me again why we're on the top floor," Amy asked as she joined them. She huffed and puffed jokingly to show her aversion to her new stairs.

Heather laughed at her bestie's antics while Amy's boyfriend Jamie joined in by pretending to wipe the sweat from his brow.

"You graciously agreed to the top floor so that my pets wouldn't have to race down a flight of stairs whenever they have to take care of business, and so that our senior friends wouldn't have to make the climb daily," Heather said.

"That does ring a bell," Amy said. "I am such a nice person."

Jamie was about to agree, and Heather was about to tease when they were both cut off by a new voice.

"Heather is nice too for referring to us as her senior friends and not as old farts," Leila said.

"We are ladies," Eva said with a twinkle in her eye. "And farts would never be associated with us. Never."

Heather couldn't help but smile. Eva and Leila were good friends of hers that felt like second-grandmothers to her family. They had made the move to Key West for some new tropical scenery, to stay by their friends, and to follow their favorite donut maker's recipes.
Eva and Leila were in the adjoining apartment to them, while Amy and Jamie were living above them all. They had already all made the joke that Amy and Jamie better not take up tap dancing, and the couple had responded that they were instead joining the cast of *"Stomp."*

Heather was so happy that they were all together. She just needed one more person to complete the party, and it sounded like she was on her way to the room. Her daughter Lilly joined them with their two pets that she had been leading around the new backyard area. Dave, the dog, was Heather's loyal companion and was a huge fan of her donuts as was evident by his canine waistline. The kitten, Cupcake, followed Dave's lead and basically thought she was a dog herself.

"I think they've sniffed every inch of the new yard," Lilly reported. "And claimed a good deal of it as their own too."

They all laughed. Dave's tail started wagging. Whenever this group got together, there were usually donuts soon to follow. Heather started petting her dog to tide his affections over until she could do some baking.

"How does everyone like the new house?" Heather asked.

"Besides the stairs?" Amy asked. Then she smiled, "I like the location a lot."

"Our faucet does need a little work," Jamie added. "It's stiff and only gives out cold water."
"That's funny," said Eva. "Right now, ours only gives out hot water."
"I'm sure these can all be fixed easily," Ryan said.

As if on cue, right after he said that, a wall lamp fell from its mooring to the ground. They all jumped.

"Paradise," Heather muttered.

Before they had a chance to clean up the mess, there was a knock at the door. Heather hadn't realized that the morning had slipped away from them so quickly but gladly opened the door to admit Rudolph Rodney.

"Hello, all," he said, with a tip of his hat. The hat paused as he saw the lamp on the floor. "Oh, dear. I was told this building was up to code when I bought it, but I never did a personal inspection of it myself. Is there anything else wrong?"

They mentioned the other issues with the house and Rudolph Rodney said glumly, "I had wanted this place to be a perk for agreeing to open up the new shop with me."

"It's all right," Ryan said. "I bet I can do a lot of these improvements myself."

"You want to be the handyman?" Heather asked.

He shrugged. "I'll need some projects on my vacation until I take up my new detective duties. And I was planning on installing a security system anyway. I know we're away from the dangers we faced in Hillside."

"We did make a lot of people unhappy when we proved they were killers and sent them to jail," Amy said happily.

"But it's better to be safe than sorry," Ryan said.

Heather nodded. She had gotten used to having a security system and was in no hurry to be poisoned or have a gun pointed at her in her own home.

"If you'd like to take on the home repairs, by all means, do," Rudolph Rodney said. "And I can reimburse you."

Ryan nodded. "How hard can it be?"

Heather felt that those were famous last words, but decided to let things run their course. She had something else that she wanted to discuss with Rudolph Rodney.

"So," she said, changing the subject. "Is it ready?"

"It's almost there. That's what I was coming to tell you," Rudolph Rodney said. "Do you want to see it?"

Heather nodded excitedly. She was out the door before Rudolph Rodney could respond.

## Chapter 2

"This kitchen is even bigger than my last one," Heather said, admiring the baking set up in her new shop.

"I know that you're going to have online orders to fill as well as donuts to sell in the shop," said Rudolph Rodney. "I wanted to make sure that you had ample space."

"Think of how many donuts she can make for us here," Eva whispered to her friend. Leila licked her lips at the thought of it.

Heather looked around the room. All of her friends, and now next-door/upstairs neighbors, fit comfortably in the kitchen. The appliances were all new and shiny. She felt a ripple of excitement pass through her and couldn't wait to get cooking. Well, maybe she could wait until after she saw the rest of the shop.
"This kitchen is perfect," Heather assured him.

"Yeah, no lamps falling off the wall here," said Amy.

Heather elbowed her friend, and then said, "Can we see the front now?"

"The fact that you had us come in through the back door," Amy said. "Makes me think the front is either so amazing that's it's going to knock our socks off, or you're trying to hide it from us."

Heather did admire that Amy was using her deduction skills. After all, they were private investigator partners. However, Heather just wanted to see it for herself.
"I'm afraid it's the latter to an extent," said Rudolph Rodney. "The kitchen is all finished, and permits are all set up. However, the front of the shop it still being finished."
He led the way to the front of the shop. There were still some projects that needed to be finished. The floorboards were in the process of being replaced. However, it was close to being

complete. Heather admired the large display case for the donuts.

"It's going to be a little more beach themed than your last shop," Rudolph Rodney said.

"I understand," said Heather. "Even if we tried to make it identical to my original shop, it would never be exactly the same. I think it's better to let this shop be its own version. Customers will probably expect a beachy theme here too."

"We're going to finish putting the beach-wood floorboards in and keep light colors on the walls. The tables will be coming in as soon as the floor is done. They'll be reminiscent of driftwood too."
Heather nodded. It was certainly different than her Hillside shop with its golden floorboards and glass top wrought iron tables. It felt strange that it would be "Donut Delights" and yet be so different.

"However," Rudolph continued. "We do have some touches to tie it back to the original. I know you have some photos that you want to hang."

Heather nodded. "I have a picture of my whole Hillside staff in front of the shop, and I have a picture of a detective donut that they created for me to look like a magnifying glass."

"We can hang them up here," Rudolph Rodney. "And I have something else for you too. If one of the gentlemen could help me?"

He walked around the counter, followed by Ryan and Jamie.

"This is so exciting, Mom," Lilly said.

Then, with a little help, Rudolph unveiled his gift for Heather and the shop. It was a bronze cash register with a clunky handle.

"It's just like my old one," Heather beamed.

"I thought you'd like it," he said. "It's my equivalent of a housewarming gift."

"A shop-warming gift," Amy offered.

"Thank you," Heather said. "I can't tell you how excited I am to open shop."

"Well, I'll leave you to get settled," Rudolph Rodney said. He shook their hands and departed.

"I think I'd like to get settled on the beach," Ryan said. "Maybe we should take a beach break."
"Not so fast," said Heather. "I need everyone's help in the kitchen today."

"But you're not open yet," said Jamie.

"That doesn't mean I can abandon my new flavor of the week," Heather said. "Hillside is counting on the new recipe, and since I need to test it out anyway, I thought we could hand out some free samples today."

"That's a smart idea," said Eva. "You'll get everyone excited about the opening."

"And get them hooked on your donuts like we are," said Leila.

"I suppose we can postpone going to the beach if it means sampling donuts," said Ryan. "The beach will always be there."

"And the donuts might all be gone if you leave me alone with them," Amy joked. "What flavor is it this week?" asked Eva.

"Something just a touch decadent," said Heather with a smile. "A Chocolate Hazelnut Donut."

"I bet I'm going to be nuts about it," joked Leila.

"I love chocolate donuts," Lilly said. "Though I guess I do love them all."

"This one has a chocolate cake base and is filled with a chocolate hazelnut spread inside," said Heather. "Then there's some chocolate frosting on top, and it's sprinkled with chopped hazelnuts."

"It sounds so delicious, I can't wait to eat them," said Eva.

"There is just one problem with that," said Heather. "We need to bake them first!"
They laughed and headed to test out the new kitchen.

## Chapter 3

Duval Street was full of shops and restaurants, and Heather was proud to be joining them. It was a busy street full of both tourists and residents. What they saw was a popular place for shopping and dining during the day, and they were told it turned into a party at nighttime. Her shop was next to a seafood restaurant and was close to a bookshop, novelty store, and bathing suit boutique.

After handing out free samples to grateful passersby (and enjoying some Chocolate Hazelnut Donuts of their own), Heather and her friends were in high spirits.

"Everyone seemed to enjoy them," Heather smiled.

"How could they not?" Eva asked.

"Yeah. They're delicious," said Amy. "And who doesn't like free dessert?"

"But Heather's donuts are priceless," Leila declared.

"And they're gone," Ryan said. "I think we gave out everything we baked."

"Almost," Heather agreed. "I have one more batch in the kitchen."

"Are they for us?" Eva asked with a mischievous smile.

"If we bring them home, I'm sure Dave and Cupcake would enjoy them," said Lilly.

"They'll have to fight us for them," said Leila. "And we'd fight like cats and dogs."

"Actually," Heather said. "I thought I'd hand them out to my new neighbors at the shops on the street."

"That's a lovely thought," said Eva.

Leila agreed, "Even if it means that we don't get extra donuts, it is a good idea."

"Many of the people we gave samples to were excited about the opening and promised to come back, but some of them are tourists and won't be here long enough to visit," said Heather. "I thought it would be nice to visit potential regulars."

"It's always good to foster goodwill in the neighborhood," said Eva.

"And I will foster goodwill with you all by thanking you for helping me today and by letting you go free now. I can hand out the final donuts on my own," said Heather.
"I'll still come with you," Amy said. "I'd like to meet everybody. And I think it'll be a better introduction with donuts."

"I think I will still head out," Ryan said. "I promised Lils I'd take her to the beach soon after we arrived, and I wouldn't mind seeing the waves myself."

"I want to do some more unpacking," said Jamie.

"And I think we'll do some window shopping," said Eva.

"Speak for yourself," said Leila. "With all these fun things to buy for our new house, I'm shopping-shopping."

Heather thanked her friends and family again and told them she hoped they had fun. Then, she and Amy collected the rest of the donuts and set out deliver donut greetings. The seafood restaurant next door was closed on Mondays, so they walked over to the next shop. It was called Bernadette's Beachy Books.

The bell above the door announced their arrival and they were soon greeted by Bernadette herself. She was a young woman with big glasses and a big smile.

"Donuts along with a good book on the beach?" she asked. "Sounds perfect."

"It does," Heather agreed. "But I'm afraid we're probably not making it to the beach today."

27

"Unfortunately," Amy agreed.

"We're too busy setting up the new donut shop that is about to open, but part of our opening plans includes handing out samples," said Heather. She opened the box and let the sweet smell waft towards the bookseller's nose.

"You brought some for me?" Bernadette asked. "That is so charming."

"They're Chocolate Hazelnut Donuts," Heather started to explain as Bernadette took a bite. "And they're—"

"Perfect," Bernadette said, before enjoying another bite. "Thank you so much for this. It's as sweet as your donut."

"Thanks," Heather said.

"Let me find a napkin. I don't want to get chocolate prints or hazelnut crumbs on the books," Bernadette said as she searched behind her counter. "I'm sorry for mistaking you for tourists. I'm as embarrassed as Olivia must be at the end of *Twelfth Night*."

"What's that?" Amy asked.

"Oh. Sorry. Shakespeare reference. I mean that I'm sorry for the mistaken identity," said Bernadette.

"It's no problem," said Heather. "They must be most of the people who wander inside."

"That," said Bernadette. "And you get to know the other shop owners and their staff. It starts to be a tight-knit group. And it can be hard to join it. They're not always fond of newcomers, especially on this corner of the street."

"I guess Rudolph Rodney forgot to mention that in the brochure," said Amy.

"Oh. You're in the place Rudolph Rodney has. He's lived in Florida his whole life, and he's pretty well liked around here. That should help,"

Bernadette said, finally finding her napkin.

"Help?" Amy asked. "We need help?"

"What's the name of your shop?"

Heather frowned and looked to Amy. "My first shop is called Donut Delights. I hadn't quite decided if I should call this one Donut Delights II or something like that."

"I'm going to call it Donut Delights the Sequel," Amy announced, giving it a cinematic flair.
"I can understand the drama of a name. I've been here almost two years now, and they still won't let me forget that this used to be Bianca's Beachy Books."

"I'm sure these donuts will go a good way to winning them over," Heather said with a little more confidence than she felt. She knew opening a second location would present challenges, but had to admit that she had never considered animosity from her neighbors because she was new as a potential problem.

"If anything could, those delicious things will," Bernadette agreed. "But I'm afraid it might be more like Sisyphus and his rock."

"Huh?" Amy asked, "Are you calling our donuts hard?"

"No. Sorry. I was making a mythology reference. I'm surrounded by stories all day. Sisyphus was cursed with rolling a rock up a hill for eternity, only to have constantly roll down before it reaches the top."

"And that's what you think this neighborhood is like?" Heather asked.

Bernadette shrugged. "No one is mean to your face. Well, most people. But no one makes you feel welcome. But I want you to feel welcome. And I want you to know that I'm very glad you're here."

"Thank you," Heather said. "We'll be sure to visit again soon."

"Good luck with the rest of your visits," Bernadette said. "Don't let them scare you away."

Heather shared a look with her bestie. What were they getting themselves into?

**Chapter 4**

After visiting a few more neighbors, Heather and Amy weren't sure what to think. The owners of a yoga studio and a hammock hut were very polite. If they hadn't been told to look out for unpleasantness, they weren't sure that they would have noticed anything out of the ordinary. However, because they had been warned, they thought they could make out traces of suspicion in their neighbor's eyes as they accepted the donuts.

"Maybe we're just being paranoid," Amy said. "We've had too many murderers chase us in the past. Now whenever we get warned about something, we assume the worst."

"Maybe you're right," said Heather. "And Bernadette was very friendly to us."

"And maybe she was being dramatic. She just wanted to make some literary references," said Amy. "Yeah. I'm sure everything is going to be fine. Let's meet our next neighbor."

They entered the bikini boutique and were greeted with, "No food inside the shop, please."

"Oh, I'm sorry," Heather said. "We're your new neighbors at the soon to open Donut Delights."

"Or Donut Delights II," added Amy. "Or Donut Delights the Sequel."

"We were trying to greet everyone in the neighborhood and give out some donuts. I'm Heather, and this is Amy."

"Delilah Lewis," the shop owner said, striding towards them. She was an attractive woman who would have looked scintillating in any of her wares. However, it looked as if she were trying to show off as much of her figure in her professional clothes as she would in the bikinis for sale.

"I'm torn," Delilah said. "They look tasty, but they're not really good for the figure. Will people want to buy bikinis after stuffing themselves with sugar?"

Heather wasn't sure what to say to this, but tried, "I think most people come to this island for fun. They'd like to eat the wonderful food offered and like to swim in the waves where they'd need a bathing suit."

"I suppose so," Delilah said. "Any maybe if people gain weight from these things, they'd be forced to buy a new bathing suit they could fit into."

Heather was becoming angry. These were terrible things to say about her donuts and about her new customers. However, she didn't want to cause a scene that the whole block would gossip about her. She was about to find a graceful way to exit when Delilah responded instead.

She grabbed two donuts and said, "Thank you for coming, but I'm afraid I really don't allow food in my shop."

"We understand," Amy said. "We don't allow bikinis in ours."

They departed, leaving Delilah with a look of confusion on her face.

The next place they visited was Juan and Don's Tacos. Juan and Don were also best friends who had opened up a restaurant together. Heather and Amy thought that they might be able to bond over their similar experiences, but the men were less enthusiastic. They commented on how too many newcomers were opening restaurants that would be in competition with them. Heather responded that tacos and donuts were different tastes and were hardly in direct competition.

Heather and Amy each bought a taco to be polite and commented how tasty they were. Juan and Don accepted the donuts and then hid how delicious they found them.

Heather and Amy were happy to leave.

"This errand is definitely becoming a chore instead of something fun," said Heather.

"I wouldn't have thought people could turn up their noses at donuts," said Amy. "Especially your donuts."

"I think it's just our block that is difficult," said Heather. "I can't imagine the whole street like this. Everyone seems so cheerful. But I suppose because of our great location people could become territorial."

"What should we do?" asked Amy.

"We'll just keep doing what we always do. We'll be nice and keep baking yummy donuts."

"And solving crimes if they pop up?"

"Yes, that too," said Heather. "But we have so much to do right now that I'm not sure we have time for a case."

"You say that now," Amy teased.

"Let's just finish up delivering these donuts to the neighbors. I think there's one more shop," said Heather.

They entered Sun and Fun Novelties and were greeted by a short older man in sandals. He leaned on a cane but moved quickly.

"Welcome to Sun and Fun," he said. "I'm Mr. Rankle. What can I help you find? Sunscreen? Hats? Key West snow globes? I know that last one sounds counterintuitive."

He gave them a large smile, and the ladies felt that they had finally found another friendly face. However, as soon as they had explained who they were the shop owner's demeanor changed.

"Get out," Mr. Rankle said scowling.

"Out?" Amy asked.

"Out of my shop," he said. "If I could get you to get off of the street, I'd tell you that too. There are too many out-of-towners setting up shops here. And now some Oklahoma broads are moving in and taking our business."

"We're from Texas," Heather said calmly. "And a donut shop won't affect your sale of snow globes."

"Get out," he said again.

This time they didn't even hand out their donut but ran from the shop as quick as possible. They walked back to their kitchen and decided to split the last donut between them. They both took a bite to lift their spirits.

"Well," Heather said. "I'm even more glad that you and our friends moved out here with me."

"Yeah," said Amy. "What a welcome to the neighborhood."

**Chapter 5**

The next morning, Heather started poking through her unpacked moving boxes, looking for her beach supplies. She had found and put on her bathing suit, but she was sure she had packed a cover up somewhere. Dave joined in the search and started sniffing around the room. However, Heather was pretty sure he was looking for leftover crumbs and not her swimwear.

Ryan joined her looking triumphant.

"I reattached the lamp to the wall," he said.

"That's great," Heather said. "Does it turn on?"

"Not yet," Ryan admitted. "But the first half of the battle is won."

"Maybe you can help me with mine," Heather said. "I'm trying to make it to the beach this morning and can't find my cover up."

"You're not coming with me this morning?" Ryan asked.

"Remind me," Heather admitted.

"I was going to visit the police station and meet my new colleagues that I'll be joining after Detective Smith officially retires," said Ryan.

"Of course," Heather said. "I definitely want to go to that. For some reason, I thought that was tomorrow."

"It's okay," Ryan said. "My days are running together too. A lot is happening very quickly."

"I'll make the visit with you, then Amy and I will visit the one neighbor we didn't meet yesterday because the seafood restaurant was closed, and then maybe after that, I can go to the beach."

"Sounds good," said Ryan. "But maybe you want to change before we go meet my new boss?"

Heather laughed. She had no intention of wearing her bathing suit to police headquarters.

***

"Does this bring back memories?" Ryan asked as they entered the police station.

Heather nodded. Before they had all moved to Key West, Heather had visited it once before. She had become embroiled in a murder investigation. She had unintentionally become a thorn in the lead detective's side until she made up for it by leading him straight to the killer.

Ryan smiled as he looked around the station. It had all the trappings of any police station, but still had a relaxed tropical feel to it.

They were greeted by a jovial man with sandy colored hair and mustache. Instead of his police uniform, he had opted to wear a T-shirt and sneakers.

"You must be Detective Shepherd," he said. Ryan recognized the voice as they shook hands.

"Chief Copeland, it's nice to meet you in person finally," Ryan said. "This is my wife, Heather."

"It's nice to meet you both. And please, call me Chet. We're pretty casual around here. Except when it comes to crime, of course," Chief Chet said. "Again, it was great meeting you. We'll be happy to have you on board when Smith retires. But if you'll excuse me, I promised a little league team I'd watch their game."

He patted Ryan on the arm affectionately and left them. Heather was about to comment on how much more friendly the people at Ryan's job seemed to be than near workplace when a voice greeted them.

"I didn't think I'd be seeing you here again," a voice said.

They turned and saw Detective Smith. Heather remembered him being a meticulous man and a good cop. She hadn't considered how old he was before but realized he was within retirement age. She briefly thought how it was a shame that Ryan wouldn't have as competent a partner as Detective Smith here. Then she remembered that Detective Smith probably wouldn't approve of her and Amy's frequent help on cases the same way Ryan did.

Detective Smith shook her hand and then Ryan's. "You're married to my replacement, I see," he said.

"And you'll be leaving Key West in very capable hands," Heather assured.

"I'll do my very best to keep the community safe and capture any wrongdoers," Ryan agreed. "And as soon as you're ready to retire, I'll be happy to take over duties."

"It will be soon," Detective Smith said, before changing the conversation. "How have you been? Been interfering with any other investigations?"

"Yes," Heather said. "But legally. I've become a licensed private detective and assist when needed."

Detective Smith nodded. "Seems about right. We couldn't keep you from investigating, and now you've found a way to keep doing so."

"How is your partner?" Heather asked.

"He's moved to Miami to be closer to his grandchildren and is very happy about it. I have a new partner now. I expect you'll meet him soon."

"I'm looking forward to it," Ryan said.

They made some more small talk and discussed Detective Smith's retirement without him saying when he was planning on officially doing it. Then they were joined by his partner.

Heather was glad that Amy wasn't there to make jokes about how young the detective looked. She was sure she would have heard something about how he looked barely out of high school, let alone police academy.

"Smith, I found the form you wanted. This was the one you wanted, wasn't it? In case it wasn't, I brought these other two. One of them should be helpful," the young detective said.

"The first one was right," Detective Smith said. "This is Ryan Shepherd who is going to be your new partner. Shepherd, this is Peters."

The young detective juggled his papers and shook hands with Ryan. "I'm Detective Peters. Miguel Peters. Or just Peters. You could call me that too."

The young detective seemed to be nervous and constantly unsure of his footing, but it also seemed like he was willing to put work into doing a good job. Heather thought that having Ryan as a partner would be good for him. It could build his confidence.

"And this is his wife, Heather," Detective Smith said.

Peters shook her hand enthusiastically too.

"She helped with a case before," Detective Smith continued. "She was good at it. But we're hoping she won't have to do any more sleuthing around here."

"Don't worry," Heather said. "I'm so busy with opening my new shop that I don't think I'll have any time for dead bodies."

"Glad to hear it," said Detective Smith.

***

"Do we have to?" Amy asked.

"Come on," said Heather. "We'll deliver a sample donut to the seafood restaurant so that we'll have greeted all our new neighbors. Then we can go to the beach."

"Fine," Amy groaned. "But only because you're bribing me with the beach."

They reached the restaurant and peeked in the window.

"I'm not just saying this to get out of work," Amy said. "But it doesn't look like they're open."

"They're supposed to open for lunch in an hour," Heather said. "Someone should be in by now."

She pushed on the door, and it opened.

"Something's fishy," Amy said.

Heather ignored the comment and entered the seafood restaurant.

"Hello," she called. "We're from the new donut shop next door."

They heard no response and crept further inside. Then, they saw something that made them stop dead in their tracks.

"I don't think we're going to the beach today," Amy said, trying to distract her from the horror before them.

The owner of the seafood restaurant lay dead on the floor.

## Chapter 6

"I thought you told me that you weren't going to investigate any cases for a while," Detective Smith said.

"I wasn't sleuthing at the time," Heather said. "We were on donut duty when we came across the victim."

"Why don't you take us through what happened," Detective Smith said. Detective Peters stood next to him and prepared his pencil to take notes in unison.

Heather recounted how they had arrived and tried to deliver a welcome donut, but had found the victim instead.

"Did you touch anything?" Detective Smith asked.

"She did tell you that we're professional private investigators now, right?" Amy asked. "We wouldn't contaminate a crime scene."

"We only touched the door when we entered," Heather said. "Before we knew it was a crime scene."

"And how well did you know the victim?" Detective Smith asked. "You had just met him?"

"We didn't even get the chance," Heather said. "He wasn't open yesterday. We came today to introduce ourselves. I think another neighbor said his name was Covens? But that's all we know about him."

"Percy Covens," Detective Smith confirmed.
"He's had the fish shop here for years and years," Detective Peters said. "I used to come here after school for the specials."

"And when was that exactly?" Amy asked.

Heather shot a look at her friend. Now wasn't the time to tease the policeman about his youth.

"Was he poisoned?" Heather asked, trying to focus on the case at hand.

"What leads you to that conclusion?" Peters asked.

"Unfortunately, we've had some incidents with poisons," Heather said, neglecting to mention that she had been poisoned by a killer herself. "And I noticed some foam by his mouth."

"The medical examiner still needs to complete his autopsy," Detective Smith said. "And we don't share the results with civilians."

"Can't you tell us?" Amy asked. "Remember how helpful we were last time?"

"I remember a deadly snake on the loose," Detective Smith said.

"And you were the people who stumbled across the body," Peters said. "That makes you people of interest."

"Come on," Amy said. "You don't really think we had anything to do with this, do you?"

"Do we?" Peters asked his partner, nervously.

"I don't really think that you've traveled across the country to murder a man you've never met," Detective Smith said. "But we will have to double check that you've never met him."

"Tell us a little bit more about him so we can make sure we've never met him," Heather said, fishing for information.

"Percy Covens was well liked by everybody," Detective Peters began. "He was one of the street's most eligible bachelors too. My sister used to have a crush on him."

"Peters," Detective Smith said, stopping the flow of information.

"Sorry," Peters said, retreating behind his notebook.

"I wonder why the killer chose poison," Heather said, thinking aloud and hoping the law enforcement agents might join in. "Does it mean that they were incapable of using a more physical means of murdering Percy Covens?"

"Maybe the killer was small or weak," Amy agreed.

"Or they wanted to give themselves a good alibi," Heather said. "If they used poison, it was definitely a premeditated murder. The killer didn't want to be nearby at the time of death. Do you know when the time of death is?"

"The medical examiner is still conducting his autopsy," said Peters. "But it was sometime this morning, probably between 9 a.m. and—"

"And we don't share this type of information," Detective Smith said.

"I'm sorry," Peters said. "It's just that they are private investigators and are related to Detective Shepherd."

"And told me this morning that they had a donut shop to set up and weren't going to get involved in any cases," Detective Smith said.

"You're right," Heather said. "We know that you can do your job and we will be very busy with my store's opening. It's just that this feels personal."

"You said that you never met the man," Peters reminded them. "Did I catch you in a lie?"

"It feels personal because he's in the building right next to me. And when did the killer strike? If we had visited with our donuts a little earlier, we might have been able to prevent this tragedy," said Heather.

"You can't blame yourselves," Peters said. "Unless you were actually the killers and poisoned the man. But, otherwise, it's not your fault."

"I saw a coffee mug," Heather said. "Could that have held the poison?"

"We have to do tests—that will not be shared with civilians," Peters said and then covered.

"It was one of those #1 Boss mugs," Amy said. "It gives me the creeps to think that it could have held something deadly."

"Remind my future employees never to get one for me around the holidays," said Heather. "I don't think I could get this crime out of my head and take a sip from it."

"Are you going to let this go?" Detective Smith asked.

Heather sighed. "We won't get in the way of your investigation," she promised.

**Chapter 7**

"There," Heather said. "What do you think?"

"I think it's hard to focus on pre-opening chores when a dead body was found next door," Amy said.

Heather had to agree. "But Detective Smith doesn't want our help on this case."

"His loss," said Amy. "We're great at finding the piece of the puzzle that others miss."

"I think we were starting to become spoiled by having Ryan hire us to help the Hillside Police."

"I don't mind being spoiled," Amy said. "In fact, I'd appreciate a little bit more of it. If they would just tell us the results of the lab test, we would probably have caught the killer by now."

"We might not like the answer we find," Heather said.

"What do you mean?"

"Detective Peters said that Percy Covens was an eligible bachelor. That doesn't sound like a wife or children wanting to kill him for their inheritance. If we ignore the family angle, which is a common motive for murder, then it has to be something else. And it might just relate to one of our new shop neighbors."

Amy shivered. "One neighbor dead, and another a killer. You know? This happened to me before. I didn't like it then, and I don't like it now."

"I don't like it either," Heather agreed.

Amy decided to go back to Heather's original question and looked at what she had written. Even though they were distracted, they had solidified their menu of regular flavors that morning. Now they were creating a "Help Wanted" ad they could post for hiring assistants in the shop. The new staff had to be pleasant and helpful with customers, they would have to bake the many flavors of donuts while following safety regulations, and they would have to keep the store sparkling clean. They would have a lot to live up to too, after how wonderful Heather's Hillside staff was.

"Do you think it adequately describes the work without scaring applicants off?" Heather asked.

Amy nodded. "But maybe we should add something about how they might have to handle store operations as a team while management runs off to solve a murder."

"It doesn't look like that's going to happen soon," said Heather. "So maybe we can work our way up to telling them about that."

"I wish Ryan was handling this case!" Amy said.

"Me too," Ryan said, joining them.

"I'd say speak of the devil, but that's as far from the truth as it could be," Heather said. "But we were just talking about you."

"I know you left me a message saying you had to talk to Detective Smith again. Does this mean what I think it does?" asked Ryan. "Has there been a murder?"

"Unfortunately, the owner of the seafood restaurant next door was poisoned," said Heather.

Ryan shook his head. "I was all set to enjoy some vacation time. I fixed our faucet this morning, so it's easier to turn."

"Did you fix the only hot water and only cold water thing too?" asked Amy.

"Not yet. But the first step has been taken," said Ryan.

"Why do I feel like there's still a marathon to run?" asked Amy.

"Eva and Leila and I were going to take Lilly to a dog beach today so she could bring Dave and Cupcake to enjoy the sand," said Ryan. "But how can I do that when I should be investigating a case?"

"Don't worry about it. This is Detective Smith's responsibility, not yours," said Heather. "Though I would be careful about bringing Cupcake to a dog beach. Most dogs aren't like Dave. They don't like kittens."

"We looked into it, and found a beach that we think will be safe," said Ryan. "But will you be safe? Is the killer after others on the street? Will he come after you two?"

"I think we're all right," said Heather. "Right now, I'd assume that the killer was only after Percy Covens. Poison is deliberate. I wish we knew the time frame of his activities though. That would help us determine when the killer had to strike."

"He's closed on Mondays," said Amy. "Could someone have broken in then? Or did it have to be set up Tuesday morning?"

"The door we entered through didn't look tampered with, but that's not to say the killer couldn't have come in another way," said Heather.

"I don't like not being able to get lab results," said Ryan. "Do you know anything about the poison used?"

"It caused some foaming at the mouth," said Heather.

"It might have been Potassium Cyanide," Ryan thought aloud. "If it caused foaming at the mouth and death after being ingested."

"It looked fast-acting," said Heather. "His coffee mug was set down, but he didn't have time to do anything else. I didn't see any cell phone at the scene, and he didn't make it to the store phone. He wasn't able to call for help."

"Are you sure the coffee mug held the poison?" Ryan asked.

"Without Detective Smith's help, no," said Heather. "But it is what makes the most sense. Coffee could mask the taste of the poison, and it was the only edible item out in the open."

"If that's what's in the #1 Boss mug, I'd hate to see what's in the #2 one," said Amy.

"If I were on the case, I'd love to talk to the employee who gave him that mug," said Heather. "Did something happen to change the employee's idea of his boss?"

"If you were on the case?" asked Amy.

"There's no reason to get involved right now," Heather said. "When we started helping in Hillside it was because we knew things about the suspects that other people didn't know. That's not the case here. We are great at finding clues and figuring out how they go together, but I bet Detective Smith and Peters are good at it too. I don't want to make trouble for Ryan at work before he even starts."

"You don't have to worry about me," said Ryan. "You've proven your skills again and again, and this police force will see that too. You're licensed now as well, and I believe Florida accepts other state's licenses."

"Maybe I will look into updating my P.I. license," said Heather. "But not today. I promised Detective Smith I wouldn't get in the way of his investigation."

"You're sure?" Amy asked.

"Well," said Heather. "Unless something forces us to get involved."

Then they heard the yelling outside.

**Chapter 8**

"There were never any murders here before," Mr. Rankle was yelling. "Not until they came here!"

Heather, Amy, and Ryan emerged from the soon-to-be Donut Delights and saw that most of the other shop owners had gathered in the street. Mr. Rankle was leaning on his cane with one hand and pointing angrily at Heather's building with the other.

The other neighbors started muttering amongst themselves. Heather noticed all of the people that they had handed donuts out to, along with a few of their staff members.

"What's going on?" Heather asked.

"As if you didn't know," Mr. Rankle said. "Percy Covens was murdered."

"Yes. We do know that," Heather said. "But what does that have to do with us?"

"Do with you? It's obvious you killed him," Mr. Rankle said.

"How can you think that?" asked Amy.

"We never had any trouble like this before," Mr. Rankle said. "And then you show up and right away a man is killed."

"Doesn't that help prove that they didn't kill him?" Bernadette from the bookstore offered. "If he was murdered right after they arrived that doesn't give them time to get a reason to kill him."
"You would side with them," Mr. Rankle said.

"I miss Bianca," Don said, and Juan agreed.

Bernadette rolled her eyes.

"And the reason is obvious," Mr. Rankle said. "They came here just to cause trouble. First, they came here handing out donuts."

"Was something wrong with the donuts?" Delilah from the bikini boutique asked. "Were they poisoned? Is this going to happen to all of us?"

"I sincerely hope not," said Mr. Rankle. "But now do you understand why I don't like newcomers? Maybe it's perfectly all right to murder your neighbors wherever they come from in Tennessee."

"Texas," said Amy.

"But it's not all right here. And we won't stand for it!" said Mr. Rankle.

"Let's all remain calm," said Ryan.

"And who are you?" asked Delilah.

"I'm Detective Ryan Shepherd, formerly of the Hillside Police, and currently transferring to the Key West Force. Now, this isn't yet my jurisdiction," he said. "But I can tell you something about the law. Gathering like this and with all the yelling you're doing is causing a public disturbance. I recommend you all return to your places of business."

The woman from the yoga studio and man from the hammock shop and a few staff member from the stores left after this speech, but the others were more reticent to move.

"You expect us to just go about our day with a killer on the loose?" asked Mr. Rankle.

"I expect you to let the police and professionals investigate this matter," said Ryan. "If you have any leads based on more than irritation about a new store opening, then report it to them. But otherwise, yes. You should return to your work."

"It's just hard to feel safe with them here," Delilah said. She gave them a dirty look and then retreated.

Juan and Don also warily left.

"I'm sorry about this," said Bernadette. "It looks like you're going to have an even rougher time fitting in than I did. But I won't ever be scared of eating your donuts."

She gave them a small smile and walked away, leaving them alone with Mr. Rankle.

"You don't fool me," he said. "And I'm going to make sure that the whole street knows that you're a bunch of cutthroats."

"Mr. Rankle, we didn't have anything to do with his murder," Heather said. "And we want justice served as much as the next person."

"It will be served when you're off of this street," Mr. Rankle said before abruptly turning around and leaving.

"We're surrounded by palm trees and shining waters," said Amy. "And yet, this day keeps going from bad to worse."

Heather didn't respond. She was scanning the area where the crowd had been, trying to determine the direction that everyone went.

"You have that look on your face," Ryan said. "Are you taking on this case?"

"Well," Heather said. "I believe I only promised that I wouldn't get in the way of Detective Smith's investigation. There's no reason for our sleuthing to interfere with his work. And yes, I think we do need to start working on it. Everyone on the street is going to blame us for Percy Covens' death unless we find the real killer."

"Hey," Amy said. "Maybe if we find the real killer, then they might even like us. Maybe we'll be heroes of the block."

"It might depend on who they end up arresting," said Ryan.

"I hope it's Mr. Rankle," said Amy. "Please, could it be him."

"So, what's your first move?" Ryan asked. "We don't have any lab results or confirmation about facts in the case."

"First, I'm going to let you take Lilly and everyone to the dog beach as you promised," said Heather.

"Really?" asked Ryan.
"You wanted to be on vacation," said Heather.

"I guess so," he said, not seeming as excited as before.

"This way you're not ruffling any feathers with the police force if they happen to get annoyed with us," said Heather.

"Not that we're ever annoying," said Amy.

"What are you going to do?" Ryan asked.

"Did you notice everyone that was in the crowd?" Heather asked. "How there

were some employees gathered as well
as the owners?"

"Yeah," said Amy.

"I think I saw someone wearing a shirt
for the seafood restaurant," Heather
said.

"He might work there," said Amy. "He
might be the one who gave Percy
Covens the #1 Boss mug."

"And he might know something about
the murder," said Heather.

## Chapter 9

Heather and Amy found the employee sitting next to the seafood restaurant looking downcast.

"We thought we saw you on the street," said Heather.

"I tried to do what the policeman said and return to work," the young man said. "But then I realized that I don't really have a place to work anymore. I don't think it will ever open its doors again. All because of a horrible murder."

He sighed theatrically. Heather sensed that he was upset about what had happened, but that he also enjoyed the drama of it all.

"So, you worked for Percy Covens?" Heather asked.

"Yes," he said. "I was his assistant. I was supposed to make sure things went smoothly when he wasn't there. But I'm not really sure I should be talking to you about this. Couldn't you both be guilty?

Am I talking to killers now? Should I be afraid? Should I scream for help?"

"I should have brought earplugs," Amy muttered.

"We had nothing to do with the murder," Heather assured him. "Back in Hillside, we actually helped solve murders. We haven't called attention to it here, but we are licensed private investigators."

"And are you going to solve Percy's murder?"

"We've been pulled into the investigation," Heather said.
"You're real P.I.s? Do you have badges? Do you have guns?"

"We have some ID cards," Heather said. "But they're in relation to the Hillside department."

She showed them to the young employee.

"These are so cool," he said. "It's nice to meet you, Shepherd and Givens. Everyone calls me Digby around here."

"How long did you work for Percy Covens, Digby?" asked Heather.

"About three years."

"Do you know anyone who would want to kill him?"

"No," Digby said. "That's why this whole thing doesn't feel right. Everybody loved Percy. And everybody loved his food. That's why when Rankle said he had important information about the murder, I went. I didn't think he'd just accuse you for no reason. I thought he might know something."

"Did Mr. Rankle and Percy Covens get along?" Amy asked, trying to hide her hope that he was behind it all.

"Rankle is not especially beloved by anybody. He only likes the locals but can hold grudges against them too. He can hide it when he's trying to sell stuff in his shop, but he hates the tourists. I guess he considers you tourists."

"Great," said Amy.

"But I think he and Percy got along all right. I really hoped that Rankle would have some information about the case, so I wouldn't have to face the unhappy truth." He turned away dramatically.

"And what is that?" asked Heather.

"That he's dead because of me," Digby said.

"Because of you?" asked Amy.

"Did you poison him?" Heather asked, prompting him to tell the whole story.

"No," said Digby. "But he wasn't supposed to be here. I was the one who called him back, and because he was here, he was able to be killed."

"Where was he?" asked Heather.

"He was on vacation for the week. He was with a woman he was seeing."

"We heard he was the street's most eligible bachelor," said Amy.

"A lot of women did like him. You know, he was handsome, and he made great food. He did date a lot. But lately, he'd been seeing more of this one lady. I think her name was Eliza."

Heather looked to Amy, and they both realized that they hadn't brought the tablet they normally took notes on about a case. That was a hazard of not completely unpacking your belongings and not planning on investigating a case. They were just going to have to remember Eliza's name and find a way to track her down. She might have a motive to murder her boyfriend.
"It was serious?"

"I don't know," said Digby. "He didn't talk about his dates too often. We talked about work things. But, he didn't like being interrupted on his vacation."

"Why did you interrupt him?" asked Heather.

"Sunday night there was a problem with the refrigeration unit. It was something I had never encountered before. I called him for help."

"It didn't smell like rotten fish when we were in there," Amy commented.

"He had me get rid of anything that might spoil and then arrived Monday to fix it. He was going to return to his vacation after he made sure our opening went smoothly on Tuesday."

"What time do people normally show up on Tuesdays?" asked Heather.

"Percy might be there at any point in the morning to make sure things were set for the day and bring in the fresh fish. Then his staff would come in a half hour before we open. Everything is cooked fresh to order, so there isn't much prep needed by them in the morning. Originally, I was supposed to come in early Tuesday, but Percy told me not to bother. I was going to come in Tuesday at my normal time when I saw the crime scene tape. I wasn't sure what to do then."

"So, the killer would have to have seen him sometime on Monday or on Tuesday morning to set up the poisoned drink," said Amy.

"Who knew he was back?" asked Heather.

"Not too many people," said Digby. "He didn't make a big announcement about being back because the reason for his return would have scared people away from the shop. They'd be afraid of bad fish. I didn't tell anyone at work because I didn't know how long he was staying around."

"So, if anyone knew he was there, it was because Percy Covens told them he was there himself. And that person could be the killer."

"Or it could be Digby," said Amy.

"No way," he said. "With Percy gone, I'm out of a job. I don't gain anything by his death."

"Who inherits the restaurant after his death?" asked Heather.

"I don't know. But Percy was the heart and soul of it. I don't see how it could survive without him there," he said. "But really, how can any of us survive without him there?"

"Did he usually drink coffee in the morning from a mug?" Heather asked.

"Yeah," Digby said. "He loved his morning coffee. And he often used a mug I got him the first Christmas I worked for him. It said #1 Boss on it. Why? Did that have something to do with his death?"

"Thank you for your help," Heather said. "We'll be in touch if we have any more questions."

"I'd be happy to help," he said. "And it doesn't look like I'll have anything else going on for a while. I'll just be job searching."

Heather and Amy walked away.

"Could he be any more dramatic?" Amy asked.

Heather chuckled. "He was very helpful though. We have some new leads to follow."

"Right," said Amy.

"It would be really helpful if we could find out if the coffee was definitely what was poisoned," said Heather.

Her cell phone rang. She didn't recognize the number but picked up and answered, "Shepherd."

Amy tried to guess who she was talking to based on one side of the conversation but was still unsure when she hung up.

"Who was it?" asked Amy. "And where are we going?"

"That was Detective Smith," Heather answered. "He wants us to come into the station."

## Chapter 10

"I'm surprised you called us in," Heather said.

"Are you?" Detective Smith asked.

"Definitely," said Amy.

"After the last time we spoke, I thought you didn't want our help on the case," Heather said.

"But it's nice to see you came to your senses," Amy smiled.

Detective Smith looked to his partner Peters who shrugged.

"We didn't call you in as back up," Detective Smith said. "We wanted to talk to you because one of your neighbors has been accusing you of murder."

"He keeps calling the station," Peters said. "He's vehement and loud."
"Can he please be the killer?" Amy wished aloud. "Then we could send him off to jail."

"We thought we had better go through everything again," said Detective Smith. "Both for appearances and to make sure that nothing was overlooked."

"It's a shame all our neighbors think we're the bad guys," said Heather.

"And they'd think it even more if they knew," Peters started. "What we don't tell civilians."
"No fair," Amy said as Peters blushed. "Are you going to let him tease us like that?"

"Why don't you tell us if you noticed anything unusual near the scene of the crime?" Detective Smith said.

"Nothing seemed out of place at the time," said Heather. "Though we are new to the area."

"The door was unlocked, but that might not be weird because employees were going to come in soon," said Amy.

"Though the refrigerating unit was not working was unusual," said Heather. "Digby said he had never encountered a problem like that before."

"Digby?" asked Peters.

"Percy Coven's assistant," said Heather.

"You spoke to his assistant?" asked Detective Smith. "That sounds like you're investigating the case."

"Maybe we were just being neighborly and expressing our condolences," offered Amy.

Heather decided to be honest. "Detective Smith, you've heard what Mr. Rankle has been saying. He's the most vocal of the group, but that's what everyone on the street is thinking. They all think that we're murderers. I don't like my name being dragged through the mud like that. And I don't like to think what that could mean for my new business venture."

"They might start telling people the donuts are what killed the guy," Amy said. "Would you buy a donut like that?"

"No," Peters said, answering the rhetorical question.

"We helped solve a case for you before," Heather said. "I'm disappointed you won't accept our help now when this is starting to affect us personally."

Detective Smith thought about it. "Despite my explicit instructions not to help before, you did help us catch a killer last time you were here. I don't expect I could stop you again. You're licensed investigators now?"

"Yes, indeedy," said Amy.

"What do you think, Peters?" Detective Smith asked.

"Me? You're asking me what I think? Well, I think," Peters stalled. "Maybe it might be all right to get their advice. They are in the middle of things now, aren't they? What with the crumbs and all."

"The crumbs?" asked Heather.

Detective Smith grumbled that information was revealed before they made their official decision to do so, but then said, "Some crumbs were found at the scene. Most likely from a donut."

"A Chocolate Hazelnut Donut?" Heather asked.

"Yes, actually," said Detective Peters. "The two ingredients identified were chocolate and hazelnut crumbs,"
"Then it came from one of our sample donuts," said Heather. "You know what that means?"

"That Mr. Rankle is going to be even more convinced that we killed the guy?" said Amy.

"It means that whoever killed Percy Covens took one of our donuts," said

Heather. "I think it was one of our work neighbors."

"Mr. Rankle?" Amy suggested.

"I just hope that the donut wasn't turned into a murder weapon," Heather said.

"No," Peters said. "You were right before. The coffee contained Potassium Cyanide. It wasn't the donut."

"So, we know how," said Heather. "Now we just need to determine who."

Heather wasn't the only one who wanted to determine who the killer was. A woman with curly blonde hair and mascara streaks from tears came up to them.

"Who killed him?" She demanded through sobs. "You're the detectives on the case, aren't you? Who killed him? Who killed my Percy?"

"Who are you?" Detective Smith asked.

"I'm his fiancé," she replied before sobbing.

**Chapter 11**

The detectives led the woman to a seat and Heather provided her with a tissue.

"I'm sorry," she said. "I'm not normally like this. I'm not one to cry. But now this week I've done it twice. Once when Percy proposed. And now again because he was taken from me. Who would do this?"

"That's what we'd like to find out," Heather said.

"What's your name, miss?" Detective Smith asked.

"Eliza Hawkins."

"Eliza," Amy mouthed to Heather. "We found her."

"You were close to Percy Covens?" Detective Smith asked.
"Of course, I was close to him," she said. "I was going to marry him."

"That's a big rock," Amy said. "I mean, a beautiful ring."

"Thank you," the woman said. "He said I deserved the best and found this truly radiant ring for me. Of course, I'd trade it back for one more day with him."

Peters was taking notes diligently.

"You two were away on vacation together?" Heather asked.

Detective Smith gave her a look. She knew more information than she was supposed to know.

"Yes," Eliza said, dabbing her eyes. "We went to Vermont. He told me it was to see the leaves change colors, but it was really so we could be alone together and so he could propose."

"That's very romantic," said Amy.

"Had you been together long?" Heather asked.

"Only a few months," said Eliza. "But we both knew it was the real thing."

"We heard he was one of the most eligible bachelors," said Heather. "That lots of women were interested in him."

"And that he was interested in lots of women?" Eliza asked.

"Was he?" Heather asked gently.

"I think he had been seeing many women for a while, but then things started to become more serious with us. He wanted to settle down. Isn't that obvious? That's why he proposed. He wanted to start a life with me."

"I'm so sorry that he was taken away from you," said Heather. "And I promise we will do everything we can to catch his killer. Do you know anyone who would want to harm him?"

"No," said Eliza. "Everybody loved him."

"All his employees?" Detective Smith asked.

"Yes," said Eliza. "He would tell me stories about his staff. He was very proud of them. Especially Digby. He was a great worker, even if he does have a flair for the dramatic."

"Digby was the one who called him back from his vacation?" Heather asked.

"Yes," said Eliza, sadly. "We were supposed to have a whole wonderful week together and then return to announce our engagement. But Digby called and said something was wrong with the fridges. Percy thought it was something he needed to deal with himself, so he came down to fix it."

"And you remained in Vermont?" Detective Smith asked.

"Until I heard about his death, yes," said Eliza.

"Your whereabouts can be accounted for the entire time?" Detective Smith asked.

"Just what exactly are you implying?" Eliza asked. "You think that I killed him?"

"He has to ask that," Heather said. "Significant others are always suspects at first. And you were Percy Covens' most significant other."

"I suppose you're right," said Eliza. "I was in Vermont the whole time. I'm sure my movements could be accounted for somehow. I went hiking with another young woman I met there to pass the time, and I played tourist for a while."

"We will check up on this," Detective Smith said. "And I'm sure it will eliminate you as a suspect."

"But you do have suspects, don't you?" Eliza asked. "You will catch whoever did this? I don't think I can sleep knowing that Percy's killer is out there."

"We have some suspects," Peters said. "And we will catch the one who did this."

Eliza allowed herself to be handed more tissues and then left the station.

"Poor lady," Peters said.

"It is really sad that he was killed right after he became engaged," Amy said.

"Yes," Detective Smith said. "Could it have any bearing on the case?"

"But who would have known about it?" Heather asked.

"And why would getting married be a reason to kill someone?" asked Amy.

"Was there anything else unusual found at the crime scene by the forensic team?" Heather asked.

"It was a public restaurant, so I'm afraid that the fingerprints and DNA found at the scene are too contaminated. The only prints on the mug were Percy Covens," Detective Smith told them.

"The only weird thing there was the donut crumbs," said Peters.
"And nothing strange on the victim?" asked Heather, grasping for clues.

"Only his wallet that was filled with the usual bits and pieces," said Detective Smith.

This made Heather pause. "No cell phone?"

"There wasn't one found on his person," said Detective Smith.

"Is that important?" Peters asked.

"Most people have cell phones these days. And if he was able to get the call from Digby about the refrigeration problem while on vacation, then I think he had a phone," said Heather.

"I'll look into that right now," Peters said, enthusiastically running off.

"The phone missing is what makes it suspicious," said Heather.

"It is possible that he just forgot it that morning," Detective Smith said. "Let's not get ahead of ourselves."

"Too late for Peters," said Amy.

"A lot of things seem funny about this case," said Heather. "Why did the killer decide to kill Percy Covens then? Who benefits from his death? And does the refrigeration unit have anything to do with the case?"

"Would now be a bad time for an "Is your refrigerator running?" joke?" asked Amy.

"Yes," said Detective Smith.

"I think we need to talk to our neighbors again," Heather said. "One of them took the donut that could have left the crumbs at the crime scene."

"Which means," said Amy. "That one of them is the killer."

## Chapter 12

Mr. Rankle was massaging his sore leg behind the counter when Heather and Amy came in. Not seeing who they were at first, he was briefly pleasant.

"I'll be with you in just a minute," he said. "This leg of mine likes to act up in times of stress. But then I can help you find what you need. What are you looking for today?"

"Answers," said Heather.

Mr. Rankle groaned as he realized who was there. "I thought I told you both that I didn't want you in my store."

"Well, we didn't really appreciate you outside on our sidewalk, trying to lead a riot against us," said Amy.

"I can call the police," he said.

"Yeah. We've heard you've been doing that a lot," Amy said.

"Mr. Rankle, you could call the police and complain, but that won't get us any closer to finding out what happened to Percy Covens," said Heather. "You could call another police station, the one in Hillside, Texas. And then you would find out that Amy and I are private investigators who have helped on numerous murder cases before."

"You bake donuts and solve crimes?" Mr. Rankle said dubiously.

Heather tried to make a joke and said, "Lots of people work two jobs these days."

"I don't believe it," Mr. Rankle said. "You're trying to trick me somehow."

"We just want to figure out who killed Percy Covens," said Heather. "And you seem to be the unofficial head of the block. You might have some information that could help us."

"That's true. I am," he said. "But I know what happened to Covens. You killed him. You and your friends from Montana."

"Texas," said Amy. "His geography is getting way off."

"Why would we kill him?" Heather asked.

"I'm not sure exactly," said Mr. Rankle. "As some sort of warning to the rest of us? Well, let me warn you: I will not back down. A man I knew and respected was killed, and I will not be quiet about it."

"So, you knew Percy Covens well?" asked Heather.

"We've both been on this street for a good long while, and we've lived in Key West our whole lives. We're not people who just popped up here one night," he grumbled.

"Did you know that he just got engaged?" asked Amy.

"That would have broken a lot of hearts," said Mr. Rankle. "But now it just adds to the tragedy."

"Speaking of those broken hearts," Heather said. "Was there anyone in particular who would have been upset by that news? An angry ex?"

"I'm not a gossip," Mr. Rankle said. "But he did have the attention of many young ladies, and he did return the attention. Tourists and locals."

"Anyone on the street?" asked Heather.

"Not that I know of, but it wouldn't surprise me," he said.

"Did Percy Covens ever have trouble with any customers or employees?" Heather asked.

"Nothing that would get him killed," said Mr. Rankle. "Every once in a while you'd get a troublesome tourist. They bring trouble with him. Then again, Covens was normally pretty good with people."

"It's a skill," said Amy, implying the man in front of her lacked it.

"Can you think of any other reasons why somebody would want to kill him?" asked Heather.

"You mean why you would want to kill him?" Mr. Rankle rebutted.

"For the sake of argument, fine," Heather said. She only just refrained from throwing up her arms in exasperation. "What are some reasons why you think we killed him?"

"Well," he said, seriously considering it. "His restaurant is right next door to yours. Maybe you wanted to kill him so that you could expand your shop. You wanted to take his kitchen over too so that you'd have one giant donut shop."

"I think the size of my shop is just fine," said Heather. "Any other reasons?"

"Maybe you wanted to get rid of some competition," suggested Mr. Rankle.

"Competition?" asked Amy.

"It was another restaurant," he said, defending his idea. "Maybe you wanted to stop people from eating there. You wanted all the little customers to flock to your place instead of his."

"I think fish and donuts are rather different tastes," said Heather. "I don't think we'd be in direct competition."

Then Mr. Rankle said, "Maybe you killed him just because that's what people do wherever you're from in Texas."

"Texas," Amy said. "Oh. Wait. You got it right that time."

"I'm right about a lot of things," he replied.

"Where were you the morning of the murder?" Heather asked.

"I was right here in my shop."

"Can anyone vouch for that?" she asked.

"If you can track down the ungrateful little boy and his mother who had to try on every single pair of sandals in the place, then yes."

"One last question," Heather said. "Did you know Percy Covens was back in town?"

"No. I don't think he told anyone. But maybe it was something a Private Investigator could have discovered," he said, giving them a dirty look.

"Thank you for your time," Heather said.

"Thank you for leaving," he replied.

Amy rolled her eyes. The two women left the store.

"I don't think we changed his mind about us being the murderers," said Amy.

"Maybe not," Heather said. "But he did give us some ideas for potential motives."

"Is there any chance he could have done it?" Amy asked. "Please, could he have done it."

"It's possible, but I don't think it's likely. Percy Covens seems like one of the few people that Mr. Rankle liked. His leg might also be a problem."

"Because of the cane?" asked Amy. "Maybe that works in his favor for guilt. He poisoned the guy because he knew he wouldn't be able to bash him over the head easily."

"But it also means that he's not especially fast. Remember how he marched off from the street crowd?" said Heather. "He might have done it. But he'd be taking a chance that someone would see him by the restaurant that morning. He would have had difficulty sneaking around."

"Maybe he knew that no one would think it was weird to see him on the street. He was just yelling at a cat or something."

"Maybe," said Heather. "But I think we should talk to more of the suspects."

"You mean more of the neighbors."

## Chapter 13

"As much as I want it to be Mr. Rankle who did it, I don't want it to be Bernadette," said Amy.

"I know," Heather agreed.

"She was the only person who was nice to us," said Amy. "I'd hate for her to end up behinds bars instead of being the only pleasant person on our street."

"We can't let our feelings cloud our judgment on a murder case, though. Anyone who took a donut could have left the crumbs at the scene and could be the killer."

"She did eat most of it in front of us," said Amy.

"We still should talk to her," Heather said. "Mr. Rankle's potential motives might hold some water. Her shop is next door to the restaurant. Maybe she wanted to expand her walls and make her shop bigger, but Percy Covens was preventing her."

"Then why was she so nice to us? It was some sort of cover?"

"It's possible," said Heather. "Maybe she was nice to us to divert suspicion away from her if she learned I was married to a detective. Or maybe she was being nice because she thought we would be suspicious. Maybe she kept the crumbs to try and frame us."

"That would go to show that you can't judge a book by its cover," Amy sighed.

"Then again, maybe she is just a nice person," said Heather. "We need to determine whether she could have poisoned the coffee."

They entered the shop. Bernadette couldn't wave because her arms were filled with books.

"Come in," she said. "It's good to see you. Give me just a moment. Sorry about this. I've got more books than I have room for."

Heather and Amy exchanged a look. Bernadette set down her pile and smiled at them.

"How are you holding up?" Bernadette asked. "I'm sorry about that crowd scene yesterday."

"Thank you for standing up for us," Heather said.

"No problem. It's silly for them to think that you had anything to do with it. If you were someone who knew Percy Covens and held a grudge against him, you wouldn't have gone through all the trouble of opening up a donut shop as a front for moving here. And if you really did come here to open a donut shop, then why would you kill a man you just met?"

"Never met," said Amy.

"Proves my point even more," said Bernadette. "Speaking of donuts, did you happen to bring any today?"

"I'm afraid not," said Heather. "I can whip some up later today, but we've been busy looking into the murder. Amy and I are both private investigators and felt compelled to help solve this case."

"Interesting," said Bernadette. "I thought you were bakers, but you're really a Miss Marple-type."

"Though not as old," Amy countered, happy to recognize one of Bernadette's literary references.

"We have to ask everyone," said Heather. "Where were you the morning that Percy Covens was killed?"

"I was here," said Bernadette. "I was actually a little late opening up shop. I overslept. And for no reason. I didn't have an exciting evening. I was home alone and went to bed."

"So, no one could confirm that you were there?" asked Heather.

"I guess not. Wow, you are good at investigating. I feel nervous now, and I didn't have anything to do with the murder."

"Did you get along with Percy Covens?"

"I told you that nobody seemed especially glad that I took over a shop on this block when I wasn't a local from the start. But Percy wasn't mean. I got lunch there sometimes."

"We heard he was a bit of a ladies' man," said Amy.

"That's definitely true," said Bernadette. "He dated plenty of people."

"You?" asked Amy.

"No," Bernadette said. "I knew he was a Willoughby and not a Mr. Darcy."

"Jane Austen?" Amy asked.

"Yes. Though I combined novels. When my love life goes poorly, which is often, she's a great one to read."

"Do you know if anyone on the street dated him?" Heather asked.

"No," Bernadette said, thinking. "There was a period of time where I thought he might have been with Delilah, but I was never sure."

"What do you mean?"

"I got the feeling that one was waiting for the other when they closed up for the day. It might have been my imagination, but it's what I thought at the time."

"When was this?" asked Heather.

"For a long time, but it stopped a few weeks ago."

"Did you notice him with anyone else recently?"

"No. But that doesn't mean that he wasn't seeing anyone. Just that I didn't seem them by the restaurant," said Bernadette. "I hope this helps in your investigation. I'd like to think I'm helping you catch a killer."

"You might be," said Heather. "We noticed when we came in today that you felt you didn't have enough space for your books."

"That's true," she said. "I can't say no to them. I have to have full shelves, but then I start to get too many and it becomes cluttered."
"I bet you'd like to expand your shop," Amy said.

"I'd love to have more space," said Bernadette. "But I think that's impossible."

"Even if Percy Coven's restaurant closes down?" asked Heather.

"I'd never be able to afford more space," said Bernadette. "This is prime real estate as it is. I couldn't expand."

Heather nodded.

"Why? Do you think I killed him?"

"We need to follow all possible leads," Heather said.

"I see," said Bernadette.

When they left the bookshop, they felt that Bernadette was acting much colder to them.

"I think we might have lost our only friend," said Amy.

"Catching the killer is more important than making friends," said Heather, but she was disappointed too.

## Chapter 14

"I'm surprised you'd dare show your face on this street," Delilah said as they entered her boutique.

"Why?" Amy asked. "Do I have frosting on it?"

"You think Percy's murder is funny?" Delilah asked. "Because I don't."

"We don't either," Heather assured her. "In fact, we're trying to solve it. We're private investigators and have decided to investigate our new neighbor's death."

"Why did you want to talk me?"

"We're talking to everyone on the street," Heather told her.

"I didn't have anything to do with it," Delilah said.
"Maybe you saw something that could point us in the right direction," Heather said, hoping to appease her and keep her talking. "Did you notice anything

unusual the day he died? Maybe someone by his restaurant that you don't normally see?"

"The only people on the street that seemed out of place was your shop," Delilah said.

"Well, you walked us into that one," Amy said.

"Did you know that Percy Covens was back in Key West?" Heather asked.

"What do you mean?"
"He was away on vacation. He was supposed to be gone for the week, but he got called back to fix something. We're not sure how many people knew he was back," said Heather.

"And so if I knew he was back, then I was the one who killed him?"

"If you knew he was back, you might know who else knew he was back," said Heather.

Delilah started organizing her swimsuits so she wouldn't have to give them her full attention.

"I didn't really notice," Delilah said. "I might have realized he was back when I saw lights on at the restaurant, but I didn't think much about it. I forgot that he was going on vacation. That was unlike him."

"So you knew him well enough to know his vacation habits?" asked Heather.

"I talked to him sometimes," Delilah said. "Our stores are close by and he was friendly."

"We heard he could be friendly," said Amy. "We heard he dated a lot."

"Already buying into street gossip, I see," Delilah said.

"Did you and Percy Covens ever date?" Heather asked.

"No," Delilah said, blushing. "Who said I did?"

"We were just wondering if he dated anyone on the street," said Heather.

"Was it Bernadette? If she said that, it's just to cause trouble for me."

"Why would that be?"

"Because I'm pretty and she's petty. Percy wouldn't even look at her. Now she wants you to think I killed him."

"That would be a change," said Amy. "Because everyone else on the street thinks it was us."

"Maybe it is. Maybe I shouldn't be talking to you. Maybe the police haven't found all their clues yet and will figure out who did it soon."

"We all want the same thing," Heather said. "Justice for Percy Covens. Do you know anyone who wanted to hurt him?"

"No," Delilah said. "Maybe someone he actually dated."

"Did he and Mr. Rankle get along?" Amy asked.

"I guess so," Delilah said. "Percy got along with everyone."

"One more line of questioning," Heather said. "Where were you the morning of the murder?"
"I was working," Delilah said.

"Can you prove that?" asked Heather.

"Actually, I can," said Delilah. "I was on a phone call with a customer that took a very long time. I'm sure phone records can back me up on that. It was the office line, so I had to be in the store to make the call."

"That's nice," said Amy. "That's one phone we know the location of."

"What do you mean by that?" asked Delilah.

120

"Nothing," said Amy.

Delilah pursed her lips, but then said, "Are you all finished with your questions?"

"For now," said Heather. "Thank you for your time."
She and Amy left the shop. They walked along the street towards Juan and Don's Tacos, discussing their prior questioning.

"I don't know how I feel about her as a suspect," said Amy.

Heather agreed. "I got the sense that she was lying about dating the victim at some point. Her face got very red and she immediately blamed Bernadette for starting the rumor."

"Then again, maybe Bernadette did start the rumor. Maybe she's been playing us."

"Well, our suspect list is certainly still remaining long," said Heather. "And we might be adding to it."

***

"We don't want to talk to you," Juan said.
"We're very busy setting up for our lunch rush," said Don.

"Interesting," Amy commented. "I bet it'll be even busier now that you don't have a lunchtime seafood restaurant a few doors down to compete with."

This made the two men pause.

"You think we killed him?" Don asked.

"Well, maybe just one of you," Amy said.

"We're talking to everyone on the street," said Heather. "We're trying to determine who might have had a motive."

Juan and Don looked at each other out of the corner of their eyes, then quickly

122

said at the same time: "We don't have a motive."

"Was that convincing?" Amy asked.
"Did we hit on something?" Heather asked. "Will your business profit from the seafood restaurant closing?"

"No," said Don.

"Another place will surely open up there," said Juan.

"And there are lots of restaurants on this street. We can all survive together," Don said.

"But," Juan started and then stopped.

"We might as well tell her," said Don. "It will seem more suspicious if we don't. And then she'll see it wouldn't be a reason for murder."

Juan nodded. "It's not a reason for murder. And we aren't happy to see him dead. We liked Percy. He was a good man."

"But?" Heather prompted.

"But," Juan continued. "Now that he's gone we can start making our special fish tacos again."

"It seemed silly to focus on them with the fish place right there," Don said. "So we just made chicken and beef."

"But we do make a great fish taco," said Juan.

"Juan has the best recipe," Don agreed.

"And so that has been something that we have been scurrying about making changes for," said Juan. "But we wouldn't kill anyone about it."

"No way," Juan agreed. "No one has to die for tacos."

"Where were you both the morning he died?" Heather asked.
"We weren't open yet," said Don. "But we were together."

"We had to go to the bank to check on something in our business records," said Juan. "I'm sure they have documentation to prove we were there."

"And do you have any idea who would want to hurt Percy Covens?" asked Heather.

She ignored Amy's whispers about wishing to hear Mr. Rankle's name.

"No," Juan said. "He was a good man."

"I'd say an ex-girlfriend, but I don't think any of them were that serious," said Don. "We couldn't think of a good reason. That's why we thought Mr. Rankle was on to something when he said you did it."

"But that was before we knew you were working with the police," said Juan.

"Well, thank you for your time," Heather said. "We'll be in touch if we have any more questions."

Secretly, she felt like they only had questions in this case and no answers.

**Chapter 15**

That evening Heather tried to spend some time unpacking but found it difficult to focus because her thoughts were still stuck on the case. Because some new house problems had developed (and this time in the kitchen), she and her friends had decided to gather together for a take out dinner together. She was trying to unpack at least a few boxes before the food arrived, but kept thinking about poison.

Ryan joined her in the room to help her unpack.

"We found Lilly's pink typewriter, so she is working on a new story before dinner," he reported.

"Another dinosaur detective story?" Heather asked.

"I think so, but I think in this story the dinosaurs are solving a mystery on the beach."

Heather sighed. "I still haven't made it to the beach. Too much to do at the shop and here and with the case."

"Well, you're about to hire employees at the shop, and that should ease the burden there. And don't worry too much about the house," Ryan said. "I've been working on the repairs, and I reattached the kitchen cabinet door."

"That's great," said Heather. "Any progress getting the light to turn on in there?"

"No," Ryan said. "But one step at a time."

"Thank you for doing so much around the house. It's starting to become a home," she said.

"Despite the problems with the house, I do like it here," said Ryan. "I'm glad we made the move."

"I am too," said Heather. "Though I'd be happier if my murder case were closed."

"This case is giving you a lot of trouble?"

"I feel like I'm missing something and I don't know if it's because I don't know my surroundings well enough yet, or if I'm distracted by my other duties, or if this killer was just smart about their crime and is, therefore, more dangerous."

"I'm sure you can figure it out," Ryan said. "I wish there was more that I could do to help. I don't think I like not being the detective to turn to."

"I have to admit that I miss it myself," said Heather.

"Is there anyone that you think is a more likely suspect than the others?" Ryan asked.

"It's possible that any of them could have done it, but right now we haven't uncovered a strong motive or who definitely could have planted the poison."

Ryan was about to ask some more questions, but they were interrupted by the doorbell.

"That might be the food," Ryan said.

"I don't like that the delivery driver is leaning on the bell though," Heather said.
Ryan frowned. "What if he's not leaning on the bell?"

They both groaned as the dinging from the bell continued on and on. They ran to the door and were greeted by Rudolph Rodney.

"Hello, Shepherds. So happy to see you both. This is rather a long doorbell ring, isn't it?"

The smile started to fade from his face as he realized the ding-dong wasn't stopping.

"Mom," Lilly said, coming into the room with her hands covering her ears. "Why won't it stop?"

"I guess it just wanted everyone to know that we had a guest," Heather joked.

She was right though because soon everyone from the three houses had entered. Eva and Leila came in joking about how now they were sure that they didn't need hearing aids. Amy and Jamie came in with the food because they had encountered the deliveryman on their way over. Dave and Cupcake also joined them in the room. Dave decided to add to the hubbub and started barking excitedly.

"I'm terribly sorry about this," Rudolph Rodney said, gripping his hat in his hands.

Ryan checked on the bell, and after playing with it a bit got it to stop ringing. His friends added some noise to the scene by clapping for him.

"Thanks," Ryan said. "But I'm not sure the bell is going to work anymore after that."

"I do apologize," Rudolph Rodney said. "I can have an electrician come out and look at it."

"I think that would be great," Ryan said. "I think I can admit that the house repairs are a tad more ambitious that I originally thought. I did take the first step in many of the projects though. I got them started."

"I'll arrange to get it all fixed soon" he assured them. "I want this place to be a home you love."

"Even with all the problems, it's well on its way," Heather said. "We do love all living here together. If I could just make it to the beach, it would be perfect."

"I just came over to tell you about how the front section of Donut Delights should be finished tomorrow."

"Donut Delights the Sequel," Amy added.

"That's great to hear," Heather said.

"I also just wanted to check in and see how you were all doing," Rudolph Rodney said. "So, if you could make up a list of everything that needs to be fixed around the house, I'll see to it that it gets done."

"Of course," Eva said. "We can make a list. I think the water temperature is the main thing that needs to be fixed in our house."

"The squeaky doors in our house is what's making me jump," said Amy. "But I guess fixing the electricity in the living room is more important."

"And we had some issues in the kitchen with the stove," said Ryan.
"Oh my," Rudolph Rodney said. "Well, get this long list written up for me and I'll take care of it. It sounds like it might be everything except the kitchen sink on the list."

"No," Amy said. "The kitchen sink is on the list too."

They laughed, but Leila added, "We don't want to scare him off. A lot of things are just fine. The appliances are mostly good. And the refrigerator is bigger than in our last home."

"The refrigerator," Heather said.

"Oh no," Leila said. "Did I speak too soon?"

"Is yours broken, dear?" asked Eva. "You can put food in ours."

"No, it's not that. It's about the case," Heather said.

"You solved it?" Amy asked.

"Not yet," said Heather. "But I think I need to talk to Detective Smith. I realized something we hadn't thought of before."

"The fridge?"

"Exactly," said Heather. "What if it wasn't an accident that brought Percy Covens back? What if the refrigeration unit was purposely broken to lure him back?"

"This really is a cold-blooded killer," Amy said.

"You can all start dinner, but I think I have to call Detective Smith."
Her friends did start setting up the food and invited Rudolph Rodney to join them who graciously agreed. However, they all kept an ear open to listen to Heather's conversation.

"This is great timing," Detective Smith said. "I was going to contact you."

"You have a lead?"

"It's about his cell phone," Detective Smith said.

"You found it?"

"We looked at the records for the phone," he said. "Most of the calls make sense. He calls work, his employees, and Eliza. However, there were also many calls to and from a phone we can't trace. It must have been a burner phone. It's not listed to a person."

"But you believe that person might be the killer?"

"I believe the timing is suspicious. There were many calls, and they suddenly stopped a week or two ago. Then there was a call the night before he died. I'm not trying to make a joke," Detective Smith said. "But that was a good call you made about looking for the phone."

"It would only be better if you could find Percy Covens' phone as well. The fact that it is missing makes me think that it's important," Heather said.
"We put a trace on it. If the phone turns on, we'll be able to track and locate it," he replied. "Wait a moment. My partner is running over to me out of breath."

Heather tried to wait patiently for Detective Smith to reveal the news.
"Peters just told me. The phone was turned on. We can track it now."

"And it might lead you straight to the killer!"

## Chapter 16

Heather and Amy stood outside of Donut Delights. Detectives Smith and Peters had traced the phone to their street. They had allowed Heather and Amy to tag along at a distance but wanted them to stay out of danger in case the killer got reckless.

The two friends watched in surprise as the detectives entered Bernadette's Beachy Books.

"It was Bernadette after all?" Amy asked. "Why couldn't it have been Mr. Rankle?"

"We're not sure it was her," Heather cautioned.

However, a moment later the detectives emerged. Peters was holding a cell phone in an evidence bag that must have been the victim's. Detective Smith was leading Bernadette out of the shop in handcuffs.

"I don't know what that phone was doing here," Bernadette said. "It's not mine."

"We know it's not yours," said Peters. "It's Percy Covens', and it was taken away from the crime scene after he was killed."

"But it wasn't me. I feel just like Jean Valjean right now. Les Mis reference." Bernadette said. "But you have to believe me. I didn't have any reason to kill Percy."

"Remember those rights I told you about?" Detective Smith said. "You might want to consider them."
He led her towards his police car, but Bernadette decided not to remain silent. She called out Heather and Amy.

"Keep investigating," she said. "It wasn't me."

***

The next day, Heather should have been excited by how far the new Donut

Delights was coming along. The floors were all finished, and the furniture would arrive soon. She would just have to fill it with donuts and employees, and it would be all set.

However, she was still distracted by the murder. Amy seemed to be feeling the same.

"Does something feel wrong to you?" Amy asked.

"Yes," Heather said. "I think we need to bake some donuts while we're here and then discuss the turn the case took."

"Sounds great," Amy said.
They began whipping up a batch of Chocolate Hazelnut Donuts. As the smells wafted around the room, Heather started to feel better already.

Then as she stirred Heather said, "I thought finding the phone would lead us to the killer, but it doesn't feel quite right."

"Bernadette didn't have a strong motive," Amy agreed. "And she was nice."

"I can't shake the feeling that maybe the cell phone was planted at her shop to make her look guilty."

"If that's true, we need to keep looking for the killer."

"Unfortunately, it doesn't shrink our suspect list either," said Heather. "She was the other newcomer on the street. She said that many people would have been happy to see her leave. Any one of our neighbors might have chosen to frame her to divert suspicion."

"When they failed to frame us with the donut crumbs," said Amy.

"I think I should check in with Detective Smith and see if he's discovered anything concrete," Heather said.

She called the station and then reported back what she had learned to her bestie. Bernadette was still professing her innocence. The detectives had examined the cell phone. No prints were found on it.

"Which is suspicious because Bernadette's prints weren't on it even though she was supposedly hiding it in her shop," Heather had remarked.

When they examined the data inside the phone, they could tell that things were deleted. The calls made to the burner phone that they had seen in the phone records were no longer visible on the phone. There was a surprisingly few number of text messages in the phone too, that led them to believe even more was deleted.

"I think the killer erased everything that could lead the police back to him," said Heather. "And then hid the phone at the bookshop to frame Bernadette."
"I think you're right," Amy agreed. "But now how do we figure out who did it?"

Heather finished putting the hazelnut toppings on her donuts as she thought of an answer. However, they were interrupted by a knock at the door.

"I bet someone smelled these donuts and can't wait for us to open," Amy said.

Heather smiled at the idea. They went to the front door and saw Digby outside.
"I hoped I would find you here," Digby said. "I didn't want to have to wander the streets trying to find you."

"What is it?" Heather asked, opening the door.

"Did you think of something related to the murder?" asked Amy.

"I thought of something else," Digby said. "I hope you won't think I'm too forward."

"Just tell us," Heather said.

"Of course," Digby said. "I have a grand idea that I think could benefit everyone involved, and – did you just make donuts? It smells wonderful."

Heather smiled. "I think we could spare one. If it's that good an idea."

They presented Digby with a Chocolate Hazelnut Donut, and he was too happy eating it to express his idea. When he could talk, he said, "I haven't felt this happy in days. I'd been feeling depressed and guilt-ridden. This is a welcome lift to spirits."

"We're glad we could help," said Heather.
"And that's why I'm here," Digby said. "Because I want to help too. At this shop. Especially after tasting these donuts. I don't have a job anymore. And I figured you were hiring. I'd be a great addition to the staff. I have lots of skills. And the fish business is comparable."

Amy wrinkled her nose.

"Please give me a chance," Digby said.

Heather smiled at him. "I suppose we could set up an interview."

"Thank you so much," he said. "You won't regret it. I worked so hard for Percy, and I will work hard for you, too. I feel so bad that his coming back for the refrigeration unit is what caused him to be here and to be *murdered*. But it was a fluke. Nothing like that had ever happened with the machines before. And it was so unusual that I didn't know how to fix it. But that shouldn't happen again."

"About the problem with the refrigerator," Heather said. "Was Percy Covens able to fix it?"

"Yeah. He was great with that sort of thing. But it did take him a while. He was upset about it too," Digby said. "He thought a tourist messed with the outside part of it."

"Someone did mess with the unit?" Heather asked. The gears were turning in her head.

"He thought so," Digby said. "Can I ask a question?"

"Go ahead."

"Can I have another donut?" Digby asked.

"Sure," Heather said, but then she realized something and paused. "She took two."

"What?" asked Amy.

"Digby have another donut, and then I need to ask a favor," Heather said. "And if you can do this, you're hired."

"Sure," Digby said. "What is it?"

"If you tell Mr. Rankle a piece of gossip, would he make sure that everyone on the street knows it?"

"Definitely," said Digby. "Rankle loves to talk."

"And yell," said Amy. "Is this a trap to prove he did it?"

"I need you to tell him what the police plan to do tomorrow."

"Sure," Digby said. "But what is it?"

## Chapter 17

"I feel silly," Amy said. "Is this really a good hiding place?"

"It is if we're quiet," Heather whispered back.

It was nighttime, and they were hiding behind a bunch of palm trees behind the back of the shops. They were keeping an eye on the seafood restaurant and waiting to see if their plan would work. It wasn't the most comfortable place they'd ever been for a stakeout because they couldn't move very much. However, their location did provide them an excellent view of the part of the refrigeration unit that sat outside.

Finally, their waiting was rewarded. They saw a figure dressed all in black was approaching the unit with a small duffle bag.

"Stop right there," Heather called out.

The figure froze and then turned to face them. Delilah gave them a dirty look.

"What are you doing here?" she snapped.

"We should be the ones asking that," Amy replied.

"I was just passing by on my way home," Delilah said. "And I don't appreciate being surprised like this. You could have given me a heart attack."

"I don't believe that's why you're here," said Heather. "I think you're here because you heard Mr. Rankle say that the police were going to do a more thorough examination of the refrigeration unit. He thought it was going to prove that we newcomers had sabotaged something because we're irresponsible. But you knew that the unit would be inspected because it related to the murder."

"I don't know what you're talking about," Delilah said angrily.

"Oh, we think you do," Amy said.

"You didn't like that Percy Covens was on vacation with another woman, so you did something to bring him back here. You sabotaged this unit so he would have to come back and fix it. Digby mentioned that Percy Covens thought that tourists had messed with it, but it was you."

"You can't prove that," Delilah said.

"You were afraid we could," said Heather. "That's why you came out here to check. You needed to make sure that the tool you used didn't leave a mark that could be tied back to you. You weren't sure quite what Percy Covens did to fix the unit, and you had to be certain you couldn't be implicated."

"And why would I want Percy to come back?"

"You were in love with him," Heather said. "All those calls from the burner phone must have been to you. You two were trying to be discreet about your relationship."

149

"I don't have to stay here and listen to this," Delilah said.

Heather was stalling now. She thought the police would have arrived on the scene by this point.

"You thought it was to avoid gossip on the street," she said. "However, for Percy, it must have been because he didn't think it was serious. It must have hurt you very much when you found out that he was engaged."

That caused Delilah to say, "How could he do that to me? I thought we were in love. Then he started ignoring me. And then, I find out that he went away with another woman. I needed him to come back. I was sure if he saw me again, he'd remember what we had."

"But instead he told you he was getting married," said Heather. "He wanted to end things permanently."

"So you decided to end him permanently," Amy chimed in.

"You visited him that morning," said Heather. "No one noticed you going there because you were both used to sneaking around to meet each other without being noticed. The only one who was suspicious of your affair was Bernadette. Is that why you decided to frame her?"

"I wanted to implicate you with the donuts, but that didn't work," she said. "I thought the police would be suspicious of the new people like Mr. Rankle was. I didn't know you were private detectives."

"You took Percy's phone after you poisoned him so you could delete your conversations," said Heather. "And then you placed it in the bookshop so they would think Bernadette was the killer."

"How did you know it was me?" Delilah asked.
"The crumbs that you used to try and implicate us," Heather said. "We handed out many donuts, but then I remembered that you took two. I started

to wonder if you had taken two so you could give one to your lover. You were planning on seeing him because you knew he'd be back to fix what you had broken."

"That's not proof though," said Delilah.

"That's true," said Heather. "But I realized that whoever broke the unit would most likely return if we started a rumor that the police were going to find evidence to catch the killer from it."

"Well," Delilah said. "I guess I'm going to have to make sure that you don't get the chance to tell anyone about this."

She quickly opened her duffle bag and revealed heavy bolt cutters. She moved towards them, ready to swing when someone else told her to freeze.

Detectives Smith and Peters were on the scene. They easily subdued Delilah, and Peters lead her away while reading her rights to her.

"Took you long enough," Amy said.

"It figures she would arrive the moment we decided to check the unit on the inside," Detective Smith said. "You did a good job keeping her talking though."

"Thank you," Heather said.

He nodded and went to join his partner. "I'm glad this is over," Amy said. "What do you want to do now?"

"Well," Heather said. "First thing tomorrow..."

## Chapter 18

Heather finally was able to set up her beach chair and enjoy some time in the sand. She was joined by all her friends and family, and wouldn't have it any other way.

"So you two finally get some time to relax?" Jamie asked them.

"Yes," Heather smiled. "The killer was caught, and justice was served. Even if she hadn't confessed and came after us."

"Which I'm not a fan of," said Ryan. "I don't like that I'm not there to keep an eye on you."

"Maybe not with a badge, but I know that you're always there to support me," Heather said.

"The other evidence?" Amy prompted.
"Detective Smith looked into her alibi. Remember she said that she had been on the phone wilth a customer the morning that the victim was killed? It

turns out the call was to the same burner phone. She had called herself and kept the line busy to give herself an alibi."

"This killer did a lot with phones," Amy said. "It's just a shame it wasn't the meanest neighbor who turned out to be worst."

"I think Mr. Rankle might never warm up to us," said Heather. "But I bet a lot of the others will. We found justice for Percy Covens, and we'll be serving up delicious donuts."

"Nobody can resist that," Eva said.

"Especially the chocolate ones," Leila said. "Can you pass another one of those Chocolate Hazelnut ones my way?"

They obliged her. Heather watched Lilly splash in the shallow water and felt the warm sun on her skin. If she ignored what still had to be done to open up her shop, it was a peaceful and relaxing moment.

However, Amy wasn't going to let her relax that easily. "There is one more thing I think we should settle."

"And what's that?"

"The shop is about to open soon. What are we going to call this Donut Delights? Is it my Donut Delights the Sequel? Is it Donut Delights II?"

"Good question," Heather said. "But I think we should just call it its name and location: Donut Delights – Key West."

"By only adding the location at the end, are you planning on opening more locations in the future?" Ryan asked.

"I can't even think of that now," Heather said. "At this moment, I just want to enjoy the sand, the surf and the—"

"So-nut?" Amy offered, making the donut dessert an alliteration.

156

Heather laughed and agreed. Surrounded by her family and friends and a few donuts, it would always seem like paradise.

**The End**

# Book 2 – Banana Chocolate & Murder

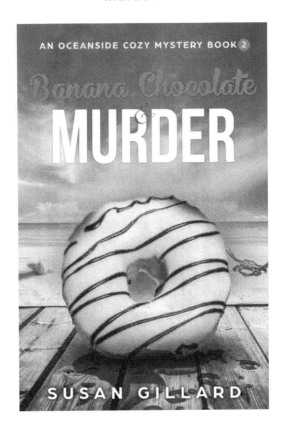

## Chapter 1 - Banana Chocolate VIPs

"I feel like a VIP," Eva said. "Entering the shop before it's open."

"It makes me feel like all the donuts are being made for us," Leila agreed.

"Well, it's the least I can do," Heather said, smiling at her friends.

Heather and her family had recently moved to Key West so she could open up a second Donut Delights shop. Eva and Leila had basically followed her there. They had wanted to remain close to their friends and the donuts that they loved. Heather was touched that the grandmotherly women had chosen to stay close to her family and, store open or not, was always happy to provide them with freshly baked donuts.

"So, what's the flavor of the week?" Eva asked.

"The flavor just for us?" Leila joked.

"I will be handing out some samples of this new flavor to drum up more excitement for our grand opening, and I will be using this recipe with the new assistants that we hire as a test run," Heather explained. "But you are my VIPs, and I did make a batch just for you."

"I can't take the suspense," Leila said, dramatically putting a hand to her forehead.

"But I can take a donut if you'll tell me what it is," Eva said with a smile.

"My newest creation is the Banana Chocolate Donut," Heather said, revealing them to her friends.

"I think I'm going to go bananas for them!" said Leila.

"And I think I'll order a whole bunch," said Eva.

Heather groaned appreciatively at the puns but didn't let it dissuade her from describing the new donut.

"The donut cake base is chocolate, but it's made with some bananas for both texture and flavor. However, overall, it should still have a rich chocolatey taste. Then the frosting is a new banana flavored icing that I created. I had to balance it so it wouldn't taste artificial, but would still have that nice yellow color."

"That's a mellow yellow I'd like to sink my teeth into," Leila said.

"And chocolate sprinkles on top?" Eva asked.

"Of course," said Heather. "I felt this called for some sprinkles."
"I think this calls for us to start eating, dear," said Eva.

Leila seconded the idea and Heather agreed. She handed out the donuts and enjoyed seeing the happy looks that always came to their faces when they tried a new flavor. At first, all Heather could make out was "mmm" but when they reached for seconds, she was positive they enjoyed them.

"It tastes like I'm dipping bananas in fondue," Eva said. "It's both rich and light."

Heather was about to respond to the compliments when she was interrupted by the appearance of her best friend, Amy.

"Am I missing donut time?" Amy asked.

"It's always donut time," Heather said, handing her a snack.

Amy was torn between making a sassy remark and eating her donut. In the end, the tasty snack won out. However, after she had devoured the donut, she said, "I needed that after all the errands I ran this morning."

"Is there still a lot to do?" Eva asked. "It really looks like it's coming along."

She gestured around the shop and Heather had to agree with her. The counters, flooring, and tables were all finished. The new location had a beachy theme that would suit the tourists in the mood for tropical donuts. It looked different from Heather's beloved first Donut Delights with golden floorboards and wrought iron tables, but she felt herself getting used to the drift wood look.

"The main thing that we still need to accomplish is hiring out staff," Heather said. "But we have some interviews set up for this week. Then we just need to stock up on a few things for the kitchen, and—"

"And Heather is using my artistic eye to finish up the décor for the front," said Amy. "I've picked up some things to help with centerpieces for the tables."

"Great," Heather said. "I'm getting used to all the driftwood, but I think that it still needs a splash of color."

Eva and Leila giggled at her use of the word splash.

Amy didn't miss a beat and said, "That's not the only splash we're going to make. Heather promised to take me scuba diving. That's one of the things I've been looking forward to the most about coming here."

"I promised that we could go after we hire an employee," Heather reminded her.
"You don't seem as excited about it," Eva commented.

"I'm not against it. We'd probably see some amazing sights," said Heather.

"But?"

"Something about it makes me nervous," Heather admitted. "I guess I feel like I don't have as much control in the water as on dry land. But it's silly to be scared of it. We'd have an instructor. And I've certainly faced more frightening situations."

The other women nodded, thinking of the many close calls that Heather had faced as part of her investigations. Heather had a knack for solving murders, but also had a knack for encountering danger.

"I'm sure it will be fun," Heather said.

"It will be incredible," Amy said. "Think of all the fish we'll see."

"We'll see your buddy the clownfish?" Heather asked.

"But his jokes aren't nearly as funny as mine," Amy said. "Now let me have another donut now. You're supposed to wait a half hour after eating before swimming, so you don't get cramps, so I better eat enough now."

"We're not going in a half hour," Heather said. "We need to hire at least one employee before we go."

"We better let you two get down to business," Eva said. "Besides, we wanted to check out some of the senior activities offered around here."

"Yes. And the quicker we get out of your hair, the quicker you can hire someone, and the quicker you can scuba," Leila agreed.

"About that," Amy started.

Right on cue, the front door opened and in walked Digby.

"Good morning," the young man said, waving to them all.

"We did already hire someone," Amy reminded her.

"Yes," Heather admitted. "But I meant after we hired someone new. From our interviews. So it felt like we had made some progress."

They had hired Digby after his employer had been murdered and he had helped them catch the killer. He was a bit melodramatic but had a good heart. He was also very excited about baking donuts.

"You might have meant that," said Amy. "But you said after we hire someone, and we hired Digby."

"You're not having second thoughts, are you?" Digby asked.

"Not at all," said Heather. "At least, not about hiring you."

"So let's give him fill out his paperwork, so he's official, and then let's dive into some scuba fun."

"Not so fast," Heather said. "You don't think I'm going to have a new assistant join the team and not immediately bake donuts with them?"

"Really?" Both Digby and Amy asked. One asked in enthusiasm, while the other asked with annoyance.

"Really," Heather said. "It's time to bake another batch."

## Chapter 2 – The Bookstore Briefing

"Digby is going to be a great addition to the team," Heather said. "He was a quick learner. He was competent."

"And he ate more donuts that I did," said Amy. "He's going to love it there."

"I think so," said Heather. "And he showed ambition by offering to hand out the free samples in front of the store."

"I think he enjoys describing the flavor," said Amy. "He thinks of it as a performance. I bet part of him wants to be an actor."

"It could be," said Heather. "But I appreciate it because it also gives us the opportunity to make our own donut delivery on the street."

She and Amy were bringing a box of donuts over to Bernadette's Beachy Books. The owner was one of the few people on the block who had befriended them, and they were eager to maintain the relationship.

168

As they walked down the street, they saw one of the people who remained unhappy to see newcomers set up shop. Mr. Rankle was standing outside his store and was giving them the evil eye as they passed. He had accused them of murdering another shop owner on the street and had been disappointed when they had caught the real killer instead of heading off to jail themselves. It seemed that the real crime to Mr. Rankle was not being a local.

"Good morning, Mr. Rankle," Heather greeted him, trying her best to thaw his icy exterior.

"Morning," he said curtly, purposely cutting off the good.

Heather and Amy walked away with Amy muttering, "I don't think we're ever going to get anywhere with him. Write him off as spoiled milk and ignore him."

"He's our neighbor, and we've got to try," Heather said. "He might come around eventually. And until then we'll be neighborly with Bernadette."

169

They entered her shop and felt cozily surrounded by books.

"I don't know who you are, but with those donuts, I'm glad to see you," a young woman with a long braid greeted them.

"Thanks, and hello," said Amy.

"I see you've met my assistant, Gina," Bernadette said, joining them.

Heather and Amy smiled at the woman they expected to see and then shook hands with the new person, before handing donuts out all around.

"You weren't exaggerating," Gina said. "These are delicious."

"Gina and I don't normally work the same shifts," Bernadette said. "But she was away last week and missed all the excitement, so I had to update her how the new neighbors cleared me of a murder charge."

170

"Too much happens when I'm gone," Gina said.

"At least you're here for the donuts," Heather said.

They chatted amicably for a few more minutes and enjoyed the snacks, and then Gina admitted that she had some work to catch up on and excused herself.

"She seems like a good employee," Heather said. "We're about to start our interviews for our new staff."

"That can be nerve-wracking," Bernadette said.

Heather nodded. "I'd conducted interviews before, but to be honest most of my staff sort of fell into my lap. They were either referred to me, or I met them while investigating a case."

"Sleuthing often leads to good employees," Amy said. "But we can't use that technique here. We need to hire in the near future."

"Well," Bernadette said. "There is something that I do when I interview potential employees. I noticed it on an interview and then used it myself."

"What is it?" Heather asked.

"I like to ask a question about my shop, but then offer a potential answer. So, if I were interviewing you, I might ask: What sort of mysteries do you like to read? Agatha Christie? And then I see how they respond. It's a balance of accepting the employer's suggestion and offering their own. There's no right answer, exactly. But if they only accept the answer I suggested, then they might not be confident enough to make suggestions on other work things."

"And if they say your suggestion is the worst thing ever or otherwise insult it," Amy said, scholarly. "Then you can extrapolate that they'll be rude to others."

172

"Right," said Bernadette.

"Though we might agree that Agatha Christie is the one that we like to read," Heather said. "I don't often have time to sit down with a book, but she is a great author. *And Then There Were None* kept me guessing right to the very end."

"And it's hard to stump Heather," said Amy.

"But see," Bernadette said. "Your anecdote proves to me that you have read her and aren't just saying the most popular thing."

"Thanks," Heather said. "This might be a good idea to try. I can ask about how they feel about donut flavors."

Amy cleared her throat, and Heather smiled.

"Thank you for your help with that," said Heather. "But truth be told, we came here for your help in another matter.

Something we thought we should ask a local about."

"What?"
"We'd like to go scuba diving tomorrow and were hoping you could suggest an instructor."

"How exciting," said Bernadette. "You'll have your undersea moment like Pierre Aronnax."

"Who?" asked Amy.

"Sorry. I should have said Captain Nemo. He's more well known. It's a *Twenty Thousand Leagues Under the Sea* reference. It's a funny thing. You know that the twenty thousand leagues don't refer to depth, but rather to how much traveling they did under the water?"

"No," Amy said. "And I don't know where to go scuba diving."

"Right," Bernadette said, thinking about it. "There are two small scuba schools that are very close by, so I'd recommend one of them. There's Shelly's Scuba School and Club Scuba. But they're both named after their owner's. Club is the man's last name."

"Would you recommend one over the other?" Heather asked.

"They are pretty similar and close competition," Bernadette said. "But Shelly comes in and finds good books. She's a sweetheart. I think I'd chose her."

"Great," Heather said, thanking her. "And Amy, do you believe now that I am going to do this with you?"

"We could go today and get it over with?" Amy suggested with a smile.

"I can't," Heather said. "I have something much more difficult to do tonight."

"What's that?"

"Make sure Lilly is set for her first day of school tomorrow!"

## Chapter 3 – Home Sweet Home

Heather and Amy returned home, which was now at the same building. They had moved into a three-family home in Key West where Heather and her family lived in one apartment, Amy and her boyfriend Jamie lived above them, and Eva and Leila were next door. It was a comfortable living arrangement because it meant that the friends never had to travel far to see one another. It was also easy to share donuts throughout the house.

It was also helping Ryan and Jamie to become better friends. The two men were watching a baseball game on the Shepherd's TV and having a good time when their significant others returned.

Heather updated them on their morning and on her reluctant plans to go scuba diving the next day. Ryan and Jamie were eager to accompany them. Heather was still a little nervous that the phrase "sink or swim" would be applicable when they tried it, but she felt a little bit better about it when she realized that three people she cared about would be there with her as she learned.

"How was your day?" she asked.

"We went to the beach with Lilly this morning," Ryan said. "But then we had to come home so that the plumber could work on the upstairs bathroom."

"It wouldn't stop flushing," Jamie explained.

"I guess I'm glad we missed one house quirk," Amy groaned.

"Don't worry," Heather said, shaking her head. "We'll be around for the next."

As much as they loved living near each other and how easy it was to travel to the beach, their house certainly wasn't an island 5-Star hotel. Their new business investor and landlord felt bad about the issue and sent professionals to fix the household problems as soon as they occurred, but unfortunately, more and more professionals had to visit. They became friendly with the plumber, and Heather thought that he didn't mind how often he had to make repairs because he was provided with delicious donuts in addition to his compensation.

"And then we started watching the game," said Ryan. "It felt like a real vacation."

Heather smiled. Ryan was waiting for a detective on the force to retire so that he could take over the position. It was supposed to happen in the near future, and Ryan had decided that since he was near the beach, he should treat the time off like a vacation. Heather thought part of him was itching to begin detective work again. He certainly could use some relaxation time, but he wasn't somebody used to sitting back and doing nothing.

"What's Lilly up to now?"

Ryan and Jamie exchanged a look.

"She's talking to her friends," Ryan said. "About what she should wear on her first day of school tomorrow."

"Uh oh. A big decision," Heather said. "Maybe I should go check on her."
Heather headed down the hall to her daughter's room. She knocked on the door, and Lilly told her to come in. She was just finishing a video chat on her tablet with her best friend, Nicolas. Heather was able to tell him that they all missed him and wished him the best of luck with his first day of school too.

Then, Heather asked, "I heard you were trying to figure out what to wear tomorrow with some friends' help. How is it going?"

Lilly sighed. "It was good to catch up with my friends, but no one was helpful. Nicolas said I probably look nice in everything and couldn't make any decisions. And Marlene was too worried about picking out her own outfit to help me much. I wanted to tell her that she's going to school with the same people

180

that she's been going to school with forever. Everyone there knows she's cool. But no one here knows anything about me. And I'm nervous."

"Honey, I don't think you have anything to be nervous about. You make friends better than anyone I know."

"But you're great with people too, mom. And your donut shop neighbors were mean to you too. Just because you were new."

"That was a little disheartening, but we managed to win most of them over. Everyone except Mr. Rankle seems to be warming up to us."

"But that's because you solved a crime on the street," said Lilly. "I don't think I'm going to be doing that."

Heather nodded. "I can see why you're nervous. New experiences are often nerve-wracking. I'm going to attempt scuba diving tomorrow and am nervous too. It's something new. And underwater."

"You're really going scuba diving tomorrow?"

"Yes. And if everything goes well, and after all the adults are certified, we can look into you going on a dive too."

"That would be amazing," said Lilly. "I bet it would be beautiful. And some types of fish have been around as long as the dinosaurs."

"See? There are lots of positive aspects to something new and different."

"I do want to go to school. And I do want to make new friends."

"Then," Heather said. "I think the best thing to do is to be yourself. It's worked before."

Lilly laughed. "I guess you're right."

"And do you want my advice on what to wear?"

"Yes, please!"

"I think you should wear whatever makes you feel good. It doesn't have to be the "coolest" thing in your closet. It should be what you feel comfortable in, and what makes you feel like you look nice."

"You know, when you put it like that, I think I have the perfect outfit," Lilly said. She pulled it out of her closet and showed her mom.

"It is perfect," Heather agreed.

Lilly smiled. "I guess I'm all set for school then. That was my only homework for the night."

"Then let's go figure out dinner. We both have busy days tomorrow and should get to bed early."

Lilly nodded. "I think tomorrow will be fine. And you'll have a great time scuba diving."

"Thanks," said Heather.

"As long as no murder cases interrupt it," Lilly added.

## Chapter 4 – Scuba and Shouting

They sent Lilly off to school with high spirits and some Banana Chocolate Donuts in her lunch. Heather was still not completely excited for her adventure that morning but felt some of the enthusiasm from the others in her group rubbing off on her.

She promised Eva and Leila to give them a detailed report of how the dive went, and the two women promised with a laugh that they would keep her updated on how their search for senior activities progressed.

"We'll also let you know if we meet any eligible bachelors," Leila said. "Who knows? Maybe they'll still have their original teeth."

"I think it will be hard to find someone to keep up with you two," said Heather.

"I agree," Eva laughed. "But don't let us keep you from your fun."

Heather nodded, hoping that she would find the outing fun like everyone else expected it to be. Why was she feeling so hesitant? Was she nervous because this was something different, or did she really believe that something would go wrong?

She tried to push her nerves and bad feelings away and traveled with her bestie and their respective partners to the beach. Amy was joking about how she would look in her diving mask and was relieving the tension Heather felt.

They saw the boat house marked "Shelly's Scuba School" and headed to the nearby dock where they were told to meet their instructors. There were a few other people there eager to begin the diving lesson. There was a newlywed couple who were just beginning their honeymoon, and three young women friends who were on a "summer's not quite over" trip. They were chatting amicably, but also began to check their watches. It was time for them to begin, but they had not been greeted yet.

"Are we sure we're in the right place?" Amy asked.

"The reservation I made said to meet at the dock," Heather said, shrugging.

Ryan scanned the area and pointed. "It looks like they're coming now."

Two people in wetsuits bearing the logo for "Shelly's Scuba School" approached them, carrying air tanks and supplies between them. The woman had short brown hair and a confident air about her. The man looked like he was still stuck in his awkward teen years even though he must have been in his thirties. He had unruly curly hair and a nervous disposition.

"Shelly isn't here?" the man asked.

"That's all right," the woman said, trying to play it off as if it were intentional. "Everyone welcome to Shelly's Scuba School. I'm Julie, and this is Micah. We're going to support you today as Shelly teaches you all how to dive.

Before you go into the deeper water, we're going to make sure you all know how to use your equipment and are adequately prepared to swim with it on. It's a multi-step process that—"

They weren't able to hear any of the steps because she was drowned out by an intentionally loud boat motor.

The boat pulled up close to the dock, and the man at the helm waved to them. He had on sunglasses and had a crooked smile.

"I see that Shelly's school is keeping you waiting," he called. "Come on over to Club Scuba where you'll all receive personal attention."

"What are you doing here, Hank?" Julie yelled.

"I'm checking to make sure that all scuba customers are cared for. If you can't care for them there, I'll take them over to my place. Club Scuba has state of the art equipment and more concern for wasting your time than Shelly seems to."

"Don't you talk about her like that!" Micah said, angrily.

"I'm sorry for this distraction," Julie said to the group. "We are getting started now."

"I didn't know this came with a show," Amy said. "We should have brought popcorn."

"And soda," Jamie agreed.

"This certainly is a dramatic start to the dive," Heather said. "Should we be worried that Shelly isn't here?"

"You're not suggesting—" Ryan started.

"I'm not suggesting anything," Heather said. "Just wondering about our instructor."

"So do I have any takers?" Hank Club asked. "I know we're close in location,

189

and price and services. So the main difference you have to consider is the instructor themselves. Do you want to entrust yourself in the care of a flaky woman who can't show up on time? Or the charismatic man who went out of his way to check that you were being cared for?"

The young women in the group on the dock were looking at one another and considering the offer.

"If you don't get out of here, you're going to be the one who needs caring for," Micah said.

"Was that a threat?" Hank Club asked. "If so, it was a very awkward one."

"It's times like this I miss having my badge," said Ryan.

"If this escalates, I don't think Detective Smith would object to your stepping in to defuse the situation," Heather said. "But I think the best thing to do would be to find Shelly. I'll go check the boat house first."

"I'll come too," Amy said.
They left the group. Shelly's assistants and Hank Club were still verbally sparring with one another. Ryan was getting ready to step in if need be. The rest of the new divers were feeling awkward about the encounter.

Heather and Amy approached the clean white boat house. She reached for the doorknob and couldn't help but notice that it was loose in the frame.

"That's odd," she commented.
As they opened the door, they saw the reason for Shelly's lateness. She was arguing with a tall man who just grabbed her by the arm.

"You'll be sorry, Shelly," he said.

### Chapter 5 – Shelly in Danger

"Don't be an idiot," Shelly said, trying to pry the man's hand off her arm.

"You're telling me I'm imagining things?" he asked.

"I guess so," Shelly said. "I don't know what you're talking about."

"Tommy is always around here. Why is that?"

"Maybe to make you mad," she said. "It seems to be working. I certainly haven't invited him here."

"Really? You're not going on any late-night dives with him again?"

"Dylan, let go of me. I have a class to teach. It's my job. Remember when you used to have one?"

"I won't let you two-time me, Shelly," he said, shaking her.

"Stop it," she said.

It didn't look like Dylan planned on letting her go, so Heather stepped in.

"I think you should know that one of the divers waiting for Shelly is a police officer, so I think you should let her go."

Dylan let go immediately. "I wasn't going to hurt her."

"Well, it doesn't look that way to us," said Heather.

Dylan walked to the door, but turned back to say, "I'll call you later, Shelly."

"Only if you regain your sense," said Shelly. "There's nothing going on between Tommy and me."

Dylan left rather than reply. Shelly took a deep breath.

"Are you okay?" Heather asked.

"I'm sorry you had to see that," Shelly said. "My boyfriend can be a jerk."

193

"Maybe he shouldn't be your boyfriend anymore," Amy suggested.

"Maybe you're right," Shelly said. "He thinks I'm sneaking around with my ex, and I'm not. I don't seem to know what I'm doing in my love life. But I do know all about scuba. I'll make sure you are all safe and have a wonderful time."

"I'm sure we will," Heather said. "We've been looking forward to it."

"We should probably move fast though," Amy said. "The Club Scuba guy is outside, trying to steal your customers."

Shelly groaned. "He's shameless. I know we're close by and are competitors, but there are plenty of people who want to learn how to scuba dive in Key West. If we both provide quality service, we both should be able to survive."

She walked up to the supply closet and unlocked its see-through door. Heather was surprised to see that it was locked with a number combination lock instead of with a lock and key. However, as she thought more about it, she could see why it made sense. Shelly had assistants who would have to get into the closet as well, and not needing a physical key meant that this was one less item that they would have to fit into their wetsuits.

Shelly entered the four-digit combination and removed an air tank from the closet. Heather noticed a small scratch in its paint.
"Come on," Shelly said, as she relocked the door. "Let's see if anyone left to join the Club."

Heather and Amy laughed, but their laughter stopped when they reached the dock. Ryan had been forced to step in as a referee for the shouting match.

"He can't say those things about Shelly," Micah was saying.

"Let's stop causing such a commotion," Ryan said. "Those that wish to go with

Club, please go now. Those that wish to stay with Shelly should remain. And then let's have the boat move along."

No one moved to take Hank Club up on his offer, and he scowled. Then when we saw Shelly, he called out, "Look who finally decided to grace us all with her presence."

"Good morning," Shelly said. "I trust my assistants have gotten you all prepped for what the plans of the day are. I'm sorry you don't have any assistants right now, Hank. As I understand it, no one can stand working for you for too long."

"I don't need anybody," Hank Club said. "And for my final offer, anyone who wants to see what real scuba diving is like is free to come by my school anytime. I'll give you a great deal."

Then he sailed off in his boat.
"Sorry about that," Shelly said. "But now I say we dive right in. But don't worry. Not into the water quite yet. First, my assistants and I will demonstrate how to

use the equipment. Then we'll get you all comfortable with it and set you up with your own. We'll slowly but surely work our way into getting you into the water and seeing some amazing sights."

The group smiled, ready to begin after what had already been an intense morning. Shelly explained about the different parts of her swimming outfit including the flippers and mask. Then she looked for her air tank to explain how breathing underwater would work. She was looking at the two tanks that her assistants had brought out, but Micah handed her the one with the scratch on it.

"Here you go," he said.

"Thanks," said Shelly, attaching it. She faced her pupils. "This is much more comfortable in the water, but I want everyone to understand how it works first. This scuba regulator takes the air from our tanks to our mouths. We're going to be using this to breathe underwater. However, it will be a little different from regular breathing on land. You'll want to pause a moment after inhaling. The pattern will be: exhale, inhale, and pause. I promise you'll all get used to it. And let me show how it works."

She put the mouthpiece in and demonstrated the breathing pattern for a few minutes. Heather was just started to feel confident in day's activities when something went horribly wrong.
Shelly started to look disoriented, and then she keeled over. Julie and Micah hurried over to her and removed her gear.

"Shelly," Micah said. "Please be okay."

Heather was in shock, realizing that something terrible had happened before they even got into the water. She shook herself into action.

"Call for an ambulance," Heather told Amy, as she and Ryan went to check on their instructor. Heather felt for a pulse and then shook her head.

"No," Heather said. "We need to call Detective Smith. Shelly is dead."

## Chapter 6 – The Other Detectives

"This is becoming a habit. How is it that you're at the scene of the crime before we are?" Detective Smith asked.

"Heather was trying to get out of going underwater," Amy joked.

Detective Smith was a meticulous man. He even wrote down Amy's comment in his notes. Heather was disappointed that such an able detective was retiring, even if it meant that Ryan would finally be able to begin work at the Key West Police Force.

Detective Peters also wrote down the comment when he saw his partner doing so. Miguel Peters was also a good detective but was young and new to his position. He often checked with his partner to make sure that he was taking the correct steps in solving the crime. Detective Peters had good investigative instincts but hadn't learned to trust those instincts yet.

"Now what did you see happen?" Detective Smith asked.

They went through the details of the morning with Ryan and Jamie explaining what happened on the dock, and Heather and Amy explaining finding Shelly in the boat house. They ended by detailing how Shelly had been showing them how to breathe with the equipment when she suddenly fell.

"The tank was tampered with, wasn't it?" Heather asked.

"It certainly looks that way," Peters said, before catching a look from his partner. "To us detectives who don't share information on a case."

"Come on," Amy said. "Are you going to go through that again? We are licensed investigators, and we did help solve your last case."

"They did, sir," Peters said.

"We saved Shelly from a fight with her boyfriend, and then we saw her die in front of us," Heather said. "This makes us involved. We want to catch whoever did this to her. Preferably with your help."

"But even without it, you'd be trying to solve the crime?" Detective Smith asked.

Heather and Amy gave him their biggest smiles.

"All right," Detective Smith said. "We can share some information with you, and you'll do likewise. However, I don't want you to do anything dangerous or anything that could interfere with leads we are working on."

"I think we have a deal," said Heather. "Was the tank tampered with?"

"Based on the description everyone gave of the events, it does look that way," said Detective Smith. "The medical examiner needs to finish his report, but it does look like there are signs of carbon monoxide poisoning."

"The killer poisoned the air in her tank," Heather said.

"This lets all the air out of our fun," said Amy. "We can't let the killer get away with this."

"We don't intend to," Detective Smith said.

"I know you'll catch him," Ryan said. "It might be one of your last cases, but you'll see it through and see justice served."

Detective Smith nodded.

"And this will be one of your final cases, won't it?" Ryan asked, trying to be delicate. "Do you have an idea when exactly you might be retiring?"

"I can't focus on that now," Detective Smith said. "I need to find out all I can about the murder weapon."

"A murderous air tank," said Amy. "Talk about dead air."

"We saw where Shelly got the air tank from," Heather said.

"Are you sure?" Detective Peters asked. "I understand the assistants also brought out some air tanks. Are you sure it wasn't one of those?"

"Positive," said Heather. "The one she took out of the supply closet had a scratch in the paint. That's the same one that killed her."

"Let's go look the closet," Detective Smith said.

Peters, Amy, and Heather followed directly behind him. Ryan hesitated a moment. He wasn't sure if, following police procedure, he was allowed to be involved because he wasn't currently on the force. However, he couldn't resist and soon joined them after making sure Jamie was still all right talking with the married couple about what had happened.

The other investigators were examining the door knob.

"It does seem loose," Detective Smith agreed. "It is possible that someone could have broken in this way to poison the air."

"Though it could be a red herring," Heather said. "If someone had a key, they could have done it as well."

"Red herring," Amy sighed. "We're not going to see any fish today."

"This is the supply closet that she took the air tank from?" Detective Smith asked, indicating to the clear locked door.

Heather nodded.

"I'll take an inventory," Detective Peters said, setting himself to the task. He started writing down everything that he could see through the door.

Meanwhile, Detective Smith looked at the lock. "I'll have forensics check that for prints. These locks aren't cleaned very often. It might be hard to find a print. But we'll try. I imagine everyone that worked her touched it, but if any other print is found it could lead to a suspect."

"Is there a chance that anyone who came out to learn to dive this morning is a suspect?" Ryan asked.

"You mean he wanted to see her die in front of him?" Heather asked. "Some killers might want to watch."

"I don't think any of them are involved," Peters said, looking up from his inventory. "I spoke to them, and they don't seem to have a motive or much opportunity to commit the crime. The newlyweds arrived this morning. The trio of friends arrived the day before and chose this tour because their hotel had a deal with this place. They all say they never met Shelly Little before and they're all from out of state, so I think they're telling the truth."

"That's all right," Amy said. "It's not like we have a shortage of suspects."

"Her boyfriend and ex-boyfriend," said Heather.

"The other scuba school competitor," said Ryan.

"And the assistants who had access to everything," said Peters.

"Well," said Detective Smith. "What are we all just standing around here for?"

### Chapter 7 – The Helpful Assistant

"Thank you for speaking with us, Miss Krabowski," Heather said.

"I don't mind at all," said Julie. "I think I'm holding up a little better than Micah is. And I want to make sure you figure out what happened to Shelly. She was a great boss and a great person."

"With not-so-great taste in men?" Amy asked.

"I guess that's right," said Julie. "No one she dated was a total brute, but she seemed to date, obsessive guys. They'd be fixated on her and get jealous for no reason."

"Was her current boyfriend like that too?" asked Detective Smith.

Julie nodded. "She and Dylan have been going out for a little over a year. They're okay together. But he gets jealous a lot. He's caused some scenes before."

"I know," said Amy.

"And who is Tommy?" asked Heather.

"That was the guy she dated before Dylan. He was obsessed with her too. But while Dylan gets angry, Tommy got mopey. He'd sit around and act sad. Then she'd have to figure out why and it'd be something stupid. Like she had lunch with us on the boat instead of eating with him when they hadn't made any plans."

"Is he still in the picture?" Detective Smith asked.
"Yes and no. Shelly didn't want anything more to do with him, but he'd show up here randomly and say how he still cared. Sometimes he'd come to the beach and watch us set out."
"Were there any other exes that caused trouble?" asked Ryan.

"No. Though there were certainly other people, who wanted to date her. Even Micah... I mean..."

"Please tell us everything you can," said Detective Smith. "It's not a betrayal to your friends or coworkers. It's helping us with an investigation."

"Well, Micah had a crush on her, I think," said Julie.

"After the way he stood up for her and wanted to fight Hank Club on the dock, I can certainly see it," said Ryan.

"These questions you're asking," said Julie. "You don't think this was an accident, do you? You think somebody killed her?"

"That is the way we are looking at it," said Detective Smith.

Julie nodded. "It's upsetting to think someone killed her, but I'm glad it wasn't somehow a mistake we made."

"When did you last use that equipment?" asked Heather.

"Yesterday and everything was working fine. Before we closed, we made sure that everything was setback up for this morning. Shelly did a thorough check, and all the tanks were filled the same way," said Julie.

"And this morning?" Detective Smith.

"We do a quick check in the morning," said Julie. "But it saves time to do it the night before. It was never a problem."

"Who has access to the boat house?" Detective Smith asked.
"Micah and Shelly and I had keys."

"Was the doorknob always loose?" asked Heather.

"Yes," Julie said. "We'd been meaning to fix it. We kept joking that someone would shake their way inside. Oh no. Do you think that could have happened? Because the doorknob was faulty someone broke in?"

211

"Does that seem likely?" Detective Smith asked.

"Oh no," Julie said, turning pale. "Yes. It seems very likely. Someone did come here late last night."

"Who?" asked Heather.

"I don't know. I mean, I thought it was Micah at the time. But maybe it wasn't Micah."

"What did you see?" asked Detective Smith.

"I live close by," said Julie. "That was a perk of the job. I could walk here. And from my bedroom window upstairs, I can see the boathouse. I saw a man there last night. I thought it was Micah. I thought he left his cell phone or a jacket there or something. He's done that before. But I realize now that I never really saw him. It might have been a different man. And it might have been the killer."

"You were at home the entire night?" Peters asked, offering a question.

"Yes. And my roommates can verify that. I was home all night. One roommate is a very light sleeper; she would have woken up if I tried to leave during the night. And I'm sure the other one would love to have me get in trouble with the police, so you can really believe her when she says I was home. We've been having a little roomie trouble. You see I do leave my socks on the floor, but she never cleans up her dishes and it... I guess after all that's happened now, that doesn't really matter."

"What time did the man go to the boathouse?" asked Detective Smith.

"It was around midnight," said Julie.

"Who knew the combination to the storage closet?" asked Heather.

"Shelly always used important dates for passwords. I think everyone who knew her knew that. Micah and I always knew what the combination was. It had been her anniversary for a while, but she just changed it to her birthday. We just had a party for her, so I think that was the reason for it. It was a really nice party," Julie said sadly, trying not to focus on how it turned into Shelly's last party.

"Thank you for all your help today," Detective Smith said. "We'll let you know if we have any other questions."

As they left her, Heather thought aloud, "If the front door could be easily broken through and everyone who knew Shelly knew her system for passwords, then there are many people who could have committed this crime."

"True," Detective Smith said. "But I'd still really like to have a word with Micah next."

They nodded. There was just one problem with the plan. Micah had run away from the crime scene. They were going to have to find him.

## Chapter 8 – Interviews, Interviews, interviews

"You have to admit that it's suspicious," Amy said.

"Of course, I do," said Heather. "I just meant that we can't assume that the killer definitely was Micah."

"He had an unrequited love thing going with Shelly. He had a key to the boat house and the code to the equipment. Julie thought that she saw him there before she said it might have been someone else. And Micah ran away from the scene of the crime."

"You're forgetting the other big thing," said Heather.

"What's that?"

"He was the one who handed Shelly the poisoned air tank," Heather replied. "She was looking at the other tanks, and he handed her that one."

"Oh. Right," said Amy. "So why don't we think he's the killer?"

"He could very well be," said Heather. "But we have three other suspects that could have done it. I just don't think we should assume the case is closed until we're certain."

"So, you want to interview the other suspects?" asked Amy.

"I do," said Heather. "But first we have some other interviews to conduct."

"Finding the right Donut Delights assistants," Amy agreed. "I sure hope we pick good ones and they don't kill us off like Micah did."

Heather groaned and was about to rebut when she saw that Mr. Rankle was outside his store and she had a good guess why. The young woman who Heather assumed was their first interviewee looked wide-eyed with fear after talking to the neighbor.

"And good afternoon to you too, Mr. Rankle," Heather said as she led the woman inside.

"Don't you have anything better to do?" Amy asked.

Rather than respond Mr. Rankle huffed in indignation and returned to his shop.

"I'm sorry. I don't know how to fire a gun," the young woman said.

"What's that?" asked Heather.

"What that man was telling me. He said you were all from Texas and that you made your donuts by shooting holes in them."

"I see," said Heather, as Amy tried to stifle her giggles. "And what else did he tell you?"

The interviewee looked at the floor and mumbled, "That you can't be trusted."

217

"And you said if we were nice to him he'd come around," said Amy.

"I said maybe. Eventually." Then Heather said to the applicant, "How about we form our own opinions about each other? And then we'll figure out if we'd work well with one another?"
"That sounds like a wonderful idea," she said.
"First things first. I'm Heather, and this is Amy."

"I'm nervous. I mean I'm Nina. I'm nervous too."

"Let's sit down and talk about something simple. Let's chat about donuts," Heather said. She decided to try out Bernadette's interview technique. "So what's your favorite flavor donut? Chocolate?"

"I think everyone like chocolate," Nina said. "But I think my favorite part about donuts are when they're filled with jelly. Not many other desserts can do that. So, I think that's what my favorite flavor is. Maybe a chocolate jelly-filled donut would be great too."

Heather nodded. Though Nina was nervous, she did give good answers to her questions. She had been going to school for pre-law but decided that the career wasn't the right one for her. She was figuring out exactly what her calling was but realized that what she enjoyed most about school was baking for charity fundraisers that were held a few times a year. While most of her classmates were doing it to pad their resumes, she discovered that it gave her great joy to bake. She hoped that baking donuts would be as enjoyable.

After the interview, Heather said, "If all the interviews are like that, we'll have a hard time deciding."

I don't know," Amy said. "She was nervous after Mr. Rankle rattled her. She might not do well knowing her boss is solving murders."

"Let's see what some of our other candidates are like," Heather said. "We'll need everyone to work as a team too."

The next interview wasn't nearly so pleasant. Amy almost agreed that she'd rather be talking to Mr. Rankle. They had been excited to talk with Charlie because he had professional chef experience. However, they liked him much better on paper than in person.

"I'm a professional chef. I do not have a favorite donut flavor. They are beneath me," he said.

"If they are beneath you, why are you applying to work here?"

"I don't have to like something to excel at creating it."

"It certainly helps," Heather countered.

Charlie shrugged. "Look, I know that I must be the most qualified applicant that you're meeting with here. I've worked in several kitchens, and I am professionally trained."

"Yes. Why did you leave those other kitchens?" Heather asked.

"Artistic differences," he said. "And now I find myself stuck on this island, and so I will grace your kitchens will my skills. Even if they are used to make little wads of dough with holes in them."

"Thank you for coming in," Heather began.

"Yes. When should I start?" he asked.

"I'm sorry. I don't think this would work out."

"You don't want me? Why?"
"Because," said Amy. "Much like our donuts, your resume has a big hole in it."

He left abruptly. Then they met their third candidate for the day who was named Mollie.

"I don't know. I don't like sweets that much. But I am great at remembering differences for food. I can keep track of the gluten-free donuts and the vegan ones and the ones made only of vegetables."

Heather and Amy exchanged a look.

"We have made gluten-free donuts before for a customer who had food allergies," Heather said. "But we don't specialize in desserts like that."

"Oh," Mollie said. "When your name was Donut Delights, I just assumed that's what the delights were."

"You know what happens when you assume," Amy started.

"We like to be able to explore every potential flavor," Heather explained. "Our donuts are delights because they have rich and varying tastes."

"Oh," Mollie said. "Delightful."

After the interviews were done, Heather and Amy sighed. They had thought that meeting potential employees and donut lovers would be fun, but this ordeal after their other ordeal was tiring.

"I'm glad that's done for the day," Heather said. "I don't want to interview anyone else today."
"Are you sure?" Amy asked.

"Why?"

"Because I saw someone that looks just like Micah walking by."

"Micah? Here?" Heather asked. She ran to the window and looked out as well. "It is him. But what is he doing here?"

Amy shrugged. They saw him enter Bernadette's Beachy Books.

"Come on," Heather said, running out the door.

## Chapter 9 – The Suspect in the Shop

Heather and Amy hurried into the book shop, not sure what they expected to happen. They were still surprised when they saw what was going on.

Micah was kneeling in the center of the room, sobbing. Bernadette was hovering nearby, offering him a handkerchief and confused help.

"I'm sorry," Bernadette said. "If you could just tell me the title of the book, I could find it for you."

"It was hers," he cried. "Her book."

"I don't know what that means," Bernadette said.

Heather took a step forward. She and Amy had informed Detective Smith of their whereabouts as they rushed over. She wasn't sure if she was about to confront a spiraling killer or a grieving loved one. Either way, with emotions running high, he might be dangerous.

"What book are you looking for?" Heather asked. "How can we help you?"

"She was reading a book this morning. It might have been one of the last things going through her mind. I'd like to read it as well," Micah said. Then he looked at them more clearly. "You. You were there."

"We were," Heather said. "And we'd like to help figure out what happened."

"She died," Micah cried. "There was something wrong with her tank, and she died."
"What's going on?" Bernadette asked.

"Shelly was murdered this morning," Heather told her. "This is one of her grieving employees. He'd like a copy of the book she just bought."

"Poor Shelly," Bernadette said. "And yes, I can get you a copy of the book. Though, if I remember correctly, it was a romance novel."

"Too fitting," Micah said.

"It was a bit of a bodice ripper if you catch my drift," Bernadette said, hesitantly.

"I'll still read it," Micah said. "For her."

"Okay," Bernadette said. She went to fetch the book, secretly happy for an excuse to leave for a moment.

Micah looked at Heather again. "Why did you say she was murdered? Because we did something wrong with the tank and we killed her?"

"I said murdered because someone intentionally filled the tank with poisoned air," said Heather.

"What?" Micah said, jumping to his feet.

"Why did you run away from the crime scene?" Amy asked.

"Why?" Micah asked. "Do you think I could have killed her? Not me. I loved her. I loved her more than anything."

"People have said that before and still committed murder," Heather said.
"I left because I couldn't handle her death," Micah said. "And I felt guilty because something happened with the tank. But I thought it was some sort of terrible accident. I didn't know she was killed. And I certainly didn't kill her."

"You went out of your way to hand her that certain air tank," said Heather. "The one that was poisoned."
"But that was because it was her lucky tank," Micah said. "She always used that one. I didn't hand her one because it would kill her. I handed her hers. So if that's the one that was poisoned, then somebody messed with that one because it was hers."

"She had a lucky tank?" Amy asked. "Is that weird?"

"A long time ago, when she was a beginner, she made a mistake while rising from the water. She almost got hit by a boat. But she was lucky. All that happened was that little scratch. She could have been killed. But she escaped with only a scratch. She also thought it was a good reminder about safety while diving. That's why I gave it to her."

"Did Julie know about this too?" Heather asked.

"Everybody knew about it," Micah said. "She loved telling us about her near-death experience and liked to remind us about safety."

"Where were you last night?" Heather asked.

"Not preparing for murder," said Micah. "Actually, last night I was at an all-night board game event. I made it to the final round too. There were lots of people there. They can back me up."

"We will look into that," Heather said. "Do you know anyone who would want to kill Shelly?"

"A monster," said Micah. "A true monster."

"What about a name?" Amy asked.

"Hank Club was a thorn in all of our sides. And he was competitive about business. You saw him at the dock. Maybe it was him," said Micah. "But most likely it was her boyfriend. He was never good enough for her."

"Why do you say that?" asked Heather.

"He made her feel bad. He would get jealous and try to make her feel guilty. For no reason at all. You shouldn't do that to someone you're supposed to love. He was really mad too about the combination lock."

"What do you mean?"

"She changed the combination lock to the supply closet recently," Micah said.

"Right," Amy said. "To her birthday."

"Well, she changed it from her anniversary with Dylan to the birthday combination. He was mad. He wanted to know why she did it."
"Do you know why she did it?" Heather asked.

"I'm not sure," Micah said. "Maybe it was because she was becoming more self-reliant and was putting herself before a man. Maybe she was starting to develop feelings for someone who had been there all along, but she never realized it until then, and she was weaning herself away from the wrong love. Or, well, maybe she just thought we should change the combination lock every year or so just in case."

Bernadette brought the book out to him. The cover picture was of a man and woman in half-dressed Victorian garb holding one another. Micah hugged the book close.

"Thank you," he said.

"Micah Crosby," Detective Smith said, entering and getting straight to the point. "You're wanted for questioning regarding the death of Shelly Little."

"I'll come with you and answer your questions," Micah said. "If I can bring this book with me. It was the last thing she read."

"Fine," Detective Smith said, as he and his partner led Micah outside.

"Sorry about all that," Heather said. "If you want, we can pay for the book."

"If that will somehow help solve Shelly's death, he can have it," Bernadette said.

Heather promised to bring over some Banana Chocolate Donuts later as a comfort food for having learned that a favorite customer had died and for facing a suspect. Bernadette said she couldn't refuse the offer of donuts, but felt guilty because she had recommended the place where a woman ended up dead.

Heather and Amy left the shop, discussing what had just happened.

"I'm sure the detectives will reach the same conclusion that we did," Heather said. "That Micah isn't the killer."
"It's a shame we couldn't get one easy case," Amy said. "It really looked like he did it."

"They can check on his alibi," said Heather. "But I don't think he wanted to hurt Shelly."

"He is a mess with her gone," Amy agreed.

"I'll tell you one thing I wouldn't mind doing," Heather said. "And that's talking to the boyfriend Dylan again."

"Micah did point the finger at him."

232

"But I'll have to do that in the morning," said Heather. "I have something important I need to do now."

## Chapter 10 – Walking and Wondering

"So," Heather asked. "How was school?"

"It was all right," Lilly said in a noncommittal tone. "How was scuba diving?"

"Oh," Heather said. "It didn't quite work out."

"Why not?"

"It's a long story," Heather said. "And I bet yours is a long story too. Let's take Dave and Cupcake for a walk, and we can discuss it all. I bet they would like the exercise."

"I think they've been enjoying lounging in the sun," Lilly said. "But you're right. There are all new things for them to sniff."

Heather attached the leash to her doggy friend Dave who had, indeed, been lying in the sun. Lilly got the kitten Cupcake ready for the walk too. Even though she was a feline, she enjoyed going on walks as much as Dave did.

As they were leaving, they were joined by Ryan. Heather was sure that he was itching for information, both about the case and Lilly's first day of school.

They started their walk but found it to be slow progress. Dave and Cupcake were determined to smell everything they walked past. They would take a step and stop to sniff.

"So, tell me more about your day," Heather said.
"We want to hear all about it," said Ryan.

"It wasn't bad," Lilly said. "Switching for my classes was exciting. But they were all in the same corridor, so it wasn't intimidating. It was the first day, so it was mostly meeting our teachers and learning where to go when the bell rings."

"Do your teachers seem interesting?" Ryan asked.

"Yes," Lilly said. "They had some fun stories. And I think I'll learn a lot. I like my English teacher very much too. I'm excited for what I'll read in her class."

"There's something still bothering you," Heather said.

"It's not a problem yet," Lilly said. "I know it's only the first day. But I felt like I didn't make any friends yet."

"Were they mean to you?" Ryan asked, hiding some anger.

"No," Lilly said. "No one was mean. In fact, everybody was pretty nice. They'd show you where to go if you didn't know the way."

"But you didn't click with anybody?" Heather asked.

"No," said Lilly. "I feel like everyone has their friends already. And I didn't know where to sit at lunch."

"I know it can be difficult," Heather said. "But you just need to get to know somebody better. I know you'll make friends soon."

"Definitely," said Ryan. "You're a great kid."

"Thanks. I'm sure it will happen soon. Right now, I just feel disappointed. I wish Marlene or Nicolas were here," said Lilly. "But now tell me about your day. What went wrong?"

"Another case dropped into our lap," Heather said. "We ended up starting to solve a murder instead of going in the water."

"Wow," said Lilly. "Do you have an idea who did it?"

"Do you still think it was the assistant Micah?" Ryan asked.

"The police are talking to him now," Heather said. "But I don't think it was him."

"Then who are you leaning towards?"

"It could be the scuba competitor or the ex-boyfriend," said Heather. "But right now, my money is on the boyfriend. He's the one I want to talk to next."

"Why him?" asked Ryan.

"He was jealous, and we saw him arguing with the victim earlier that day. He also knew what the combination to the supply closet where the air tanks were kept was," said Heather.

"Well, that sounds like a solid lead," Ryan said.

Heather could tell that he was disappointed he wasn't officially a part of the investigation. He normally would be tracking down leads on his own at this point in a case.

"I'm sure Detective Smith will retire soon, and then you will be the new detective in town," Heather said.

"It's fine," Ryan said. "I know that the Key West police will solve this case, especially when they have you and Amy helping them. And I'm enjoying the time off."

He was half-believable.

"You're lucky to have the time off," Lilly said. "I'm in school now. There are so many exciting things to do here, and I don't know when I could do any of them."

Heather thought about it. "Lilly brings up a valid point. We can all end up rather busy. With school, and detective work and the donut shop. Maybe we should choose one afternoon where we all make sure we are free and go do something touristy."

"Like what?" asked Lilly.

"Saturday afternoons let's all do something fun in Key West together. This weekend we could all go to the Southernmost Point."

"I'd love to see that," said Lilly. "Can Eva and Leila come too?"
"Of course," said Heather. "Everybody can come."

Dave and Cupcake looked up at her expectantly.

"Well, with you two furry friends, it will depend on where we go."

They wagged their tails as their humans laughed. Heather was happy for the plan. It was nice to look forward to a family outing, and if they made it a weekly thing, they were sure not to miss out on anything that the island had to offer.

Heather crossed her fingers. She hoped she would have the case solved by then. She wasn't sure she could fully

enjoy the afternoon, knowing that a killer
was still out there.

## Chapter 11 – The Jealous Boyfriend

They found Dylan Newhart's address, and he greeted them unhappily at the door.

"What are you doing here?" he asked. "Come to check up on Shelly and me? There's no need. She died yesterday."

"Yes, we know," Heather said.

"We were there," said Amy.

"You were?" Dylan asked. "Can you tell me? Did she suffer?"

Heather wasn't sure of his motivation for asking that question yet but decided to answer him and see where it led. "It was over in a few minutes. I don't believe there was any undue suffering."

He nodded. "But, then, if you knew she was dead, why are you here?"
"We're investigating her murder," Heather said.

"And just who are you? Some wannabe scuba divers who are playing detective?"

"Oh no. We're licensed private detectives," Heather said, introducing themselves. "And we received Detective Smith's blessing to follow our own leads on this case, seeing as we felt involved."

"That will happen when you see someone murdered in front of you," Amy said.

"Can we ask you a few questions?" Heather asked.

Dylan crossed his arms and thought about it.

"Of course, if you'd rather talk to Detective Smith, we can call him," Heather said.

"He might get cranky though," Amy said. "Being called from one lead to come and talk to you because you didn't want to talk to us. That might put him in a bad mood for the interview. But if that's what you want."

243

"No," Dylan said before they could walk away. "Come on it. We'll talk."

As they entered, Heather wished that they could have conducted the investigation outside. To call Dylan's home a pigsty was an insult to pigs. Every flat service was covered with junk, and there were food wrappers all around.

He led them to the living room and pushed some empty Chinese food containers off the couch so they could sit down. They gingerly did. Amy cringed and kept her bag on her lap so it wouldn't touch the mess. She took a tablet out of her bag so that she could take notes about their questioning.

After their move, they had been without the tablet for a case because it had been hidden in a moving box. They were glad to have it back so that they could refer back to their notes as they gathered enough information.

"What do you want to know?" Dylan asked.

"Let's start with what you were fighting about the day she died," Heather asked. "What did we walk into?"

"I thought she might be cheating on me," Dylan said. "Her ex had been hanging around a lot. And I wanted to know why."

"And what did she tell you?"

"That she wasn't cheating and she didn't want her ex around," he said. "I wasn't sure that believed her or not. But now, I guess it's true."

"You think of her fondly and trust her now that she's dead?" Amy asked.

"Because she was murdered," Dylan said. "It must have been Tommy who did it. He wasn't able to win her away from me, so he killed her."

"Did Tommy do anything specific to make you think this?" Heather asked.

245

"Not exactly," said Dylan. "But he was obsessed with her. And he used to be really jealous when they were dating."

"Who does that sound like?" Amy muttered.

"I loved Shelly," Dylan said.

"Mr. Newhart, you said you saw her ex around frequently. Where did you see him? And when?"

"When seemed to be real often," said Dylan. "And where? Most often on the beach. Within walking distance from the boat house. I thought he and Shelly were meeting up, and he was leaving when I arrived. But he might have been stalking her. You need to talk to that guy."

"Mr. Newhart, did you often grab Shelly the way we saw this morning? Grabbing her arm when she told you to let go?"

Dylan took a deep breath. "I get angry sometimes. I admit I can get jealous.

246

But I never hurt her-hurt her. I loved her so much."

"Someone mentioned that what might have set you off this time was that the combination in the boathouse was changed," said Heather.

"It used to be our anniversary," Dylan said. "Did they tell you that? The combination was our anniversary. I thought it was so sweet at the time. And then she went and changed it. Why would she do that?"

"Maybe because the lock was no longer secure if everyone knew the combination was your anniversary," Amy said.

"You think it could have just been that? Because everyone knew about us. And how important I was to her?"

"Maybe," Amy shrugged.

"Did you know what the new combination was?" Heather asked.

"It really wasn't anything related to another man," Dylan admitted. "She changed it to her birthday. She always used important dates as her passwords and combinations. But we used to be the important date."

"And you do know when her birthday was?" Heather asked.

"Of course," Dylan said indignantly.

"Did you have a key to the boathouse?" asked Heather.

"Why would I have a key to her job?" he asked.
"Maybe in case there was an emergency," Heather suggested.

"No, I didn't have a key. But I knew where she kept her keys when she was home. If she forgot it or something, I could have grabbed it for her. I did have a key to her apartment."
Heather nodded.

"Why?" he asked. "You can't think I killed her, can you?"

"I think that we saw a suspect fighting with the victim the morning of her murder. Now we've learned that he would have easily been able to unlock both the door and the closet where air tank that killed her was kept."

"When you put it like that, it does sound like I could have done," Dylan said. "But I didn't. I—"

"You loved her?" Amy finished.

"Where were you the night before she died?" Heather asked.

"I was home," he said.

"Can anyone vouch for that?" Heather prompted.
"Shelly didn't come over," he said. "She was tired. I just came home, cleaned up and went to bed."

"Cleaned up?" Amy asked, looking around the messy living room.

"Yeah," Dylan said, not understanding her skepticism.
"Shelly mentioned that you were between jobs?" Heather asked.

"Yeah," Dylan said. "But I have some promising leads."

"Do you know who inherits her business and belongings? Or collects any life insurance?" asked Heather.

"I don't know. I'd guess her parents," said Dylan.

Heather thanked him for his time and then she and her bestie left.

"I don't like him," Amy said.

"Neither do I," said Heather. "But I'm not sure if he's the killer."

"Why not? Like you said he had access to the tank and had no alibi. He was a jealous guy and was angry with her. For no real reason, but he thought there was one."

"I've been thinking about the fight he had with her this morning," said Heather.

"More motive," said Amy.

"If he knew he was going to kill her because he executed his plan the night before, why would he fight with her where others could overhear them arguing?"

"Because he couldn't control himself?" Amy suggested. "Because he's an angry person who is capable of murder."

"That could be true," said Heather. "But it would have been sloppy. He was setting himself up to be a suspect."
"So, what now?"

"We'll keep him on the suspect list, but we should keep talking to the other suspects."

"Right now?"

Heather looked at the time. "Nope," she said. "We need to get back to Donut Delights."

"Oh," said Amy. "For more delightful interviews."

## Chapter 12 – Who to Hire?

This time Heather and Amy were able to intercept Mr. Rankle and stop him from scaring away their applicants. They baked some Banana Chocolate Donuts just to be certain that they wouldn't be frightened off easily. The shop smelled delicious, and the applicants were happy to come in.

However, Heather and Amy were becoming more disheartened after their interviews.

"No one is terrible," Heather said.

"Some of them are terrible," Amy disagreed.

"But they're not jumping out and making me feel like I have to hire anyone."

"I liked the juggler," Amy said.

"I liked Nina," Heather said.

"Imagine the juggler throwing the donuts up in the air and catching them. It could be pretty entertaining."

"And pretty unsanitary."

"Maybe he could do it in gloves," Amy suggested.

Heather sighed. "Why is this so hard?"

"I think it's because of your last staff," said Amy. "They were all so good it's hard not to compare the new guys to them. But somebody will prove their worth."

"Do I smell donuts?" Digby asked, poking his head inside the shop.

"You better get used to it if you're going to be working here," Heather laughed.

"Oh, I think I could get used to this," Digby said as he grabbed a donut.

"Were you just waiting on the street to see if we were making samples?" Amy asked.

"Maybe," Digby admitted.

"This is the level of enthusiasm I like," Heather said. "Though there will be much more work after we open."

"I'm looking forward to it," Digby said.

Heather smiled.

"How have your interviews been going?" he asked. "Do we have more of the team yet?"

Heather sighed. "Unfortunately, no."

"We have had some interesting candidates though," said Amy.
"Yes, the professional chef who thinks making donuts is a waste of his time," said Heather.
"Has he tried these donuts?" Digby asked, aghast.

"We had a sculptor who wanted to use the donuts to make displays," said Heather. "It seemed promising at first, but she wouldn't want customers to ever eat any of them."

"And we had an ex-used car salesman that had started baking, but for some reason, we didn't trust him," Amy said.

"Sounds rough," said Digby.

"I was telling her that because we liked the first staff so much it's hard to replace them," said Amy.

"And a lot of our staff joined us as we were working on other things, but they proved to us that they could become good bakers," said Heather.

"Well," Digby said. "If you'd like to interview some more candidates…"

"Are you offering someone new?" asked Heather.

"Don't hold back," said Amy.

"My friend's mom is looking to get back into the workforce," he said. "I don't know how she is with donuts, but she made amazing birthday cakes. She's not enjoying having an empty nest and is looking for a job. I know that she was reliable with any projects she took on, and would always be on time when she picked us up when she was little."

"We'd love to meet her," Heather said.

"Great," said Digby. "I'll get in touch with her."

"Thanks," Heather said, as he left. "Maybe something is working out?"

"She has a different background from anyone on your last staff," said Amy. "But maybe that's a good thing."

"Could be. And I'll be happy if we're almost finished with these interviews. We still have more interviews to conduct for our investigation."

"Right," said Amy. "Let's get going."

## Chapter 13 – The Ex

Heather and Amy discovered that Shelly's ex-boyfriend Tommy Mercer was not at his house or his job, so they had to expand their search for him. They found him on the beach by Shelly's boathouse. It must have been the spot that both the assistants and Dylan had seen him watching Shelly.

Instead of watching anyone this day, he was laying the sand morosely. It was clear that he was truly sad, but it was difficult to take his sorrow too seriously because of the way he was dressed. He was wearing short shorts, a large brimmed hat and had thick white sunscreen on his nose. He was dressed like someone on vacation but was teary-eyed.

"Tommy Mercer?" Heather asked.

"I was Tommy Mercer," he said. "But my soul is dead now. It left when my true love left this world."

"Can we still ask your body questions?" Amy asked.

"Who are you?"

"I'm Heather Shepherd, and this is Amy Givens. We're private investigators approved by some detectives with the Key West Police to investigate the murder of Shelly Little."

"Good," Tommy said. "I'm glad they're treating this seriously. The whole force should be out looking for her killer. They should be locked away forever."

"We certainly hope to catch the killer," Heather said. "Maybe you can help us."

"I'd love to, but how?"

"We heard that you were often on this beach," Heather said.

She and Amy sat down in the sand to make him feel more comfortable. Amy took out the tablet to take notes, careful not to let it get sand-covered.

"Yes," Tommy said with a sigh. "It's a good beach."

"Did you notice anything unusual around here recently? Before her death?"

Tommy thought about it. "That other scuba guy had started heckling Shelly's Scuba School. He'd drive his boat by and try to recruit her customers."

"Don't remind me," said Amy.

"Did you ever see Hank Club on land or near the boathouse?" Heather asked.

Tommy shook his head. "Of course, I'm not out here every day."

"Why do you come out here?" Heather asked.

"It was to see her," Tommy said. "I missed her."

"She didn't want to see you?"

"No. And it was breaking my heart. So I came here to watch and make sure she was okay."

"You know that you being out here was causing her trouble?" Heather asked.

"So you were causing her not to be okay," Amy explained.

"How?" he asked.

"You were upsetting her new boyfriend and causing friction in the relationship," said Heather.

"Good," said Tommy. "Dylan was no good for her. He didn't deserve her."

"Why did you break up?" Amy asked.

"She told me I was too jealous and too passive aggressive," said Tommy. "I told her that I could be more active-aggressive if that were what she wanted. She didn't like that response either."

"Was Dylan jealous too?" Heather asked.

"I never directly met him, but he seemed like a bad guy. He was always trying to catch Shelly in a lie or trick her into doing something wrong. That's not a good relationship."

"So, you'd watch the two of them together?" Heather asked.

"Occasionally I might catch sight of the two of them together. And I saw that they were not a happy couple. I hoped that Shelly would come to her senses and realize how much she missed me. But I didn't set out to watch them. I wasn't following them."

"You just followed her to her job," Amy muttered.

"I know what her assistants say about me," Tommy said. "I'm not a stalker. I just liked seeing Shelly sometimes."

"Mr. Mercer, where were you the night before she died? Were you on the beach?"

"That night I went to a bar for a drink and then went home."

"Alone?" Heather asked.

"Of course," Tommy said. "I was waiting for Shelly."

"What time did you arrive home?"

"About ten o'clock. It was an early night."

Heather nodded. Even if he did go to a bar, he could have made it to the boathouse by midnight.

"Did you have a key to the boathouse?" Heather asked.

"No," Tommy said. "And they didn't want me there. This distance at the beach was as close as I got."

"One last locking question," said Heather. "Did you know what the combination Shelly used on her storage closet was?"

"It used to be our anniversary," Tommy said. "But that was a long time ago."

"You don't know the new combination?"

"No," said Tommy. "But she always used important dates for them. I bet that's what she did again."

"Do you know anyone else that would have wanted to hurt her?" Heather asked.

"I don't have to know anyone else," Tommy said. "It's obvious who killed her."

"So obvious," said Amy. "Who do you think it was?"

"It was Dylan, of course. He was a bad boyfriend to the end."

"You don't think he treated her well enough, and that's why you think he's the murderer."

"That," Tommy said. "And he used to work in some sort of science lab. That's where you can get poison to put in an air tank, isn't it?"

"Yes," Heather said.

"It sure is," said Amy.

## Chapter 14 – Sharing Donuts and Information

"I feel like this could be a break in the case," Heather said. "If we can verify it."

Heather and Amy had brought their new information straight to the detectives at police headquarters, or almost straight to them. They had made a quick stop to pick up some Banana Chocolate Donuts on their way. They felt they needed a sugar boost and that they deserved a snack after all their hard work. Detective Peters, especially, enjoyed the treats.

"It is new information for us, and we thank you for bringing it to our attention," Detective Smith said. "But you're right. Verification is key. Right now, we only have the word of a rival lover. He didn't mention which lab Dylan worked for, did he?"

"Unfortunately, no," Heather said. "But if we talk to Dylan again, I'm sure we can get him to tell us."

"Then we can find out why he doesn't work there anymore," Amy said. "Maybe he was fired for stealing some carbon monoxide."

"I think Detective Peters and I should talk to him," Detective Smith said. "We can bring him into the interrogation room."

"Yes, sir," Peters said, standing up. Detective Smith indicated that he should wait a minute, and his partner hovered for a moment before deciding to sit again.

"Good idea," Heather said. "He might be more willing to talk in a formal setting. We'll come up with some more questions to ask him. Working at the lab is an important new lead that could establish creating the murder weapon, and his alibi is quite weak."

"You don't have to come up with any questions," Detective Smith said. "We appreciate your help so far, but we can take it from here. We can interrogate Dylan Newhart on our own."

"Are you kidding?" Amy asked. "You wouldn't be talking to him again if it weren't for us?"

"I said we appreciate your work, but I think continuing this lead should be a police matter," said Detective Smith.

"But," Amy began.

"We agreed that you could investigate as long as you didn't interfere with any of our leads or aspects of the case we're working on, didn't we?" asked Detective Smith.

"I guess we did," said Heather. "We also agreed to share information. We clearly shared ours."

"Yeah," Amy said. "So, what do you have to update us on?"

Detective Peters checked his notebook and reported. "We confirmed both Micah and Julie's alibis. There was too much foot traffic in the sand to determine footprints. Fingerprints in the boathouse indicate many people had visited it before, including the assistants, Shelly, Dylan Newhart, Tommy Mercer. There were also a variety of unknown prints, which were most likely dive customers. There were no prints on the storage closet lock, except for partials of Shelly's and Julie's."

"Which means the killer wiped the lock after sabotaging the tank the night before. Then Shelly and Julie must have used the lock in the morning," said Heather.

"It looks that way," said Detective Peters.

"Anything else?" asked Amy.

"We had been looking into how the carbon monoxide had been put into the tank," said Detective Peters. "But if the killer had it already bottled from a lab, that would be the easiest answer."

"What are some other answers?" asked Heather. "You could collect it from your car?"

Peters nodded. "Carbon monoxide can be produced when you burn fuel in cars or other small engines. It could come from furnaces or fireplaces or a stove."

"Those are things lots of people have access to," Amy commented.

"Yes," said Detective Smith. "But as you pointed out, there is only one suspect who might have had access to pure carbon monoxide. And I think we should go talk to him now."

Heather and Amy allowed themselves to be ushered out so that the detectives could go about their business.

"Why do I feel like we've been locked out of the detectives' club?" Amy asked. "We were the ones who brought them the lead."

"I know. It feels unfair," said Heather. "But we did bring it to their information because they have the means to check with many labs and to make them share their records."

"But now what do we do? They're going off to catch the killer, and we're left twiddling our thumbs. I don't like twiddling."

"Don't worry. You won't have to twiddle," Heather said. "There's someone else we've been meaning to talk to, and now is as good a time as any to talk to him."

"Who's that?"

"The owner of the rival scuba school, Hank Club."

"Great," Amy said. "If he's not the killer, could we try scuba diving with him. I know he was a little obnoxious, but I still really want to dive."

"Let's just focus on one thing at a time," Heather said.

## Chapter 15 – Welcome to the Club

"You look very familiar," Hank Club said, as they entered his establishment. It had a similar layout to Shelly's but was trying to look more upscale. His storage area was more spread out and made to look like displays. Seven wetsuits hung up next to six air tanks and fourteen flippers. The masks had colors on them and were arranged to look like a fish.

"Well," Heather said. "We were going to go scuba diving with Shelly. You called out to our group on the docks."

"Yes. That's it," said Hank. "I'm glad my advertising worked."

"Advertising. Yelling. Same difference," Amy shrugged.

"I believe I offered you a deal. I'm pleased you came over to claim it."

"Of course, that's not the only reason," Heather said. "It's impossible to learn how to scuba dive from a dead woman."

"So you know about that," Hank Club said. "And the incident didn't scare you off from learning how to scuba?"

Here Amy shined. "Not at all. I've wanted to scuba dive since I came to Key West and nothing will deter me. I want to see all the fish up close. I want to be able to see what's below the water and feel like I'm flying as I swim through the water. And when I get good enough at diving, I want to explore sunken wreckage and feel like a treasure hunter."

Hank Club smiled at her enthusiasm. "It is one of the most amazing feelings. And I am happy that I can be a part of it all."
"I'm very gung ho about all this," Amy said. "But my friend is still a little nervous. Maybe you could reassure her a bit?"

"What is it that worries you?"

Heather was able to tell the truth, even though they were performing a bit as part of their sleuthing. "I was nervous about it before for some reason. But seeing the instructor die and still be on dry land has frightened me a good deal."

"I can understand why, but you really have nothing to worry about."

"I don't?"

"No, ma'am," he replied. "What happened to Shelly was a fluke. It could never happen to you. I heard that the police are treating it as a murder. So, it wasn't equipment malfunctioning or something wrong with scuba in general. It was somebody who wanted to kill her."

"But why would anyone want to kill that sweet woman?" Heather asked.

"She wasn't all that sweet," Hank let slip.

"What do you mean?" Heather asked.

"Nothing," said Hank Club. "I shouldn't speak ill of the dead. And she wasn't a bad person. But it's hard to hear how nice and sweet she was when she was my biggest competitor. She'd steal business away from me by acting like she was a kind instructor and only cared about her customers and the sport of scuba. She tried to make me look like I only cared about the money. Which is not true."

"That must have been hard," Heather said.
"It didn't look like you all got along at all that day on the docks," said Amy.

"No. We didn't really. And her assistants were no better. They were like trained puppies, doing whatever she said."

"I think that day she mentioned that you didn't have any employees," said Heather. "Is that a problem?"

"No problem at all in regards to your safety. I take out smaller groups so that way I can give more individualized attention."

"Then why would she say that?"

Hank Club cleared his throat. "I have had trouble holding onto employees. Maybe I'm a difficult employer, but if so it's only because I'm so thorough about my instruction. When I felt a little desperate about not having a staff, I might have approached her assistant Julie to see if she was interested in leaving Shelly for me. She wasn't. At any price."

"That's disappointing," said Heather.

"But then I realized I didn't need a staff, and that business could go quite well with only me running things."

"How has business been?" Heather asked.

"It's consistent," Hank Club said. "Tons of people have been scuba diving before, and no one had an incident like Shelly. You'll be perfectly safe."

"How has business been after her death?" Heather asked. "Has it improved?"

"That's a strange question to ask," Hank Club said, suspiciously.

"She's obviously stalling," Amy said. "Avoiding going in the water."

Hank Club laughed. "I do know the type. If it makes you feel better, I will answer your question. I think there might be an increase in business with her school gone. There will be less competition in the area. But it's hard to tell right now. People might be scared away from diving because of the incident like you are."

"That poor woman," Heather said.

"Yes," Hank said. "But I do remember hearing that she had trouble with men. Jealous lovers and that sort of thing. It must have been one of them that did her in."

"Oh dear."

"Yes. I remember a big commotion at her birthday party. Her assistants had thrown her a party, and there were balloons. They were using it as an event to drum up more business too. It was silly. And something I clearly couldn't repeat. Nobody cares how old I am. But, they had the party. And I think one of the jealous lovers caused a big scene. Very unfortunate."

"Unfortunate indeed," said Heather.

"Now are there any other questions I can answer to assuage your fears and get you into the water?"

"I do have one more," said Heather. "Her equipment that killed her must have been sabotaged during the night while nobody was around. Where were you at night? Were you protecting your equipment?"

"You don't have to worry about that. My shop is very secure. And yes, actually, I am here very late usually. Yesterday I was here 'til past one o'clock in the morning. I make sure that everything is taken care of."

"Did you work late the night she died too?"

"Yes," Hank Club said, narrowing his eyes.

"And without employees?"

"Yes," said Hank Club. "Now are we going to go scuba diving or not?"

"I just can't," Heather said, dramatically. "I'm still too afraid."

She hurried out the door as Amy shrugged. "Well, I can't go without her."

Outside, they broke into nervous giggles, excited that their ruse had worked so well.

"He could gain financially from Shelly's death," Heather said. "And he knew what day her birthday was so he could know the combination for the lock."
"I hope it's not him though," said Amy. "I do still want to go diving."

"He must think we're really weird," Heather said.

"Well, that's okay," said Amy. "He can think we're weird as long as he's not trying to kill us."

Heather's phone rang, and she answered it. When she finished the call, she said, "That was Detective Smith. They can't find Dylan Newhart."
"Why is everyone running away in this case?" Amy asked.

"Wait a second," Heather said. "I think I might know where he is. And if I'm right, we better hurry."

## Chapter 16 – A Lovely Beach for Fighting

"How could you do it?"

"Me? How could you do it?"

Heather and Amy were nearly out of breath, but her hunch was proved right. They saw that Dylan had arrived on the beach where Tommy was still laying around. The two men were shouting at each other, and it was starting to get heated.

"I loved her," Dylan yelled. "And you took her away from me."

"You took her away from me," Tommy yelled back. "Twice."

Heather called Detective Smith to alert him of the situation and was pleased to hear that he was in the area as part of his search.
"They'll be here soon," Heather said.

"I just hope it's fast enough," said Amy. "This situation looks ready to explode."

"She was the best thing in my life. How could you kill her?" Dylan asked.

"How dare you accuse me, you lying rat! You're the one who killed her." Tommy retorted.

"Take that back!"

"I think you're right," Heather said. "I think we might have to intervene."
Tommy and Dylan were facing off, about to fight each other. Heather ran up to them.

"Stop it, both of you," she said. "The police will be here soon."

"Then I don't have a lot of time," Dylan said, starting to punch Tommy. "I'll kill you for what you did to her."

"I knew you were a killer," Tommy said, fighting back. "And I'm going to get your first."

"Didn't you understand that we said stop?" asked Amy.

Heather reached into her bag and found her Taser. She had started carrying it after finding herself in one too many dangerous situations with a killer she was closing in on her. She pointed it at the two men fighting.

"Stop fighting now, or I'll use this," Heather threatened.

Luckily, she wasn't forced to carry through on her threat. Detectives Smith and Peters arrived on the scene and subdued the two men.

"We'll take them to the station," Detective Smith said. "If nothing else, we can hold them for this fighting."

"But most likely, one of them is the killer," said Peters.

Before they led the two men away, Detective Smith said, "Good work today. Why don't you call me in a few hours? I'll let you know what we discovered during interrogation."

"Thanks," Heather said.

"Was it any better today?" Heather asked.

Lilly shrugged. "I still don't know who to sit with at lunch. No one would turn me away from their table, but I'm still not part of any group."

"I know that you're likable and friendly. And I know that it takes time to make meaningful connections," Heather said. "But recently I've been thinking about something else too."

"What?"

"I've been having some trouble finding my new staff for Donut Delights – Key West. Now, these employees need to have certain skills and need to be personable. But overall, I was still having trouble finding people that I felt were right. Then Amy made me realize something."

"Even if she makes a lot of jokes, she can be smart," Lilly said.

Heather nodded. "She made me realize that I might be comparing the new employees to the old ones. And that's not fair. I love my Hillside staff. But this staff could be great too. It's just going to be different. I might have subconsciously been trying to fill the same spots like before. You know how Jung is an archer? Well, we interviewed a juggler."

"So, you think you were looking for new Jungs and new Maricelas instead of new employees?"

"I think I might have," Heather said. "Not completely. But enough for me to think I should stop comparing. And I was wondering if maybe you were doing that with new potential friends too."

"Like I'm holding back from making friends because they're not Nicolas or Marlene?" Lilly asked. "Maybe there's something to that."

285

"Just remember that making new friends doesn't mean your old ones are any less important," Heather said.

"That's true. But my old friends are pretty great."

"That's definitely true," said Heather. "But remember, they're not perfect. Like how they weren't any help picking out your first day of school outfit?"

"They were no help at all," Lilly laughed.

"Maybe try looking for someone different and see if they're a good friend," Heather said. "That's what I'm going to try at the store. We're meeting someone with a different background for an interview tomorrow. Most of my employees have been young adults, but this woman might even be older than me."

"As Eva would say – age is just a number."

"Very true," said Heather.

"Thanks, mom," Lilly said. "It helps to think that I might have been holding myself back from making a new best friend because it's something that I can overcome. I'm just going to dive right in at school tomorrow."

"Please don't use that phrase," Heather joked.
"You're that against scuba diving now?"

"No," Heather admitted. "But it reminds me that I still haven't cracked the case yet."

"Don't worry. You will."

Heather smiled at her daughter. "Thanks."

Then her phone rang, and it gave her less hope about solving the case. Detective Smith was updating her on what he had learned from his interrogations. Both Tommy and Dylan still had means, motive, and opportunity. However, Dylan's means wasn't as airtight as they had thought it was.

287

Dylan did work for a lab, but it didn't look as though he had stolen any carbon monoxide from there. The lab didn't notice anything missing from their inventory. They did inform the detective that Dylan was fired because he wouldn't show up for work. Most likely, he was skipping work to visit Shelly.

Heather thanked him for the information. She reminded herself that he still could have gotten the carbon monoxide from a car or other source near his home.

However, she had to admit that she felt like she was missing something.

## Chapter 17 – A Cupcake Clue

"Thank you for seeing me. I was so excited when Digby told me about the job."

"We're happy to meet with you too, Mrs. Lopez."

"Please call me Luz."

Heather and Amy sat across the table from their newest applicant.

"The first thing I'd like to ask is what your favorite donut is," said Heather. "Chocolate?"

"Oh my," Luz said. "I'm afraid I don't have a simple answer. For all desserts, my favorite is usually the one I've eaten last. For specialty donuts, the last one I had was a variation on Cherries Jubilee. It was fantastic. Then for simpler donuts, of course, both chocolate and vanilla are sublime. Though if those Banana Chocolate Donuts are delicious as they smell, then I think I've found a new favorite."

"Please, take one and see for yourself," Heather offered.

Heather was pleased. She liked the woman at once. The interview only further proved that she thought they would be the right fit. Luz's experiences were comparable to what would help her at Donut Delights. She was friendly and competent.

The icing on the cake was literally icing as Luz had prepared some cupcakes for them to sample her baking.

"I know cupcakes are different from donuts, but I wanted to show you that I do know my way around a kitchen. These are Tres Leches Cupcakes."

"They're delicious," Heather said. "What a wonderful idea. Would you mind if I used these as an inspiration to create a donut of this flavor?"

"I'd be honored," Luz said. "I haven't done professional baking before. I'm so excited for this opportunity."

"You even have such a cute travel bag," Amy said.

"Thank you," Luz said. "It's important to have the gear to transport things."

"What's that?" Heather asked. A thought was forming in her head.

"Because you don't want your desserts to get squished. That's why I have the plastic container and the cute carrying bag to carry it in."

"That's right," Heather said. "How could I have missed it? You need to travel with it. It's not just air."

"What is she talking about?" Luz asked.

"She gets like this when she's thinking," Amy said. "You get used to it."

"We have to go," Heather said.

"Oh. All right," Luz said, uncertainly.

"I mean," Heather said. "You're hired. Definitely. We'd love to have you on the team. But I do have to leave now. I think I solved the case. I just need to check one thing first."

***

Julie looked up as Heather and Amy approached her.

"Hello again," she said. "Is everything all right? Is the case solved?"

"It's very close," Heather said. "I need to ask you a few more questions about the night before Shelly's death."

"Sure," Julie said.

"You saw the man by the boathouse door around midnight, is that correct?"

"Yes. And I'm so glad it wasn't Micah," Julie confirmed.

"Did you see how the man arrived at the boathouse?" Heather asked.

292

"No," Julie said. "He was already there when I looked out my window."

"How do people normally get to the scuba school?"

"I walk from my house," Julie said. "If you're coming from further away on the island, you could ride a bike or drive. There's a parking lot right before the sand starts."

"Is it a long walk from there to the beach?" Heather asked.
"Not really," Julie said. "I walk further from my house and think it's fine. However, I guess it could be awkward if you're carrying stuff. I see some tourists get frustrated with the trek and are towing a bunch of beach chairs and umbrellas."

"Thank you," Heather said, nodding. "That's what I thought."

"I don't understand," Julie said.

"I have one more question," Heather said. "And I need you to think very carefully about it."

Julie nodded solemnly. "I'll do my best."

"When you saw the man outside the boathouse, was he carrying anything?"

Julie thought about it. "Yes. He was."

"Big or small?"

"Big," said Julie. "Is that important? I can't believe I forgot about it. I thought it was Micah at the time, and I remember briefly thinking why did he have such a large bag with him. If he forgot something at work but had that big bag, then he should still be fine."

"Thank again," Heather said.

She hurried away with Amy at her heels.

"Okay, what's going on?" Amy asked.
"I need to call Detective Smith about what happened," Heather said.

"Sure. But first, tell me. What was in the big bag?"

"I realized that the killer needed to transport the carbon monoxide in order to put it into Shelly's lucky tank. I can't believe I didn't think of it before. It would be difficult to travel by air, and it needed to be pumped into the killer air tank."

"So, what was in the bag was how the killer brought the poison to the office to replace the good air with?" Amy asked.

"Yes," Heather said. "He brought his own air tank and used some sort of pump to get it into Shelly's tank."

"His own air tank?"

"Yes," said Heather. "And that's also how we're going to prove who it was. With air."

## Chapter 18 – Catching a Killer and Seeing Some Sights

"So, you've returned?" Hank Club said as he saw Heather and Amy enter. "You're ready to finally start your scuba lessons?"

"Sadly, no," said Amy.

Detectives Smith and Peters entered as well.

"Officers, what can I help you with?" Hank Club asked. "Are you interested in diving?"

"We're interested in some of your gear," Detective Smith said.

"Look, one air tank is missing," Peters pointed out.

They looked at the display and saw that one tank was indeed missing. There were seven wetsuits and only six air tanks."

"It became faulty," Hank Club said. "I had to dispose of it for safety."

"Convenient," Amy said.

"What is this all about?" Hank Club asked.

"It's about the murder of Shelly Little," said Heather. "And we figured out how you did it."

"How I did it?" Hank asked. "Are you crazy? It had to be one of her boyfriends who did it."

"We thought so for a while," Heather said. "But it was you all along."

"Officer, are you going to let her say these things?"

"Let's see what she has to say," Detective Smith said.

"Julie saw a man with a large bag near the boathouse the night before the murder. She didn't see how they arrived, but I figured it out. Carrying an air tank and pumps would have been awkward to pull from the parking lot, across the beach, and to the boathouse. And the killer might have been seen during this trek. It would have been much easier to arrive by boat."

"This is nonsense."

"You were able to break into the boathouse because the knob was already loose. You learned that Shelly used important dates for her combinations. After you learned her birthday, you had a good idea of what the combination for the storage closet would be. I'm guessing you had a backup plan in case you were wrong about the combination, but you were lucky and opened it with the code. You wanted it to look like someone who knew her well had committed the crime."

"Why would I do all this?" he demanded.

"To get rid of your rival and make more money," Heather said.

"It also helped that you didn't like Shelly or her assistants much," Amy added. "That probably made it easier to carry out your plan."

"How would I be sure that Shelly was the one who used the tank?"

"You knew the story about her lucky air tank as well as anyone. You pretended not to know too much about her, but you did. The two of you insulted each other with knowledge of one another's businesses and personal lives," said Heather.

"He probably didn't care if he accidentally killed anyone else anyway," said Amy. "A murder at the scuba school would still have shut her down. That was all he wanted anyway. More money."

"These are terrible things to say," said Hank Club. He smiled. "And there's no way you can prove any of it."

"You might have disposed of the air tank evidence," Heather agreed. "But that's not the only evidence from the crime."

"What do you mean?"

"Well," Detective Smith said. "While we were in here talking, a forensic team has been taking samples of the exhaust from the boat."

"Don't worry. We have a warrant," Peters said.

"I bet you didn't know that every engine is slightly different. We'll be able to compare the samples from your boat with what was found in Shelly's air tank. I think they'll be a match," said Detective Smith.

Hank Club considered running but gave up on the idea. He allowed himself to be read his rights by the detectives. Before he left, he asked Heather, "How did you know?"

"You were the one with the right equipment for the murder," she said. "You had a way to carry and change the air."

The detectives led him away.

"It was lucky you were right about the boat being how he collected the carbon monoxide for the murder," Amy said.

"It was the only thing that made sense," said Heather. "It was an engine he could run without arousing suspicion."

***

"Look, there is it," Lilly said, pointing.

Everyone smiled. The Saturday outing idea was proving to be a big hit. Eva and Leila started snapping pictures of the Southernmost Point as soon as Lilly pointed it out. Jamie was regaling Amy with facts about it.

"This marks the southernmost spot in the continental United States," Jamie said. "There used to be just a small sign

301

to mark the location, but now they have this giant concrete buoy that was erected in 1983. It's suffered some storm damage from hurricanes, but it still remains standing strong."

"I like the way it looks," Lilly said. "It's taller than us, and it has those distinct striped on it."

"We'll have to take a picture of all of us there," Eva said.

"I'm photo ready," Leila joked, making faces.

They milled around the other happy tourists, eager to also step foot at the most southern point in the USA. When it was their turn to take a photo, they all smiled wide.

After it was taken, Heather couldn't stop smiling. She was surrounded by the people she loved most, enjoying the sights of their new home. She also felt proud that because of her, another dangerous killer was now behind bars.

She was also happy that they had made some decisions about her new staff. She had officially now hired Digby, Nina, and Luz Lopez. She thought this would be a strong team to start with, and she was sure it would grow as they expanded their donut making.

Then Amy said something that was threatening to take the smile away. "So," said Amy. "When are we going scuba diving?"

"What?" asked Heather.

"We were supposed to go after we hired one employee and now we have three. When are we going to scuba?"

"You still really want to go after everything that happened?" Heather asked.

"If we let a murder case stop us from everything we wanted to do, we'd never do anything," said Amy. "We'd probably have to stop eating donuts too."

Heather sighed. "Fine. We can still go. But we need to find a better way of picking the place we go to."

"No problem," Amy said. "We can do as much research as you want beforehand and make sure that no killers are lurking nearby. Because, next time, nothing is stopping me from making a splash."

Heather groaned, but her smile had returned.

**The End**

## Book 3 – Tres Leches & Murder

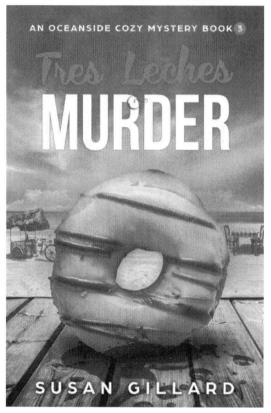

**Chapter 1 – In the Kitchen with Donuts**

"Are you making Tres Leches to celebrate having three amazing donut-making assistants?" Digby asked Heather with a smile.

"Hey!" Amy said, realizing that there were four of them there besides Heather.

"No disrespect meant," Digby said to her with hands raised in apology. "We don't think of you as an assistant. You're a higher up. A partner."

"That's true," Amy agreed. "I'm Heather's partner in both private investigating and in best friendship. And I don't mind being thought of as a second boss around here. I can give orders. You, bring me a donut. And you, clean the counters. On second thought, forget the counters. You, also bring me a donut."
They all laughed.

"I'm glad everybody is still in such high spirits after such a long day," Heather said.

"I think everyone is excited about the grand opening," Luz said. "I know I am."

"We're going to make sure we put the *grand* in the grand opening," Digby said.

"It is a little nerve-wracking. It's arriving so quickly." Nina said. "But it is exciting too. I can't believe it's happening tomorrow."
"Me neither," Heather agreed, though the timing felt different for her.

She had been extremely busy, so in some ways, the time felt like it flew by. In addition to having the donut duties on her plate, she also had to juggle moving into her new home and some sleuthing. However, it also felt like a lot of time had passed since she arrived. She and her family and best friends had moved to Key West relatively quickly so she could open up a second Donut Delights. She thought she would be able to open up shop right away, but it had actually taken a few weeks to finish the decorating, hire the proper staff and train them, and to advertise the opening. Add to that, that she had already helped to solve two murder cases since she moved in and it felt like she had been in town quite a long while.

"I think the other thing that is keeping our enthusiasm going is the smell of those donuts," Amy said.

"That's the case for me," Digby said. "But you never did answer my question."

"I certainly could have chosen Tres Leches as my flavor to celebrate my three new employees, because I know you will all be wonderful. You've helped me so much with setup and are becoming pros at making all the different donuts," Heather said.

She smiled at them, grateful that she had made the right decision in her hiring. Digby was a little dramatic but would be great with customers, and his fervor for the delicious flavors would be infectious. Nina was a little nervous but was a natural in the kitchen. Luz would excel at both aspects. She was an empty-nester who was a natural fit for Donut Delights. In fact, she had been the inspiration for the latest flavor, which Heather shared with the group.

"But the reason I chose to make a Tres Leches donut was because of Luz." Heather explained, "She created a terrific Tres Leches cupcake that encouraged me to try and make a donut version of the dessert."

"I couldn't be prouder," Luz said. "I knew my family enjoyed my baking, but it feels wonderful to be part of something official now. And to know that I inspired this donut – well, I just can't help smiling."

"I hope we all feel the same tomorrow," Heather said. "Hopefully, it will be very busy."

They heard the door open, and all moved towards it.

309

"I think it will be," Amy said. "They're already breaking down the door to get in."

However, they soon saw that the customers were Heather's friends Eva and Leila. The two older women started out as her favorite customers at her Donut Delights shop in Hillside, Texas, but had become close family friends. The two senior besties had followed them to Key West citing five main reasons: the weather, the company and "donuts, donuts, donuts."

"I guess this is the last time we're going to enter the shop before it opens," Eva said.

"Tomorrow we'll be just like all the other regular Joes that come in during business hours," Leila agreed.

"There's nothing regular about you two," Heather said.

"Great compliment," Amy said, rolling her eyes.

"I mean," Heather amended. "That you'll always be special. You're my favorite customers, and I don't think there's any way around it."

"We'll have to figure out what our new regular table is," Eva said, eyeing the setup of the room. Leila joined her as they moved around the space. They were discussing the pros and cons of each table.

"The lighting here might be good for reading the local paper," Eva said.

"But there might be a lot of people maneuvering around this table to get to the others," Leila pointed out.

Amy was getting bored. "The longer you take to pick a table, the longer you have to wait for donuts."

Eva and Leila promptly sat down at the table they were closest to.

"I think this is it," Eva said.

"The perfect table," Leila agreed.

"Now, what donut do you have for us today?"

Heather held back her giggles to explain the new flavor. "It's a Tres Leches Donut."

"That means three milks?" Eva asked.

"Maybe we should make it four milks," said Leila. "And get some coffee with milk in it to go with them."

Even though she was half-joking, Digby quickly started preparing some coffees. Heather was very proud of her staff picks.

"Yes," Heather said about the dessert. "A Tres Leches cake is made with condensed milk, evaporated milk and heavy cream. It's a light cake, so I had to work carefully to capture that consistency in my donut base. It's made to be like a sponge cake. It should be both creamy and light. But of course, with a rich, creamy frosting."

The two women took a bite, and then they took several more. When they could pry themselves away from the deliciousness, they complimented the snack.

"Tres cheers!" Leila said.

"Yes," said Eva. "Hip hip hooray! And well, I'd keep cheering to three, but then I'd have to stop eating."

Heather smiled and then turned to her staff. "Why don't you all enjoy another donut too? Then we'll clean up for the night and head home. Everyone should get a good night's sleep because it might be crazy tomorrow."

Her assistants happily agreed, and each grabbed a Tres Leches Donut. They seemed happy with the perks of their new job.

"So, what are you up to after you finish your donuts?" Heather asked her friends.

"We'd actually like to take a donut with us for a friend if we can," Eva said.

"There is actually a friend," Leila said. "We're not just grabbing more for ourselves to be greedy. Though I wouldn't mind a few more for ourselves."

"We've been enjoying some of the activities for seniors here, and we made a friend at the community center. A very dear woman named Betty," Eva said. "She has to go to physical therapy several times a week and is very tired afterward, but she does love visiting with people. We thought we'd bring some donuts to her and her son and chat for a while before she takes a nap."

"Of course, you can have some donuts," Heather said. "But she'll have to promise to come in and visit the shop when she's feeling up to it. I'd like to meet her."

314

"I'm sure she'd be glad to," Eva said.

"Especially after she tastes these donuts," Leila agreed.

She prepared a boxed sample of donuts for her friends made of what her staff had been practicing baking all day. Then, she helped her assistants finish closing for the day.

When only she and Amy were left, she turned to her best friend and said, "I can't believe it's really happening. I hope this second one is as good as the first."

"It will be different, but I think it will be just as delicious," her bestie said.

## Chapter 2 – Is this Opening Grand?

"Heather, I'm so happy we decided to do this, aren't you? I'm practically shaking I'm so thrilled. I'll contain myself and focus on shaking your hand," Rudolph Rodney said.

Heather gladly shook his hand back. She had been fortunate to have worked with several people who believed in her business before, but Rudolph Rodney was the investor who convinced her to open a second location in Key West. He was so confident that the new Donut Delights on Duval Street would be successful that he had even bribed the Shepherd family to move there by offering them a house. Even though the house had some quirks, it was a smart enticement to offer because it was a three-family house. This allowed Amy and her boyfriend, and Eva and Leila to have adjoining homes to Heather.

Rudolph Rodney had been a fan of Heather's donuts since he sniffed the air in her Hillside shop. She hoped that his belief in them would pay off when they opened the doors that morning. Heather was always proud of her creations, but couldn't help but feel a little nervous about the new endeavor. Her friends and family had moved there to support her with this store. If it failed, she would have moved them across the country for no reason. This was a new town. What if they didn't like her donuts as much as Hillside did?

Rudolph Rodney didn't look nervous though, so Heather tried to reflect his confidence. He was a fan of hats and today was wearing a Stetson Fedora for the occasion. It didn't shade his face so much that you couldn't see his huge smile.

"Are you all ready?" he asked.
"As ready as I'll ever be," Heather said. "I mean, yes. We'll be ready to open on schedule today. The front is ready for people to come in and sit down with the donuts. And the staff is hard at work preparing the donuts for the day."

"I do love the little artwork that you added to the tables," Rudolph Rodney said, indicating to the table settings. They were napkin holders that were decorated to match the beachy theme of this location. They were painted to look like oysters, but instead of holding pearls they were holding a greater treasure: donuts!

"Amy made those," Heather said, proud of her bestie's talent.

"That's wonderful," Rudolph Rodney said. "She's very artsy."

"I'm glad you didn't say crafty," Amy said, joining them. "Because that could have a double meaning."

"No, no," Rudolph Rodney said. "I know you aren't crafty and dishonest. Maybe the killers that you both catch are. I'll never forget how you cleared my name of that false murder charge. I don't know how to thank you. First that and now you're going to make me a successful donut investor," Rudolph said.

"Fingers crossed," Heather said, trying to make the butterflies in her stomach take a rest from flying around.

Ryan and Jamie entered the shop, and the butterflies formed in her stomach for a whole other reason. Heather and Ryan had been married for a while now and had adopted a child together, but he could still give her a romantic fluttery feeling when he appeared unexpectedly. "You're early," Heather said, greeting Ryan with a kiss.

"We were too excited to stay home," Jamie said after properly greeting his girlfriend, Amy.
"And I have to admit there wasn't much for me to do anyway," Ryan said.

Heather squeezed his hand. Ryan was a detective but hadn't started on his new police force yet since the move. He was waiting for the current detective to go into his promised retirement. Ryan maintained that he was enjoying the time off, especially because they were on an island with beautiful beaches, but

Heather knew he was itching to start work again.

"You said we would be back up today if the grand opening event today got too busy. We realized that it certainly would happen as soon as one person tasted your donuts, so we decided to come," Ryan said. "I can help out until Lilly gets out of school. But I'll be sure to bring her by. I know she wants to see the new shop up and running."

"I really appreciate it," Heather said. "You could help with the register today if we get stuck in the kitchen."

"Then we'll definitely have business," Amy said with a wink. "People will come for the donuts and for the eye candy."

Heather laughed, and the men pretended to be offended by her response. Ryan and Jamie were both very handsome, but she had trouble taking the phrase "eye candy" seriously.

Rudolph Rodney took the opportunity after the humor to talk to Jamie. "I'm very glad to see you again," he said. "After it quiets down with Donut Delights after the opening, we'll talk about setting you up with your pet grooming van business."

"I'm looking forward to it," Jamie said. "Befriending this group of people ended up being the best business decision I ever made," Rudolph Rodney declared. "And now tell me that everything is settled with the house and that there are no new problems."

Ryan and Jamie exchanged a look. While the setup of the new house and its location was wonderful, it did keep presenting problems that needed plumbers and electricians to be brought in. Rudolph Rodney was quick to bring someone in to repair any damage but felt disheartened that his "dream home" for them was occasionally a nightmare.

"Nothing that can't wait until after the opening," Ryan said.

"We might be having another problem," Amy said, looking out the window. "This could be trouble."

## Chapter 3 – The Rankle Problem

Heather had a terrible feeling as she looked out the window where Amy pointed. She was glad to see that her fears that a crime was being committed were allayed, but was frustrated for her business by what she saw.

Many of her shop neighbors on the street had made peace with here after initially giving her a hard time about being an out-of-towner setting up a shop in their prime real estate. It might have had something to do with her solving the murder of another neighbor, or it might have had something to do with her kind disposition and her yummy donuts.

However, one neighbor that had never warmed to her was Mr. Rankle of Sun and Fun Novelties. He could pretend to be pleasant, but she learned that in general, he was a cranky old man. However, she had never thought that he would stoop to the pettiness of his most recent stunt.

He had set up a display on the sidewalk in front of his store of heartburn and stomach medication. It proclaimed that it was for anyone that needed it after trying something new. Though he wasn't outright saying it, Heather knew that the display was aimed at her donuts. She was pretty sure that potential customers on the street would make this association too because of all their "Grand Opening - New Donut Shop" flyers.

"Well, I never," Rudolph Rodney said indignantly, without finishing the sentence.

"What part of Sun and Fun does this fit under?" Amy asked. "Fun for him to be a jerk?"

"What should we do?" Ryan asked.
"I'll have to go talk to him," Heather said.

"Great idea," Amy said. "Let's go."

"Not so fast," Heather said. "I think you should stay here."

324

"Why?"

"Because you get very passionate when you're angry. And you already start out on a pretty high sarcastic level. And I need to calm him down and rationally persuade him to put his display away."

"Fine," Amy said. "But if he doesn't listen to reason, make sure to tell him that he leaves as bad a taste in my mouth as some of those gross medicines."

Heather nodding, acknowledging to herself that it was a good idea that Amy stay behind. Rudolph Rodney insisted that as her investor he should accompany her. Heather agreed to that but suggested that everyone else stay behind too. She didn't want to make it look like they were ganging up on the old man.

"Good morning, sir," Rudolph Rodney said, trying to keep his tone even as he approached Mr. Rankle.

"Good morning," Mr. Rankle replied, jovially. "I see that you were visiting that new donut place. Do you need something to quiet your indigestion? I have many options to choose from."

"I certainly do not," Rudolph Rodney said. "I am an investor in this fine establishment and its honorable owner. Her donuts are so delicious that I had them brought over all the way from Texas to share with people here. And quite frankly, I find this little display of your distasteful."

"You're entitled to your opinion," Mr. Rankle said, dropping his smiling façade. "But here on this block, we find it distasteful for strangers to come in from off the island and steal our business."

"My donut shop won't take away from the sales of your sunglasses and snow globes," said Heather. "And if you really believe that all this stomach medication is necessary after eating my baked goods, then it would seem that I'd actually be creating more business for you. If, however, you are setting up this display just to hurt my feelings and my business, then I think it is something you might want to reconsider."

"I like my display the way it is," Mr. Rankle said. "I'm keeping it. And there's nothing you can do about it."

"We'll see about that," Rudolph Rodney said. "I'm going to Town Hall and then perhaps to the police to register a complaint."
"Why don't you take some heartburn tablets to go," Mr. Rankle suggested. "You might need them if you've been eating her mainland recipes."

"Just wait until you are eating some humble pie or, even better, a humble donut," Rudolph Rodney said, before turning on his heel to make good on his Town Hall threat.

"Mr. Rankle, don't you think this is rather silly?" Heather asked. "Can't you let my business be tested on its own merits instead of trying to sway customers against me? Can't we both work together on this street?"

"Can you please move out of the way of my display?" Mr. Rankle asked. "I'm expecting a surge in business today."

Heather thought to herself that with all her employees, staff and friends, she would have enough people to completely block this awful display from view. However, instead, she walked back to her shop, determined to keep her head held high. She would just have to do what she suggested should happen. She would let her donuts be judged on their own merits, and perhaps she would have to create her own street display.

## Chapter 4 – First Customers

The grand opening did not go exactly as Heather had hoped, but it was not a complete disappointment. In order to combat Mr. Rankle's sidewalk smear campaign, Heather came up with her own idea: sidewalk sampling.

She had her staff quickly set to work baking donut holes to hand out on the street. She wanted passersby to have a taste of her donuts and be induced to come inside and buy a whole one or maybe several whole ones.

"Did I mention I have the best job ever?" Digby asked as he came inside to get more donut hole samples to hand out. He had also been told that he could eat one every so often to assure others that what he was handing out would not make anyone sick. He was attacking the assignment with gusto and had been attracting some customers into the shop.

"Just be careful," Heather warned. "You don't want to eat too many all at once that you'd get sick and tired of eating them. That would make the plan backfire completely."

"Get tired of donuts?" Digby asked as if something so outrageous could ever be suggested.

"All right. Enjoy the work then," Heather said. "But let Nina have a turn after you."

Jamie and Ryan helping at the register really did help because it allowed Heather to show the others the different techniques for making the donut holes. She wanted them to be as tasty as their prized donuts.

Heather was happy to see that not all of the other shop owners on the street were supporting Mr. Rankle's efforts to undermine her. Heather's new friend Bernadette from Bernadette's Beachy Books made sure to stop by for the grand opening.

"It smells as wonderful as I imagine Mr. Wonka's factory would smell,"

Bernadette said. She was a friendly woman with large glasses who couldn't keep herself from making book references. "Though I am sorry about Mr. Rankle. He's a regular Ebenezer Scrooge."

"We're trying not to let it get to us," Heather said.

"I'm trying not to let it force me to go out and knock his tables down," Amy countered.

"My assistant and I are telling everyone who comes into our store to visit you," Bernadette said. "Nothing goes better with a good book than a donut snack."

Some other neighbors also visited the store, including Harmony from the yoga studio and Brogan from the hammock hut. Juan and Don who owned a taco restaurant also stopped in. They still were wary about newcomers on the block but didn't want Heather to think that they supported Mr. Rankle's exhibition. In fact, they were afraid that it might affect their business to because they were also nearby the display.

The visit that warmed Heather's heart the most was when Ryan brought their daughter Lilly in to see the grand opening. She told her mom that she was very proud of everything she was doing and that she was glad that they moved. Heather felt this validation from her daughter came a moment when she needed it.

Another visit she was happy to see was from Eva and Leila's new friend Betty Turner. She was accompanied by her son Theodore.

"I'm so happy to meet you," Heather said. "Any friend of Eva and Leila's is a friend of ours."

"I'm very glad to have a friend like you after tasting those delicious donuts that they brought to me yesterday. We couldn't wait to have some more, could we, Teddy?"

"That's right," Theodore said. "Mom loves sweets. This will probably be her new favorite place."

"Eva and Leila have already claimed their new regular table, and I'm sure they'd love to have you join them," Heather said. "They should be in soon."

Betty said she would love for that to happen. She explained how it was sometimes hard for her to make friends because she had to go to physical therapy a few days a week and one of the days was Wednesdays, which was the most popular day for activities at the senior center. She also had to go Thursday evenings and would have to go there later that day, and so wanted to enjoy some donuts before she started all her exercises.

She had some mobility issues that she was improving through therapy, but she was currently handling them with the use of a walker and the help of her son on long trips.

It was clear how much she appreciated her son. They lived in the same house together, and he was her caretaker when needed. Theodore seemed a bit embarrassed by attention when his mother complimented him.

He turned the attention back to her by telling them what a card shark she is, how she taught him to play cards, and how that's how the three ladies became friends. Finally, there was someone who could give his mother a run for her money in gin rummy and bridge.

There was suddenly a loud musical ringing. Amy jumped.

"Wait," she said. "Am I hearing things?"

"No," Theodore said. "Mom. It's your phone."

"I'm sorry," Betty said, digging in her purse. "I have trouble hearing my phone sometimes."

"Sometimes," Theodore teased.
Betty batted her son away playfully and answered the phone. When she hung up, she said, "That was Eddie. Your brother made better time with his drive

than he thought. He just arrived in town."

"Great," Theodore said, trying to mean it. "I guess we'll get going then. Wouldn't want to miss a minute with the bro. Do you want to bring him some donuts?"

"Does a royal flush beat a straight?" she retorted.

Theodore laughed. "We'll take a dozen."

Heather brought them their donuts. She was handing out donuts for the rest of the day and felt that it had been a decent day at the shop. If it had been a regular business day, she would have been quite content with it. However, knowing that Rudolph Rodney had put a decent amount of effort into grand opening advertising, she felt a bit disappointed.

It was clear that Rudolph Rodney felt the same. He was pleased and proud of Heather's quick thinking with the donut holes but was annoyed that Mr. Rankle's sidewalk display had affected their business. He was also annoyed that his visit to Town Hall or the police station had not helped alleviate the problem. Hopefully, Mr. Rankle would grow tired of his display and put it away for the next day.

"Oh well," Heather said to herself. "I'll deal with problems as they come up. Luckily, I don't have any investigating to do so I can focus entirely on a strong start for the business."

This was true for a little while.

## Chapter 5 – A Resolution to Relax

After a long day on her feet working at the shop and after putting Lilly to bed, all Heather wanted to do was take a hot bath. Unfortunately, the current problem with their house involved the tap on their tub, so she wasn't able to.

Instead, she curled up on the couch with her other doggy best friend, Dave. He appreciated the attention and allowed her to hug him and pet his white fur even though she didn't have any donuts that he could beg for and slobber over.

"Am I interrupting anything?" Ryan asked, entering the room.

"I don't mean to make you jealous with the other man in my life," Heather laughed. "You're welcome to scratch his belly with me too."

Ryan joined them, and Dave was in doggy heaven. His foot twitched appreciatively as they pet the sweet spot on his tummy. Then they let him fall into a happy sleep between them.

"I think I'm going to fall asleep as quickly as that when I get into bed," Heather remarked.

"The rest of the day was as crazy?" Ryan asked.

"It could have been busier," Heather said. "And I think we managed well with the hand we were dealt today, but it was stressful. It makes me sad to know that someone wishes for our failure, even if it's someone as cranky as Mr. Rankle."

"I don't mind him wishing it," Ryan said. "But I don't like his acting on it. Is there some way to get him to put away that heartburn display?"

"Rudolph Rodney said that because it doesn't mention us specifically and because it's on his property, the town can't make him take it down. I'm hoping he gets bored with messing with us tomorrow and stops it. If not, we're going to have to figure out a way to make him be reasonable," Heather sighed.

"I wish there were more I could do to help," Ryan said.

"You're a great help," Heather assured him. "You and Jamie working the register saved me when I needed to come up with a Rankle damage control plan. And Lilly loves the extra time you've been able to spend with her. The pets love it too. Right, Dave?"

Dave snored on cue.

"Thanks," Ryan said. "I needed to hear that. "I feel like I haven't been doing much lately."

"That's okay," Heather said. "You're entitled to a vacation. After all, how many cases did you break in Hillside one right after another?"

"Around sixty," Ryan said. "But I had some help."
He gave his wife a kiss.

"You'll be an official detective again soon and will be solving all sorts of cases," Heather assured him. "It's all right to enjoy the time off and relax."

"You don't get to do any relaxing," Ryan pointed out.

"That's true," Heather said. "It seems like I'm always running around with one thing or another. But I am going to do some relaxing tonight. Even if I can't take a hot bath, I'm going to relax. I think I'll take a hot shower instead. Then, how about we pop in a movie and enjoy a good film and snacks until we're ready to fall asleep?"

"That sounds perfect," Ryan said.

However, before they could execute their plan, there was a knock on the door. Heather opened it to see Eva and Leila, looking very pale. She ushered them into the living room, and handed them both a donut for comfort before asking, "What's wrong?"

The fact that they didn't immediately start eating their donuts told her that the answer would be that something was very wrong.

"It's Betty," said Eva.

"Something terrible has happened," Leila said.

"Oh no," Heather said, bracing herself for the news. The women were hesitant to start talking, so she continued, "I saw her this afternoon. She was such a kind woman. Did she pass away?"

"No," Eva said. "She called us. She wanted to cancel our plans for tomorrow, which was very levelheaded for having just faced a tragedy."

"I don't think it quite hit her yet," Leila agreed.

"And we also thought that maybe the real reason she told us was that she knew how close we are to you, and we did mention that you were a private investigator. Maybe she thought she might need one," said Eva.
"Why?" asked Heather.

"Her…" Leila began. "Oh, I just can't say it."

Eva took a deep breath and said the words, "Her son was killed this evening. He was murdered."

## Chapter 6 – Comforting Betty

They arrived at the hotel room where Betty Turner had told Eva and Leila she would be staying at while her home was still deemed a crime scene. The room door was ajar, and Betty told them to enter.

While earlier at the donut shop Betty had seemed full of life, she now seemed subdued. She wasn't crying, but the sorrow was evident. Her small figure seemed to be sinking into her chair, and she had no desire to pry herself from the seat. She had lost a child, and nothing now seemed to matter.

"We're so sorry for your loss," Eva said.

"We felt like we couldn't just say that over the phone," said Leila. "We felt like you needed to know we're here for you in whatever way we can be."

"And we brought Heather," Eva explained. "She's brought some donuts in case they can provide any tiny bit of comfort."

"It is important to eat and keep your strength up," Leila said. "The times we feel the worst are when we need to remember to eat."

"And Heather is an excellent private investigator," said Eva. "She's solved more cases than I can remember. She's helped us on many occasions too."

"She caught the arsonist who burned our house," Leila said, supplying an example.

"If you feel you need any help on the case, she'd be happy to help," said Eva.

Heather bit her lip. She wasn't sure how she felt about her services being volunteered so readily. She was happy to help if needed, but the current detective in town wasn't a huge fan of her interfering, even though it had helped catch some murderers in town. Heather had thought that they were coming over to offer comfort to the woman and not sleuthing services. However, it seemed that Eva and Leila thought that the best way to comfort her was the find the killer.

"Detective Smith is a wonderful investigator," Heather assured Betty. "And I'm positive he will figure out what happened. If you need me, of course, I'll help. But I'm afraid I only know the vaguest details right now, and I don't want to pry at this time."

"I can tell you what I know," Betty said. "It still doesn't feel real. I wish it weren't real. It was my Teddy. He was shot tonight."

"At your house?" Heather asked.
"Yes," said Betty. "My other son Eddie arrived this afternoon. After we had all visited for a while, Eddie volunteered to take me to my physical therapy appointment so Teddy could have a little time to himself. Someone must have come after him that night."

"Who would come after him?" Heather asked.

"I knew that he liked to gamble," Betty said. "A mother isn't blind to her children's faults. But I liked cards as next as the next person. And I didn't think it was a real problem. I thought he had control of it. I knew that sometimes he would pawn some of his items, like a TV or a watch. But he never took anything from me. I don't want his name dragged through the mud if this comes up. He never stole anything from me. He never used any money that wasn't his. He was a good boy, and he cared for me. He moved here after my husband died so I could keep my house and he could help me regain some mobility. He was my son, and he never stole from me."

"We believe you," Heather assured her.

"But maybe he should have," Betty said. "I didn't think it was serious, but he must have owed money to the wrong person. Someone who killed him for it."

"That's who you think killed him?" Heather asked.

"It's the only reason there could be," said Betty. "Except for the cards, Teddy was a saint. The way he cared for me. I mean, Eddie would have cared for me too. But he would want me to move to Santa Monica with him. Teddy left his job in Orlando to care for me. And Letty. She's very busy in Virginia. She's a doctor. Oh no. Oh, I have to tell Letty about her brother."

The door opened and a man with similar features to Theodore came in.

"Eddie, we have to tell Letty about what happened."

"I already did, Mom. She's trying to see if she can take off of work," he said.

"If she can take off of work?" Betty asked. "Of course, she should be able to. Her brother was just killed!"

"I'm sure she'll be here soon," he said. "And who is here?"

"I'm Eva, and this is Leila. We're friends from the community center. And this is

Heather. We thought she might be able to help."

"Edward Turner," he said, giving them all a powerful handshake. "Help how?"

"Donuts," Heather said, quickly. "Eva and Leila were afraid that she wouldn't be eating."

"Thank you," Edward said. "I think my mother needs to get some rest now. I'll make sure that she eats enough. I'll care for now. I think you should go to bed now, Mom."

"I don't think I can sleep," Betty said. "Not after what happened, and not when I'm out of my own bed."

"Well, we can't go to the house until the police say it's okay."

"I'm not sure I can ever go back there," Betty said.

"Then you can come home with me," said Edward. "But let's not discuss this now. This isn't the time for big decisions."

"I guess you're right," Betty said.

The other women told her to let her know if there was anything they could do to help and left the hotel room. Edward closed the door quickly after them.

"Poor Betty," Leila said.

"What do you think?" Eva asked Heather. "Are you going to get involved?"

Heather thought about it. She was busy opening her shop and dealing with Mr. Rankle's sabotage, but she couldn't forget the sorrow she saw on Betty Turner's face. She would at least make sure that Detective Smith had some solid leads on the case.

"First thing tomorrow, I'm going to check in with Detective Smith," she said. "I'm going to make sure that this killer is brought to justice."

### Chapter 7 – Dealing with Detectives

"There's no chance that you came just to deliver some donuts, is there?" Detective Smith asked.

"He is a good detective," Amy said.

"We are celebrating our grand opening. And we did bring Tres Leches Donuts," Heather said, displaying a box of the frosted delights. "But we also came to ask about a case."

"Is it about the man with the indigestion stand in front of his store on your street? Because I'm afraid, there's not much we can do about that unless his actions escalate."

"No, we're not here about him," Heather said.

"Though if you could do anything about him, that would be great," Amy said. "Rankle is worst."

"We're here about a murder," Heather said.

"Why am I not surprised?" Detective Smith said. However, he didn't seem as annoyed as he had in the past. He took one of the offered donuts.

"Eva and Leila are friends with Betty Turner. They wanted us to make sure that her son's death was on track to being solved," said Heather.

"Does it being on track mean that you're investigating it?" Detective Smith asked, putting his donut down to give them a serious stare.

"Not necessarily," Heather said. "But if we can be of any help, then we do want to do what we can. Betty is obviously upset by what happened to her son. And we and our friends are concerned about her."

"Do you have any leads?" Amy asked.

"Yes, we do," Detective Smith said. "But I'm not sure I should share them."

"We shared our donuts," Amy pouted.

Detective Smith held his half-eaten snack out towards them, inviting them to take it back.

"If you could assure us that you'll catch the culprit soon, then we don't have to get involved," said Heather. "We are already pretty busy with Donut Delights – Key West opening."

"And we do have a Rankle annoyance to deal with," Amy agreed.

"Telling us your potential leads could reassure us that we're not needed," Heather said.

Detective Smith relented. "Theodore Turner was shot to death inside his home yesterday. We believe the shooting occurred between six and seven p.m. last night."

"Your medical examiner was able to pin the time of death down to such a small window of time?" Heather asked, impressed.

"The victim made some phone calls last night that help us shrink the time frame," Detective Smith explained.

"Who did he call?"

"His mother and brother," said Detective Smith. "People that would be able to recognize his voice."

"Who do you think did it?" Amy asked.

"We're going to follow up on a potential lead. Apparently, Theodore Turner liked to gamble. He might have owed money to someone who got tired of waiting to be paid and took drastic and deadly measures," Detective Smith said.

"I better make sure I don't forget to pay anyone back," Amy said. She turned to Heather. "I paid you back for new chairs in my house, didn't I?"

"Yes," Heather said. "But I wouldn't kill you over that."

"Worse," said Amy. "You might cut me off from my supply of donuts."

"The first thing we're going to do is find out who the gun belongs to," said Detective Smith.

"The killer left the gun behind at the scene of the crime?" Heather asked.

"He dropped it in the trash can," said the detective.

"That seems like a dumb move," Amy commented.

"Not completely dumb though," he said. "The killer did wipe away any fingerprints that were on it."

"Well," Heather said. "I suppose that if the gun is able to easily lead you to the killer, then you don't really need us on this one."

"Thank you for the vote of confidence," Detective Smith said, wryly.

"I know you'd like to work on a case with just you and your partner," Heather admitted. "Since it might be your last."

355

"Do you think this will be your last case?" Amy asked.

"I don't know. I just focus on one case at a time," he replied.

"Yes," said Amy. "But while you're focusing on this case, could you determine whether it's the last or not? I know the other detective is excited to get on the job."

Detective Smith said neutrally, "I will be retiring soon."

Before they could get any other information about his retirement date, they were interrupted by his partner Detective Peters. Peters was a young officer with a great work ethic and strong sense of duty. However, he was also new in his position and could be unsure of himself.

"I think we've hit a snag, sir," he said, joining them.

"Be careful who you say that in front of," Detective Smith said. "But what's the issue?"

"I found out who the gun belonged to."

"And?"

"And it belonged to the Theodore Turner. It was the victim's gun that shot him," said Peters.

"Looks like finding the gun's owner isn't going to lead to an open and shut case," Amy said.

"That's right," said Heather. "Now we're not sure if the killer went to Theodore Turner's house with the intention to kill him, or if it was the result of a fight that got out of hand. Did Theodore Turner bring the gun out to protect himself and it got taken away from him and used on him? Or was the gun part of the killer's plan? Did he know where it was in the house and planned on picking up the murder weapon at the scene of his soon-to-be crime?"

Peters listened to her questions and began writing them down in his notebook. "Good questions," he commented.

"I suppose you're not going to be walking away from this case now," Detective Smith said.

"I'm sorry," Heather said. "But with a more complicated crime, I think you need all hands on deck to get justice for the Turners."

Detective Smith sighed. "Very well," he said. "Peters, why don't you take them to visit the crime scene?"

## Chapter 8 – The Crime Scene Search

"It's a mark of confidence that Detective Smith is letting me bring you here on my own," Detective Peters said. He was only half-talking to them, and half-reassuring himself. "I will make sure that you do not disturb any evidence in your search and keep a careful eye on the area. He trusts me to handle the situation. And it's good for me to handle these sort of tasks on my own. He's preparing me for when he retires so that I can be more self-sufficient."

"Don't be nervous," Amy countered. "He probably thinks that this is a waste of time, and is letting you babysit us."

"Do you think so?" Detective Peters asked, sounding less nervous but somewhat crestfallen.

"We've helped with other cases before," Heather said. "He wouldn't allow us all to go here if he thought it was a complete waste of time. And I think we can find something useful."

Peters smiled. They arrived at the Turner house. Instead of walking up the path to the front door, the detective led them around to the back.

Heather hesitated just for a moment. "It seems strange for our first visit to Betty's to be through the back and to examine a crime scene."

"Yeah," Amy agreed. "Based on the conversation you had in the shop, I expected it to be playing cards with her and Eva and Leila."

Heather shook her head to clear it. "Now we just need to focus on who killed Theodore Turner and stopped that happy gathering from happening."

Detective Peters took the lead. He showed them the broken window on the back door.

"This is where we believe the killer entered from," he said. "He broke the glass so that he could unlock the door and sneak inside."

"The glass was already collected by the forensic team?" Heather asked.

"Yes," Peters said, consulting his notebook. "The glass was found inside the house, indicating that the force came from outside. That is consistent with someone outside breaking their way inside. So far, no fingerprints or DNA have been found on the glass."

"What about any fibers?" Heather asked.

"There were some black threads recovered," said Peters. "They might have gotten caught in the glass when the killer broke it. But unfortunately, the threads are very common. They are used in several popular shirts and jackets. It might help if we find a suspect and determine their black outfit was ripped, but it doesn't provide us with a starting point."

"That's a shame." Amy joked, "Why couldn't the killer have worn his one of a kind shirt made from only certain silkworms that came from a store that keeps excellent records?"

Heather was examining the door. "What was used to break the glass?"

"A rock," said Peters. "We think it came from this yard. There are other rocks over there in a display around the palm tree that match it."

Heather and Amy looked at circle of stones around the tree.

"It's missing one there too," said Amy. "It must have come from there."

"Which means that the killer used what was nearby to break inside. He didn't bring anything with him that could be used to incriminate himself," said Heather. "But did he do that because he was a smart criminal that planned on using anything nearby to accomplish the task without providing a link to his identity? Or was he familiar with the yard, and knowing the rocks were here, planned to use them?"

Amy groaned. "We're finding more and more questions, but not enough clues to answer them."

Heather nodded. "Can we look inside now?"

Detective Peters showed them inside, careful to make sure that the scene wasn't disturbed.

"The body was found over here," he said, showing them to an area of the hallway. "He was shot in the chest. We believe he was facing the killer."

"This spot is in the center of the house," Heather said. "Both the killer and the victim could have been coming from any room."

"If it was his gun, Theodore Turner might have been going to get it," Amy said.

"We'll have to determine where the gun was kept," Heather said.

"The victim might have been moving to get his cell phone," Peters said. "It was charging on the table in there."

They moved toward the sitting room area that was situated between where the body was found and the broken back door. There was a charger still on the table that must have been connected to the victim's cell phone before the police took it into evidence. However, that was not what was attracting Heather's attention.

"What are those cards doing on the floor?" she asked.

"It's a card table, and games must have been played there," Peters said. "We thought the wind from the hole in the door blew them off the table. It was a little windy last night."

"I don't think that's why those cards are there," Heather said. "There's five of them."

"What does that mean?" Peters asked.

"Ames, you know poker, don't you?"

"I know the rules," she said. "I'm an okay player, but believe it or not, I'm not great at bluffing."

"What hand is made from those cards on the floor?" Heather asked, hoping to verify her idea.

"Let's see. They're all the same suit. All hearts," Amy said. "And there's a king, queen, jack, ten and nine. That's straight flush."

"Is that good?" Peters asked.

"You don't play poker?" Amy asked.
Peters shook his head. "My friends don't play cards. If we play a table game, it's most likely a co-op strategy board game like where you battle zombies or search for a cure to a disease."

"Well," Amy said. "The cards all in order and the same suit. It's the second highest hand you could ever get. It would only be higher if there were an Ace instead of the nine."

"You said that Theodore Turner might have had a gambling problem and that he owed money to the wrong person?" Heather asked.

"That's a theory we're working on," Peters agreed.

"Well," Heather said. "I think that person left us a message. We just need to determine exactly what it means."

## Chapter 9 – Another Turn with the Turners

"Thank you for talking with us," Heather said. "I know this must be difficult for you."

"If it helps catch whoever did that to my Teddy, I can brave anything," Betty said. "The worst has already happened to me."

"We hope to make it a little bit better by finding the man responsible," Heather said.

"And we hope to make the questioning a little bit better by offering you donuts while you answer them," Amy said.

Betty picked up a Tres Leches Donut and took a big bite. Then she braced herself, and asked: "Now what can I tell you that would be helpful?"

Amy took out her tablet so that she could take notes about the interview. She nodded to Heather to let her know that she was also ready.

"The first thing we'd like to know about is the gun," said Heather.

"Teddy got that gun to protect us. He knew I would have difficulty fighting off any intruders because of my legs," Betty said. "I can't believe it was turned against him. Are the police sure of that?"

"I'm afraid they are," Heather said. "Where was the gun kept?"
"It was kept in the kitchen," said Betty. "It was in one of the drawers so it was low enough that I could grab it. It was in a box with a latch, but it wasn't locked."

Heather nodded. "And who knew about this gun?"
"Well, the family knew about it," Betty said. "Letty was quite upset about it being in the house. She didn't like the idea of me shooting a gun."

"Letty is your daughter?"

"Yes. My daughter Leticia. She should be coming down to join us soon.

Apparently, it was difficult for her to get off of work," Betty said.

"Did anyone else know about the gun?" Heather asked. "Maybe Theodore's friends? Or people he gambled with?"

"I'm not sure," Betty said. "I don't think he would tell people he didn't know about it. But sometimes he could be a bit of a bragger. I bet he would tell the guys he was playing poker with if he thought they would be impressed."

"Speaking of poker," Heather said. "Do you know of any significance for a straight flush from a nine to a king?"

"That does sound familiar," Betty said. "I think my Teddy had that hand before. But I can't remember the circumstances. He played so much. I can't recall exact details."

"That's all right," Heather assured her as the older woman started to fret. "I have another question I would like to ask.

369

How was Theodore set with money? You think he owed someone?"

"We were all right with money in general," Betty said. "My husband was rather wealthy. He left some money to all of our children. And he left enough for me to be cared for. Theodore was in charge of my money. He was very honest. I know this for a fact. I always believed in him because he's my son and I knew him. But objectively too, I can prove it. His brother Eddie was worried that he might be skimming some money off the top and hired a man to look into the matter, and the accountant or investigator came to the conclusion that my Teddy wasn't doing anything untoward."

"So, he never touched your money," Heather said. "How was he with his own money?"

"Not as wealthy as his father. But he did some work with computers to make ends meet. And because he helped me so much I insisted that I pay for the house and all utilities," said Betty. "Teddy would gamble, but I think it was more for the thrill than anything else. Sometimes he would lose, and he'd pawn something of his. But I never expected him to lose enough that it would have gotten him killed. But what else could it have been? That was his only vice."

Edward Turner returned to the room with some beverages.

"Are you almost finished with this discussion?" he asked. "I know it must be draining for my mother, and I'm afraid I need to have another unpleasant talk with her after you leave."

"What do you mean?" Amy asked.

"I mean that I don't think that my mother can stay on the island without Theodore to take care of her," said Edward. "I think we're going to have to seriously discuss moving."

"I can't move now," Betty said. "We haven't even had the funeral yet. They're still investigating the murder."

"And hopefully it will all be concluded soon," Edward said. "But we do need to start planning for the future. You need someone to care for you. And I'd like that person to be me. You could move closer to me. I know some wonderful senior living facilities. And even better physical therapy classes. And we could see each other all the time."

"Let's discuss this after the killer is caught," Betty said, firmly.

"Fine," Edward said. "But we need to discuss it."

"What else do you need to know?" Betty asked, turning her attention back to Heather and Amy.

"Where were you both at the time of the death?" Heather asked.

"Eddie took me to physical therapy class that night," Betty said. "So, Teddy could have an evening off. He brought my purse to the car when I forgot it inside the house, he drove me there, and he stayed in the waiting room while I was with my therapist."

"I wasn't in the waiting room the whole time," Edward said. "I was talking with some of the nurses and therapists at the desk for a good long while. They should remember me. I was somewhat displeased with her current plan. Which is another reason why I think the move would be good for her."

"Eddie, stop it."
"Fine," he said. "And I also did take a phone call from Theodore. He asked me to pick up some laundry detergent on our way home, which we did."

"I had missed a call from him," Betty said. "While I was waiting for them to take me in the therapy room, he must have called me. Then he called Eddie later to make sure the message got through. I wish I could have heard my phone ring. I would have loved to hear his voice one more time."

She started to tear up, and Edward moved closer to her.

"I think we're done for today. She's been through enough," he said.

"Just one more question," said Heather. "Do either of you know the names of the people that Theodore played poker with?"

"Not most of them," Betty said. "He'd go over to their houses instead of having them at home so I could rest early."

"And he'd leave you home alone," Edward grumbled.

"He left when he knew I'd be sleeping. I have a pendant that I could push in case of an emergency. And I'm not an invalid," Betty said. "He was allowed to have his own life too. You and Letty certainly did."

"But I want to care for you now," Edward said.

Betty looked at Heather. "I only know one of the players because he mentioned it when we went to visit Donut Delights. It was a man from the taco place on your block. He was a player. Don."

Heather and Amy exchanged a look.

"Why are we having such troubles with our neighbors?" Amy asked.

## Chapter 10 – Don's Denial

"Look, we said that we don't support what Mr. Rankle is doing," Juan said. "But there's nothing we can do about it."

"He wouldn't listen to us," Don agreed.

"And we'd rather not wake a sleeping beast if we know it won't do any good," said Juan. "But if you'd like a taco, we'd be happy to serve you."

"Our new fish ones are really good," said Don.

"And maybe we can form some sort of tacos for donuts exchange between us?" Juan suggested. "They were actually very good."

"That does sound like a good idea," Heather said. "But it's something we're going to have to discuss later. We've come here to talk to Don."

"To me?"

"To him?" Juan asked. "Why just him? What's going on?"

"Don't look at me," Don said. "I have no idea."

"We'd like to talk about Theodore Turner," Heather said.

"Who?" Juan asked.

"Yeah," said Don. "Who?"

"One of the regulars in your poker group," said Heather.

"Don doesn't play poker," said Juan.

"That's right," Don agreed. "I don't know what you're talking about."

"Well, the man you don't play poker with was murdered yesterday," said Amy.
"Murdered?" asked Don.

"You don't know who he is, do you?" Juan asked.

Don shook his head. "Sorry I can't be of any help."

Heather and Amy left the taco shop more confused than before.
"Why would Don be lying?" Amy asked. "Could he be the killer?"

"I don't know," said Heather. "But I think that if we wait around here for a moment, we might find out more."

Her hunch was correct. A few minutes later, Don quietly snuck out the back door and ran into them.

"I was heading to your donut shop to find you," he said.

"So, you do know Theodore Turner?" asked Heather.

"Yes," said Don. "And I can't believe he's dead. You think he was murdered?"

"We know he was murdered," Amy said. "He was shot in the chest."

"Why did you lie about the poker games?" Heather asked.

"Because of Juan," Don said, embarrassed. "I didn't want him to know about the games because I didn't invite him when they started up."

"So you were willing to interfere with a murder investigation because you didn't want to admit that you didn't invite someone to a game?" Heather asked.

"I came to find you right after," Don said. "And yeah. I didn't want to hurt Juan's feelings. He's my best friend. But I needed something for myself. We work together every single day, and we hang out all the time. I wanted one night with some other people. Can you understand that?"

Heather and Amy looked at each other. They also worked together, solved cases together, and loved hanging out and having movie nights. They shrugged.

"Where does Juan think you are when you disappear every week?" Amy asked.

"I made our poker nights on the day his favorite show plays on TV. It's a wartime fantasy show that he knows I'm not into," said Don.

"Who normally hosts the games?" Heather asked.

"Usually me. And sometimes O'Malley. The other guys were married, and Theodore had his mom, so it was easier to have it at one of our houses."

"Was there any animosity in the group?" Heather asked.

"No," Don said. "It was always a friendly game. It never got out of hand."
"I'll pardon the pun," Amy said.

"I don't think it could have anything to do with his death," said Don.
"Even when people are upset they're losing money?" asked Amy.

"But it was never that high stakes a game," he said. "The highest we ever went was a thousand. But usually, it was only a couple hundred between us. It was just about having a night out with the guys to play cards. It wasn't really about winning."

"And how did everyone in the group get along?" Heather asked.

"Fine," said Don. "We might not have been the best of friends, but we liked seeing each other. O'Malley might have had a temper occasionally, but he was a jokester too."

"We'd like to talk to him too," said Heather.

"I can give you his contact information," Don said. "But I really don't think they could have had anything to do with his death."

"Where were you last night?" Heather asked.

"Juan and I went on a double date," said Don. "We went out for drinks after a movie and dinner. It got to be pretty late."

"Do you know where any of the other poker players were?" asked Heather.

"Actually, most of them were out of town this week. The married guys' wives are all friends, and another of their friends was getting married. All of them were at a wedding in Port St. Lucie."
"Who wasn't there?"

"Just Theodore, me and O'Malley."
"Did you and O'Malley know where Theodore Turner lived?" Heather asked.

"I guess so. Sometimes we'd carpool and have a DD if we felt like having some beer."

"Did Theodore ever mention that he had a gun?" asked Heather.

Don nodded. "It's come up before. He said he kept it in the kitchen."

Heather thought about it. If Don knew where Theodore had kept the gun, then probably everyone in the poker game knew it too.

"One more question," Heather said. "Does a straight flush of hearts mean anything to you?"

"No," Don said. "But it would be a great hand to have."

## Chapter 11 – Rankle Remains

Heather and Amy walked back to Donut Delights, thinking about everything that they had learned about the case. However, as they got closer to the shop, they were greeted with another unhappy sight.

Mr. Rankle had enlarged his display of stomach medication and was now offering information on what to do if you discovered signs of food poisoning.

"Is he serious?" Amy asked.

"It looks like he didn't get bored of his sabotage," Heather said.

They walked up to Mr. Rankle, who looked perfectly satisfied, sitting at one of his heartburn tables.

"How's business?" Amy asked.

"It's going great," Mr. Rankle said. "There's been an upsurge in sales of these products. Must be the new food that's causing a need."

"Must be that you're scaring people into thinking that they need it," Amy said.

"Would you like to purchase something?" Mr. Rankle asked.

"I'd like you to stop this pettiness," said Heather. "What can we do to get you to put away this display?"

"You can close up your shop and go back where you can from," he replied.

"Don't you think you might be hurting some other businesses on the street beside ours? Maybe some other food places that are owned by people you've deemed locals?"

Mr. Rankle looked nervous for a moment, but then said, "I don't believe I am. And I'll make sure I won't."

"There are locals working at the donut shop," Heather said. "And very excited to be too. If you hurt our business, you're hurting them too."

"I'm sure they can find a job with the next out-of-state person who plans on trying to take over my block," said Mr. Rankle. "Now if you're not going to buy something, please move along."

Heather sighed. She pulled her bestie away from the display before she could do anything rash. Then, they both returned to Donut Delights.

"Tell me Mr. Rankle's display isn't really affecting business," Heather said to her staff.

"I'm afraid it might be," Nina said.
"We still are getting customers," Luz assured her. "It's just not as big a gathering as Mr. Rodney had hoped."

"But we will survive and overcome," Digby said with a dramatic hand movement.
"Mr. Rodney was really mad," Nina said.
"He said he was going to go fishing to clear his head," Luz said. "And based on the terms he used, it's clear he's no

fisherman. He was thinking about using donuts as bait."

"That would catch me," Amy said.

"But a donut won't last in the water for long," Luz pointed out.

"Not with me after it," Amy joked.

"We'll have to figure out a way to deal with Mr. Rankle," Heather said, both for her sake and her investor's. "The reason he doesn't like us is because we're from out of town. Is there any way to overcome that?"

"I don't know. But we could easily overcome his table by flipping it over," said Amy. "Just saying."

"Has he even tried any of the donuts?" Digby asked.

"No," said Heather. "When we first tried to deliver some to him, he refused."

"That's a shame," said Nina. "Their taste might win him over."

"Maybe I could convince him to try one," Luz mused.

"Anything you could do to win Mr. Rankle over to our side would be appreciated," Heather said. "I feel as stuck in that situation as I do on our case."

"Are you really trying to solve a murder?" Nina asked. "That sounds scary."

"We have had some close calls before," Heather admitted. "But I wouldn't call our investigations scary. I think it's important work. And we seem to be good at it. We like to make sure that justice is served, and if we can help do so, then we will."

"We're really good at it," Amy amended.

"How is this case going?" Luz asked. "Was it really a nice customer's son who was killed?"

"Yes," Heather said. "That's why we're on the case."

"But if you're on a case, doesn't that mean that the killer might realize that and come after you?" Nina asked. "Or come after us?"

Digby hummed some dramatic theme music to accompany her questions.

"You'll all be fine," Heather assured them. "The problem for you to focus on is Mr. Rankle. If you have any time, in between serving donuts, to come up with a plan, let us know. Now we're going to follow up on a lead for the case."

"A lead. How exciting," said Digby.

Heather wasn't quite sure whose side to take. Was it exciting that they were going to follow a lead and talk to O'Malley? Or were they putting themselves in danger by talking to a suspected killer?

### Chapter 12 – A Gamble on O'Malley

O'Malley opened the door and immediately greeted them with an offer. "Twenty bucks I can guess who you are and why you're here?"

"No deal," said Amy. "We called before. You know who we are."

"You might have been mailmen or salespeople," O'Malley said as he admitted them inside. "It was still a little gamble for me. But you are the investigators?"

"Yes. We'd like to talk to you about Theodore Turner," said Heather.

"Of course," he said, as they sat down at a table. "I heard he had been killed. Want to lay down odds that I can guess what the murder weapon is?"

"I don't think that's appropriate," Heather said. "But I am interested to hear what your guess is."

"Fine," he said. "I'd guess a wrench."

"Why do you say that?" Heather asked.

"Like in the board game," he said. "And I figured he was hit on the head. Someone panicked when he was home and not taking his mother to her doctor and had to act quickly."

"You know a lot about his schedule," said Heather.

"Everyone who knew him did. His mother was on a tight schedule with her doctors, and he made sure she made every appointment. We almost changed our poker night, but he couldn't because of some doctor thing with his mom. Actually, Don was weird about it too."

"So, you're guessing that the killer didn't mean to kill Theodore Turner?"

"Why would anyone want to kill him? He was a good guy. Took care of his mom."

"Never cheated at cards or didn't pay a debt?" Amy asked.

"We didn't play on credit here," said O'Malley. "It wasn't big enough stakes. And it was just for fun. Theodore was a good guy. And no, he never cheated."

"Somebody was angry enough at him to shoot him in the chest," Heather said. "There must have been a reason."

"Somebody shot him?" O'Malley asked. "I never would have guessed that."

"Even though he had his own gun?" asked Heather.

"Especially because he had protection," he said. "Do you think I had something to do with this?"

"Does a straight flush of hearts mean anything to you?" Heather asked.

"It's a poker hand," said O'Malley. "But other than that, no. Why?"

"The cards were laid out at the crime scene," said Heather. "Did Theodore ever win big or lost big with that hand?"

"Not that I remember," he said. "So I don't think it was a significant event."

"Was there any fighting within the poker group?" Heather asked.

"That's why you're talking to me," he said. "I get it now."

"You do?"

"This is about the pair of twos," O'Malley said. "Look, I did get mad about that. Theodore was good at bluffing that day, and I folded. I ended up folding for a pair of twos. I threw a beer can at the wall. I was mad. But then I realized it was a game and how silly it all was. I accused myself of alcohol abuse and licked the wall to save the beer."

"This is why I don't play regularly," Amy said.

"But that was a while ago," O'Malley said. "And I never would have killed over it. And like I said Theodore was a good guy."

"Where were you last night?" Heather asked.

"I was home."

"Alone?"

"Yes. Is that a crime? I was watching TV."

"It's no crime," Heather said. "But it means no one can vouch for your whereabouts."

"I guess not. But I didn't have anything to do with the death."

"Who might have?"

"I don't know," O'Malley said.

"We heard that Theodore Turner was in debt to someone. That he had pawned his TV before," said Amy. "If it wasn't for the poker game, who was it for?"

O'Malley looked uncomfortable. "I mean, I wouldn't know that, would I?"

"I've got a feeling you do," said Heather. "Was he gambling on something else?"

"Maybe," said O'Malley. "It's possible that he might have liked to do some sports betting. And it's possible that I might have given him the name of a guy who takes bets. But it's impossible for me to give you his name."

"Why?" asked Amy. "Did he change it to a symbol?"

"If I give you his name, I won't be able to bet with him anymore. And I need that."

"And I think we need that name if we are going to figure out who murdered your friend."

"I'm sure he had nothing to do with it," O'Malley said.

They stared at each other, no one ready to budge.

Then, Amy said, "Okay. You like to make bets, right?"

"Occasionally."

"So, we'll make a bet," said Amy. "And if we win, you give us the name. And if you win, I'll give you all the money I have in my wallet."

"What's the bet?" O'Malley asked. "I want something where I make the decision."

"Okay," Heather said. "I might have an idea. I have a box I've been carrying around. Can you guess what is inside it?"
"Three guesses?" O'Malley asked.

"Sure," Heather said.

He agreed. "You're private investigator ladies looking into a murder. So, my first guess is it's the murder weapon."

"No."

"What about evidence bags from the scene?"
"No."

"A magnifying glass?"

"Nope," said Heather. "We're also bakers. It's a box of donuts."

O'Malley groaned. "Do they at least knock someone out when they eat them or something?"

"Try one and see," said Amy.
"They're regular donuts," Heather said. "Well, regular in that they are normal desserts. Not regular in their special flavor."

O'Malley accepted a donut and accepted defeat. "The man's name is Max Brookston."

"Do you have his number?"
"That wasn't part of the deal. And I can't do double or nothing on info I already told you."
Heather thanked him, and she and her bestie left.

"It was a good thing we won," Amy said.

"The name could help us catch the killer," Heather agreed.

"That," said Amy. "And he would have been disappointed if he won. I didn't have any money in my wallet."

They both laughed.

## Chapter 13 – Senior Wisdom

Heather and Amy realized that O'Malley's home was close to the community center where Eva and Leila had started joining in activities. They decided to stop in and see what the ladies were up to that day.

"It's so wonderful to see you," Eva said.

"Yes," agreed Leila. "With or without donuts."

"Thanks," said Heather. "We are with donuts, but only a few."

"I think that's all right," Amy said. "Doesn't look like there are many people here. Is that usual?"

"There are lots of activities to be part of," Leila assured her. "But today most people have opted to be part of the trips. There's a bus that transports people who can't take themselves."

"We could have gone to the beach with one group," Eva said. "But somebody didn't feel like getting sandy today."

"I'm sorry, but I just didn't. With the shoes I'm wearing, the sand would have dug right in," said Leila. "And we could have gone bowling."

"You two love bowling," said Heather.

"But somebody wanted to avoid the romantic advances of a certain gentleman."

"Firstly," Eva said. "There is nothing wrong with wanting to avoid romance at this stage in my life. I've been widowed, and I've had to say goodbye to Soupy. I'm not looking for anything right now, and I am fine with everyone knowing that. Secondly, they weren't romantic advances."

"He asked if they could share a lane," Leila said.

"How scandalous," Amy teased as Eva blushed.

"And he said he would pick her blowing shoes out for her if she went," said Leila.

"Like Cinderella," said Amy.

"Oh for goodness sake," said Eva.
"Is he handsome?" Heather asked.

"Very handsome," said Leila.

"But he knows it too," said Eva. "I'm sure he's something of a player. He must have been seeing if he could get anywhere with the new girls."

"I didn't get that feeling," Leila said. "I thought he was very polite and he liked your smile."

"Let's stop this line of conversation. I don't know anything about that man. And I am not interested in romance anymore. I am perfectly happy spending time with best friend," Eva said. "Usually."

401

Heather and Amy laughed.

"So, what brings you here?' Eva asked, focusing on what she deemed more important things. "Have you made any progress with the case?"

"We went to visit Betty this morning, but her son shooed us out quickly," said Leila.

"They said that the other child should be arriving tomorrow," Eva said.

"That's good," Heather said. "I'd like to talk to her as well."

"We felt a little bad going to activities while she was suffering, but we weren't sure what else we could do," said Leila.

"We do have our phone near us in case she calls," said Eva.

"And I think our Saturday afternoon plans are still in place," Leila said. "Unless you think we should cancel them."

Heather and her friends and family had decided that every Saturday afternoon they would see the sights of Key West. They thought that putting aside a few hours every week would guarantee that they didn't get too busy to appreciate what the island had to offer or to spend time together. This Saturday they were planning on riding a special train that would take them around the island and point out key sights.

"Unless there is something specific that we can do for the Turners at that time, I'd rather not cancel our plans," Heather admitted. "This sightseeing is something I'd like to do with Lilly every week. She's very excited about it."

"Maybe taking a break will help us see the case in a new light," said Amy.

"I guess so," said Heather. "We've made progress on the case in some ways. But in others, it feels like we're going in a circle."

"A big donut circle," said Amy.

"We've found one man he played poker with who might have had the opportunity, and we found out the name of a bookie who might have taken bets from Theodore," said Heather. "I think we'd have trouble tracking him down on our own though. We should update Detective Smith on what we've found out."

"Maybe he'll have some news for us too," Amy said.

"I hope so, dear," said Eva. "It's so terrible that this happened to Betty."

"It looks like she's going to have to move away too," said Leila.

"We'll do the best we can," said Heather.

"Then you will solve it quickly," said Eva. "You're very good at what you do."

"I just hope Detective Smith thinks so too."

"You've certainly been busy," Detective Smith said after they informed him of all their interviews.

"Do you think you can find this Max Brookston?" Heather asked.

"It might take a little while, but we will," Detective Smith assured her.

"You think that this bookie might be who Theodore Turner owed money to?" Peters asked. "And he could have killed him for not paying him back?"

"Or sent someone after him," Amy suggested.

"Let's not get ahead of ourselves," Detective Smith said. "Let's find the man and then question him."

They all nodded.

"We'd have to find out if Brookston knew where Theodore Turner lived," said

Heather. "And whether he knew about the gun or not."

"But Theodore might have been going for the gun himself and the killer took it from him," Amy suggested. "Maybe he planned on killing him a different way but then thought the gun would be easier."

"There wasn't much evidence of a struggle inside the house," Heather said.

"So, what does that mean?" Amy asked.

"Well," Heather thought aloud. "Either the killer surprised the victim, so he didn't have time to react. Or Theodore wasn't scared of the killer. At least, at first."

"That sounds it could be one of his poker buddies," Amy said.
"Again," Detective Smith said. "Let's not get ahead of ourselves."

"I feel like we need to catch up to ourselves at the point where we're solving the case," Amy said.

Heather nodded. "Tomorrow we'll focus on talking to the other sibling, and you can find the bookie. Hopefully, one of them will have the information we need to get to that point."

## Chapter 14 – Sisterly Love

"Are you sure we have time for this?" Amy asked.

"We'll just have to find her quickly," Heather said.

They had just over an hour until they had agreed to go on the train ride around the island. They had already made sure that Donut Delights was all set for the day, albeit with no solution to Mr. Rankle's ugly display of attention. He had upped his game by being more specific about who he was accusing of having bad food, still without using their name. Heather's comments about hurting the other restaurants on the street must have struck a nerve with him after all. He had now added his circular pool floats to the display. Of course, he chose ones that were colorful and reminiscent of donuts.

Rudolph Rodney had stormed off to Town Hall again after seeing the display, Heather and Amy had opted for trying to solve the murder case as a distraction.

They were close to the hotel where Betty was staying at when they saw a woman with the same hair colors and cheekbones as her brothers.

"I think that's her," Amy said.

"Letty Turner?" Heather called out.

"It's Leticia," she said warily. "Only my mom calls me Letty. Who are you?"
"I'm Heather Shepherd, and this is Amy Givens. We're private investigators looking into the death of Theodore Turner."

"So you are real?" Leticia said. "I was afraid mom was hallucinating when she started talking about how you were on the case. Edward was annoyed, so it was hard to tell how he felt."

"Before I get to questions about the case, I'd like to ask how your mom is doing," Heather said.

"I don't think there's anything I can tell you about the case," Leticia said. "I have a medical practice in Virginia. And I'm very busy. I haven't seen Theodore in about a year. I mean, we'd talk on holidays. But I don't know very much about what he was up to. And as for my mom now, she's a mess. She's trying to hide how badly she's heartbroken. I think it will be good for her to get out of the area once this is all settled. Edward wants her to move by him."

"Yes, we know," said Amy. "He was very insistent. Even while we were still there."

"He's wanted her to move closer to him for years," Leticia said. "But she wanted to stay on the island. And Theodore was there for her."

"Why did he want her to move towards him?" Heather asked.

"He always says it was because there were better doctors. But if it were really about doctors, don't you think they should have asked my opinion? Don't you think I would have some really valuable insight about that? I am a doctor myself. And a genius one too."

"Right. And so humble," muttered Amy.

"Part of me thinks he wants to control her money. And part of me thinks he just misses his mom," said Leticia. "But it doesn't matter. I can't do anything to help right now. I have patients I'm away from while I'm here. And I'm constantly busy. I can't be the one to take care of her. If Edward wants to, be my guest."

"I'm not getting a great impression of this family," Amy whispered to Heather. "I think we lost the best member."

Heather shushed her and then got down to business.

"Where were you the night of the murder?" Heather asked.

"In Virginia," said Leticia. "I usually work late. I'm sure someone at the desk could look into my exact schedule on that day if needed."

"You said you hadn't spoken to your brother in a while?"

"That's correct."

"What about your mother? Was she worried about Theodore in any way? Or mention any troubles?"

"She seemed to think everything was fine. I heard he gambled a bit, but that was reading between the lines. Mom would never say anything bad about any of her kids, especially Theodore after he moved there to be with her. He was the only one who came to her."

"What do you know about his gambling?"

"Very little," said Leticia. "He was taking care of mom. That was all that mattered. To me, at least."

"What does that mean?"

"Edward is a bit of a perfectionist. I guess by that I mean that he wants things done a certain way. His way. He and Theodore used to rub each other the wrong way."

"We heard Edward hired someone to make sure that Theodore wasn't stealing from his mother," Heather said.

"Yeah," Leticia said. "Edward was trying to convince me that something must be wrong and that we needed someone to investigate. I wasn't convinced and didn't really care what he was saying. That was the way Edward worked. He looked for evidence to support his theories. Usually, his theories were there for him to get something he wanted."

"And he and Theodore didn't get along?" Heather asked for confirmation.

"Right," said Leticia. "But, I mean, he didn't kill him. They were brothers."

"One more question," Heather said. "Does a straight flush of hearts mean anything to you? From nine to a king?"

"Only that it's the second-best hand in poker," Leticia shrugged.

Heather thanked her for her time. Then she and Amy hurried to make their train.

## Chapter 15 – Train of Thought

The small train they boarded looked like it appeared out of a movie. The group slid into their seats and enjoyed the gentle rhythm as the engine started moving them forward. It was a beautiful day to be in the open-air cars, and the views promised to spectacular. The guide on the train was going to tell stories about historic Key West, as well as where the best shopping was on the modern-day streets.

Heather and Amy had arrived just in time to board. Lilly was excited to see all the landmarks that would be mentioned and thought this would be a wonderful tool for planning future outings, as well as being a fun one that day.

The adults were also excited. Eva and Leila had their cameras ready to start snapping photos. Ryan and Jamie sat next to their significant others and were content to sit back and see the sights that Key West had to offer.

Heather and Amy found themselves still distracted by the case and couldn't stop themselves from whispering about it. The conductor and guide was telling the train about a man named Mel Fisher who had searched all his life for sunken Spanish galleons, and how he had finally found millions of dollars' worth of treasure. They were interested in the treasure, but more so in the murdered.

"It sounds like Edward had a motive to murder his brother," Amy said quietly to her friend.

"That's true," said Heather. "With him out of the way, he could finally persuade his mother to move closer to him. And he could control her money."

"He'd also get a larger share of inheritance after she passes with his brother gone," Amy said.

"But," Heather pointed out. "He has an alibi, remember? Detective Smith said the time of death occurred between six and seven. He was at the physical therapy appointment with his mom. And he was bothering the nurses, so they remember him."

"Ladies," Ryan said. "Can we discuss the case after the family outing?"

"Sorry," Heather said, squeezing his hand.
She listened to the guide describe the unique architecture of the buildings along the street. Eva and Leila were taking pictures, and Lilly would pose with a happy smile for any that included her in the shot.

They heard about how cigars would be hand rolled in Mallory Square and how the process worked to create perfect ones. Then Amy couldn't contain herself anymore and leaned over to her bestie.
"Don had an alibi, but the other poker player O'Malley didn't," Amy said.

"That's true," said Heather. "He said there was no reason to kill Theodore, but they were gaining and losing money every gathering. He also had a bit of a temper."

"He threw the beer at the wall and licked it," Amy said. "That sounds like a man who might break into a rival's house and let things get out of hand."

"But what are the odds that he's the killer?" Heather asked.

"I'd say even odds," Amy said, smiling.

"The tour," Jamie gently reminded them. They listened as the guide listed and gave fun tidbits about the many famous people who had visited the island before. The list was historical and extensive. It included Ernest Hemingway, Tennessee Williams, and John Audubon. Harry S. Truman had also stayed there in a place that was dubbed "The Little White House."

Heather felt her mind wander to the list of suspects bouncing around in her head. She leaned over to Amy to discuss another one.

"Then there's also the mysterious bookie," Heather said. "If he's the

418

reason that Theodore was pawning his stuff, then there could be a serious money issue."

"And he could have killed to get it back," Amy agreed.

"Mom," Lilly said, giving her a playful nudge.

"Sorry," said Heather, hugging her daughter. She tried to give her full attention to the tour.

Then she listened to the stories about the natives who had lived on the island and about how the warriors had left the bones of their enemies there on the sand. It accumulated so much that the nearby beach was called Bone Key.

It was an informative and interesting ride. Heather was very happy that she hadn't missed the outing but did wish she wasn't so distracted during it. She considered hopping on the train again after the case was solved so she could fully absorb all the information about pirates and explorers and conch shells.

When they disembarked from the trolley, the group decided to get lunch together.

"As long as it's nowhere that gives me heartburn," Leila joked.
Heather groaned. "Don't remind me about Mr. Rankle."

Amy said, "We've been so busy trying to crack this case that we haven't had a chance to deal with that nut."

They found an eatery that looked appealing while they were on the train and sat down at a large table that they set up for the group. They were looking over their menus when Heather received a call from Detective Smith.

"They found the bookie," Heather said.

"Do you have to go right now?" Lilly asked.

Heather shook her head. She told Detective Smith that she would be over after lunch to hear what he had found out. She was proud of her restraint and how she was trying to balance all the aspects of her life together.

Then Detective Smith told her that the suspect should be in custody by the time she finished and they would interview him at the station. It was perfect timing. Heather smiled to herself.

"So, what appetizer should we get?" Heather asked.

They decided on getting some samplers, and then Ryan said with a laugh, "If you two need to discuss the case now, you can."

"Who? Us?" Amy asked. "We know how to shut off our sleuthing senses for a little while to enjoy the experience with our loved ones."

"And," Heather chuckled. "We won't get much further until after we talk to the new suspect."

## Chapter 16 – The Bookie

"You've got nothing on me," Max Brookston said. He wore a Hawaiian shirt and a determined expression.

"Even as we tried to bring you in for questioning, you tried to get Detective Peters to place a bet on a football game," Detective Smith said.

"I was just testing to make sure that you were honest cops," Brookston said "You passed. But you are wasting your time with me. Nothing I do is illegal."

"Not even murder?" Peters asked.

Heather and Amy watched the exchange on the other side of the two-way mirror. She was disappointed that they couldn't be in the room with the detectives and suspect but knew that even allowing them to watch was a big step for Detective Smith. She looked over at Amy to see how she felt about it, but she was fidgeting with her bag.

"What's wrong?"

"I think there's a hole in my purse," Amy said. "I hope I didn't lose anything."

"I'll help you look after the interrogation," Heather offered. Then she focused back on the suspect.

"I didn't have anything to do with that," Brookston said.

"Don't you want to know who it was?" Detective Smith said.

"It doesn't matter," Brookston said. "I didn't have anything to do with any murder."

"Fair enough," Detective Smith said. "We'd like to talk to you about Theodore Turner."

"What about him?"

"How well did you know him?" Detective Smith asked.

"We met a few times," Brookston said. "To discuss sports."

"Discuss and bet on sports?" Peters asked.

"To discuss," Brookston said again. "He wasn't someone I spoke with regularly."

"What about recently?" Detective Smith asked.

"No. It had been a few weeks since we chatted."

"Why the pause?" Detective Smith asked. "Did one of your conversations go poorly?"

"No," Brookston said. "Our conversations were always amiable, and brief, and left no room for further discussion."

"So, you wouldn't send someone after him to finish one of your discussions?" Detective Smith asked.

"Officers," he said. "Firstly, I'm someone who is easy to get along with. And I would never have the problems that you two seem to be implying. Secondly, this is Theodore Turner that we're talking about, right?"

"Right."

"I know that gambling with money is frowned upon and perhaps illegal in some areas," Brookston said. "But you would not begrudge us a friendly sportsman bet of shaking hands, would you?"

"Fine," Detective Smith said, eager for the information. "For the sake of argument, you only bet handshakes."

"Well, this Theodore Turner. He would only bet twenty, maybe fifty handshakes. We're not talking thousands of handshakes here. It was kid stuff."

"You're saying that Theodore Turner never made any substantial bets with you?" Detective Smith said.

"That's right, officers. I'm sorry, but you're barking up the wrong tree. Not that I would harm anyone, but I had absolutely no reason to harm that young man."

It looked like the detectives were about to finish their interrogation. Heather banged on the glass, hoping they would remember the question she wanted them to ask. Her banging seemed to work. Max Brookston jumped at the table, surprised by the sound, and Detective Smith asked another question. "Does a straight flush made of hearts from nine to a king mean anything to you?"

Brookston shrugged. "It's the second-best hand you could get. I mean, it's a great hand to get. There's only one higher than it. Then again, if that one higher hand comes out, then it can still lose. Why are you asking this?"

"Peters wants to learn to play poker," Detective Smith said, dismissing the question. He and his partner got up to leave the room.

"I think I just figured something out," Heather said.

"Where my phone is?" Amy asked, still looking through her bag. "I hope it didn't fall out on the train."

"The significance of the cards," she said. "It wasn't referring to specific hand that was dealt during a game, but it was still leaving us a message. I wonder if it was intentional."

"You've lost me," Amy said. "Just like I've lost my phone."

The detectives joined them.

"I'm afraid that didn't go quite the way we hoped," Detective Smith said. "I told us not to get ahead of ourselves."

"I think he's telling the truth," Peters said. "At least, about the murder part. He is definitely organizing some gambling that goes beyond handshakes."

"Now that he's on our radar, we'll have to keep an eye on him," Detective Smith said. "I mean, that you will have to. I'll be retiring soon, so it will be up to you."

428

Peters gulped and then smiled.

"Do you happen to have an idea of when you will be retiring?" Heather tried to as gently. "I'm sure Ryan would like to know."

"I can't think about that until this case is solved," said Detective Smith.

"Then you're almost there," said Amy, digging through her bag. "Heather figured out the card thing. Maybe you can get her to tell you what it is. But it's only a matter of time until she busts the rest of the case wide open. Meanwhile, I'm dealing with another mystery without any help. What fell out of my bag since this hole developed? And where is my cell phone?"

"Oh, calm down," Heather said. She took her cell phone out of her own bag and dialed Amy's number. They heard the ringtone, and Amy realized it was in her jacket pocket.

"I normally don't have pockets big enough to do that..." she said. "But

429

great work, investigators. And hopefully, I didn't lose anything else through that hole. Could you see why I was concerned though?"

"The phone," Heather gasped.

"Yeah. It's right here," Amy said, waving it around.

"No," Heather said. "It's not that. I just figured out the case. I know who did it."

"Who?" asked Amy.

"The real question is can we prove it?" Heather said.

**Chapter 17 – The Arrest**

Heather and Amy arrived at Betty's hotel room, hurrying to get there ahead of the detectives. Both Leticia and Edward were there. Leticia was answering emails on her phone while Edward was still trying to convince his mom that she would have to move in with him.

"Could we take Betty for a little walk?" Heather asked.

"We think some fresh air would do her some good," Amy agreed.

"Are you crazy?" Edward asked. "She's not going anywhere with you two."

"Then maybe you want to step into the hallway," Heather suggested.
"Why?"

"You don't want what's going to happen to be in front of her," Heather said.
"This is ridiculous," Edward said.

However, then Detectives Smith and Peters arrived on the scene. Detective

Smith told him he was under arrest for the murder of Theodore Turner and read him his rights.

"No," Betty said. "This is impossible. He was with me a physical therapy at the time of the murder."

"He was with you at the time we thought the murder was," Heather said. "But the reason we were able to pin the window of opportunity down to just an hour was because of the phone calls."

"Right," said Betty. "Teddy called us. So, he was alive then."

"Your phone went off in Donut Delights before, do you remember?"

"Yes."

"You had trouble hearing that ringtone," Heather said. "But it was quite loud to many others in the shop. You always keep it at that volume, don't you?"

Betty nodded.

"Then Edward would have heard your phone ring," Heather said. "But he didn't respond to the sound. He didn't want you to pick it up."

"But he spoke to Teddy."

"He told us that he spoke to Theodore," Heather said. "But he was just providing an alibi for himself to mask when he actually committed the crime."

"And when was that?" Edward asked.

"Betty, you said that you left your purse inside, didn't you?" Heather asked. "So your sons helped you inside the car. And then they went inside. Edward was gone for a few minutes and then re returned with your bag."

"He was sweating," Betty said. "I thought it was because he was hurrying to get me to my appointment on time."

"It was, mom," Edward said. "I could never hurt my brother."

"You used his own gun and shot him when he wasn't expecting it. Then you quickly broke the glass on the back door and took his cell phone," said Heather.

"This is crazy," said Edward.
"When I called Amy's phone to help her find it, I realized how you did it. You called both your mom's phone and your own from Theodore's cell phone to give you an alibi. All you had to do was hit a button, and everyone believed Theodore was killed later than he was," said Heather.

"The cell phone towers will confirm this," Detective Smith said. "They have records of what the closest one it. And a call from the Turner home would be different from at the doctor's."

"You replaced the cell phone on the charger before the police arrived when your mother was distracted," said Heather.

"But he had so many enemies from his gambling," said Edward.

"That's what you wanted us to think," said Heather. "But he never gambled much money, and there was no reason for anyone to go after him. You just set the scene to keep us searching in the wrong direction. You placed the poker hand on the floor so we would assume the killer was after him because of a gamble gone wrong. But this wasn't related to a specific hand in a game he played. It was you planting evidence."

"No," Edward said. "It must have been a bookie or another gambler."

"The hand you placed on the ground was telling whether you meant it to be or not," said Heather. "You placed the second-best poker hand on the floor. Whether this was an intentional message or subconscious, you were saying that you thought Theodore was the second-best son. You thought you were the best."

"I am the best," Edward said. "All I ever wanted was my mom's welfare. But she chose to stay with a gambler and a hooligan. I needed to get her away from him. It was for her own good."

"And it had nothing to do with the money?" Leticia asked.

"I only wanted to make sure she was protected and cared for. I could do it so much better," Edward said. "If she'd only move to me."

"If you really wanted to protect and care for her, then you'd also care about what she wanted. She wanted to live where we grew up. And she wanted her other son alive," Leticia said. "Don't pretend this was about anything besides you getting your own way."

"Mom, you believe me, don't you?" Edward asked. "I did it for you."

"Oh, Eddie," Betty cried. "How could you?"

Detective Smith led Edward away, as Leticia hugged her mom. Peters paused and looked at an open suitcase.

"Is this Edward's suitcase sitting here in plain sight?" he asked.

Leticia nodded.

"Then I'm going to take this black jacket into evidence," he said. "And look at that, it looks like there's a tear on the arm."

"Take it," Betty said. "Take whatever you want. Nothing matters anymore."

Detective Peters bowed out of the room with the new evidence. Leticia was still hugging her mom.

Heather caught her eye and tried to convey a message without saying anything. Surprisingly, it seemed to work.

"I've been a bad daughter," Leticia said.

"No," Betty said.

"Well, not as bad as Edward, obviously," Leticia said. "But I haven't been there for the family when I should have been. And I regret that more than anything now. I want to be there for you."

"Thank you," Betty said. "And I think I would be willing to move to be closer to you after all this. If you'd want me too."

"No," Leticia said. "I don't want you to."

Amy took a step forward, ready to fight until she heard the next words Leticia said.

"I want to move here to be with you. I feel like I've been a path for a little while that has made a bit self-absorbed. And I don't like that. And I missed opportunities to be with you and with Theodore. I don't like that either."

"Letty, you don't have to do this."

"I want to. But if it makes you feel better, we can sleep on it for a few days. And you can decide if you want to go back to the same house or not."

"Thank you, Letty."
They hugged, and Heather and Amy started heading out.

"Wait," Betty said. "I need to thank you too."

"We're sorry it turned out the way it did," Heather said.

"But you did find out what happened to my son," said Betty. "And you gave me back my daughter."

"Key West could be fun," Letty said. "I'm sure they could use another doctor."

Then, Heather and Amy did leave the family.

"That was a sad case," Amy said.

"At least there was some silver lining to it in the end," Heather said.

"At least one problem is solved," Amy said.

"One problem?"

"Yeah. We still have the other to deal with."

Heather groaned. "Mr. Rankle."

## Chapter 18 – The Grand Regular Business Day

"My attempts to win him over with the donuts failed," Luz said. "Even when I told him I'd lived here for my entire life and that this shop was allowing me to try baking in a professional setting, he wouldn't be swayed."

"He's a hard one to sway," said Amy to the others crowded in at Donut Delights.

"Everyone has tried admirably," Heather said "But I think he's not listening to you because you all work for me. What I think we need to try it get him to respect the person above me. We need him to like you, Rudolph Rodney."

"It will be hard for me to reciprocate with everything that he's done," Rudolph Rodney responded. "But if it will get rid of that egregious stand I'll try anything."

Rudolph Rodney marched over to the Sun and Fun heartburn display, followed by Heather and Amy.

"Don't you get tired of going through the same song and dance?" Mr. Rankle asked.

"Then stop calling for an encore," Amy said.

"I don't know if you two have every officially met," Heather said. "Mr. Rankle, this is Rudolph Rodney."

"Your investor," he grumbled.

"And a Key West native," Heather said.

"If he's a local, how come I haven't seen him around? Nice try," Mr. Rankle said.

"I did grow up here," Rudolph said. "But as a young man, I made my travels across the country and eventually found my fortune. I returned here to make peace with my sister but discovered I was too late and that she had passed. I continued making business decisions, but then I went in search of other family members. I found my nephew in Hillside, which is where I met these donut makers and were won over by their wares. I needed to bring them back with me."

"You really grew up around here?" Mr. Rankle asked. "Your sister. She couldn't be Ms. Rodney that taught in the grade school?"

"Must be," said Rudolph Rodney. "She taught second grade. But that was a long time ago."

"My son was in her class," Mr. Rankle said. "She was his favorite teacher."

"You don't say," said Rudolph Rodney. "I missed so much time with her."

"I think I have some class photos," Mr. Rankle said, rising. "Let's go look at them."

He started towards his store, but Rudolph Rodney remained. He looked pointedly at the display.

"Sure, sure," said Mr. Rankle. "Grab a box or tube, and we'll bring it inside."

"And you won't set it up again?" Rudolph Rodney asked.

443

"I can't promise to like these Texans," Mr. Rankle said. "But why would I do anything to harm Ms. Rodney's brother?"

Satisfied, Rudolph Rodney helped bring the heartburn display and supplies inside, and then went to look at pictures of his sister.

"Well, he's not going to like us," Amy said.

"As long as he's not trying to convince new customers that we'll make them sick, he doesn't have to like us," Heather said. "And maybe with a little prodding some Rudolph Rodney he'll eventually try a donut and come around."

Amy didn't look convinced.

"Well, I said maybe," Heather commented.

They returned to Donut Delights and were greeted by a round of applause.

"Our fearless leader saved us," Digby said.

"Rudolph Rodney's sister saved us," Heather said.

"What?"
"Never mind," said Amy. "Let's celebrate by eating some donuts before all the customers start flocking in."

They agreed and happily Amy's prediction did come true. Without Mr. Rankle's display to dissuade customers, they were piling in to try the exciting new donuts.

Even though Heather was exhausted by the end of the day, she was happy with how business had been and how everything had turned out in general.

However, she was most excited by the arrival of her favorite customers. Eva and Leila came in and sat at their new usual table.
Leila decreed that they needed to have twice the number of usual donuts in

445

order to properly break in their new seats. No one quite understood the logic, but they were happy to supply the donuts.

"The best news of a bad situation seems to be that Betty is planning to stay in the area with her daughter," said Eva.

"And something else was solved for us today," Leila said. "Remember how it came out that Theodore had pawned some items?"

"Yes," Heather said. "But it looks like his gambling debts were never that high."

"Right," said Eva. "It turns out that Theodore had been pawning things to have a little extra cash so he could afford a gift for the family. He ordered it to arrive when he thought Edward would be arriving."

"What is it?"

"A boat."

"Wow," Heather said.

"Just a small one," said Eva. "But one with a proper ramp so Betty could get on board. He knew she missed going on the water."

"And she's invited all of us to go out with her on it to remember Teddy," said Leila.

"That's a lovely idea," Heather said. "I'm sorry we didn't get to know him better."

"But thanks to you we still will be able to get to know Betty. She won't be stolen away by her evil son," said Leila.

"Stop it," Amy said. "Bringing up that unhappy case is giving me heartburn. And no way am I going to buy anything to help it from Mr. Rankle!"

Heather laughed, and her friends joined in. Donut Delights felt officially open.

### The End

# Book 4 – Blackberry Cream & Murder

## Chapter 1 – The Aquarium Outing

Lilly giggled. "It's different from petting Dave or Cupcake. No fur. And much wetter."

Heather grinned at her daughter. She expected petting a sea creature to be very different from petting her beloved dog and kitten. She wasn't expecting it to be as enjoyable as the smile on Lilly's face declared it to be.

"I'll give it a try too," Heather said, moving closer to the Touch Tank. She had listened to the guide's instructions and put her hand into the water. She gently touched the sea star.

"Is it slimy?" her best friend Amy asked.

"No," Heather assured her. "And the guide told us that nothing would bite or pinch us. Why don't you try?"

"I'd like to," Eva piped up.

"And I'll dip my toes in," Leila said. "Sort to speak."

It wasn't every day that Heather got to pick up hermit crabs and pet sea cucumbers. She was usually either covered in sugar baking delicious donuts or looking for clues in an investigation. However, today she was visiting the Aquarium with her friends and family.

They had decided that they would have an outing together every Saturday to make sure that they enjoyed every exciting activity that their new home in Key West had to offer. They had recently moved to the island so Heather could open up a second Donut Delights shop. Though it had been a bit of a bumpy start, they were now open and were providing freshly baked donuts to happy customers.

They made for a large group at the Aquarium, and Amy kept joking that they were like a school of fish in their own right. The Shepherd family consisted of Heather, her husband Ryan and their daughter Lilly. They were joined by their senior friends Eva and Leila who kept joking about how they wanted to swim with the sharks for a thrill. Amy's boyfriend Jamie was also part of the group.

Jamie joined them at the Touch Tank and allowed a giant hermit crab to crawl over his hand. "I don't think I'd have any of these animals as clients," he said. "But they sure would be easy to bathe."

Jamie was going to talk to their investor friend that afternoon about starting his own pet grooming business in the area. He was a little nervous about it and kept making comments about the sea creatures in relation to his business.

After they finished getting up close and personal with the Touch Tank and washed their hands, they tried to decide where they wanted to go next. They had already watched the stingrays' feeding and saw tropical fish swim around in a living mangrove ecosystem exhibit. The colorful fish had trickled in and out of the mangrove tree roots and some quick ones had only looked like flashes of red or yellow.

"What should we see next?" Heather asked, consulting a tour map.

"Anything except the Man-Of-Wars," Amy said, making a face. Those deadly jellyfish had been used as a murder weapon in a case they investigated before, and Amy was not eager to see them again. Heather nodded. It wasn't the animals' fault that they had been used to kill, but she also couldn't look at them without thinking about the case. Today wasn't a day for looking murderers but was for spending time with loved ones and sea creatures.

"How about the sea turtles?" Lilly suggested, and they all agreed.
"They have a conservation tour that will tell us how they save the turtles that need help," said Ryan. "And I think they even have a turtle with a prosthetic flipper."

"Let's swim on over there and see it," Amy said.

They started walking over to the exhibit.

"This has been such a nice visit," Eva said. "Watching the fish is both fascinating and soothing. And we've learned so much about the different types."

"And how some of them feel to the touch," added Lilly.

"It's nice to just get out of the house," said Heather.

"Especially right now," agreed Ryan.

They loved their new house because it allowed the three families to live next to one another, and because of its beautiful location. However, there kept being problems with their new home in paradise. This weekend it was the air-conditioner in the Shepherd house that was on the fritz and had instead started blowing heat into the home. It was sweltering inside their place, and they were told that a maintenance specialist couldn't fix it until Monday. They were going to have to sweat it out.

"It will be all right, dear," Eva said. "We can find more comfortable arrangements for everyone. You can either stay with Leila and me, or with Amy and Jamie."

"I hate to intrude, but if it stays this hot, then I think we will have to accept the offer," Heather said.

"Dave and Cupcake already did," Amy said, reminding her that her pet dog and cat were already staying in the upstairs apartment to stay cool. "I just hope that they aren't making themselves too much at home and marking it as their own."

"I'm sure they'll behave themselves," Heather said. "They know if they misbehave, they won't be getting any donut treats when we get home."

"I could use some donut treats myself," said Eva.

"After the Aquarium, I'm going to head over to Donut Delights to whip up a batch of my new flavor to try to deliver at a bed and breakfast," Heather said. "You're welcome to join me."

"You don't need to ask me twice," said Eva.

"But first, the sea turtles," said Lilly.

"Yes," Heather agreed. "First, the turtles."

The gang headed over to the exhibit and watched the sea turtles swim. They learned about the conservation efforts to keep them safe from boating accidents.

Heather loved the exhibit. She was happy to see how the graceful creatures were being protected in their moment of need.

Lilly leaned against her as they watched the animals and she hugged her daughter. She was grateful that she was able to enjoy this experience without any other responsibilities hanging over her head. However, based on how busy she usually became with both her donut business and her investigations, she was certain that this peacefulness wouldn't last for long.

## Chapter 2 – Blackberry Cream Planning

"How is it going today?" Heather asked as she entered Donut Delights and saw her three assistants.

"No trouble from Mr. Rankle. He's given up on any pranks today. And business has been pretty good. People are grabbing donuts on their way to the beach," Digby reported happily.

"And they are loving the new flavor," Luz said. "Blackberries don't seem to be used in too many desserts, so it seems exotic."

"I wanted to try out some new berry flavors," Heather said. "I thought it would go well with the bed and breakfast we're trying to impress. These flavors should complement the jellies that they serve with their toast and waffles."

"Then I'm glad that we're trying to impress them," said Luz. "Because you created something delicious for it."

"How were the fish?" Digby asked.

"It was a lot of fun at the Aquarium," said Heather. "And I think we're going to have an influx of business soon because the rest of my group are following me here with the promise of fresh donuts."

"I'm a little worried about this," Nina said. "We've been keeping up with supplying the shop with donuts even when it gets busy. But if we're going to start filling the online orders as you said we would, then we might end up short-staffed."

"Don't worry," Heather said. "The online orders will be split between here and the Hillside location so that we won't get overwhelmed. But if it does start to seem too busy for you all, then I promise to hire some more help."

Heather was willing to fulfill this promise but wasn't looking forward to the hiring process again. It had been quite an ordeal finding the proper staff, but she was more than pleased with the results. Her new staff was exactly what she needed at the shop.

She knew they would be able to face any challenges that came their way, and she knew they would be able to handle the increased baking by filling online orders.

This had been one of the main reasons that Heather had agreed to the move and second location. Besides the excitement of the change, it also made sense to open Donut Delights – Key West because it meant that there would be two kitchens to fulfill the rapidly growing online orders instead of just one.

However, Heather thought it was more important to deal with the orders in front of her. She started filling a box for the bed and breakfast order but paused as her family and friends entered. Then, she joined her assistants putting the flavor of the week on plates for them.

"Just one for the road," Jamie said. "Then I need to go meet Rudolph Rodney."

He enjoyed one bite of the donut and then kissed Amy goodbye. She commented on how sweet his kiss was and then turned to the rest of the group. "So, tell us about this flavor," Amy said.

Heather smiled. "You are all about to enjoy the Blackberry Cream Donut."

"You used blackberries in a recipe?" Ryan asked.

"I told you people thought it was exotic," Luz piped up before going to serve another customer.

"They can be a tart berry," Eva commented. "But I'm sure you've done something to make them sweeter."

"That's right," said Heather. "The donut cake base is a blackberry and cream flavor, and the rich, creamy taste keeps the berry from being overpowering."

"Good." Leila joked, "I wouldn't want to be overpowered by a berry."

"Then it's filled with a blackberry jelly. And it's topped with a creamy frosting that keeps everything tasting sweet," Heather finished.

"I like the way it looks too," said Lilly. "Normally only the chocolate donuts are dark colored, but this is a purplish-black color that's pretty."

"Not too pretty to eat though, I hope," said Heather.

Lilly shook her head definitively. She was planning on eating it.

"You know the phrase "You can't have your donut and eat it too"? Well, let's choose to eat them," said Amy.

The group agreed and started eating. Only after they had finished one and were reaching for seconds were they able to compliment the taste.

"I always loved strawberries and cream," said Eva. "But this might be my new favorite berry."

"Yes," agreed Leila. "I love it berry much."

"You're lucky this donut has put me into too good of a mood to groan at that," said Amy.

They all laughed. Then, their topic of conversation led to a discussion of what to do at the house that night.

"Leila and I were thinking that we'd love for Lilly to sleepover at our part of the house tonight," Eva said. "She's promised us a new dinosaur story."

"It's true," said Lilly. "Seeing all the fish and sea turtles and alligators today made me want to write one of my stories about the aquatic dinosaurs. I could have a Pliosaurus character."

"Gesundheit," Amy joked.

"Or an Elasmosaurus," said Lilly.

"What long names," said Leila. "With our mouths full of donuts, I'm surprised you can say any of them."

"Lilly is great with scientific names," Eva said. "She's a very bright child to be so adept at both science and literature."

Lilly blushed. "I only know a few of the dinosaurs that lived the in water. But I would like to write a story about them."

"We'd be happy to let you sleep over there and read the story," Heather said. "As long as I get to hear it too."

"Of course," said Lilly.

"And we could set up the blowup mattress for the pair of you to keep you out of the heat of your home," said Eva. "Would you like it in our living room or Amy's?"

"If it's my room, I might have to insist that we watch *Beaches*," said Amy. "We haven't watched it since we arrived.

463

And, hello, we're surrounded by beaches now. It's a sign we should watch it."

Heather laughed. "How about I decide after I deliver these donuts to the B&B By The Sea? I need the owner to sample them to see if she'll become a regular customer."

"I can come with you to help you carry things," said Ryan.

"And I can come with you to help eat the things," said Amy.

"I think we'll head home and rest for a bit," said Eva. "And we can check on the pets for you."

"Do you mind if I go with them too?" Lilly asked. "I want to get started writing on my pink typewriter."

Heather agreed, and the group started to go their separate ways, but not before Heather had filled some donut travel boxes. One was for the bed and breakfast, but the other was for midnight snacks.

## Chapter 3 – B&B By The Sea

"They do smell good, but the taste is everything."

Heather nodded, waiting for the owner of B&B By The Sea to sample a donut. Bea was a middle-aged woman with a tight bun on her head. She wore a festive apron and Heather suspected that she had a variety of options to choose from. Today's apron was decorated with a sugar and spice theme.

"I usually do all my own cooking and baking, but I've wanted to leave some things to snack on out in the dining room in the afternoon, and these might be just the thing."

"I think they're a great afternoon snack," Amy said.

Bea raised the donut to her mouth but then paused. "I wasn't sure I wanted to contact you. I know that you're new to the area."

Heather and Amy exchanged a look. Their one shop neighbor Mr. Rankle had given them quite a hard time about opening shop without being a lifelong local, but they had hoped that the sentiment wasn't held by everyone.

"But Bernadette from the bookstore said that you were very nice and made good food. I get all my coffee table books from her, so I know she has good taste," said Bea.

"We've found her to be a good neighbor," said Ryan.

"But I do have very high standards about what I serve here," Bea continued. "So, this would have to meet those standards."
"Why don't you just take a bite?" asked Heather.

Bea relented and tasted the Blackberry Cream Donut. Her eyes lit up. "I think we can do business together."

"I'm very glad to hear that," said Heather. "I've brought several samples of our jelly donuts. Besides the Blackberry Cream, I've brought Classic Strawberry, Wild Raspberry, and a few others. When Bernadette mentioned your bed and breakfast to us, she mentioned that you have wonderful jellies to go with your pancakes."

"I try to serve fine jellies," said Bea, proudly. "You wouldn't happen to have an elderberry donut, would you?"

"I'm afraid not," said Heather. "But I could experiment with the taste and come up with one. It could be one of my weekly new flavors."
"No. It's all right," said Bea. "I didn't expect you to have it, but one of my guests is very insistent on having elderberries."

"I didn't think it was that common," said Heather.

"It's not," said Bea. "I'm having one heck of a time finding elderberry jelly that I can serve to him in the morning. I think I finally have a lead and can have it for breakfast so I won't have to hear another tirade. Thankfully he's only here for the weekend."

"I'm sure he'll like one of these donuts," Amy said.
"If he has proper taste buds, he will," Bea agreed.

"Thank you," said Heather. "So, should we bring more donuts over tomorrow for your dining room?"

A thought occurred to Bea. "If I haven't scared you off with my description of the grumpy guest, I'd like to invite you to stay over tonight and see how my breakfasts usually work. I'll provide this breakfast in exchange for some donuts, and then I will buy them properly for future meals."

"Yes," Heather and Ryan said immediately. Then, they couldn't stop from laughing.

"Sorry," Heather explained. "Something is wrong with our heating and cooling system in our home. It's pumping in heat, so it's way too hot right now."

"And we already made arrangements for our daughter to stay with friends," said Ryan. "So this sounds perfect. We'd love to."

"That is," said Heather. "If you're sure you have room for us."
"I do," said Bea. "When school just starts, it gets slow for a few weeks. I have a dozen rooms between this house and the carriage house and less than half are full."

"Really?"

Bea considered her guest list. "Yes. The man I told you about and his wife have a room. And his secretary has another. They're all on a working vacation. Then there's a young couple having a romantic vacation. And one other young woman has a room, but I'm afraid she's not been feeling too well. She probably won't join us for meals."

"Then we'd love to accept the invitation," said Heather.

"Sure. You guys get all the fun," Amy grumbled.

"I could give you a room too," Bea offered, and Amy immediately smiled.

"I'm sure Jamie would love to join me."

"Oh," Heather said. "But can we leave the animals with Eva and Leila too last minute?"

"If it's a dog, he's welcome to join you. But I'm afraid I'm allergic to cats," said Bea.

Heather nodded. Maybe Dave would come on another adventure with them.

They were just settling on the details when there was a commotion at the door.

"Why are we here?" a female voice whined. "I want to stay at the big hotel."

"This will be romantic," the male voice reassured her.
"It better be. It looks small."

Heather followed the sounds of the voices and saw the couple in the hallway. For all the complaining about the size of the hotel, they didn't have much luggage that they were going to need to fit inside. All they had was one small bag between them.

"Can I help you?" Bea asked.

The young man looked like he had rolled right out of bed and came there. The young woman had spent more time on her outfit. Her dress and shoes matched perfectly. She moved her large sunglasses up on top of her head to hold back her blonde hair.

"Hello," the man said. "I'm Mike Crown, and this is my girlfriend Kylie. We were hoping that you might have a room available."

"If you don't, it's okay," Kylie said.

"We'll see ourselves out and let you deal with this," said Heather.

"I'll see you tonight," Bea said, letting them know that this turn of events hadn't affected her invitation.

Heather, Ryan, and Amy left.

"Those two seem like they might cause some drama," Amy said. "Are we sure we want to stay there?"

But for Ryan and Heather, the answer was still a resounding yes.

## Chapter 4 – A Late Night Fight

"This place is adorable," Amy said. "Everything in the rooms at this B&B is beachy and cute. Look at all the seashells. If we're not careful, I'm going end up moving in here."

"Don't tempt me," Heather said. "If we don't get our air conditioner fixed soon, I might consider the option."

"I really don't want to move all our furniture again," Ryan joked.

Heather, Ryan, and Amy laughed. Amy nudged the quiet Jamie in the ribs.

"Sorry," he said. "What?"

"Um," Amy said. "We're moving into the bed and breakfast, and we've nominated you to move all our stuff."

"Ha. Ha," Jamie said. "But I am sorry I'm distracted. Rudolph Rodney was telling me about all the permits I'll need to my pet grooming van going. I have a feeling

474

I'm not going to be approved. I'm sorry I'm not good company right now."

"You're always good company," Amy assured him.

"I'm just worried it's not going to work out. And I really wanted it to. I was looking forward to working with all the dogs," Jamie said, sadly.

Dave went over to cheer him up. The wagging tail did work. Heather was glad that they were able to bring Dave to the bed and breakfast. So far he had been on his best behavior. It might have been because he was happy to be allowed to go on an outing with Heather again, or it might have been because he smelled the Blackberry Cream Donuts in her bag.

The friends and their canine companion chatted for a while longer and then split into their separate rooms for some shut-eye.

Heather was luxuriating in the cool room and fell asleep quickly. However, she was woken up that night by Dave licking her hand.

"What's going on?" she asked groggily.

Heather saw Dave's white furry form run to the door. She figured he needed to go out and pulled herself out of bed.

"I'll be right back," she told the sleeping Ryan. He responded without hearing her and without making sense in his reply.

Heather hooked a leash on Dave and was ready to take him outside. However, once she opened the door, he didn't pull her towards the exit door. Instead, he froze in place, listening. Heather listened too.

"Good dog," she said.

She heard voices arguing, and they were starting to become heated. She didn't want to pry into someone's private business, but she did want to make sure that this fight didn't escalate into something more serious. She had investigated her fair share of "heat of the moment" murders and was not eager to have one occur under the same roof as her.

"I can't do this," a female voice was saying, trying to remain quiet.

"No time like the present," a male voice replied. "Or maybe in the morning?"

"I hate you more than I thought possible," she said.

"Then you do have feelings for me," he replied.

"Why here?"

"Why do you think?"

"You know what? It doesn't matter. If you don't leave tomorrow, then I will," she said.

"You can't run away," he said.

"Watch me."

She heard movement down the hall and realized that the woman must have walked away. It seemed that the fight wasn't going to turn deadly. Heather breathed a sigh of relief.

Then, she saw the man from the lobby early walking down the hall. Mike hurried back to his room, not noticing Heather.

When he was gone, Heather turned to her dog. "Never a dull moment, huh?"

He wagged his tail.

"Did you just want to show me that in case it was a clue on one of our cases?" she asked. "Or do you want to go out too?"

He wagged his tail and started moving as if to say, "Well, since you're offering…"

Heather and Dave started towards the exit when they saw another figure in the hall. This one was a few inches shorter than Heather and was wearing a thick robe.

"Who's there?" she asked.

"I'm Heather. One of the guests here. I'm taking my dog out."

"I heard voices," the woman said. "Angry voices."

"I think there was a lover's quarrel," Heather said. "But it's over now."

"Oh," she said. "It woke me up. I was worried."

"It looks like everything is all right now," Heather said.

"This has not been the vacation I was looking forward to," the woman said. "I've been sick as a dog. And now my rest is being disturbed."

"I'm sorry," Heather.

"Agnes," the woman said. "Agnes Stewart from Minnesota. I'm sorry I can't be more sociable, but it is late, and I'm not feeling well."

Heather wished her a goodnight and Agnes returned to her room. Heather took Dave outside and let him sniff in the night air as a reward for his good watchdog skills.

Heather was glad that she had brought him. She had a feeling that would need him again while they were staying there. Though it was cool, The B&B By The Sea was not as calm as she thought it might be.

## Chapter 5 – The Other Guests

"I was just walking the dog," Heather said.

"It sounds pretty close to your sleuthing," Ryan said. "And if you were going to investigate anything, especially in the middle of the night, you should have woken me up."

"There was nothing to investigate," said Heather.

"I may not officially be on the force right now because Detective Smith is taking his time retiring, but I could be of help," he said.

Heather relented. She had thought that Ryan was annoyed because her habit of putting herself into harm's way was acting up again. However, he was starting to trust her ability to get out of those situations more and more. What was bothering him now was really that he felt like he wasn't able to help on cases anymore. While he had at first enjoyed being in Key West and waiting for his job to start, the longer it took, the less it felt like a vacation. Ryan was getting bored.

"I promise you didn't miss anything," Heather said. "You can ask Dave."

That made Ryan chuckle. "He would back up whatever you say anyway. You're his mom and the bringer of donuts."

"Did you mention donuts?" Amy asked in the doorway.

Dave barked, but Heather said, "Not exactly. Are you ready to go down to breakfast?"

"Definitely," said Amy.
The humans started down to the breakfast table. Dave was told that he'd have to stay in the room while they ate, but he was content to be left with a donut on his own.

They were greeted with a wonderful smell wafting in from the kitchen as they sat down at the table. A couple was already seated.

"Good morning," the man said cheerfully. "Would you like some coffee?"

"I'll have some more," the woman said.

The man was bearded and exuberant but looked concerned as he looked at his partner. Her dark hair was pulled back in a ponytail, and she had some dark circles under her eyes. He poured her another cup.

"Are you feeling all right?" he asked.
"I didn't sleep very well," she said.

"I'm sorry," he said. "I slept like a rock."

"It's all right. I'm sure I'll sleep better tonight," she said. Then she turned to the group. "I'm Trish, and this is Travis."

"Nice to meet you," Travis agreed and started pouring coffee for everyone.

They thanked him and introduced themselves.

"We're here for a romantic weekend," said Travis. "We're from the mainland, but wanted to get away. What about you? What brings you here?"
"We're actually newly locals," said Heather. "But we were invited to stay because we're donut makers that are going to be baking for the breakfasts."

"That sounds nice," said Trish.

"We're figuring what we'd like to do today," said Travis. "There are so many options."

"Maybe we should head out now," Trish suggested. "Get a head start on the day. That way we can fit more activities into it."

"We can't miss breakfast," Travis said.

"That is half the name of a B&B," Amy commented.

"I'd be fine with just coffee if you were," Trish said.

"I'm sure the food will be done soon," Travis said. "And it does smell delicious."

The others agreed.

Then a young woman in a business suit entered the room and frowned at the table that was not filled with food. She headed towards the kitchen and called in.

"Mr. Ridgefield would like to know if breakfast will be served soon. He doesn't like to be kept waiting after he's sat down."

In response, Bea entered with plates of waffles and eggs and bacon.
"I remember. And he can be served as soon as he likes. Breakfast is ready," Bea said. "And you can tell him that I did manage to track down some elderberry jelly. So, everything should be to his liking."

The woman gave a slight smile. "He'd never agree that everything is to his liking, no matter the circumstance."

She left to tell Mr. Ridgefield the news. Bea handed out the meals, and the table thanked her.

"I can't wait to dig in," Travis said.

"Should we wait for the others?" Heather asked.

"You go right ahead and eat," said Bea.

"Besides we might end up losing our appetite if some of the guests are as difficult as they seem," Amy said.

"Most of us are here anyway," said Bea. "Agnes won't be joining us. She told me that she's still not feeling well. Poor thing."

"We're all here?" Trish asked, perking up.

"The Ridgefields and the secretary you just met will be down soon," said Bea. "And…"

"Looks like we're just in time," Mike said, entering the room with his girlfriend.

"Great," Kylie said, unenthusiastically.

Bea added some jars of jelly to the table, and then put her hands on her hips. "Now don't be eating the elderberry jelly until Mr. Ridgefield has had some. This was a special request of his."

"That's fine," Heather said. "Everything else looks fantastic anyway."

Jamie was looking in better spirits surrounded by yummy food instead of worried about potential permit problems.

"What type of jelly would you like?" Travis asked his significant other.

"It doesn't matter," Trish answered.

"Doesn't it?" Mike asked. "I think a proper pairing is very important. Don't you think so too, sweetie?"

"Sure," Kylie said, but she was bored and was playing with her cell phone.

Amy whispered to Heather, "I'm not sure why there's tension, but I do have a butter knife here if we want to cut it."

"So, what do you think we should do first today?" Travis asked Trish.

"I don't know," Trish said.

"We went to the Aquarium yesterday," Ryan said. "It was a great trip."

"Then you can see how there's plenty of fish in the sea," Mike said.

"We were thinking of taking a bike tour around the island," Travis said.

"Then you'll be able to see everything that is available to do and see some scenic sights," Heather agreed.

Travis said, "And we were thinking of visiting the butterfly conservatory."

"We haven't done that yet," said Amy. "Maybe we should go there too."

"And we definitely want to spend some time on the beach," Travis said.

"I want to do that too," Mike said. "Kylie looks amazing in a bathing suit."

"Thanks," Kylie said.

Mike rose from his chair to stand behind Kylie. He started massaging her shoulders. The rest of the table started to feel awkward that this was happening at breakfast.

Then the Ridgefields arrived. Before they saw them, they heard Gideon Ridgefield's voice yelling, "They better be prepared!"

He was referring to breakfast, but the other guests knew that they had better prepare themselves to meet this picky man.

## Chapter 6 – Pickiness and Poison

"Marigold, where's my meal?" Mr. Ridgefield barked.

The secretary hurried to pull a chair out for him to sit down on and then hurried to the kitchen. Before she had to call, Bea arrived with more plates for the trio that had arrived.

"About time," Mr. Ridgefield said.

He gave the impression of being a crotchety old man but was still only middle-aged. His wife was the same age but was trying hard to look younger.

"Good morning," Travis said, giving them the same kind greeting that he had given Heather's group. "I'm Travis, and this is Trish."

"Gideon Ridgefield. Of Ridgefield Industries. This is my wife, Cara."
"Charmed," Cara said, nodding at the table with grace.

"And my secretary Marigold."

"We're here on a bit of a working vacation," Cara explained. "Gideon must conduct business during the day. But in the evening, we can have some pleasant relaxation time together."

Heather doubted whether any time spent with Gideon Ridgefield would really be pleasant. He was lifting his plate of food up to his face and grimacing.

"Where's my jelly?" he asked.

"Bea said that she found it especially for you," Marigold said.

"Of course, she did," he said. "Who else would have so sophisticated a palate around here?"
Ignoring the insult, Mike continued introductions, "I'm Mike, and this smoking hot lady here is my girlfriend Kylie. We're here for a romantic weekend. Because this is our special place to go."

"I guess so," said Kylie.

Heather thought it was only proper to finish the introductions and told the newcomers their names.

"Donuts, eh?" he said. "I never understood donuts. The hole in the middle always made me think I was being cheated out of some of the pastry."

"Then maybe you'd like the jelly or cream filled ones without the hole," Heather said calmly.

"Maybe," he said. "Marigold, open this jelly for me."
He handed it off. Marigold obliged and opened the jar for her employer. Then he waited for her to spread the jelly on his pancakes for him.

"Poor Marigold," Cara said. "Always working."

"I don't mind," said Marigold.

"No, I suppose you wouldn't," said Cara.

Heather and her friends tried to focus on their breakfast but found there was drama commencing on both sides of the table. Gideon Ridgefield was being picky about how his jam was spread on his pancakes but was refusing to do it himself. After the two couples finished comparing who was going to have a better day on vacation, Mike was trying to convince Travis to arm wrestle him.

"I thought it was usually dinner and a show," Amy commented.
"After we eat, we can skedaddle," Heather whispered.

"Do we have to?" Ryan asked quietly back. "I know it's not the company we expected, but the heater isn't pumping hot air into the rooms here."

"That's enough," Mr. Ridgefield said, making Marigold jump aside.

Marigold and Cara finally began their meals as Gideon Ridgefield took his first bite.

"I'm not sure about this," he said. "I've always loved elderberry jelly. It was what I've always preferred on my vacations. But I'm afraid this tastes off somehow. Is it fresh?"

"Yes," Bea assured him. "I bought it yesterday, and you can see the expiration date on it somewhere. It is fine. I tasted a spoonful yesterday."

"Well, that's if I am to believe your taste buds," he said. He continued eating, but also continued looking grumpy.

Bea returned to the kitchen, and the others kept eating. Travis offered to pour some more coffee, but Mike grabbed the pitcher and started pouring instead.

"Cara, try this jelly," Gideon Ridgefield said. "I think it tastes strange."

"What a wonderful reason for her to try it," Amy said.

"I don't want any," Cara said.

"Try it," he demanded again.

"I don't like elderberries," Cara said. "I've told you this a hundred times before. It seems you never do listen to me. It will taste strange to me regardless because I don't like it."

"Fine," Mr. Ridgefield said in a huff. He turned to Marigold. "You try this."

Marigold took a bite, but then shrugged. "I'm not sure what it's supposed to taste like. It is a little bitter."

"No help at all," Mr. Ridgefield grumbled. However, he continued to eat his meal.

"It's Trish, isn't it?" Mike asked.

"That's my name."

"What is it you see in this guy?" Mike asked.

Travis stepped in. "Is this your idea of friendly breakfast table conversation?"

"No disrespect meant," Mike said. "Just since we're all so in love, I thought I'd ask."

"Travis is a great guy," Trish started. However, she didn't get to finish her reasons for being with Travis. Mr. Ridgefield beat his fist on the table, and they all turned to face him.

He fell out of his chair and onto the floor, flailing around.

"Jamie, go call 911," Heather said. She and Ryan ran towards Gideon Ridgefield.

"I'm a police officer," Ryan told him. "Someone is calling for help now."

Gideon kept flailing and moaning.

Ryan stood up. "This is clearly a medical emergency. Bea, lead everyone into the other room."

"An ambulance is on its way," Jamie reported.

"Go outside and direct the EMTs where to go when they arrive," said Ryan. Without a moment's hesitation, Jamie ran outside.

"I'm not leaving my husband," Cara said.

"Then you can stay, but to the side," Ryan said. "We need to give him space."
"What can I do?" Heather asked.

"Keep an eye on everything on the table and make sure no one takes anything," Ryan said. "Because you know what this looks like?"

Heather nodded. "Poison."

## Chapter 7 – Breakfast Table Crime Scene

The EMTs had done their best, but they were unable to combat the fast-acting poison. Gideon Ridgefield was dead.

Detective Smith arrived on the scene with his partner Detective Peters. He paused when he saw Heather.

"What are you doing here?"

"I was hoping to have a quiet breakfast, but it wasn't meant to be," said Heather.

"Our being here did mean that we were able to secure the scene for you," Ryan said. "Heather and Amy made sure that nothing from the table was removed by any of the guests. There's a good chance that whatever killed him is on the table."

"Our forensic team will run the necessary tests," Detective Smith said. He was a meticulous man and a good detective, except when it came to announcing his official date of retirement. Ryan was waiting for him to retire so he could take over the position.

"I'd start with the elderberry jelly," said Heather.

"Why is that?" Detective Peters asked, taking out his notebook. He was a young detective who was eager to solve cases, but still occasionally felt unsure about the best way to do so.

"That's the one thing that Gideon Ridgefield definitely ate," Heather said.

"He made a big stink about it," Amy agreed.
"And it was something that wasn't being eaten by everyone at the table," Ryan agreed.
"Except for the secretary, Marigold," Heather said suddenly. "She had a bite of it too. We should have a doctor look at her."

"Don't worry," Detective Smith said. "She's already being examined. She told the EMTs she wasn't feeling well. We assumed it was because of the shock, but now there might be another reason. Peters, will you tell them to check for signs of poisoning?"

Peters nodded and left.

"She should be all right," Detective Smith said. "A small bite shouldn't be lethal."

"I hope you're right," Heather said.

"I'm glad we don't like elderberries," Amy said.

"Now, why don't you take me through what happened?" Detective Smith asked.

"Everyone was at the table for breakfast," Heather said. "Well, except for one guest. Apparently, Agnes has been ill the entire trip. She isn't leaving her room much, though I did see her last night. We had both heard a commotion in the hall."

"And what commotion was that?" asked Detective Smith.

"The guest Mike was having an argument with a woman. I thought it was his girlfriend Kylie at the time, but I'm not positive. I only saw his face," Heather replied.

Detective Smith nodded. "I suppose we'll have to make sure we know what exactly was poisoned. If it was the elderberry jelly like you suspect, then would that have been the best murder weapon to kill Gideon Ridgefield? Or was the intended victim someone else?"

"If it was the elderberry jelly, then I believe the killer succeeded in killing the man he wanted. The jelly was a special request for Gideon Ridgefield," said Heather.

"And others knew this?"

"Apparently, he made a scene about it at breakfast yesterday," said Heather.

"And if we saw him when he got what he wanted, I'd hate to see what it was like when he didn't get it," said Amy.

"We can check with the owner Bea, but I believe the other guests were there for it or heard about it during the day. The only ones who checked in after the incident were Mike and Kylie," said Ryan.

Heather nodded. "They checked in after we were offered rooms. It looked like they didn't have any reservations."

"If the killer came here to kill Gideon Ridgefield," Detective Smith said. "Then we will have to look at who decided to come here after Mr. Ridgefield already made his reservation."

Ryan nodded. "Because they would have to know that the victim would be here in order to murder him."

"You said we," Heather noted. "Does this mean that you don't mind our help in this investigation?"

"I suppose this time I can allow the help," Detective Smith said. "You're already guests here. And you might be able to pick up on things we might miss because you know how the other guests were acting before the murder took place."

Heather smiled. "We won't check out until the case is solved."

"So first we want to figure out when people planned to come here?" Amy asked. "To see if they were planning the murder."

"I think that's a good starting place," said Heather. "But there is also the chance that this location wasn't vitally important for where it happened."

"You mean that the killer could have had access to the victim regularly, but just chose this place in the hopes of casting some doubt on what happened?" Detective Smith asked for clarification.

"You mean it could have been the wife?" said Amy.

"She did refuse to try the jelly," Heather answered. "But there are many suspects in this case."
"That's true," said Ryan. "There were many people under this roof last night. They all might have had access to the jelly."

"We'll have to find out where the jelly was kept," Heather said. "And if there was any security that could have prevented the murderer from completing their plan. For example, if Bea locked the fridge overnight, then there would only be a small window of time where the killer could have added the poison."

"There is another possibility," Detective Smith said. "You said that this man was a tough customer?"
"That's one way to put it," Amy said.

"Could the cook have gotten so frustrated that she wanted to get rid of him?" Detective Smith asked.

"I think either way," said Heather. "We should go talk to Bea."

## Chapter 8 – A, Bea, See

"I can't believe this is happening," Bea said as they entered her office.

Bea sat in her usual spot at her desk. Heather, Amy, and Ryan stood to the side as Detective Smith took out his notebook to begin his questioning. Detective Peters was keeping an eye on the other suspects.

"How could he just keel over like that?" Bea asked. "Is there a chance it was a medical condition and not something that went wrong in my kitchen?"

"Right now we're treating this as a murder investigation," Detective Smith said.

"Murder?" Bea asked. "How can that be?"

"That's what we're going to find out," Heather said.

"And you here," Bea said turning to her. "I invited you to show off my business, and this happens. You'll never want to provide donuts now. I'll be back to square one with my brunch spread. Then again, I might not have any customers."

"Don't worry about us," Heather said. "This isn't going to scare us away from a business deal. But the important thing right now is figuring out what happened this morning."

"Plus, we're kind of used to this sort of thing," Amy admitted.

"Had you ever met Gideon Ridgefield before he stayed here this weekend?" Detective Smith asked.

"No," Bea said. "It was his first time staying here. And I didn't know him before his visit."

"I understand he was a difficult guest," Detective Smith said.

"That's an understatement," Bea said. "He was picky about everything. How he wanted his room. And how he wanted his secretary's room. And especially about his breakfast."

"I could see how that could be frustrating," Detective Smith said. "I could see how someone could be driven to deal with a difficult person in a drastic manner."

"You can't think that I had something to do with this, can you?" Bea asked. "This is going to be terrible for my business. Who will want to eat a place where a man died eating? And who will want to sleep under the same roof that a killer did?"

"Calm down," Heather said, gently. "We'll catch whoever did this, and that will help business go back to normal."

"Yes," Detective Smith said seriously. "We'll catch whoever did this."

"We have a few questions we need to ask you," Heather said. "Who has access to your kitchen?"

"Technically, anyone in the building," Bea said. "There is the screen to discourage guests from bothering me while I am cooking, but it doesn't stop them from entering. And it doesn't have a lock. I never thought it was necessary until now."

"So, anyone here could have poisoned the ingredients last night," Amy said.

"I suppose so," Bea said turning pale. "I do have precautions to keep people from entering if they're not a guest and don't have a key. But any of the guests could have committed the murder. Oh. I knew some of them were troublesome with their orders and the last-minute couple was a bit obnoxious. But I didn't think anyone was dangerous."

"Could you tell us more about the elderberry jelly?" Heather asked.

"Yes," said Detective Smith. "This was a special request from the victim?"

"He was very specific about it," Bea said. "And it was hard to find."

"Where did it come from?" Ryan asked.

"I had to special order it to get it in time. There was a place that sold unique preserves about an hour away, and I had it brought down. A delivery boy brought me the jar. I can find the name of the place," Bea said. She looked on her desk and found a business card. "Here it is."

"When did the jelly arrive?" Heather asked.

"It was around eight p.m. last night," Bea said. "It arrived sealed. I tried a spoonful of it last night, and it tasted fine to me."

"And it was in the kitchen all last night?" Heather asked.
"Yes," said Bea. "I went to my room around ten o'clock, so I wasn't watching the kitchen after that. I fell right asleep."

"When did the Ridgefields make their reservation?" Detective Smith asked.

Bea consulted a document on her computer. "Marigold Fanning made the reservation for her room and the Ridgefields two months ago. They said he had some business meetings this weekend."

"And what reservation were made after theirs?" Ryan asked.

"Besides ours," Amy joked. "I think we can be eliminated as suspects."

Bea clicked a few more buttons on the computer and then said, "All the other reservations were made after his."

"All of them?" Heather asked.

Bea printed out the list of reservations and handed it to the investigators.

"Trish Hathaway booked the room a month ago for two people," she said. "That poor sick woman Agnes booked two weeks ago. And then that other couple arrived last night looking for a vacancy."

"We saw them as they came in," Heather agreed. "Based on their baggage and look of preparation, it certainly looked like a last-minute trip."

"What does that mean about the booking dates?" Bea asked.

"Sadly, nothing helpful," Heather said. "We can't rule anyone else based on it."

"I really can't believe that one of my guests would kill someone," Bea said. "And at my breakfast table. With my jelly."

"We'll have to confirm it is the jelly," Detective Smith said. "But it is a good starting point."

"You know, now that this all happened and I think about," Bea said, remembering. "I did hear someone walking about last night. I checked to make sure no one needed help, but all I saw was an outline. I think it was one of the female guests. I thought maybe she wanted a midnight snack, but she was moving away from me."

"Could she have been in the kitchen?" Heather asked.

Bea nodded. "I didn't think so then, but she could have been."

"But you're not sure which of the female guests it was?" Ryan asked.

Bea shook her head. "I'm sorry. I wish I did." She turned to Heather. "Could I ask you something?"

"Sure," said Heather, thinking it would be related to the case.

"Could I have another of your donuts?" asked Bea. "They were very tasty. And I can't see myself cooking anytime soon. I think I could really use one."

"I'll get us some more Blackberry Cream Donuts," said Heather. "And then I'd like to get some more clues."

## Chapter 9 – Clues to Feast On

"No offense. You look terrible," Amy told Jamie.

He had returned to his room after the chaos but had invited doggy Dave to join him so he wouldn't be alone. The two of them had been staring at the ceiling forlornly until the others joined them.

Dave jumped up to greet Heather and Ryan while Amy sat next to Jamie.

"I feel a little terrible," Jamie sighed. "But it's my fault too. After everything that happened, I came up here. But then I've just been thinking about death and permits. Not very happy thoughts."

"Next time think about me," Amy joked.

"I'll try that," he said, returning the smile. "How is the investigation going?"
"Maybe you can help us," Heather said.

"How?" he asked, sitting up.

"We've been trying to remember everything that happened at breakfast," Heather said. "Maybe one of us noticed details that another didn't. What exactly did Gideon Ridgefield eat?"

"Obviously, he had the pancakes and elderberry jelly," Jamie said. "There was no way we could have missed that."

"Could the pancakes have been poisoned?" Amy asked.

They all thought about it.

"I think the pancake plates for the latecomers were brought out around the same time. It didn't look like a specific plate was delivered to Mr. Ridgefield," Heather said. "But maybe the killer was sneaky."
"If it were the pancakes, it would have had to be Bea who poisoned them," Ryan said.

"You're right," Heather said. "Because it would have had to be specially added to the batter. And it would have to be done carefully, so no one else was poisoned. But I don't think Bea did it. This is going to hurt her business. She would need a better motive than being annoyed by a customer."

"And if she talked to Bernadette before she invited us to stay then she would know that we were private investigators," said Amy. "Why would she invite us to the beds if she were going to poison the breakfasts?"

"Did Gideon Ridgefield drink anything?" Heather asked.

"No," Jamie said, proud that he remembered. "He had coffee in his cup but didn't drink it. I remember thinking that maybe he would be in a better mood if he had a sip. I feel bad about thinking that now."

"But it's very helpful that you did," said Heather. "I'm pretty sure it was the elderberry jelly that was poisoned."

518

"Which means Gideon Ridgefield was indeed the target," said Ryan.

"And now we need to figure out who wanted him dead," said Heather. "But first I want to check on Lilly."
Heather and Ryan called Eva to see how the sleepover had gone. Everyone had a good time, and they loved Lilly's new dinosaur story. Heather said she couldn't wait to read it.

"So, when do you think you'll be home, dear?" Eva asked.

"Well..." Heather began.
"Did you get involved in another case?" asked Eva.

"I'm afraid so," said Heather. "They do keep falling into my lap."

"Don't worry about us," Eva assured her. "We're having a lovely time. You and your friends catch that murderer. And just let us know if you plan to be home by dinnertime."

"I'm hoping we can solve this case quickly," Heather said. "All the suspects are in the same building, but figuring out who did it could be tricky."

"I'm sure you, Amy, and Ryan can figure it out," said Eva. "And you have Dave there to help."

After Eva had wished them luck, and they had listened to Lilly's account of a fun evening, Heather and Ryan were ready to focus on the case again.

"I was just telling Jamie about how Detective Smith said he would accept our help on this case," Amy said. "I think he's coming around and realizing what a valuable resource we are."

"He's conducting the official interrogations," said Heather. "But he invited us to question the guests a little more subtly too. I think we might be able to uncover some secrets the guests are hiding."

"I just hope this is for real," said Amy. "And he's not just telling us we can do this to keep us out of his hair."

"I think Detective Smith is a man of his word," said Heather.

"In every way except in regards to his retirement," Ryan chuckled.

Dave ran to the door before the knock occurred.

"Good boy," said Heather.

She opened the door and saw Detective Peters.

"Do you mind if I come in?" he asked.

"As long as you have information about the case," said Amy. "And you and Detective Smith aren't hiding things from us."

"I'm sharing information," he said. "I came to tell you about the jelly."

Amy gracefully waved him inside.

"Was it the murder weapon?" Heather asked.

"Yes," Detective Peters nodded. "Based on your suggestion, we told the lab to test the elderberry jelly first. Both the jelly on the pancakes and in the jar contained poison."

"What a terrible breakfast," said Amy.

"Anything else?" asked Ryan.

"We also looked at the fingerprints on the jar. As we've been questioning the guests, we've been asking for prints for comparison. And we've found our matches already," Peters said.

"Matches?" said Heather. "How many?"

"Three," said Peters. "The prints match Gideon Ridgefield, Bea, and the secretary Marigold."

"That matches what we saw at the table," said Ryan. "Bea brought out the jelly. And the Marigold and Mr. Ridgefield were the ones to use it on his pancakes."

"That means that the killer must have planted the poison last night and wiped their prints off of it," said Heather. "There are no longer any prints from the person who delivered the jar to Bea, so it was wiped clean before she picked it up this morning."

Peters made a note of this in his notebook. Then he said, "I better get back to work. Good luck on your end."

He left, and the group considered who they wanted to question first.

"You know who I'd like to talk to?" Heather said. "Both as a suspect and to make sure she's okay."

"The other person who ate the poison?" Amy asked.
Heather nodded. "Marigold Fanning."

**Chapter 10 – The Other Victim**

"How are you feeling?" Heather asked as they entered Marigold's room at the bed and breakfast.

"Very sad," Marigold said. "Gideon Ridgefield was a great man."

"I meant about the poison you ingested," Heather said.

"Oh," said Marigold. "I'm all right. Just tired physically. They said I had too small an amount to do any real damage. They treated me and thankfully said I didn't have to stay at the hospital overnight. But the police say we're not allowed to travel home. So, I'm stuck here, in the same building he was killed."

She looked frail under her blankets. She looked pale, and even her green eyes looked dull.

"This must be so hard for you," Heather said.

"He must have been a great boss," said Amy.

"Yes," said Marigold. "A boss."

Amy, Ryan, and Heather with Dave on a leash moved further into the room.

"You said you were a cop at the table when Mr. Ridgefield fell," said Marigold to Ryan. "But you're not the detective on the case?"

"No," said Ryan. "Not officially. But we said we would help in any way we can. And we wanted to make sure that you were doing all right."

Marigold still looked uncertain about opening up to them.

"Dave isn't a therapy dog, but he has made people feel better before," said Heather. "Would you like him to come closer?"

Marigold considered and then nodded. "My mother always used to say that wagging tails and wet noses were the surest sign there was good in the world."

Dave jumped up on the bed and allowed Marigold to pet his ears.

"Dogs are so much better than people," she said. "People are terrible. One of them could murder Gideon."

"You two were close?" Heather asked.

"I worked for him for six years," said Marigold.

"Were you in love with him?" Heather asked.

Marigold stopped petting Dave to look Heather in the eyes. "He was in love with me too."

"So, you were having an affair?" Ryan asked.

"I knew he wasn't going to leave Cara, but that didn't mean what we had wasn't real. We might not have been able to start a family together, but we were in love. We'd been officially together for two years."

"Officially but secretly?" Amy said.

"No one knew," Marigold agreed.

"His wife didn't know?" Ryan asked.

"We kept things looking professional on the surface," Marigold said. "She couldn't have known."

"So, you'd still take orders from him in public and run errands for him and prepare his breakfast," Amy said.

"Yes," Marigold said sadly, petting the dog again.

"Don't take this the wrong way," Amy said. "He seemed like a difficult man to work for and to be in a relationship with."

"He could be particular," Marigold said. "And he could be grumpy at times. But I found it charming. When it was just the two of us, I would tease him about it."

"Romantic," Amy muttered.

"Don't you see what it means?" Marigold said. "He picked me. He was so particular. And so picky. But he picked me. I was good enough. And he loved me."

"Miss Fanning, you must realize that the police will consider you a suspect because of your relationship with him," Heather said.

"But why would I kill him?" Marigold asked. "I've lost the love of my life and my job because of this. I was also almost poisoned myself."

"Maybe you got tired of sharing him with his wife?" Heather suggested.

"If that were the case, I would have killed Cara and not Gideon," she snapped. "But I didn't. And I wouldn't. I wouldn't kill anyone."

"Where were you last night after nine p.m. until breakfast time?" asked Heather.

"Gideon and I weren't able to meet last night. He had to stay in his room with Cara. So I was in my room by myself. I read for a while and then went to bed around eleven. I was up for about an hour and a half before breakfast, getting ready for the day. Then I checked on the Ridgefields, and they told me to see if the meal was ready."

"And you never left your room last night?" Heather asked.

"No. There was no reason to."

"Did you know Mike Crown before today?" asked Heather.

"I still don't know who he is."

"He's part of the couple that arrived last night," said Ryan. "He was in a T-shirt at breakfast and is with the blonde woman."

"I never met him before today, and it wasn't a very good meeting what with everything that happened," said Marigold. "I'm getting pretty tired."

"We'll let you rest," Heather said.

Marigold gave Dave a kiss on his head, and then the others left her to rest up.

"What do you think?" Amy asked.

"I think she's still a viable suspect," said Heather. "She knew about Gideon Ridgefield's particular breakfast tastes, and she has a potential motive."

Ryan nodded. "She could have been upset that Mr. Ridgefield wasn't going to leave his wife for her."

"And no one could account for her movements during the night," said Heather. "But she did allow herself to eat the poison."

"That's dedication to the crime," said Amy. "It might be the perfect cover."

"It is tough to gauge," Heather said. "On one hand, she didn't even flinch when Gideon told her to eat the poisoned jelly. On the other, if she did poison it, she would know that a small amount wouldn't kill her. And it might help clear her of suspicion."

"But not for us," Amy joked. "We're suspicious of everyone."

"Then again, there was someone who flatly refused to try the jelly," Heather said.

"And someone who might not mind if both her cheating husband and his mistress ate the poison," said Ryan.

"I think it's time we talk to the wife," said Heather.

## Chapter 11 – Wife Turned Widow

Mrs. Ridgefield was already dressed in black when they arrived at her room to talk to her. She seemed devoid of any emotion rather than sad.

"Yes?" she said. "What do you want?"

"First, we'd like to offer our deepest sympathies on your loss," said Heather.

"And secondly, you'd like to ask some questions?" asked Cara Ridgefield. "That young detective said that you might. I get the sense he says more than he should at times."

"Normally that's helpful in a murder case," said Amy. "If only all the killers would just blurt out their mistakes, then we'd have an easy time of it."

"You're here to ask if I killed my husband," said Cara. "I didn't."
Dave started scratching his ear, and Cara jumped back.

"I don't want white fur on my black dress," she said.

"Did you pack that black dress for your vacation?" asked Heather.

"Yes," said Cara. "But I don't like what you're implying. I didn't bring it because I knew that I'd become a widow. I brought an evening dress for when I went out to dinner with my husband. I find black to be slimming."

"Why did you refuse to taste the elderberry jelly?" Heather asked.

"It's not that I had any suspicion about poison," Cara said. "I don't like elderberries. I know I might have seemed heated about it at the table. But it wasn't because I was avoiding it and the danger. I was annoyed because he's been confusing my tastes with someone else. Another woman."

"He was having an affair?" Ryan asked.

"Don't play dumb," Cara said. "I'm sure everyone could tell. He was sleeping with his secretary. It was obvious. And I didn't like when he confused me with her. Bringing me chocolate covered strawberries when he knew for years that I don't like anything with seeds that could get caught in my teeth. It was her who liked them."

"How long has this affair been going on?" Ryan asked.

"Probably years," said Cara. "But he'd become more careless recently. Maybe he realized that I wasn't going to leave him. That I don't believe in divorce."

"There are other ways to get rid of a husband," Amy said.
"I wanted to save my marriage," Cara said. "Not kill it off. That's why I started insisting that I accompany him on his business trips. I thought I could keep him away from temptation. And who knows? We might enjoy one another's company."

"Do you inherit everything after his death?" Heather asked.

"Wives normally do," said Cara.

"It's a good deal of money?"

"Yes and no," said Cara. "Gideon was wealthy. But the money was tied up in his business. I don't know how I'm going to access it. It's going to be a very confusing process."

Dave took another step towards her and Cara backed up towards the wall.

"I mean it. I don't want white fur on me."
"Do you know anyone else who is staying at this bed and breakfast?" asked Heather.

"I only knew Gideon and Marigold," said Cara. "That's it."

"But that's two people who were hurting you," said Amy. "I bet you're disappointed that Marigold didn't have more of the jelly."

"What a terrible thing to say," said Cara. "I was a loyal wife. I never did anything to hurt him. Or to hurt anybody. But now, maybe I deserve some happiness. I think I'll enjoy widowhood. And maybe I'll find another man who agrees with what loyalty and monogamy should be."

"This killer sure did her a favor," Amy muttered.

"One more question," Heather said. "And I need you to be honest, or I'm going to let Dave shed near your dress."

Dave gave a full body shake at the moment to drive the threat home. Cara gave them a hard look.

"What do you want to know?"

"Did you leave your room at all last night?"

"No," Cara said "I was in my room with Gideon all night. Unfortunately, he's not here to back me up on that. But it's true. I wanted to keep him from crawling away down the hall to see that cheap secretary of his."

She nearly cowered as Dave moved closer, but Heather thanked her for her time, and they left the room.

"She certainly has a motive," said Ryan. "And no bitterness about the death," said Amy. "Plus, she refused to eat the jelly."

"She did have a good reason for it," said Heather. "But if she had been planning this, it would have given her time to come up with a reason."

"The money being tied up makes the inheritance less of a motive," said Ryan. "But even if it takes a long time to receive her money, it might be worth the inconvenience if it gets a cheating husband out of the way."

Heather frowned.

"What's wrong?" asked Ryan.

"We haven't eliminated any of the guests as suspects yet," said Heather. "And I still don't know if that argument in the middle of the night had anything to do with the death."

They were just thinking that they should talk to Mike next when they heard a woman's voice from the other room saying, "I can't go through with this. How could I have let this happen?"

They hurried around the corner, but the woman was faster than them. She was gone by the time they reached the sitting room.

## Chapter 12 – And the Trail Leads To...

Heather was once again pleased that they had brought Dave with them. She told him to follow the trail of the woman who had been in the room, and he had led them off down the hall. She supposed it was entirely possible that he was just using this as an excuse to lead his human friends around on an inside walk, but it certainly looked convincing. It looked like he was tracking the scent.

He stopped at a bedroom door, and they knocked.

"There better not just be donuts inside," Amy teased.

However, the door opened, and two people were revealed. Travis greeted them with a friendly wave while Trish asked, "What do you want?"

"Were you just in the sitting room?" Heather asked.

"Why?" she responded.

"That's still allowed, isn't it?" asked Travis. "We're not allowed to go out and enjoy our vacation with the plans we made because of this tragedy, but surely we can move around the building. She needed to clear her head for a moment. This was a very upsetting incident. We've never seen anyone die before. And then to learn it was murder."

"Yes," Trish said. "The murder is very upsetting. It's been weighing on my mind."

"Did you know Mr. Ridgefield?" Heather asked.

"No," said Trish. "But you could still be upset about someone dropping dead in front of you. And to know that if we ate the wrong thing we could have been killed too."

"That did scare me too," said Amy. "Because I like to eat most everything."

"Did you know anyone else here?" Heather asked. "The wife or secretary? Or any of these other guests?"

"I don't like these questions," Trish said. "Why are you asking them? Everyone is asking us things. We don't know anything about this murder. Why don't you just leave us alone?"

"Trish, they're just trying to figure out what happened to the man," Travis said. "They don't mean anything by it. And they'll soon find out we didn't have anything to do with it. That we were just here to have a romantic weekend. We don't have any secrets."

"I need some air," Trish said.
She left them. Travis wanted to follow but remained in place.

"I guess I should give her a little time."

"Is this normal behavior for her?" Ryan asked.

"What's normal when a murder has just occurred?" asked Travis, but then he frowned. "Though, actually, she has been acting a little strange recently. She had been so excited for this trip. Then yesterday she started suggesting that we leave early."

"When was this?"

"Well," Travis said, unsure if he wanted to share the information. "It was right after we saw the Ridgefields in person for the first time. We had an early breakfast on Saturday, so we left before we saw them. We had a fun day out and about. Then we arrived back at the B&B By The Sea. She went in ahead of me because I needed to get some more sand out of my shoe. When I came in, Bea was dealing with the Ridgefields in the lobby as the man complained about the breakfast. And Trish looked upset. But she said she was just tired."

"That doesn't sound like she doesn't know the Ridgefields," Ryan said.

"We've been together almost a year, and I never saw her with them or heard her mention them," said Travis. "It might have been a coincidence."

"I usually don't trust coincidences of a murder case," said Heather. "Something upset her last night."

"I know Trish," said Travis. "She's a wonderful person. She couldn't have had anything to do with a murder."

"Wonderful people have been pushed to it before," Heather said. "We need to look at the facts. But we promise to be objective as we can. If you're certain she didn't have anything to do with this, then you can keep telling us the truth without feeling guilty."

"I am certain that she didn't have anything to do with it," said Travis.

"Did she leave the room at all last night?" Heather asked.

"Yes," Travis said. "But only for a little while."

"At what time?"

"I'm not sure," he said. "But it was rather late. I had fallen asleep but woke up when I heard her. She was having trouble sleeping and wanted to take a shower. She said she was going to try and find an extra towel so we'd have a dry one in the morning."

"So, she went out in search of a towel in the middle of the night?" Amy asked.

"It's not a crazy thing to do," said Travis. "She thought there was a good chance Bea was asleep, but that the linen closet might be marked and easy to find."

"Was it?" Heather asked.

"No," Travis said. "She came back a little while later saying that she couldn't find it. She decided to try and go to sleep. I tried to comfort her, but then I fell asleep and was out for the rest of the night. I didn't realize that she didn't fall asleep right after me until this morning when she mentioned it at the table."

"Did you know anyone here besides Trish?" asked Ryan.

Travis shook his head. "That was how we wanted it. We wanted a weekend away for just the two of us."

"Thank you for all your help," Heather said.

"I hope it was helpful," Travis said. "I know Trish didn't kill anybody."
They wandered away from his room and down the hall.

"Are we certain that Trish didn't kill anybody?" Amy asked.
"Right now, I'm not certain of anything," Heather responded.

## Chapter 13 – Asking Agnes

"Bea?" Agnes asked, peeking her nose out of her door. Instead, she saw Heather, Amy, Ryan, and Dave in the hall.

"I'm sorry," she said, starting to retreat. "I thought it was some food being brought up."

"It's good to see that you're feeling well enough to open the door," Heather said.

"Yes," said Agnes. "But I'm still not back to normal. I think I had better lie back down until the food arrives. I thought it would have been here by now."

"Since we've run into you, do you mind if we ask you a few questions?" Heather asked.

"Well," Agnes hesitated.

"You're welcome to lie down while we talk," said Heather. "And if your meal hasn't arrived by the time that we're finished we'll run down and get it for you."

Agnes agreed. Heather helped the small woman back to her bed, and then Dave decided he should join her. He wriggled up next to her so that she would pet his head. Her green eyes lit up as she scratched his belly and his tail wagged.

"Dave could become a professional," Amy said.

Agnes smiled. "My mother used to say that wagging tails and wet noses were a sign that there was—"

"Good in the world," Amy finished.
"Did your mother say that too?" Agnes asked. "It must be a common expression. But a true one."

"I can agree with it," Heather said.

Agnes began to cough. Heather filled up a cup of water for her, while Amy tried not the breath in any potential germs.

"We know that you haven't been feeling well and haven't been out of your room much," Ryan began.

"That is the truth," Agnes said. "I've been feeling so lousy. And so weak."

"What's wrong with you exactly?" Amy asked.

"The doctors at home weren't quite sure," said Agnes. "After several treatments didn't work, they suggested it was stress and that I should go on a vacation. I know it sounds very old-fashioned. To head towards the sea for better air. But they suggested I try and relax. But the travel didn't help me at all. I've been feeling worse since I arrived. They don't seem to think I'm contagious, but I do understand if you don't want to stay with me for too long."

"We can brave it," Heather said. "When did you book this vacation?"

"Oh, about two weeks ago," said Agnes. "That was about the time my doctor suggested the salt air."

"Why did you settle on this location?" asked Heather.

"I had always wanted to visit Key West," said Agnes. "I heard it was one of the most beautiful and fun places. I felt certain I could relax here."

"And why this bed and breakfast?" asked Ryan.

"You're going to think it sounds silly, but I chose it because of the name. It had "by the sea" in its title, and I thought it was a sign. Because that was exactly what I was looking for."

"I guess that makes sense," said Amy. "Sometimes I just close my eyes and point at a spot on a map to make traveling decisions."

"Of course, now I don't believe it was a sign," said Agnes. "A man has died here, and I feel like I'm at death's door myself."

"Would you like for us to get you a doctor?" Ryan asked.

"No, no," said Agnes. "I don't want to be any bother. Besides, there are so few doctors I really trust."

"We know you didn't socialize much while here," said Heather. "But do you know anyone else staying here?"

Agnes had another coughing fit but then collected herself.

"No. I'm afraid not," she replied. "The owner of the hotel, Bea, has been very kind to me. But I don't know anyone else. I've barely seen anyone else here. I've kept to myself mostly, trying to recuperate."

"Have you heard anything unusual while you've been in your room?" Ryan asked.

"No," said Agnes. "Perhaps if the killer had used a gun, I might be more helpful."

"What about anyone moving around last night?" asked Ryan.

"There was something that woke me up last night," said Agnes. "I heard voices in the hallway, and they frightened me. I went into the hall to see what was happening. And that's when I ran into you."

Heather nodded. "I told her that it sounded like a lovers' quarrel. Of course, now I'm not so sure."

"And I was feeling so poorly and was so frightened that I didn't give this furry fellow the proper attention," Agnes said, petting Dave's head. "I wish I had noticed him. He might have made me feel better then too."

Then Agnes began coughing so badly that she scared Dave off the bed. Heather helped her to sit up and handed her some more water.

"Thank you," Agnes said. "I'm sorry about this."

"It's all right," Heather said. "I think we'll go and check on your meal now and let you rest. I think we've asked enough questions. Unless you can think of anything else that might help us figure out who snuck into the kitchen and added the poison last night."

"Well, there is one more thing," Agnes said. "After you had left with your dog, I went to check that my door was locked and heard someone in the hall. I thought it might have been one of the people from the argument. But now you have me considering that they were actually planning a murder."

"Did you see who it was?" asked Heather.

"I don't know anyone's names, I'm afraid," said Agnes. "Except for the victim's family from the police questioning."

"What did he or she look like?"

"She had dark hair," said Agnes. "One of the young ladies here with her boyfriend."

"That sounds like Trish," said Heather.

"And she looked upset," Agnes said. She coughed and then asked, "Does that help at all?"

"It just might," said Heather. "I think we need to talk to Trish one-on-one."

"Three-on-one?" Ryan asked.

"Three and a furry puppy on one," said Amy.

"Regardless," Heather said, trying not to laugh. "We need to get some answers from her."

## Chapter 14 – The Couples

"Trish?" Heather called, as she and her team searched for her around the bed and breakfast.

"I didn't think this place was that big," Amy said. "But after wandering all around it, now I'm tired."

"Trish?" Ryan called.

"Why are you looking for Trish?" Mike asked entering the room.

"We'd like to ask her some questions," Heather said.

"About what?" asked Mike.

"The murder," Amy said as if it were the most obvious thing in the world.

"She didn't have anything to do with it," said Mike. "And why are you asking questions?"

"Detective Smith said we could investigate on our own," Heather said. "We're licensed private investigators."

"And who hired you to come here?" he asked. "Did you know I was coming here? I can't believe it. You were here when I arrived."

"Why would we come after you?" Heather asked.

"Sure. Play dumb," Mike said. "She's trying to gather some blackmail too. Fight fire with fire. But I'm a bigger inferno. You'll just see."
"Hey, hot-head," said Amy. "What are you going on about?"

"As if you don't know," said Mike. "We'll just see who finds Trish first."
"You're blackmailing her?" Ryan said. "That's quite an offense. I think we should call in Detectives Smith and Peters."

"Wait," Mike said. "I never said that. I never said I was blackmailing her.

You're trying to put words in my mouth. I didn't do anything."

"Hey, Ames," Heather said. "How much of a jump is it from blackmail to murder?"

"Depends on the person," Amy said. "But I think he'd be willing to take a running start and jump."

"Wait a minute," Mike said. "Let's all just calm down now. Take a breather. I didn't kill that guy. I had no idea who he was. Let's all relax."

"Mike!"

They turned and saw Kylie storming into the room.

"Mike," she said. "This is the worst vacation ever."

"I'm sorry," he said. "I couldn't plan on there being a murder investigation."

"Even before he died, this was boring. I thought this was going to be so exciting. I thought that sure, we're a new couple. But he's so spontaneous and romantic. He wants to go Key West for the weekend. Then we arrive. You're hot, and you're cold. And I'm bored. And now, we can't even leave the stupid bed and breakfast. Which if you remember, I didn't even want to come to."

"She's right," said Amy. "We heard her say she wanted to go to the big hotel."

"But he was insistent on staying at this specific bed and breakfast?" Heather asked.

"Yeah," Kylie said. "We passed several that looked nicer too. But he insisted we stay here. And look what it became - the murder lodge!"

"Kylie, just calm down. I promise to make it up to you," he said. "Now why don't you go back to the room?"

"Why? So you can ignore me some more? Go off on late night walks without me?"

"He left you alone last night?" Heather prompted.

Kylie didn't need any other encouragement. She went into a tirade about how this had been her worst vacation ever and how Mike was fast becoming her worst boyfriend ever. Mike had convinced her to go on a whirlwind vacation at the last minute but then had started acting weird. He had been leaving her on her own for what she thought were secret meetings.

"And I want to walk out on him, but we're not allowed to leave this stupid place," Kylie finished.

"Kylie, calm down," Mike said. "And stop talking so much. You don't know what you're talking about. You're making it sound like I might be a killer."

"Were you meeting someone last night?" Heather asked.

"No," said Mike.

"Let me rephrase that," said Heather. "I heard the end of an argument late last night and saw you walking away from it. Who was the woman you were talking to?"

"Another woman?" Kylie asked. "Should I even be surprised? You're the worst."

"When I heard the woman say that she couldn't do something and you suggested it happened in the morning, what were you talking about?" asked Heather.

"Not poisoning some stranger," said Mike. "It was a personal matter."

"How personal?" asked Kylie with her hands on her hips. "Are you cheating on me? How dare you? We're done."

"You want to be done, fine. We're done," Mike said. "We never really were anyway. I just brought you here to try and make Trish jealous."

"What?"

"Yeah," Mike said. "I was just trying to get my ex back."

"This was a pretty messed up way to do it," Kylie said. "And you're terrible. And I'm glad I'm getting away from you. And I am totally hotter than her. Your loss."

With that, she stormed out of the room. "I have to agree with the messed up part," said Amy.

"You don't understand," said Mike.

"Then help us understand," said Ryan. "If it doesn't have anything to do with criminal activity, then we can leave it alone."

Trish entered the room with a red spot on her face. "Kylie just slapped me in the face. I've never been slapped before."

Heather reached into her bag and found an instant cold compress that she had been carrying around since Field Day at Lilly's school in case any of the kids had fallen down. Trish accepted the compress, but there was still fire in her eyes.

"I broke up with her," Mike said. "I told her I was in love with you."

"I'm not in love with you," Trish said. "I can't stand you."

To prove her point she threw the cold compress at his head. He ducked and then moved closer to her.

"Why don't we get back together?" Mike asked. "We were good together. And you always come back. I'm the only one who understands."

"I'm in love with Travis," she said.

"Then it would be a shame if he found out, wouldn't it?" Mike asked.

"This does sound like blackmail," said Heather. "Would you like to press charges?"

"We'd be happy to help you," Ryan assured her.

"No," Trish said. "I don't want Travis to find out. If he learned I'm being blackmailed, then he'd try and figure out why. I don't want Travis to know."

"To know what?" Travis asked, entering the room.

## Chapter 15 – Not Quite the Vacation They Were Planning

"Nothing," Trish stuttered, replying to Travis's question. "Nothing at all."

Heather, Amy, and Ryan all took a step back from the lover's triangle forming in front of them. Dave wanted to stay in the center of attention but allowed himself to be pulled back with a few tugs on his leash.

"As soon as he learns, he'll leave you," Mike said. "But I'll be right here to catch you. I'll always love you."

"Trish, who is this man?" Travis asked.

"My ex-boyfriend," she said.

"That's why you wanted to leave early? Why didn't you just tell me?" Travis said.

"It's not that simple," said Trish.
"Not with the secret she's carrying," said Mike.

"You stay out of this," said Travis.

"Remember at breakfast when I said I had a butter knife for the tension?" asked Amy. "I think now we need a broadsword."

"I don't know how he found out we would be here," Trish said. "But he always does this. He finds me and scares off my boyfriends."

"You posted about your trip online," Mike said. "When I saw the name of the bed and breakfast, it was easy to find out where you were."
"I'm not going to be scared off," Travis told her.

"You say that now," said Trish.

"I mean it."
"Are you super curious about what it is?" Amy whispered to Heather. "Because I am."

"I'm not sure if it had anything to do with Gideon Ridgefield's murder or not," Heather replied. "If it does, then we need to hear about it."

"You don't have to tell me," Travis said.

Amy tried to contain her gasp. She was dying to hear Trish's secret and didn't want him to stop the reveal.

Travis said, "We can pretend this never happened."

"But can we really?" Trish asked. "Won't it always be in the back of your mind now?"

"It doesn't matter," Travis said. "Nothing is going to change how I feel about you. I love you, Trish Hathaway."
"Well, there's your first problem," said Mike. "Her name isn't Trish Hathaway."

"Quiet," Travis told him.
Trish sighed and then started explaining. She kept her eyes on the ground as she said, "He's right though. My name isn't Trish Hathaway. It used to be Trish Bundaloo."

"I could see why she changed it," Amy muttered. "It sounds like a cartoon character. But is that what she's being blackmailed for?"

"I changed it to separate myself from my father, Bryan Bundaloo," Trish said. "I was dating Mike at the time that the scandal broke out. I'm sure you remember the tabloid articles saying: BundaLoopHole. And things like that. He swindled thousands of people out of their life savings. And a lot of people lost their money and lost their homes. I didn't understand it at the time. I didn't know about his business, but maybe I should have. I was a freshman in college when he was found out. I had my name legally changed after the trial. The testimony against him was heartbreaking. He's one of the most hated men in America. And I'm his daughter."

"But Trish, that's him. That's not you," said Travis.

"It scared everyone else away," said Trish.

"Not me," said Travis.

For the first time since they met her, Trish looked happy.

"Now you've tried your worst and caused no damage," Travis said to Mike. "We're in love, and you're not breaking us up. Now get out of here before I cause you any damage."

"Wait a minute," Heather said. "Before we go off to our happy ending or just desserts, there is the little matter of the murder that we need to discuss."

Travis nodded. "Of course. That takes precedence."

"Now, Mike and Trish, you met last night to talk. Is that right?" Heather asked.

"When Travis and I returned from our day out, he had to deal with his shoes, so I went in ahead of him. Mike was there and told me we had to meet that night, or he'd tell Travis everything. I think I was still in shock that he had come here when the Ridgefields came down and started complaining about their breakfast."

"And I thought you looked upset because of the Ridgefields," said Travis. "But Mike must have left before I came in."

"And did either of you go anywhere near the kitchen?" Heather asked.

"No," Trish said. "I went straight from my room to the sitting area where Mike wanted to meet. And then right back."

"I was the same," said Mike.

"Did either of you see anyone else out that night?" Heather asked.

They both shook their heads. Then Trish said, "Wait. I think the sick lady opened her door when I went by. I'm not certain."

"That makes sense with what we've heard," said Heather. "Well, thank you all for your help."

"Thank you," Trish said. "If your investigation hadn't pushed this into the light, I might never have learned how loyal and true Travis really is."

"And I'm glad that no one will try and use your family's past against you," said Travis.

They left together, holding hands happily. Mike looked less than pleased.

"I can't believe I paid for this whole vacation for this to happen," he said. "I wonder if I can make it up to Kylie."

"Fat chance," said Amy.

Mike left anyway.

"Well, that was an unexpected turn of events," said Heather.

"I'll say," Amy agreed. "Blackmail. Love."

"Trish Hathaway isn't Trish Hathaway," said Ryan.

"And it looks like all the fighting and strange behavior between the four of them was because of this romantic drama and family secrets," said Heather. "It doesn't look like it had anything to do with the murder."

"So, this was all a red herring?" Amy asked. "Bring it back to the aquarium! It's in our way."

"So, if the four lovers aren't involved in the murder because their behavior is explained and their movements are now accounted for," Ryan said. "It means we have four fewer suspects."
Heather nodded. "But I'm still not sure who did it."

Amy shrugged. "Wife or mistress?"

## Chapter 16 – Conferring with the Detectives

"How has your investigation been going?" Heather asked.

"It's been smoother than some other cases because we weren't stepping on each other's clues," Detective Smith said.

He and Peters sat on one side of the dining room table while Heather, Amy, and Ryan were on the other. Dave was sniffing to see if there was anything that the forensic team had forgotten to clean up. Thankfully, the forensic team was very thorough, so he wasn't finding anything. They had also placed a tarp over the area where the poisoned jelly might have hit the carpet.

"But difficult in other ways," said Detective Peters.

Detective Smith reluctantly nodded. "It seems that anyone in the house had the opportunity to enter the kitchen and plant the poison last night, but no one was seen doing so. We only know that Mike Crown was out because you saw him, and we think that the woman he argued with was Trish Hathaway based on what Agnes Stewart saw."

"About that," Amy said. "Trish Hathaway isn't Trish Hathaway, and that explains why they were out last night."

"What?"

Heather explained the situation about the lover's triangle and potential blackmail, but how things had righted themselves in the end. Unfortunately, this meant that they were no closer to discovering who had been sneaking around at night to kill.

"The other problem in this case," Peters said. "Is that the suspects either have no motive at all or too much motive. The two couples and the sick woman didn't know Gideon Ridgefield."

"They've told us that, and we've done some preliminary research. There don't seem to be any ties between those guests and Mr. Ridgefield. Though we will keep combing through their backgrounds, and we will look under the name Trish Bundaloo now."

"And Cara Ridgefield and Marigold Fanning both have major reasons to want to hurt Gideon Ridgefield," said Peters.

"The other woman," said Amy.

"Exactly," he agreed.

"But there's no evidence to link them murder right now," said Detective Smith. "Marigold Fanning's prints were on the jelly, but you all saw her touch the jar at breakfast. Other than that, there is no concrete piece of evidence to point out who planted the poison."

"Well," Amy said. "What about we start from a gut reaction? Who do you think did it?"

"My gut is confused," admitted Heather. "Both of them had means, motive, and opportunity. But I don't have a strong feeling that one of them did it."

"The wife didn't seem especially upset about her husband's death," Amy said. "And not that she didn't have reason to be mad at him. But she was more upset by Dave's fur than the need for a funeral."

"And she did refuse to eat the jelly at breakfast," Ryan said. "We can't forget about that."

"Everyone else at the table could have had the jelly if they wanted to deal with Mr. Ridgefield, but she was the only one who was asked to try it and refused," said Amy. "Though I would have done the same thing if that guy told me something tasted funny and to try it."

"Everyone else at the table," Heather repeated to herself.

"Did you think of something?" Amy asked.

"Not yet," said Heather. "An idea, but not fully formed. But don't stop on my account. What do you think of Marigold as the killer?"

"She also had a motive," said Peters.

"And because she was alone, no one could back up her alibi of being in her room all night," said Detective Smith.

"I can't decide if her eating the jelly was an accident that luckily didn't turn into another tragedy, or if it was a clever move to avoid suspicion," said Ryan.

"Again, I have to say, it's not working," Amy said. "We're still considering her a suspect."

"Because she was also the one who piled the jelly on top of his pancakes," said Ryan.

"But apparently by this time everyone had heard about how he wanted this special jelly," Peters said.

"I don't know if it's her," Amy said. "Dave liked her a lot."

Heather suddenly shot a look at Dave. He wagged his tail in response.

"A wagging tail and a wet nose," she said.

"What's that?" asked Detective Smith.

"Have you ever heard the saying that wagging tails and wet noses were the surest sign there was good in the world?" Heather asked.

"No," the detective said. "It's a nice little saying, but I haven't heard it before."

"I don't think it is that common," Heather said.

"You have that look on your face," Amy said. "Did you solve it? Was it Marigold?"

"Trish Hathaway wasn't Trish Hathaway," Heather said. "I wonder if it could happen again."

"So, Trish did have something to do with it?" Amy asked. "I thought we cleared her of involvement."

"Where's the background information that you have for all the guests so far?" Heather asked.

Detective Smith handed her a file. Heather flipped through it.
"Aha," Heather said when she came across a copy of a driver's license. "Ames, how tall would you say Agnes Stewart is?"

"I don't know," Amy said. "She was shorter than you."

"Exactly," said Heather. "She's not five foot ten."

"What does this mean?"

"It means that Agnes Stewart is lying. And I think I might know why."

## Chapter 17 – Confession

Heather entered Agnes's room and saw the woman was in bed again. Amy and Ryan followed her inside.

"How are you feeling?" she asked.

"About the same, I'm afraid," replied Agnes.

"You must be feeling somewhat better," said Heather. "You started packing."

"I've been working on it for little bursts of time," said Agnes. "I still feel weak, but I'd like to go home when this is all over."

"I'm afraid that's not going to happen," Heather said.

"What do you mean?"

"I mean that we know that you killed Gideon Ridgefield and you'll have to go to prison for it."

"That's ridiculous," Agnes said. "I've been sick all weekend."

"The perfect cover for not being at the breakfast table and having to avoid the poisoned food," said Heather. "But I know you had another reason as well."

"What reason could I have for killing a man I never met?" Agnes demanded.

"It's true that Agnes Stewart never Gideon Ridgefield before. But you're not really Agnes Stewart, are you?" Heather asked.

"Of all the rude things to imply," Agnes said. "I'm a liar and a killer and fraud. Is that right?"

"That's right," said Amy.
"I'm not feeling well, and I'd like to lay down," Agnes said. "I think you should leave."

Agnes began coughing, but this time they did nothing to help her.

"We know you're not sick," said Ryan.

"We came to give you the opportunity to confess before we had to take action to prove what you've done," said Heather. "Do you want to take the opportunity?"

"I have nothing to confess," said Agnes.

"Very well," said Heather.

She looked to the door and saw Detectives Smith and Peters supporting Marigold as she walked through the door.

"I still don't understand any of this," Marigold said. She looked even more confused as she saw who she was facing in the bedroom. "Rose?"

"Shhh," Agnes said, quickly jumping out of bed. "My name is Agnes Stewart."
"What are you talking about? What is going on here?" Marigold demanded, "Why has my sister been brought here?"

"Marigold, you're going to ruin everything," Agnes said.

"I'll deal with this, Rose," Marigold replied. "Detectives, why did you drag my sister here? I can't tell you any more about the case. And I didn't kill Gideon."

"We know," said Peters.

"And we didn't drag your sister here," Detective Smith said. "We'd like you to meet the other guest here. The woman who has been sick in her room the whole time. Agnes Stewart."

"I told you that you were going to ruin everything," Agnes / Rose said angrily.

"I don't understand what's going on," said Marigold.

"Did your sister know about your affair with Gideon Ridgefield?" Heather asked.

"Yes," said Marigold. "She thought it was a bad idea. She didn't approve."

"How could I?" Rose asked. "He treated you badly as a secretary, and he treated you worse as a significant other. He was never going to leave his wife."

"I didn't ask him to."

"You weren't going to get what you wanted from him," Rose said. "You were never going to have a family with him. All you would ever get was a paycheck."

"Take that back," said Marigold.
"It doesn't matter now," Rose said. "You're better off now. You're free of him. Now you can find somebody who will treat you right."

"And that's why you killed him?" Heather asked. "To protect your sister from a bad relationship?"

"You killed him?" Marigold asked. "No. Tell me you didn't."

"It was for you," Rose said. "I was trying to save you."

"I ate the jelly too. I could have been killed."

"I didn't think that would happen," Rose said. "You've complained about him before. You told me about how he wanted that special jelly when he went away. You said he didn't like to share it."

"He thought it tastes funny so he asked me to try," Marigold said.

"You see how much better off you are without him?" Rose asked.

"But why did you have to kill him?"

Instead of answering her, Rose turned to Heather. "How did you know it was me?"

"In the end, it was the height of the identity you chose to impersonate," Heather said. "You did look an awful lot like her picture, but you were much shorter."

"I tried to only talk to people when I was laying down," Agnes said. "But you kept catching me when I was up."

"I'd like to think that's why we didn't pick up on that detail earlier," Detective Smith said. "But Heather saw right through the disguise."

"You and your sister have the same color eyes, and you both mentioned the expression that your mom used about dogs. It's not an extremely common expression. I started to wonder if you had the same mom," said Heather.

"Once one puzzle piece fit into place, the others followed," said Amy. "You pretended to be sick so no one would bother you."

"And to avoid bumping into the one person who would recognize you. Your sister," said Heather.

"Last night you went downstairs and poisoned the jelly you thought only Gideon Ridgefield would eat," said Ryan. "You ran into Heather in the hall and told her that you heard angry voices. It was a great cover story. And later, it had us spending a lot of time chasing the couples around. Because who would suspect the poor sick woman stuck in her bedroom?"

"It almost worked," Rose said. "And I knew there would never be enough evidence to convict Marigold. You would never know if it was her or Cara. It almost worked."

Detective Smith began reading Rose her rights as Detective Peters escorted her out. She stopped to turn to her sister and say, "I wanted to save you from heartbreak."

Then the police led her away. Heather called for Dave to come in from the safety of the other room. He came in and comforted a crying Marigold, and Heather told him what a good boy he was.

## Chapter 18 – Bed and Breakfast at Home

Heather and he crew arrived home late that night, but they decided to celebrate by having breakfast for dinner in Eva and Leila's apartment.

"Since your time at the bed and breakfast wasn't the cool and relaxing time you thought it might be, we decided to bring the breakfast home to you," said Eva.

"As long as there's no elderberry jelly, I'm good," said Amy.

Heather nodded in agreement. Her friends had created quite a spread. There were pancakes, waffles, French toast, sausage, bacon, eggs, and fruit. There were also, of course, donuts that they had picked up from the assistants at Donut Delights.

"It wouldn't be home without the donuts," Eva said.

"And I was still craving the Blackberry Cream ones," said Leila. "So we needed some more."

"What shapes are these pancakes in?" Heather asked as she noticed the unusual sizes.

"Well, those were our attempts at making dinosaur pancakes," said Eva. "We were trying to be festive. But some were more successful than others. Some do look like dinosaurs."

"And some look like the asteroid," said Leila.

They all laughed. Then Heather suggested that they hear Lilly's new dinosaur story. She was more than pleased to read it to them. It was a dinosaur detective story where the T-Rex land detective had to team up with a Pliosaurus water inspector so they could solve a mystery on the beach. Working together, they uncovered the dastardly caper and saved a triceratops from being accused of theft.

"That was a wonderful story," Heather said. "I don't know how you come up with them."

"I don't know," Lilly said. "Maybe the same way that you're able to come up with answers to cases."

Heather smiled. "Here, have a stegosaurus pancake."

"It doesn't look a stegosaurus," Lilly said.

"Maybe if you squint," Heather suggested.

They enjoyed their meal and their time together, and there were no terrible tragedies to ruin this "breakfast."

In fact, Jamie had good news.

"Rudolph Rodney called me this afternoon. He spoke to one of his friends that works in the permit office. It's not going to be such an uphill climb after all. His friend said it should actually only be a few simple forms and choosing the proper vehicle."

"That's great news," said Amy. "See? You were worried for nothing."

Dave barked.

"Do you want to be my first client?" Jamie asked.

The kitten Cupcake felt like she had been ignored for too long and made her presence known at the table.
"Or do you want to be my first client?" asked Jamie. "How do you feel about baths?"

Cupcake made her feelings about baths know by leaping away from him and traveling to Lilly for support. Lilly laughed and pet the kitten to let her know she was safe from baths, at least for this day.

"Now tell us a little more about this case," said Eva. "You solved it very quickly."

"Well," Heather admitted. "There were five of us investigators and one smell-hound on the case. And all the suspects were under one roof. So I guess we were prepared for it. It didn't feel quick though."

Amy agreed. "It felt like we were knocking on doors and figuring out who snuck out for a midnight murder instead of a midnight snack forever."

"But we did catch the killer," said Ryan. "And Bea's bed and breakfast business will be all right in the end. Soon she'll be serving donuts to keep the customers there happy."

"After she installs some more security in her kitchen," said Heather.

"Come on," said Amy. "What are the odds of this ever happening again?"
"How did you know that the person there wasn't who they said they were?" asked Lilly.
"Well, one of the other suspects had legally changed their name, and that got

me thinking whether anyone else could have used a pretend name. The only reason why we knew people were who they said they were was because of their say-so," said Heather.

"But they were already lying about other things," agreed Amy. "Mike was lying about bringing Kylie there for a spontaneous romantic trip. Trish lied about her parents. Cara lied about knowing about her husband's infidelities."

"Right," said Heather. "So, I started thinking about what lie would make the most sense if someone were committing a murder. For this case, it was pretending that they were a person that didn't know the victim. Then it was just figuring out how they were able to maintain this lie. And figuring out the real motive."

"Maybe I'll use that in one of my stories," Lilly said. "A Brachiosaurus could be pretending to be an Apatosaurus so they could commit a crime."

"It sounds like a classic," said Heather.

However, after they finished their doughnut desserts, Heather announced it was time for bed. It was a school night, and Lilly had to get some sleep. After the long day they had all had, the adults were ready to call it a night too.

With a murder solved and permits looking hopeful, Amy and Jamie returned to their upstairs apartment with peace of mind. Lilly went to sleep on the small bed in Lilly and Eva's guest room, while Heather and Ryan set up a blow-up mattress for them to use.

"Goodnight," Eva said.

"Don't let the bedbugs bite," said Leila. "Though I'm sure you'd catch them. You catch every wrongdoer."

Heather and Ryan wished their friends a good night too and then settled in to sleep for the night.

"That was a long day," Ryan said. "But it felt good to be involved in an investigation again."

"You be officially again soon," Heather assured him. "And then you can solve all sorts of cases."

"Will you still be at my side?" Ryan asked.

"Of course."

"Then I can't wait."

They smiled at each other.

"I also can't wait to be back in our own bed," Heather said. "Do think the air conditioner will be fixed tomorrow?"

"I hope so," said Ryan. "These housing problems are adding up."
Heather nodded. Then they both reached for another blanket.
"You don't think it's getting colder in here, do you?" Ryan asked.

"Could the air conditioner be malfunctioning here too?" Heather asked. "But in the opposite way?"

Ryan groaned and pulled the blankets over them. "Just bundle up tonight, and we'll deal with it tomorrow. We already have a professional coming to look at one problem. Why not two?"

Heather was considering whether they really should do something about it that night but fell asleep before she could come to a firm decision. From breakfast to breakfast, it had been a long day.

**The End**

# Book 5 – Pumpkin Glaze & Murder

## Chapter 1 – Donuts and Costumes

"Boo!"

"You don't like the new Pumpkin Donut flavor?" Heather asked her best friend.

Amy laughed. "I love it. I was hoping to scare you so I could sneak off with what you already baked."

Heather returned the laughter and handed her another donut. "You're my bestie. You don't need to scare up donut opportunities."

"It was also more fitting for the season," Amy said before gobbling up her donut.

"Uh oh," Digby said, entering the Donut Delights kitchen. "Amy's here."

"What's that supposed to mean?" Amy tried to ask. It was difficult because her mouth was still full of donut and she was trying to remain dainty and ladylike.
"Just that we're going to need some of these new donuts for the customers," he teased.

"I can't help it if I love all things Halloween, and I love donuts. These Pumpkin Donuts are combining my two favorite things," she said. "I think I'm entitled to some."

"You are," Heather said. "And you can't help loving them. But you can help me whip up another few batches. Digby is right. Our customers are going to want to buy up this flavor."
They began work on the new batch as they continued chatting.

"It's delicious like all your flavors are. And it's perfect for the holiday," Amy said. "I can't believe it's almost Halloween."

"Me neither," said Digby.

"Do you have big plans?" asked Heather.

"My friends and I are going to finally see that cult Halloween movie that's been playing at the classic theater this month *Zombie Pirate Caper.* And then we're having a small party. I'm going to make sure I order some of these donuts for it."

"They're the perfect party snack," said Heather.

"But I still need to finish making my costume," said Digby. "I wanted to be a superhero this year. Because, you know, I am super."

"Super dramatic," Amy joked.

"A super assistant," Heather said instead. "You'll just have to make sure that you don't get your cape stuck in any batter if you wear it here."

"My dilemma has been not wanting to wear tights," said Digby.

"I'm having trouble with my costume too," Amy said. "Jamie has an idea for a couple's costume, but it's silly. I'm trying to come up with a better idea for us, but if I don't, then I'm going to be stuck wearing it."

"What is it?" Digby wondered.

"I'm not telling," Amy said. "And I'm hoping I won't have to show it either."

"Fine," Digby said. "What about you, boss?"

Heather wrinkled her nose in annoyance. She had mentioned how at her first Donut Delights location her employees had called her "boss" to tease her, and now the new shop was picking up the habit.

"My costume is all set," Heather said. "But I'm keeping it a surprise. My bigger dilemma is finishing Lilly's costume. She gave me a tall order. And I do mean tall."

"Giraffe?" Digby guessed.

"Apatosaurus," said Heather.

"Lilly is the most awesome kid," Digby said.

"I'm glad you think so," said Heather. "I agree. And I can't wait to go trick or treating with her this year."

"Hopefully it's all treats like these," said Amy. "And no tricks. We've had enough tricks with our investigations this year."

"Boss?"

Heather looked up and saw Nina, another assistant, poking her head into the kitchen.

"There are some people here to see you," Nina said. "But a duo you'll be happy to see."

"A treat already," Heather said. "Digby, will you finish these donuts up?"

"Of course," Digby said. "I am a super assistant."

Heather and Amy followed Nina to the front of the shop and saw their favorite customers and friends were visiting. Eva and Leila were two senior ladies who, at the moment, were trying to contain their giggles.

"What are we walking into?" Amy asked. "Is something going to jump out at us?"

"Of course not," said Eva.

"We just wanted to see what you thought of our Halloween costumes," said Leila.

Heather and Amy exchanged a look. They hadn't noticed that the women were wearing a costume.

Heather put her keen eye towards examining their ensembles, and her sleuthing senses kicked in. She laughed and shook her head.

"They're wearing each other's clothes," Heather explained.

"We're dressing up as one another," Eva said.

"And so, when we're in costume if you call out Leila, then both she and I will respond. Me because I'm the real Leila, and Eva because she's pretending to be

Leila. And if you call out Eva, then Eva will respond. But I will also be Eva."

"I'm glad you didn't choose a confusing costume," Amy said wryly.

"You know," Heather said. "If you're really going to sell this costume you're going to have to switch to each other's hairstyles and colors as well."

"I suppose she's right," Eva said.

"If we can't find an appointment with a hair stylist, it's going to be rather difficult on our own," said Leila. "It's a distinctive shade of blue."

"Perhaps we should figure out another costume," Eva sighed. "If it took a moment for our best friends to realize what we were dressed as, it might be impossible for the people we just met."

"I know someone who will recognize it," Leila said.

"Oh, don't start that," said Eva.

"Who?" asked Amy.

"A certain gentleman at the senior center who has been trying to impress Eva," Leila blabbed.

"Trying and failing," said Eva. "I'm not interested in romance right now. Especially from the likes of Vincent."

"He is going to be all the Senior Halloween Ball," said Leila. "And I think that's why she wants to change costumes now. To look impressive there."

"I do not," said Eva. "I don't care what he thinks. And we could dress as slugs for all I care."

"As slugs?" Leila asked. "If we start crawling around on the ground, I don't think we'll ever get up."

Eva groaned. "Heather, can you end this fight for us? Can you provide us with some donuts to stop our mouths from running when they have to chew?"

Heather promptly presented them with some donuts, and the women smiled at them.

"They're orange," Eva said. "Is it the flavor I think it is?"

"This is the Pumpkin Donut," said Heather. "A simple and sweet pumpkin flavored based, covered with a sugary glaze."

"Pumpkin perfection," Eva declared.

"Pretty, pleasing and perfect," Leila added.

"Please," Heather said, adding one more "P" to the conversation. "You'll embarrass me."
"We'll stop with the alliterations if we get some more donuts," Leila said.

Heather happily handed them another one, and then asked, "If you go to the Senior Halloween Ball, will you still be free to go trick or treating with Lilly and us?"

"Yes," Eva assured her. "We wouldn't want to miss that."

"Especially in her dinosaur costume," Leila said.
"The senior party is in the afternoon," Eva said. "So, we can still go to the parade with everyone in the morning and trick-or-treating that evening."

"I'm excited about the parade," said Amy.

"It does sound fun," said Heather. "But I'm most excited for going door to door with candy with Lilly. I hope nothing gets in the way of that."

"Don't say that," Amy said. "That's like inviting something to come along and disrupt our plans. And since it's Halloween, it's bound to be something scary."

Even though it was a clear and tropical day, they could have sworn they heard a boom of thunder. Then a woman in black flowing skirt sauntered inside.

## Chapter 2 – The Woman in Black's Invitation

"Is anyone else getting a strong witch vibe?" Amy asked.

Heather shushed her. Even though it was the week of Halloween, most of the residents and tourists on the streets were still wearing shorts and T-shirts. This woman was in a full-length layered black dress and corset. Her hair was also long and black. She had dark eyeliner on but refrained from black lipstick. Instead, she wore a dark maroon color on her lips.

She looked out of place is the bright and cheery Donut Delights shop. She also didn't look pleased to be there. She glared as she glanced around the store at the clean and colorful donut display.

"You're sure this is the right place?" she asked as another woman joined her. The only black this other woman was wearing was a T-shirt that advertised for a Halloween "Boo"ze Cruise. She had her pale hair pulled back and looked annoyed with the situation.

"Yes," she said. "I'm sure."

The woman in black surveyed the donuts. Nina was nervously cleaning the counter, afraid that the woman might cause a disturbance.

"Can I help you?" Heather asked.

"Possibly," the woman said. "I am Lucrecia Gravely."

"Gravy?" Amy asked. "Like what goes with potatoes."
"Gravely," said Lucrecia. "Like a grave. Like where corpses are buried."

"Oh. That's different," said Amy.

"I'm the party planner for a Halloween booze cruise operating this week. We're going to have to add some more desserts to our menu because our guests have been hungrier than anticipated. My assistant suggested I come here."

"I'm Tanya," said the assistant. "I heard that you have specially flavored donuts. I thought you might have something for Halloween."

Digby arrived at that moment with the fresh batch of Pumpkin Donuts. The doubt disappeared from Lucrecia's eyes as she smelled the freshly baked pastries.

"Why don't we have a seat?" Heather suggested.

Eva and Leila said their goodbyes after Heather promised to update them on whatever happened with the ladies from the cruise.

Heather and Amy sat down with Lucrecia and Tanya who happily sampled the new flavor.

"I'm sorry I doubted you," Lucrecia said. "When I entered and didn't see any decorations, I thought that you weren't enthused for Halloween. It made me suspicious of the treats you'd make."

"I suppose we could add a few decorations to the shop. At least a pumpkin or two," said Heather. "I suppose I wasn't focused on the décor because we opened so recently. I'm still getting used to the regular beachy theme of the place."

"Now," Amy said. "You've been to the donut pumpkin patch. Are you going to pick them?"

"I would love to order a large order of these donuts from you," Lucrecia said. "I think they would be perfect for our cruise."

"What sort of cruise is it?" Heather asked.

"It's an evening cruise," Lucrecia explained. "It's not a multi-day cruise. It's a ship that goes out for a few hours in the evening so guests can dress up and party. We operate all Halloween week. Obviously, some nights are busier than others, but there are some people who like to party every night. And we do have a lot to offer."

"Like what?" asked Amy.

"There are, of course, fun drinks and snacks," said Tanya.

"And you're on the deck of a ship with a view of the waves with the moon above it and surrounded by the crisp night air," said Lucrecia.

"And in addition to all the joys of a regular booze cruise, the Halloween one has some fun activities," said Tanya. "There's a dance floor and some black light dances to make things feel creepy. There's some bobbing for apples if you feel like a classic game. And the Captain will give a prize to his favorite costume at the end of the night."

"There will also be a screening of that cult classic that has been playing so successful after its restoration: *Zombie Pirate Caper*," said Lucrecia.

"How could I forget that?" asked Tanya. "It's been so popular lately."
"We've been so busy with the shop and investigating cases that we haven't had a chance to go to the movies," said Heather. "Is it good?"

Tanya shrugged.

"It's a little cheesy," said Lucrecia. "But it is enjoyable. It was made about thirty years ago but was just remastered and rereleased. Actually, one of the men from the classic movie theater helped with its release: Jason Myers. We're presenting it on our ship because of his help too."

"It does sound like a good time," said Heather.

"I'd love to invite you both to it," said Lucrecia. "You'd have to pay for drinks, but I can give you tickets to board. For both of you and your dates. Then you can see what a great time it is."

"Thank you so much," said Heather.

"I can give you tickets to any day except Halloween," Lucrecia said, realizing.

"That's fine," Heather said. "I have plans with my daughter on Halloween anyway."

"Then we'll be pleased to see you all and hope that you dress up," said Tanya.

"But beware," said Lucrecia with a twinkle in her eye. "There might be dead bodies on board."

Then, Heather and Amy caught each other's eye and shrugged.

"I suppose we've seen our fair share of them," Heather admitted.
Lucrecia hadn't expected that response, but still said, "Our musicians are all dressed as skeletons."

## Chapter 3 – Preparing to Board

Heather looked at herself in the deerstalker hat in the mirror's reflection and smiled. She didn't need the magnifying glass in her hand to tell it completed the look. She and Ryan had agreed to dress up as Sherlock Holmes and Dr. Watson for Halloween and were putting on their costumes early for the Halloween Boo-ze Cruise that they were going to board that night.

She made sure that her red hair was hiding in the cap and practiced the line, "Elementary, my dear Watson." She knew that he never really said that phrase in the book series, but it would be expected of her to say it.

She was excited about the cruise. She hadn't been on boats very often and thought this was a fun opportunity to board one. She was looking forward to dancing with her husband and was dying to see what Amy and Jamie had dressed up as. She also never gave up the chance to see her donuts enjoyed at events.

"What do you think?" Heather asked as she modeled for her daughter.

"I better not commit any crimes because Sherlock Holmes would find me," Lilly answered happily.

"You better not be committing crimes anyway," Heather teased.

Ryan entered the room ready to show off his costume as well but then froze in his tracks. He was also in a deerstalker hat, coat with a cape and balancing a pipe in his mouth. Heather was staring at a second Sherlock Holmes.

"I thought we were going to be Holmes and Watson," Ryan said.

"Me too," said Heather.

Then they both burst out laughing.

"I guess we both think that we're the master detective," Heather admitted.

"And we both are really skilled," said Ryan.

"Technically, Holmes was a consulting detective and not on the force," said Heather. "I guess that might be why I thought I'd be him."

"Either way," Ryan said. "We couldn't solve our cases without our partner at our side."

"Eva, check my temperature. I'm seeing double," Leila said as they entered the room.

"I'm seeing double detectives too," said Eva.
"We seem to have had a miscommunication," said Heather. "So, they'll be two Sherlocks tonight."

"Hopefully, the cruise won't need your particular sleuthing talents, and you can enjoy the evening," said Eva.

"Thanks," Heather said. "How is your costume planning coming along?"

"Not so well," Leila admitted.

"But we hoped that Lilly might be able to help us with some ideas when we babysit tonight," said Eva.
"I'd be glad to," said Lilly.

There was a knock at the door, and Heather hurried to open it and see what her bestie's couple's costume was. She stood puzzled for a moment and then grinned.

Amy was dressed as a black cat, complete with a long tail and pointy ears. Jamie was dressed as a spotted dog with long ears. They were both wearing galoshes and holding umbrellas.

"Raining cats and dogs?" Heather asked.

"I told you that they'd know what it was," Jamie told his girlfriend.

"That wasn't my concern," Amy retorted. "It was that this is a silly phrase to dress up as."

Jamie shrugged. "I think it's cute and no one else will have the same costume."

"I think you're right about that," said Amy.

"And it might even help my business," said Jamie. "It would be easy for me to talk about my new pet grooming business opening soon if I'm already dressed as a dog."

Dave and Cupcake ran out from the other room to join the gathering. The dog and kitten stared at Amy and Jamie with their heads tilted. Then Dave wagged his tail.
"I think they like your costumes," said Heather.

"I'm glad someone does," Amy muttered. But then she smiled at Jamie and said, "Sorry. I'm being catty."

He groaned but otherwise accepted the apology.

"Wait a second," Amy said. "Why are there two Sherlocks?"

"We didn't investigate properly," Heather said.

"But we should get going," said Ryan. "We don't want to ship to set out without us."

"Bon voyage," Eva said.

The costumed friends smiled and departed while Lilly, Eva, and Leila waved goodbye. Dave and Cupcake danced around, excited for the night's babysitting because they were sure that there would be donuts involved.

***

Ryan parked, and the friends emerged from his car near the ship's dock.

"That's impressive," Amy said. "I don't think we're going to need a bigger boat."

"This is going to be fun," said Jamie.

"Halloween dancing and donuts," said Heather. "What more do we need?"
"Well, maybe we can check out that movie that everyone has been talking about," said Amy.

They started walking towards the ship when suddenly Heather shivered.

"What's wrong?" Ryan asked. "Don't tell me you're scared of the Halloween party."

"No," Heather said. "I just had a creepy thought, and I suppose it scared me."

"What was it?"

"Well, if a murder occurred tonight, we'd be stuck on the ship out at sea with no way to escape," said Heather. "We'd be trapped with a murderer."

"That's scarier than the vampires and ghosts and goblins," said Amy, holding her umbrella close.

"But I'm sure we won't have to worry about it," Ryan said. "And if we did, there would be two Sherlocks on the case."

## Chapter 4 – Arriving at the Party

Heather and her friends walked up the ramp to board the ship but had to pause as the line in front of them stopped too.

"I think they're checking bags before we board," Ryan said.

"Maybe they're checking to make sure that no one is really a werewolf or a ghoul," Amy said, and then she looked at the crowd. "Or a zombie pirate."

They looked at the other partygoers in line and noticed a distinct trend. Most of the men were wearing shabby blue pirate coats, tall black boots with a bone seeming to come out of one, and a large feathered hat with a skeleton parrot sitting on it. The degree of zombie makeup on their faces varied from monster to monster.

The women were dressed in short red dresses, wigs with long black hair and big pirate hats. They were also wearing varying degrees of zombie makeup, and most of them were carrying a fake sword.

"I guess we missed the memo," Amy said.

"It must be from that movie we keep hearing about," said Heather.

"Well," Amy said to Jamie. "You were right. No one has the same costume as us."

They made their way easily through the security checkpoint when it was their turn, and then they saw Tanya right before they boarded.

"I'm checking tickets and reservations. It's also a booze cruise, so I do need to check IDs to make sure that everyone is over twenty-one," Tanya said.

"Does she really not think we're over twenty-one?" Heather asked, realizing she was approximately double that particular age.

"I'm not complaining," Amy said.

Tanya finished checking them in. She placed a sticker on each of their costumes to prove that they were cleared to enter and wished them a spooky and fun evening.

The friends walked onto the ship and admired how detailed the decorations were. There was a graveyard area and a haunted house area, and as promised the band was dressed as skeletons.

"I'm pleased to see some variety in costumes," Lucrecia said when she saw them. She was dressed as a vampire. There were some touches of red in her mostly black outfit. Her long black hair was pulled back into a braid. There were fangs on her teeth, and her makeup made it look as if blood had dribbled from her mouth.

"Thanks," Jamie said. "I was pretty proud of this idea."

"It's cute," Lucrecia said. "There are so many pirate zombies. They must have heard the news."

"What news?" asked Heather.

"Jason Myers is onboard tonight," said Lucrecia. "He might give a little talk before the movie plays. However, I think he is here mostly as a guest. I hope the other guests aren't disappointed to find him drinking and dancing instead of talking about zombie pirates all night."

"Well, we won't be disappointed," Amy said. "We still haven't seen the movie. Though we've seen tons of zombie pirates on board tonight."

"They won't be eating brains tonight though," said Lucrecia. "They'll be enjoying the dessert spread that includes your donuts."

"I hope everyone enjoys them," Heather said.

"I'm sure they will. Unless their taste buds have died," said Lucrecia. "But I should get going. I should make sure that all my bat wings are fluttering properly and that we're all set to sail."

"You do pay attention to every detail," Heather said. "Your décor is amazing. I can see why you were disappointed by what was in our shop."

"I love Halloween," Lucrecia said simply. "The monsters, the horror, the death. What's not to love?"

With that, she left them. Amy shrugged.

"Part of me feels the same," she said. "I do love the contained creepiness. But I would mention candy rather than death."

"Why don't we check out the candy and snacks now?" suggested Heather. "And then we can decide what else we want to do. Movie or dancing."

"I think I'd like to try one of those poison apple martinis," said Amy.

They were headed towards the food when they ran into a man in a captain's uniform.

"Are you the captain or in costume?" Heather asked.

"Captain Braxton," he said, shaking their hands. "Captain of this ship and the chaos of the evening. Though Lucrecia tries to keep the party in order for me, so my first mate and I can focus on the sailing."

"Tell me, Captain," Amy said. "Are you concerned about all the pirates on board?"

Captain Braxton laughed. "I think we'll survive. Even if they are zombie pirates."

"People sure seem to love this movie," Heather commented.

"Yes," the captain said. "The one thing I'd be concerned about is having Jason Myers onboard. I wouldn't want fans to get unruly trying to talk to him. He's a bit of a local hero because he found and saved the movie. If you don't mind a bit of gossip from an old seafarer."

"Not at all," Amy assured him. "As long as it's not too salty."

He smiled, but then said, "I heard the fame is going to his head. He's become a heartbreaker. There were disturbances at his theater from his ex-girlfriends."

"Do you think it's possible that one of them boarded tonight?" Heather asked.

Captain Braxton shook his head. "Jason Myers gave us the names of the women who caused the disturbances, and Tanya has been checking IDs as guests board."

"So, she didn't really think there was a chance we were under twenty-one?" Amy asked, sadly.

"I'm afraid she was matching whether the guests who made reservations had identification to prove they were the person they said they were," he said. "But you do both look lovely."

"This does seem like rather a dramatic situation," Heather said. "Setting out a ship with a man who has many friends and many enemies."

"I'm sure it will be fine," said Captain Braxton. "Everyone has come here to party and not to cause trouble."

Then they heard an ear-piercing scream.

## Chapter 5 – Screaming and Yelling

"This way," Ryan said, starting to lead them by the ambient battery-operated candlelight towards the source of the scream.

"Wait," Captain Braxton said.

"Don't worry," Ryan said. "Even though it looks like it, we're not just blindly running towards danger. I'm a detective soon set to join the Key West Police Force. And these women are talented private investigators."

"I'm just a dog groomer," Jamie admitted. "But I help where I can."

Captain Braxton followed them as they hurried towards where the scream originated. They breathed a sigh of relief when they saw that it was all part of a Halloween show, and not a person really in need of help.

A skeleton band member had screamed to get their attention. When she had it, she said, "Well, we know you're all dying for the music to start. So, we're not going to make you wait anymore!"

The band started playing, and Lucrecia's bats fluttered to life. The guests enjoyed the show, and some started dancing.

"I'm sorry," Captain Braxton said. "I tried to let you know."

"It's all right," said Ryan.

"We're just glad that nobody really needs our help," said Heather.

"Now that I know that I have detectives ready to help if I do have any issues, I'll be sure to call for you," the captain said. "It's nice to know they're not just costumes."

He thanked them and left to prepare for departure.

"Well, I could really use that drink and those snacks now," said Amy. "And then I think I want to sit down for a while."

"I'm fine with that," said Heather. "Let's stock up on snacks and then check out the movie."

"The food is afoot," Ryan joked in his best English accent.

***

Heather and her friends enjoyed their snacks and then moved into the area designated for the movie viewing. It was decorated like an old theater. There were fake cobwebs amid the curtains and candelabras, and Heather wouldn't have been surprised to see a phantom make a grand entrance.

"This movie better be good to drag me away from the donut table," Amy said.

"You brought half a dozen with you," Heather pointed out.

"I didn't know how long the movie would be," she responded.

"I'll take one off your hands," said Jamie.

"You're taking one of my donuts?" she asked.

"Don't fight like cats and dogs," Heather teased.

Before Amy could do anything more than groan at the comment, a man stood up in front of the crowd assembled to watch the movie. He was also in the costume that so many men were wearing, complete with the blue pirate jacket and boots.

"Hello everyone," he said with a dramatic wave of his big hat. "I am Jason Myers, the man responsible for finding this treasure and sharing its bounty with you all. Based on your costumes, I can tell that you're all fans. And, you're welcome."

He sat back down. The crowd grumbled, but only one person let their annoyance at the short introduction bubble over into action.

One female zombie pirate in a red dress with a foam sword jumped to her feet and stomped over to where he was sitting.

"That's the speech you're going to give? That's the speech you give to the people who support you and back you? You're welcome? That's it?" she demanded.

"Celia, get out of here," Jason Myers said.
"Oh? So now I can't even be in the same room as you?" she yelled. "I knew you were a lousy cheating boyfriend, but I didn't know you were going to cheat all your fans too. And now you think I can't even be in the same room as you? You're too high and mighty to associate with me?"

"You can't be here because you're causing a scene," he said.

"Good," she said. "My scene will be a whole lot better than this stupid movie!"

Ryan and Heather were on their feet, ready to help with the situation. However, Lucrecia beat them to the punch and prevented any violence. The vampire led the zombie pirate lady out of the room.

"An interesting pre-show," Amy commented.

The rest of the film was somewhat entertaining. Heather realized that most of the fans of this movie loved it because it was so easy to mock and laugh at rather than being a truly scary movie.

The two pirates that the guests dressed up as were the main characters of the film. They were pirates slowing turning into zombies that were plundering to find a cure. They planned a heist to steal a potion from a mansion, but it failed to help them.

In the end, the female pirate in the red dress stabbed the male pirate in the stomach, hoping to end his cursed life.

However, this was a not a fatal blow, and a huge fight occurred. Eventually, she severed his head and killed the other zombie. Then she tied herself to an anchor and threw herself into the sea, hoping she would never kill any other humans.

"What was scarier?" Amy asked when it was over. "The storyline about the zombies? Or the special effects?"

Heather shrugged. "I'd like to get another drink and another donut."

"Then, may I have a dance?" Ryan asked.

"I bet you can guess my answer, Sherlock," Heather said with a smile.

The friends had some snacks and then headed towards the dance floor. They had some fun swaying to the music.

"No bones about it," said Amy. "This skeleton band plays great."

Then the lights went out. They weren't concerned that this was anything other than a Halloween party trick because robotic spiders also chose this moment to start dancing around their webs that had suddenly started glowing.

"This must be for that black light dance that Lucrecia mentioned," said Amy.

"Look, I'm glowing too," Jamie said, pointing to the white on his costume.

"Do you want to keep dancing?" Ryan asked, as more guests headed onto the dance floor for the special dance.

"Why don't we look at the waves for a while?" Heather suggested. "That should be calming and romantic."

The other agreed and headed towards the railing. They only enjoyed the peacefulness for a few minutes, however. Then they heard another scream. It was followed by several others.

"Could this be another part of the Halloween show?" Amy asked.

"I've got a feeling it isn't," said Heather. She was soon proved right when another voice joined the screams. Someone yelled, "He's dead!"

## Chapter 6 – The Dead Zombie

Heather and Ryan ran to the dance floor, followed by their friends. The lights had turned back to normal, and this time it was clear that the horror was real. Many dancers had backed away from the dead body, but some were still gathered around it.

Ryan moved forward. "I'm Detective Shepherd. Please clear a space."

The zombie pirates and other costumed guests moved back, and they were able to see who the victim was. Jason Myers lay on the ground with a sword sticking out of his chest.

"The captain needs to be informed," Ryan said.

"I'll tell him," Jamie said, before hurrying away.

Heather moved closer to her husband and surveyed the scene. "I don't think we'll need a medical examiner for this case. The cause of death looks pretty clear."

"Hopefully there were enough witnesses that we can get an idea of what happened," said Ryan.

"What happened?" repeated Amy. "I'm pretty sure the guy was stabbed with a sword. Just like in the silly movie."

"But who did it?" said Heather. "There were many people on the dance floor. That's why we left."

"We'll see what the captain wants to do for the remainder of the voyage," said Ryan. "He'll obviously want to return to shore. But should we keep everyone out in the open where we can see what everyone is doing? Or should we carry on as normally as possible, knowing that the killer cannot escape unless they jump overboard?"

"I can't believe this," Captain Braxton said, as he joined them. He was out of breath after running to get there. "How could this have happened?"

"We should have been worried about the pirates," Amy muttered.

"He was clearly murdered," Ryan said. "Based on the angle, I don't see how this could have been an accident."

"A murder on my ship," Captain Braxton said. "I don't see how this could happen. It was supposed to be a party."

"Captain, how would you like to handle this situation?" Heather asked.

"I don't mind admitting to you I'm out of my depth," Captain Braxton said. "I've been dealing with these party cruises for many years now. There were occasional fights and one or two impromptu weddings. However, I've never encountered this situation before."

"We'll obviously want to return to land," Heather said.

"Yes. Of course," said the captain. "However, this is the most inopportune time in the cruise path. We basically sail out to a certain point and then turn around and return. We're at our furthest point from the shore. We can't speed up our return time by much safely."

"That is bad luck," agreed Heather.

"I suppose you'll have to investigate," Captain Braxton said.

"Are you sure you want us to do that?" Ryan asked. "Not that we aren't willing. But we would understand if you'd want to wait until we return to land and have access to all the police resources."

"No," Captain Braxton said. "A killer is on board, and if we have a chance to catch him earlier, then I want to do what we can."

Ryan nodded.

"We can interview the guests who were dancing and determine what they saw," said Heather.

"And we already saw somebody with a motive to kill Jason Myers," said Amy. "That angry ex of his who yelled at him before the disappointing movie."

"But, Captain, you told us before that you were worried about the crowd," said Ryan.

"That's right," he said. "Though I obviously wasn't worried enough. I never thought it would escalate to murder. But I was concerned both about fans who loved the film too much and any jilted lovers. Though I thought the ones that Jason Myers was worried about wouldn't be allowed on board."

"We'll have to speak to Tanya about the boarding process," Ryan said. "To see if someone could have slipped past her or tricked her."

"Is there anyone we can rule out?" Heather thought aloud. "Besides us."

"My first mate was at the helm with me," said Captain Braxton. "We can both vouch for one another. And if we had both left the controls, then all you passengers would notice."

"I have to admit that because you asked us to investigate immediately, it made me discount you as a suspect," Heather said. "It's great to have a firm alibi to back up my gut feeling though."

"I'll have to talk to Lucrecia and see what exactly she had planned for the evening. I think we should keep the guests away from the dance floor. I want to give them something to do so they don't panic. But I don't want to do anything in poor taste. I wouldn't want the skeletons to jump out and remind people there is a real dead body on board," said Captain Braxton.

"Why don't you show the movie again?" Heather suggested. "For those who want to watch it. We could say it is a memorial."

"Classy move," said Amy.

"And we could see if anyone acts suspicious around the film again," said Heather. "Maybe it will shake something loose."

"Like if it's an obsessed fan, he'll need to watch the movie again. But someone with a guilty conscience might not want to be near it," Amy said.

"But I think the captain's idea about talking to Lucrecia is a good idea," said Heather. "She was so fast dealing with the ex before the movie, and yet she hasn't come to check on this disturbance yet."

"Does she have a sinister reason?" asked Amy. "Could she be the killer?"

"She had as much chance as anyone on this ship," said Heather.

## Chapter 7 – Interview with the Party Planner Vampire

"The veil between the living and the dead has become even thinner this eve," Lucrecia said.

"Sure," Amy said. "But we're trying to figure out who did it."

Heather, Amy, and Ryan had finally found Lucrecia who seemed not to be aware that anything had happened. Her hair was mussed as if she had been wearing a hat, and was surprised to see the trio descend upon her so purposefully.

She had to be informed of the murder but seemed to take it in stride. She led them to a table where they could sit down and discuss the evening's horror.

"They really took things too far," Lucrecia said. "We might celebrate the dead and the undead at this time of year, but we shouldn't cause people to join their ranks. We're not the monsters we dress up as."

"You're the party planner so you know how everything should happen," said Heather. "Did anything go not according to plan before the murder?"

"Overall, things went smoothly. Except for the woman who interrupted the movie," said Lucrecia.

"Right," said Heather. "Her name was Celia, wasn't it?"

"Yes. Celia Curtis," said Lucrecia. "She was one of the women that we were supposed to stop from boarding. Jason Myers said that she had caused a scene at his theater too."

"She was an ex-girlfriend?" Ryan asked.

"It seems like it," said Lucrecia. "But there were suddenly many ex-girlfriends that were angry with him. I think he was seeing many women at once and then they found out about one another. Jason Myers was only concerned about a few of them causing him trouble though. He gave us three names of women to watch out for."

"We'd like to have those names," said Ryan.

"Of course," said Lucrecia. "I only remember Celia Curtis's off the top of my head because of the incident. But I do have the list, and I will get it for you."

"If she wasn't supposed to board, how did she get on the ship?" Heather asked.

"You'll have to talk to Tanya about that," said Lucrecia.

"You think she made a mistake?" asked Heather.

"It's possible," said Lucrecia. "She started off as such a good assistant, but she's been making mistakes recently. She's been distracted. Boy troubles, I think. That's why we had to order your donuts so last minute. She had been in charge of dessert and miscalculated. I thought she redeemed herself by finding your Pumpkin Donuts. But it's going to be hard to redeem herself if she let a killer on board."

"So, you do think it was possible that Celia Curtis's behavior could have escalated to murder?" asked Heather.

"It seems the most likely possibility at the moment," said Lucrecia. "He wasn't killed by any of the ghosts on board. It had to be a person who had a problem with him. However, I don't think that Jason Myers believed his life was in danger. He wanted us to watch out for his exes, but if he really thought there was a chance that someone was going to kill him, he wouldn't have been dancing."

"Where did you take Celia after you brought her away from the movie?" asked Heather.

"I took her to the nurse's station," said Lucrecia. "I told her to lie down on the cot and collect herself. I thought she stayed there, but there wasn't an armed guard by the room. I had to leave her after a while, and I suppose she could have left and committed the murder."

"Where did you have to go?" asked Ryan.

"That's right," said Amy. "You weren't on the dance floor."

"I was taking care of other things," said Lucrecia vaguely.

"This is a murder investigation," said Ryan. "We don't have the luxury of keeping secrets about the party or one's whereabouts."

"After I left Celia, I checked to make sure that everything was ready for the black light dance," said Lucrecia. "The band was still set, and Tanya was going to flip the light switch. Then, after I saw that everything was set for the special dance, I had to visit the storeroom."

"What did you need from there?" asked Heather.

"I was looking for more tombstones to add to the front of the ship," Lucrecia said.

"We had to do some searching to find you," said Heather. "And we didn't see any new tombstones."

"I wasn't able to finish setting them up," said Lucrecia quickly. "Because of the murder."

"I thought we were the ones who told you about the murder," said Amy.

"You were," Lucrecia said. "And so, I wasn't able to continue decorating. I needed to stop and talk to you. I suppose now it doesn't matter. There will be no saving this party tonight."

"Miss Gravely," Heather said. "Did you know Jason Myers before tonight?"

"Yes. We met a few times in regard to his movie and showing it on the ship. Much like my visit to your Donut Delights, I went to his theater. And I offered him tickets to any night of the cruise. He chose tonight."

"Oh, I see," said Amy. "He got to choose any night that he wanted to go. We didn't have the option of choosing Halloween."

"We have Halloween plans anyway," said Heather.

Amy shrugged. "So?"

"Wait a moment," Heather said. "When did Jason Myers choose to come tonight? How many people knew about it?"

"He decided a few weeks ago after we made the deal to show the movie," said Lucrecia. "But we just announced it on our website the other day when he told us that he would make a little speech before the film."

"Yeah. Some speech," said Amy. "Short and pointless."

"This was originally a slow night for the cruise, but after we announced that, we had an influx of ticket sales. Basically, everyone who dressed up as the zombie pirates bought their tickets because of the announcement," said Lucrecia.

"Well, thank you for all your help," Heather said. "We'll be back if we have any more questions."

"Of course," said Lucrecia.

Heather, Ryan, and Amy left her and started walking. They were near the front of the ship, and Heather stopped short.

"What's wrong?" Amy asked.

"The décor here," said Heather. "It's pumpkins."

"Does it make you crave a Pumpkin Donut too?" asked Amy.

"It makes me wonder about what Lucrecia said about the storeroom," said Heather. "She said that she wanted tombstones for the front of the ship. But this is the pumpkin patch section. The two styles of décor would clash. And Lucrecia is very detail-oriented."

"So, she was lying?" Ryan asked.
"I think so," said Heather. "But does it relate to the murder?"

"Let's talk to the witnesses on the dance floor first and see what facts we can establish about what happened," said Ryan. "Captain Braxton and Jamie should have separated the witnesses by now so we can talk to them."

"Yes," said Heather. "Let's question them and see how dancing led to stabbing."

## Chapter 8 – The Crowd of Witnesses

"I'm just glad I could help," Jamie said after they thanked him for his efforts.

Captain Braxton started to explain how they had set things up. His first mate was steering the ship while he dealt with the passengers. They were replaying *Zombie Pirate Caper* for those that wanted to watch it as a memorial. Tanya was keeping an eye on the crowd there.

Captain Braxton had separated the partygoers who had been on the dance floor during the murder into a separate room where they were provided with coffee. Jamie was keeping an eye on them to make sure that they didn't start talking about what they saw before they spoke to the investigators. If they began discussing what they saw with one another before giving their own account, then it was possible that the description of the event could be swayed or altered. "There's a lot of witnesses to talk to and not a lot of time," Ryan said. "Should we split up?"

"Good idea," Heather nodded.

"And I think we should split the Sherlocks up," said Amy. "That way we don't spend half of the interview explaining why there's two of you."

"You and Amy can work together. You're already partners," said Ryan. "Captain Braxton, will you conduct interviews with me?"

"I'd be happy to," said the captain. "I know two rooms that we can use to have these meetings."

They all agreed and were soon set up in the two rooms. Heather and Amy spoke to their first witness. He was a man named James McDonald, and he was one of the many men dressed as a zombie pirate in a blue jacket.

"Is there any chance that this is all part of some sort of Halloween prank?" he asked. "If anyone were going to fake their death, I'd guess it was Jason Myers."

"I'm afraid there's no chance of that," Heather replied. "He's definitely dead."

"But, of course, you would say that if you were in on the trick," he responded. "And you're already dressed up as Sherlock. That's a nice touch."

"And I thought we wouldn't have to discuss the detective costumes," Amy sighed.

"I'm sorry. This isn't a prank," Heather reiterated. "We're treating this as a murder, and we would appreciate your help in telling us anything you noticed on the dance floor."

"Well," James said, trying to recollect everything that happened to determine whether he really believed it was murder or not. "The regular lights went down, and the black lights turned on, so I knew the black light dance party was going to begin. There were some spiders dancing about, and it was cool."

"That was about the time we left," Amy muttered. "Because it was getting crowded."

"There were a lot of people on the dance floor," James said. "And lots of pretty pirate ladies."

"Did you notice Jason Myers on the dance floor?" asked Heather.

"No," said James. "Now that I think about it, it makes sense that he was there, being a part of the party. But I didn't realize it at the time. It was dark. And there were a ton of zombie pirates dancing."

"That is true," Heather said, frowning.

"Hey," James said. "This was even more dangerous than I thought it was before. There were a bunch of us zombie pirates dancing. I have the same coat as him. What if the killer had stabbed me by mistake?"

"It was really dangerous having a sword on the dance floor," Amy said.

"But it was a part of so many of the costumes," said James. "It's an important part of Scarlet Zombie's outfit. That's why it didn't seem weird to see it until it stabbed the guy."

"You saw the whole incident?" asked Heather. "Please tell us everything."

"I was dancing and trying to impress a Scarlet Zombie nearby. Then I saw another Scarlet Zombie with her sword out. I thought it was fake. Like I thought it was a prop at the time. I still didn't think it was a good idea to have it out in case someone bumped into it. But then she walked over to the zombie guy who turned out to be Jason Myers, and she stabbed him," said James. "I think most of froze. We weren't sure it was part of the show or not. Until we saw the guy on the floor. I was looking at him and didn't see what happened to the killer. She just blended in with the crowd and got away."

"But it was someone dressed as the zombie pirate lady who killed him?" asked Amy. "Great. There's only about fifty of them on board."

"Did she have any distinguishing features?" Heather asked.
"In the dark and with the crowd, the only thing I noticed that was unusual was how shiny the sword was. It ended up being for a deadly reason and not just to look cool," said James. "She had the same red dress as everyone and the boots and the long black hair."

"Could you see her face?" Heather asked.

James frowned. "Most of the ladies had makeup on to look like zombies. It might obscure some features, but you could still see their faces. Now that I think about it, she wasn't wearing makeup. She had a zombie mask on."

"The only time you could get away with wearing a mask and not have anyone notice," said Amy, "is at a Halloween costume party."

They asked if he could remember anything else, but he couldn't recall anything helpful. The killer was dressed like the many other women and was average in her size.

Heather and Amy questioned the rest of their half of witnesses and then met up with Ryan and Captain Braxton. They all had similar accounts. A woman dressed as the female zombie pirate in red had stabbed Jason Myers. She was wearing a mask, and no one noticed anything special to differentiate her from the other zombie pirate partyers.

"So, the only thing we're sure of is that the killer is a woman?" Captain Braxton asked.

"And that she had access to a costume and a sword," said Heather.

"Though I didn't get a strong killer vibe from any of the ladies we interviewed as witness, any of them could have been the murderer," said Amy. "And there were a bunch more in the same costume that were on other parts of the ship."

"There was something interesting that our first witness said," Heather thought aloud. "He said it was dangerous because the wrong pirate might have been stabbed."

"I guess he was right," said Amy. "There were a lot of people in costume."

"Exactly," Heather said, starting to walk away.

"Where are you going?" asked Captain Braxton.

"I'm going back on the dance floor," she said.

## Chapter 9 – Dance Floor Crime Scene

The dance floor was a much less happy place than when they first arrived on the ship. Earlier there had been toe-tapping music and creepy décor. Now the lights were shining brightly on the silent area that had been roped off.

A plastic tarp had been secured over the victim and the immediate area to protect it until a forensic team was able to process it properly.

"Do we really have to come back here?" Amy asked, playing with her costume cat tail nervously.

"It was what the witness said about him being concerned that he could have been stabbed by mistake," said Heather. "That got me thinking."

"But can't we think back where we were?" asked Amy. "I've reached my maximum quota for seeing dead bodies for the day."

"What did it make you think?" Ryan asked, ignoring Amy's concerns.

"There were so many people in the same costumes," said Heather.

"And it worked to the killer's advantage to blend in with the crowd," Ryan agreed. "We don't know which female pirate is the killer right now."

"But there were also many male zombie pirates," said Heather. "How do we know that the killer meant to stab Jason Myers? Could the killer have wanted to stab another male zombie pirate? Did the victim not matter, and the killer just wanted to kill somebody? Or did the killer have a way to find Jason Myers in the crowd?"

"Those are an awful lot of questions to find an answer to," Captain Braxton said.

"It does make sense for Jason Myers to be the intended victim because he was the person who was causing drama on the ship," said Ryan. "Fans were eager to see him and could have been disappointed by the speech he gave. At least one ex-girlfriend made her way onboard and caused a scene. Other women were displeased with him. And Lucrecia told us that most of the tickets were sold after they announced that he would be speaking."

"That's right," Heather said. "But that doesn't change the fact that many other men looked like him on the dark dance floor. He was an average height and was wearing the same jacket and hat as everyone else. He was also wearing a decent amount of makeup to give him scars and a green coloring, like many other guests."

"So, if he was the intended victim like we believe he was," said Ryan. "Then we need to determine how the killer found him on the dance floor."

"Exactly," said Heather. "And I have an idea."

"Is everything all right?" Lucrecia asked, approaching the group.

"Besides a man dying on our watch?" Captain Braxton asked. "I suppose so. We're making some progress in our investigation."

"I can get out of your way then," said Lucrecia. "I just wasn't sure if there was something I should be doing now that the party is on hold. I can leave you though."

"Wait," said Heather. "You can help us with something?"
Lucrecia smiled at the thought, showing off her vampire fangs again.

"Can you turn on the black lights again?" Heather asked.

"Tanya was the one to turn them on before," Lucrecia said.

"But you do know how to do it?" Captain Braxton asked. "You could turn them on for us?"

"Of course," Lucrecia said.

She flipped a switch, and the others saw the lights abruptly change, and the spiders on the glowing webs begin to dance.

Heather turned back to thank Lucrecia, but she was already gone. Heather dismissed it. She wanted to find out if her theory was right before she started chasing down suspects.

"Amy, you're going to want to look away because of your quota," Heather said.

Amy groaned and turned away.

"We looked at body already," Ryan said, and then he realized. "But not in the black light."

"I thought maybe the killer had another reason for choosing this time for the kill," said Heather.

Heather, Ryan, and Captain Braxton carefully removed part of the tarp and allowed the black light to shine on the victim.

"What am I missing?" Amy asked, still not looking.

"We discovered how the killer found the right male pirate zombie in the dark," said Heather.

"How?"
"He was marked with a paint or something that can't be seen in regular light but can be seen in black light. It's on his jacket and must have been how he was found in the crowd."

"So, he was marked for death?" Amy asked.

"Yes," said Heather. "And you're going to hate this too."

"What?"

"The marking on him was an X," said Heather. "X marks the spot."

## Chapter 10 – Undead Ex-Lover

"What's going on?" Celia asked.

Heather, Ryan, Amy and Captain Braxton found her sitting in the nurse's station. It was a small room with a cot and some simple medical equipment. Captain Braxton had explained that because they were never too far from shore, they didn't have a real medical professional onboard but that the whole crew was certified in first aid and CPR.

Celia rose. "Am I in real trouble? There are four of you here. One is the captain, and two are Sherlock Holmeses. All I did was yell at somebody. Sorry that it was at a movie event. But he deserved it."

"Did he deserve anything else?" Amy asked.

"Maybe to be thrown overboard," Celia suggested. "Why?"

"Jason Myers is dead," Heather said.

"What?" Celia asked. "How?"

"He was murdered," said Heather.

Celia sat back down and looked pale.

"Where were you after being escorted from the film?" Ryan asked.

"Here," said Celia. "I was here with the vampire lady for a while, and she told me to calm down. Then I just stayed. I was in a bad mood. I didn't feel like seeing anybody or pretending to have fun."

"Can anyone vouch for that?" Heather asked.

"I'm not sure," Celia said. "But I was here."

"Why did you decide to come on the cruise tonight?" asked Ryan.

"I thought it would be fun," Celia said. "I still love *Pirate Zombie Caper*."

"And Jason Myers being on board had nothing to do with it?" Amy prodded.

"I figured if he were on board then maybe I would see if he was stringing anyone else along romantically," Celia admitted. "But I wasn't planning on confronting him. It just happened because of how lousy his speech was. He wasn't giving anything back to the fans of the film."

"He only found it," Amy said. "He didn't create it."

"He's the one who saved the film from never being seen," said Celia.

"Yeah. Thanks for that," said Amy.
"You and Jason Myers had dated?" Heather asked.

"Yes," Celia said. "He made me think I was the only one. But then I started to realize that he didn't want to bring me by his theater anymore. The reason was that he had to keep all his dates separate."

"So he was cheating on you?" Heather prompted.

"He was a dog. He became successful and started having affairs," said Celia.

"I can see how that would upset you," said Ryan.

"Of course it did," said Celia. "He's lucky I didn't consider us to be any more serious. Or... I guess he's not so lucky anymore anyway. How was he murdered?"

"He was stabbed with a sword," said Ryan. "By someone who was wearing the same costume as you."

"Stabbed with a sword? Like in the movie?" Celia asked.

"I suppose that's right," said Heather. "He was stabbed like in the movie, but in real life, he didn't get back up."

"It couldn't have been me," said Celia. "This is my sword for the Scarlet Zombie costume. I still have it. And it's only foam."

She showed them her sword and then forced it into Captain Braxton's hands. He squeezed it and then handed it over to Heather.

"This is foam," Heather said. "But that's not to say that you couldn't have used another sword as a murder weapon and kept this for your costume."
"Where would I have gotten a sword?" Celia asked.

"Where did you get the pirate hat and dress?" Amy countered.

"All right. He was my ex. And he was a bit of a jerk," Celia said. "But I wouldn't have killed him. All I did was yell at him. And it would have stupid to do that and then kill him."

"Unless you were just really, really angry," Amy said. "And you couldn't help it."

"Just because someone was in the same outfit as me, doesn't mean I'm a killer," Celia said, crossing her arms.

"I have another question," Heather said. "I'd like to know more about how you were able to board."

"What do you mean?" Celia asked.
"Your name was on a list to intercept before you got on the boat," Captain Braxton began.

"What?" Celia yelled, displaying the same volume she had when she confronted Jason Myers before the film. "He cheats on me, and now I'm not allowed certain places? Who does he think he is?"

"He gave the crew some names of people to watch out for because they had caused disturbances at his theater," said Ryan. "Did you cause a disturbance?"

"Again. Just yelling," said Celia. "And I thought it was fair game for his patrons and fans to learn he was a dirty, rotten cheat. Because it's true."

"I'd still like to know how you boarded when they were checking IDs before you were admitted," said Heather.
"What name did Jason put on the list?" Celia asked.

"Celia Curtis," Captain Braxton said.

"Curtis is my maiden name," Celia explained. "And that's the name I told Jason. But I haven't legally changed my surname back since my divorce. My ID still says Dozier."

"I wonder if anyone else could have snuck through the checkpoint in a similar way," Amy said.

Heather frowned. She was thinking the same thing.

## Chapter 11 – Talking to Tanya

"Are we doing well?" Captain Braxton asked. "I've never been involved in this sort of thing before? I can't tell if we're getting close to solving the case."

"We've made some progress," Heather said. "Unfortunately, we still have many suspects."

"A horde of suspects," said Amy. "A zombie horde."

"We know that Jason Myers was the intended victim because his jacket was marked so he would glow on the dark dance floor and the killer could find him," said Heather. "And we know it was a woman dressed up as the red zombie pirate."

"She was either wearing a costume already," said Ryan.

"Which is possible because there are a ton of those pirate zombie ladies already on board," said Amy.

"And just added a mask," Ryan continued. "Or she put the costume on only to commit the crime and blend into the crowd, and then she could have changed her outfit again."

"The killer also had a real weapon," said Heather.

"But she didn't use it to eat the victim's brain," said Amy. "She just killed him."

"I think we're doing all right," Heather assured Captain Braxton. "And if we don't figure out who the culprit is before we reach land, then the police will be able to take over. At least we know that the killer can't escape. And without the party distractions and everyone on guard, I don't believe she'll be able to hurt anyone else."
"And not without the sword that Jason Myers is holding onto for us," Amy said.

"We'll know more after we talk to Tanya," Heather said.

They had been walking towards the movie screening as they spoke and finally arrived to meet Tanya. She was standing by a door, watching the crowd.

"Everyone had been very subdued," Tanya reported. "No one had been unruly. However, I'm not sure if anyone has been acting with a guilty conscience. They all seem to just be quietly watching the movie."

"Thank you for keeping an eye on the guests," said Captain Braxton. "But these investigators have some questions for you."

Tanya nodded and followed them to another room to talk. She smoothed her pale hair and gave herself a hug.

"I didn't expect this cruise to be so scary," Tanya said.

"You helped to plan the party, didn't you?" Heather asked.

"I was Lucrecia's assistant, so I did help plan things. I was in charge of the food. That was why I came to you about the donuts," Tanya said. "I didn't realize you were investigators too."

"They're not skills that always go hand in hand," Amy admitted. "But we're pretty good at both."

"Where were you at the time of the murder?" Ryan asked, focusing on establishing everyone's whereabouts.

"I was near the dance floor. I had to turn on the black lights for Lucrecia when the special dance started, and then I stayed by the switch. I was watching the crowd to make sure they were having fun. And then I was waiting to see if Lucrecia would come back and have anything else she wanted me to do before the apple bobbing game."

"But she never came back?" Heather asked.

Tanya shook her head.

"What could you see of the murder?" Heather asked.

"Not very much," Tanya said. "There was a crowd of people dancing, and I couldn't see through them. I thought everyone was having a good time until the yelling and screaming started. I realized that someone must have died because of what the crowd was yelling. And I knew it wasn't part of the planned Halloween show."

"What did you do when you realized someone was killed?" asked Ryan. "We didn't see you when we arrived on the scene."

"I turned the regular lights back on," Tanya said. "That was me. I thought it would be helpful to see more clearly. But then I just stayed by the lights. I didn't know what else to do. I'm only an assistant party planner. Not a police officer. I just waited until somebody told me what I could do to help."

"Because you were a little further back from the crowd, maybe you could see something that the others couldn't," Heather said. "Did you see anyone leaving the dance floor after it happened?"

"It was still hard to tell what was going on," Tanya said. "A lot of people were backing up. I think I saw one of the women dressed as the Scarlet Zombie hurrying away from the floor. It seemed like a natural reaction to me, though."

"Where was she headed?" asked Heather.

"I'm not sure," said Tanya. "Towards the front of the ship."

"Towards the bow," Captain Braxton said, using the proper nautical term.

"Right," Tanya agreed. "I'm sorry I didn't notice more. It all happened so fast."

"That's all right," Heather assured her. "Now we do need to ask something of a delicate nature."

"I didn't kill anybody," Tanya said.

"Lucrecia had mentioned that you had started out as a model assistant, but that recently you've been getting distracted and making some mistakes," said Heather.

"That doesn't have anything to do with what happened," Tanya said. "And it wasn't anything crazy. Lucrecia is just a perfectionist. We needed to order some more desserts. It wasn't a big deal."

"She said this was because of boy troubles?" Amy asked.

"I broke up with my boyfriend," Tanya said. "But I don't think I was doing my job poorly. I think the cruise was a huge success. Until, you know, the murder."

"Is it possible that you made any other mistakes?" Heather asked.

"Like what?"

"Like admitting people on board who you were told shouldn't be?" Detective Braxton asked.

"I checked everyone's ID," said Tanya. "And no one matched the names on the list."

"Celia did say that she used an ID with a different last name," said Heather. "That wouldn't have been Tanya's fault if she let her on."

"Could anyone have boarded without going past your checkpoint?" Ryan asked.

"All the guests that came up the ramp went through me," said Tanya. "I don't know if anyone could have snuck on another way or been a stowaway before the boarding started."

"No," Captain Braxton said. "I always do a check of the ship before any voyage."

"And you checked every guest?" Heather reiterated.

"Yes," said Tanya. "I made sure that they had paid for a ticket and that they were over twenty-one. I checked IDs."

"If Celia could have entered with a different name, is it possible that others could have done the same?" Heather asked.

Tanya frowned. "I supposed it is possible. Most of the guests had zombie makeup on. As long as they had an ID and looked enough like the picture but maybe missing some scars, I thought it was all right."

"Was there anyone who seemed suspicious to you?" Ryan asked.

"Now that you mention it," Tanya said. "There were two women who were acting a bit strangely when they boarded. Most people were talking about how fun the party would be or about the drinks. These two women were talking about a mortgage. And it was if they wanted me to hear about it."

"Could a mortgage have anything to do with the murder?" Ryan asked.

"I think it's time to have a little chat with them and find out," said Heather.

## Chapter 12 – Suspicious Characters

"This is outrageous," one woman said.

"Ludicrous and sensational," the other agreed.

"Just wait until we call our attorneys," said the first one. "Our high-powered attorneys."

"Or our wealthy fiancées," agreed her friend. "They will be most displeased by this."

"You should probably just let us go."

"Ladies, please calm down," Ryan said. "Captain Braxton is in charge of this vessel, and because of our qualifications, he has asked us to look into this case until we reach the shore."

Beneath their heavy eyeliner and zombie makeup, the two women looked pale. One was dressed as the lady pirate in a short red dress, and the other was dressed in a sexy version of the blue outfit.

"But we had nothing to do with Jason Myers's death," said the woman in red.

"We just wanted to have a good time," said her friend.

"Let's establish the basics," Ryan said. "You are Wanda Quigley from Tallahassee?"

They both nodded.
"I mean, I am," said the one in red.

"I just got nervous," said the other.

"You're Lori Atlas from Milwaukee?" Ryan asked.

"Yes. That's me."

"What brings you to Key West?" Heather asked.

"We thought the booze cruise would be fun," said Lori.

"And you came all the way from Milwaukee for it?" Amy asked. "You must have gotten a better drink than I did."

"Well, my friend Wendy is also here," said Lori.

"You mean Wanda?" asked Amy.

"Wendy is my nickname for her," Lori said quickly. "Because…"

"Because I love Peter Pan," said Wanda.

"Did you travel all the way for this cruise not because you thought it would be an evening of fun, but because you knew Jason Myers was going to be here?" Heather asked.

"When you say it like that, it sounds like we might have had something to do with it," said Lori. "Travelling so far."

"I mean it was nice that he was here," said Wanda. "But we would have come anyway. We just wanted to celebrate Halloween."

"Where were you at the time of the killing?" Ryan asked.

"We were getting some drinks and deciding if we wanted to dance some more," said Lori. "We weren't killing anybody."

"Why did you decide to dress as the characters from the *Zombie Pirate Caper*?" asked Heather.

"It's a popular movie right now," said Wanda. "And we thought we could look hot in the boots and hats."

"It's a popular movie in Key West right now," said Heather. "Because that's where the man who found and restored it was from. I know it's starting to make the rounds at other theaters. I didn't realize it had gotten to Tallahassee and Milwaukee."

"Good films travel fast," Wanda suggested.

"And you chose to dress up in the same outfit that the killer did," said Heather.

"I should never have listened to you," Wanda said.

"Me?" Lori retorted. "This was your dumb idea."

"We're going to go to jail. Or like pirate jail," Wanda whined.

"The brig," Captain Braxton added helpfully.
"I don't want to go to brig jail," said Lori.

"No martini is worth this," said Wanda.

"Ladies," Heather said, starting to catch on to what was happening. "Do you have anything you want to confess?"

"No," Wanda said.

"Yes," said Lori. "I'm sorry. I can't keep this up. They think I'm from Milwaukee. I don't know anything about Milwaukee. And I'm a little drunk to begin with."

"Did you kill Jason Myers because you had been drinking?" Amy asked.

"No. We didn't kill anybody. We lied a little bit because we wanted to drink on a cruise, but we didn't kill anyone. We're not Wanda and Lori from Milwaukee and Tennessee."

"Tallahassee," said Amy.

"I knew I couldn't keep it up. We're not from there. We're from the community college. We borrowed fake IDs, so we come on board and party. We thought it would be really fun. We didn't expect anybody to die."

"But that's not our fault," said her friend. "He didn't die because we were underage drinking."

"Please don't arrest us. I think we learned our lesson, really."

Ryan sighed. "I don't think we need to send you to jail. But I do want to impress upon you the seriousness of what you did."

"It's been impressed upon us."

"Very seriously."

"What do you think, Captain?" Heather asked.

"I think they should tell you anything that they saw that might be helpful," said Captain Braxton. "And then they should help the bartenders wash the glasses from the night as penance."

The girls agreed quickly but didn't have much helpful information to add about the crime. They had been by the bar area at the time. They heard screams but didn't know what caused them and didn't see any Scarlet Zombie hurry past them as if they were escaping the crime scene.

The captain led the teens off to go help the bartenders, and the others looked to one another.

"Do we still feel like we are doing well with this case?" Amy asked. "Because I'm not so sure anymore. It's another dead end."

## Chapter 13 – Bag Check, Please

"You think that we didn't do our jobs."

"We think that during a murder investigation, we need to check every aspect of the crime," said Ryan.

"And one aspect is the murder weapon," said Heather. "We need to determine how the killer brought the sword on board."

"I still think it sounds like you don't think that we did our job right."

The investigators were crammed into a small room that the two men who had conducted the bag checks when they boarded had been staying. Because they did not have much to do during the actual cruise, they had been playing cards together.

"Do you really have nothing you're supposed to be doing during the cruise except playing cards?" Amy asked. "This sounds like a dream job."

"We could have stayed on land and only helped with boarding and disembarking," said the smaller of the two men. "But Lucrecia asked us to stay on board in case there were any issues."

"If she forgot we were on board and didn't ask us to do anything, that's not our fault," said his coworker.

"If you're trying to impress the captain, it's not working," Captain Braxton warned them.

"Sorry, sir," they both said, hiding their cards.
"Freddy and Norman have been working with my ship for a while," Captain Braxton explained. "The ship runs for other events besides Halloween parties. They usually are very helpful."

"We just weren't asked to do anything," Freddy said.

"We would have helped if we knew what to do," said Norman.

"We thought we were just supposed to help carry big things or something like that and were waiting for the call," said Freddy.

"You didn't leave this room at all?" Ryan asked.

"No," said Freddy. "We were playing cards."

"But we did keep the door open so we could be found," said Norman.

"Lucrecia walked by at one point but didn't talk to us."
"What time was that?" Heather asked.

"Maybe eight-thirty or nine," said Freddy.

"That would be around the time of the black light dance," said Heather.

"And the murder," said Ryan.

"She was hurrying like she was in a rush or scared or something," said Freddy.

"What was she wearing?" Heather asked.

"Her red and black vampire costume," Norman said. "And yeah. She was in a rush."

"Maybe she really needed those tombstones," Amy said.

"Huh?" Freddy asked.

"She told us that she was in the storeroom trying to find some more tombstones for decoration," Heather explained.

"That's not the way to the storeroom," Norman said.

"Yeah. She was heading in the opposite direction," Freddy agreed.

Heather looked at her fellow investigators. "So, Lucrecia was lying about where she was."

"Suspicious," Amy said, voicing the thought that was running through all their minds.

"I still want to know more about this bag check though," said Captain Braxton. "Is it possible that a guest brought the sword on board?"

"We did do our jobs," Freddy said.
"Yeah. Just because we were playing cards after our jobs were done doesn't mean we didn't do them," Norman agreed.

Captain Braxton gave them a look that made them quiet down.

"Why don't you take us through how your bag check worked?" Ryan asked.
"You went through it," Freddy said. "When a guest boarded, we checked them. If they had a bag, we asked them to open it so we could make sure they weren't bringing anything dangerous on board."

"And nothing dangerous came on board?" Amy asked.

"Not through us," said Norman.

"Did some guests bring weapons on as part of their costumes?" Ryan asked.

"Yeah. A bunch did," said Freddy. "There were a lot of fake pirate swords that were brought on. Especially the ladies in the red dresses."

"That's what we were afraid of," said Amy.

"The guy was killed with a sword?" Norman asked. "Like a real one?"

"Yes," Heather said.

"I'm positive we only allowed fake ones on board," said Norman.

Freddy agreed. "We checked all the swords. They were foam or plastic. The one metal one that we came across, even though it wasn't sharp, we told the lady that she couldn't bring it on board because we didn't want any accidents."

"And she understood. She went back and put it in her car and boarded without it," said Norman.
"We also didn't let anyone bring anything that could be used as a club to hurt someone," said Freddy.

"We wouldn't have thought someone would have done something on purpose. Like what happened. But we were told to stop weapons from coming on. And we knew they'd be alcohol. So, we made the big swords stay off the ship too," said Norman.

"And you're sure nothing could have slipped past you?" Heather asked.

"How big is this sword we're talking about?" asked Freddy.

"Like sword-sized," said Amy before gesturing with her arms.

"There's no way something that big could have slipped past us," said Norman.

"And you saw how short the dresses were for the lady pirates," said Freddy. "Where would they hide it?"

"Especially if it's sharp?" pointed out Norman.

"What if she had an accomplice?" Ryan thought aloud.

"We checked every guest who boarded," Freddy reiterated. "Men and women. Pirate and cat. We didn't let any weapons on board."

"If that's true," Heather started.

"It is true," said Freddy.

"We did our job," said Norman.

Heather continued her train of thought undaunted. "Then it wasn't a guest who brought the weapon on board. It was somebody else."

"Somebody with long dark hair?" Amy asked.

Heather nodded. "I think we need to talk to Lucrecia again."

### Chapter 14 – The Search

"There are definite reasons to suspect Lucrecia," Heather said.

"Besides the fact that she's hiding from us?" Amy asked.

"We don't know that she's hiding," Heather admitted. "We don't know where she is. And are having trouble finding her. But that might not be her intention."

"I still think she probably did it," Amy said. "I got a funny vibe from her the first time we saw her at Donut Delights."

"Well, she did look out of place," Heather said. "But I wouldn't have considered her a killer at the time."

Heather and her bestie were discussing the case as the investigators searched for Lucrecia's whereabouts. Captain Braxton was leading the way with Ryan at his side, as they looked in all the rooms and hiding spots in the ship. So far, they had covered most of the ship, and their search had been unsuccessful.

"Lucrecia knew how the party's events went from start to finish," said Amy.

"That's right," Heather agreed. "And she knew exactly when Jason Myers was going to be on the ship."

"If she wanted to kill him, it would make sense for her to do it when she had some control over the evening," said Amy. "And she controlled when the lights went out."

"As the party planner and someone who communicated with Jason Myers about playing the movie on board, I'm sure she could have come up with an excuse to come close enough to mark the X on him. And it would have been invisible until the lighting changed," Heather thought aloud. "But what could her motive be?"

"Maybe she was a jilted lover too," Amy said. "It sounds like the victim was collecting exes. Maybe he just didn't consider her a threat. Or thought playing the movie was a peace offering. It just turned out to be an offer she refused."

"It's possible," Heather said.

"There are other reasons to think she did it too," said Amy. "Her costume already had some red in it, and she'd have an opportunity to change."

Heather thought about it. "She does have long black hair like the zombie pirate character. And it was a little disheveled when we saw her after the murder as if she had been wearing a hat."

"A pirate hat just like the killer?" Amy suggested. "But of course, the main reason, I think she did it right now, is because we cannot find her."

Heather hurried to catch up with Ryan. "No luck?"

He shook his head. Captain Braxton opened another door, but Lucrecia wasn't inside. Instead, the skeleton band was sitting there in various states of costume. Most of them were half in their skeleton costume and half in street clothes. All were looking confused.

A female guitarist who was dressed in all bones except her face came up to them.

"We weren't sure what we should be doing, Captain," she said. "We knew we couldn't stay by the stage area because of the dead body. We didn't know if we should set up somewhere else, but then we thought that maybe the music was unwanted because of the death."

"What you're doing is perfectly acceptable under the circumstances," Captain Braxton said. "We've been looking for Lucrecia. Do you know where she might be?"

"No idea," the guitarist replied. "If we saw her, we would have asked her what we should be doing."

"I think it's fine if you want to get out of costume and pack up your instruments," the captain told them. "I think you're right about the music for tonight. I don't think anyone will be dancing this evening."

She nodded. "All right. Thank you. I'll tell everybody."

"Before we go," Heather said. "You and your bandmates didn't notice any particulars about what happened tonight, did you?"

"We were focused on our music until everyone started yelling," she said. "I'm sorry."

"Thanks anyway," said Heather.

They left the band to pack up and continued their search.

"I don't see where she could be," said Captain Braxton. "I know Lucrecia could be a little odd, but I thought it was fitting for the Halloween party. I thought she was a nice and capable lady. But not being able to find her is making me nervous."

"We should be back on land soon. Shouldn't we?" Ryan asked.
"In a little over an hour," Captain Braxton said.

"If we can't find her soon, I'm sure a full police force searching the place will," said Ryan.

"Unless," Heather said suddenly, having a troubling thought.

"Unless what?" asked Amy.

"Are there any lifeboats on board?" asked Heather.

Captain Braxton nodded. "Of course. We have some rafts in case of emergency."

"Are any missing?" Heather asked.

"We better check," the captain agreed.

They rushed over to where the safety boats were kept, and Captain Braxton greeted them with some unhappy news. "One is missing One raft that inflates when a string is pulled."

"How could we miss that escape?" Ryan asked.

"I suppose we were distracted at times," Heather groaned.

"This means that the killer got away?" Amy asked. "Lucrecia escaped?"

"It seems like it," Heather said.

"It doesn't make any sense," Captain Braxton said. "If a life raft were blown up to full size and deployed and set on the water, my first mate should have seen it. And he would have told me right away."

"What does that mean?" Amy asked.

"That the killer was either very skilled at their escape and could fool the first mate," said Heather. "Or the killer is holding onto that life raft until a more opportune moment to escape."

"It would be easier for her if she were closer to shore," Captain Braxton agreed.

"But where is she hiding now?" Amy asked. "If she's on board, where is she? Where haven't we looked?"

## Chapter 15 – Lucrecia's Lies

After a disappointing search, they were starting to lose hope. Lucrecia was their main suspect, and if she couldn't be found on the ship, then it was likely she has escaped overboard after all.

"Then it won't matter if we reach land or not," Ryan said glumly. "If she escaped on our watch, then they'll have to get a team to search the seas."

"But if she did escape in a life raft, then she'd have to know it makes her look guilty," Heather said. "When she came home, she'd be caught by the authorities."

"I think Lucrecia Gravely is pseudonym for the Halloween events," Captain Braxton said. "You'd have to track down her true identity."

"Really?" Amy asked. "She chose Gravely as her scary fake name? Does it not make anyone else think of gravy and potatoes?"

Heather shook her head. "But maybe you're just getting hungry. I feel like I haven't had a donut in forever."

"This has been a long night," Ryan said.

"I don't see where she could be hiding," Amy said. "But wherever she is, I hope she's coming up with a scarier last name."

"It's possible that she was moving around while we were moving," Heather said. "Maybe we missed her in our search because we were going in opposite directions."

"Great," Amy lamented. "Let's go do exactly the same thing we did before in case we missed her."

"If she didn't leave the boat, that probably is what happened," Ryan said. "But was it an accident? Or is she purposely avoiding us and hiding?"

"I think before we go on another wild vampire search, I want to fix my cat makeup and have a Pumpkin Donut," said Amy.

"Do you need to do that now?" Heather asked. "We don't have much time left."

"But we're going around in circles," said Amy. "Literally. All around the ship. I might as well fix my makeup, so my confusing, silly costume makes a little bit of sense."

"All right," Heather agreed. "We'll run to the ladies' room for a moment."

"The head is that way," Captain Braxton said.

Heather and Amy entered the small bathroom with two stalls and a large mirror in it. Amy started fixing her cat eyes when Heather noticed something.

One of the stall doors was locked. She looked at the bottom and saw the black shoes that were visible. They were Lucrecia's. She pointed them out to Amy.

Amy shuddered. "I was so convinced that Lucrecia was the killer. But now that we're standing on the other side of the door with those unmoving shoes, I'm scared she's dead."

Heather took a deep breath and then knocked on the stall door.

They waited a moment and then the door opened. Lucrecia pushed some large headphones off of her ears and stared at them.

"What's going on?" she asked.

"We were looking everywhere for you," Amy said. "And I thought you were the killer, and then I thought you were dead, and now I don't know what to think."

"Well, I'm neither of those things," Lucrecia said.

"Have you been hiding here listening to music?" Heather asked.

"I've been here for a bit," Lucrecia admitted. "Listening to something."

"Lucrecia, we were looking for you because we're trying to figure out who killed Jason Myers. The guests' bags and costume weapons were all checked. You're one of the few people who could have gotten a real sword on board," said Heather.

"And you've already got the long black hair that matches the description of the killer," said Amy. "And we saw how it had gotten mussed before. Like you were wearing a hat."

"I wasn't wearing a hat," Lucrecia said. "If it was mussed, it was because of these headphones. Not because I was wearing a pirate disguise to kill someone."

"So, you were listening to the music earlier too?" Heather asked.
"Yes. I suppose I was," said Lucrecia.

"That might account for what we saw," said Heather. "But why were you in here listening to it when so much was happening?"

"What are you listening to anyway?" Amy asked. "Any good music?"

"It's not music," Lucrecia said. "It's a tape to calm your nerves and make you feel more in control. It's therapeutic."

"I could see why you'd need to calm your nerves now after the murder and all the chaos that has happened," said Heather. "But why did you need to listen to it earlier?"

"Unless she needed to calm her nerves because she had just killed somebody!" Amy said.

"No," Lucrecia said. "That's not it."

"Can you tell us what it is?" Heather asked. "We're not trying to pry into your personal business. We're just trying to solve a murder."

Lucrecia must have been doing what her tape had earlier instructed her to do. She counted to ten and took a deep breath. Then, she told them, "I've been facing my biggest fear."

"What's that?" asked Amy.

"Spiders," said Lucrecia.

"Really?" asked Amy. "You seemed to love everything creepy and Halloween-y."

"Not things with eight legs," said Lucrecia. "I've always been terrified of those hideous little things."

"Then why did you include them as part of the party?" asked Heather.

"Because tonight was supposed to be mildly terrifying," said Lucrecia. "And spiders make a wonderful addition to the terror. Their webs also glowed beautifully in the black light. But I couldn't face them. That's why I had Tanya flip the lights. And it's why I left right after. I needed to relax myself and listen to my calming tape."

717

"Why couldn't you just tell us before?" Heather asked.

"That would have been great advertising for my horror businesses," Lucrecia said. "Admitting I'm scared of bugs."

"A lot of people are scared of spiders," said Heather.

"But I'm supposed to be the one instilling the fear with my events," said Lucrecia. "My name is Lucrecia Gravely, for goodness sakes."

"About that," said Amy. "Why Gravely? Why not Gravestone? Or Gravington? Or just Graves?"

"Graves?" Lucrecia repeated, trying it out.

"Gravely only makes me think of gravy," said Amy.

"Lucrecia Graves," she repeated back. "I like the sound of it."

"I solved one thing that's been bothering me," Amy said.

"I wish we could solve another," said Heather. "But if we've just dismissed Lucrecia as a suspect because she was in the bathroom the whole time."

"And that must have been where she was headed when Freddy and Norman saw her," Amy added.

"Then we still have no idea who the killer is," said Heather.

## Chapter 16 – The Case

Heather, Amy, Ryan, and Jamie were seated around a table, eating donuts to make them feel better about not having the answer to the case. Captain Braxton was checking on the guests and on his first mate.

"I can't believe we're going to be bested by a zombie," said Amy.

"Well, pirate zombies can be very tricky," Jamie said.

"It makes me feel like they did take our brains," said Amy as she took another bite of the donut.

"We were pressed for time if we needed to solve this on our own before we returned to shore," said Ryan. "But we have already done a lot in a short period of time."

"Then why does it feel like the killer is going to get away?" asked Amy.

"Because of the missing life raft," said Heather.

"Why don't you go through what you know so far?" Jamie asked. "Maybe I can help. And I'm all ears."

"In that costume, it's true," said Amy.

"We know it was a woman dressed in the red pirate zombie outfit," said Heather.

"And that she wore a mask, so no one saw her face," said Ryan.

"And that she had a real sword that she used to kill the man," Heather said.
"And she marked him with an X that could only be seen in the black light," said Amy. "So she could find him on the dance floor."
"Could you eliminate any of the pirate lady suspects?" Jamie asked.

"We did dismiss some teen pirates who boarded illegally," said Ryan. "They're working as dishwashers now to make up for it."

"I don't really think it's Lucrecia anymore," said Heather. "The story she told us makes sense and explains her hair and her location. Plus, she never had a good motive."

"The ex-girlfriend Celia had a good motive," said Amy. "But the sword she had was definitely foam. And the bag checkers are adamant that a guest couldn't have snuck a weapon past them."

"Do you believe them?" Jamie asked.

"I think so," said Heather.

"They were a little lazy when we saw them but seemed to take pride in their work. I don't think they let anything slip by," Amy agreed.

"Then it wasn't a guest," Jamie said simply.

"Well, thanks for all that help," Amy said sarcastically.

"Wait. He's right," said Heather. "When you put it like that, then it's simple. If a guest didn't bring the sword on board, then it had to be an employee. They wouldn't have had to bring their things through bag check."

"And she could have hidden the sword until she wanted to use it on the victim," said Ryan.

"It might have been easier for an employee than for a guest to mark Jason Myers with the X as well," said Heather. "She could have come up with business sounding reason to touch him for a moment, and that's when she applied the marker."

Captain Braxton joined them and asked, "Any breakthroughs?"

"Unfortunately, we realized that it had to one of the employees on the ship who killed him," Heather said. "That's the only way the sword could have been brought on board."

"I hate to think it was someone who worked here," Captain Braxton said. "That someone on my crew could murder somebody like that."

"How do we figure out which employee it was?" Amy asked.

"It had to be a woman," Ryan said.

"Does anyone jump to mind?" Heather asked. "Is there anyone you noticed acting strangely today?"

Captain Braxton shrugged helplessly. "Everyone acts a little strangely around Halloween."

"Captain?"

They looked up and saw the female guitarist from the skeleton band.

"What is it?" Captain Braxton asked, inviting her to join them.

Amy looked to Heather and raised her eyebrows. "This is a female employee," she whispered.

"But the band was playing on stage," Heather whispered back.

"Oh. Right."

"Captain," the guitarist said. "We discovered something strange while we were putting our instruments away. And since you're still investigating, I thought I should tell you. It might be nothing. But maybe it's a clue. We thought it was weird."

"What is it?" Heather asked.

"After we all put away our instruments, we noticed that there was an extra guitar case. It's not mine. And it's not anyone else's in the band."

"What was inside it?" Heather asked.

"Nothing," said the guitarist said. "There was no instrument. And nothing else."

Heather stood up. "But I bet there was something inside."

"The murder weapon," Ryan agreed.
"I think a sword could fit into a guitar case easily," said Heather. "And it was a good hiding place for it. An extra guitar case didn't seem suspicious until it was time to pack up for the day."

"Was it a special case that we could trace?" Ryan asked.

"No. It's a cheap guitar case that you could get pretty much anywhere," the guitarist informed them.

"A costume could have been kept in there too," Heather said. "So an employee could have hidden the costume and sword on board, marked Jason Myers with the X, and then disguised herself and found the victim on the dance floor to kill him."

"But who did it?" Amy asked. "Who decided to actually use an X to mark the spot?"

Realization dawned on Heather's face. "I think I just realized when he was marked."

"When?"

"At the same time that we got our stickers that cleared us for entrance," said Heather. "That's when an employee could have touched Jason Myers without arousing any suspicions. She placed the stickers on us."

"Captain, we have a problem," Freddy said. He and Norman piled into the room with them.

"Please tell me that it's only that you found out about the extra guitar case too," said Captain Braxton.
"What?" asked Freddy. "No."

"Remember how you told us to stop playing cards and to keep an eye on the guests and the ship?" Norman asked.
"Yes," said Captain Braxton. "Right after we interviewed you both, I told you that you should help with the situation."

"And we did," said Freddy.

"That's right," Norman said. "We did our jobs."

"But when we went to check on the crime scene area, someone had broken through where it was blocked off," Freddy said. "And so we went to go check on it."

"That's when we saw the dead guy," said Norman. "That's a terrible thing to see."

"But that's when we also saw something else," said Freddy.

"Just get to the point," Amy said. "I can't take the suspense. What happened to the victim? He was already dead."
"It's the sword," Freddy said. "Somebody took the sword."

"Oh no," Heather said. "She must have realized that we were getting close to an answer. She's going to make a break for it."

"With the sword," said Amy.

"And the raft," said Ryan.

"And unfortunately, if my hunch is right," Heather said. "With a hostage."

## Chapter 17 – Hostage Situation

"Tanya?" Heather called.

"I don't like this," Amy said. "Searching for a killer is bad enough. But searching for an armed killer?"

"The guests and band and bartenders are all accounted for according to Freddy and Norman," said Heather. "But Lucrecia is missing."

"Maybe she's just hiding the bathroom again, listening to nice, relaxation tapes," said Amy.

"Or maybe she's in real trouble," Heather said.

"I feel like we're about to get into real trouble too," Jamie said nervously.

Captain Braxton had said that there were two areas of the ship where casting off on the raft would be easiest. He and Ryan had gone in search of one, while Heather, Amy, and Jamie went to the other one.

"Tanya?" Heather called again. "Lucrecia?"

"Stay right there," Tanya yelled as they came into view.

Heather contained her panic as she saw the situation in front of her. Tanya was holding the sword so it was pointed at a frightened Lucrecia.

"Stay there, or I'll make her walk the plank," said Tanya.

"We're getting close to shore. That might not be such a bad idea," Amy said. "That's why you want to raft away, isn't it?"

"Not now, Ames," Heather said.
"Sorry," said Amy.

"We're not coming any closer," Heather announced. "In fact, Jamie is going to leave right now."

She whispered something to Jamie who nodded and ran away.

"What did you tell him?" Tanya asked.

"To tell the captain what happened," Heather fibbed. "You're not going to get away with this. You should just let her go."

"I am going to get away," Tanya said. "I've got a life raft and a weapon and a hostage. I'm getting off this boat and getting to shore. Then I'll figure out a new life. If the others tonight could get a fake ID, then I could too. I can disappear."

"It sounds like you have it all planned out," said Heather, taking a tentative step forward.

"I don't want to kill her, but I will," Tanya said, gesturing with the sword.

"Like you did Jason Myers?" Heather said.

"No," said Tanya with a depraved smile. "I wanted to kill him."

"He was the ex-boyfriend that you mentioned," said Heather.

"And he deserved to die," said Tanya. "He did the same thing to me that he did to a bunch of others. He told us we were the only one, but it was a lie. He broke my heart, and he didn't care at all. He would have kept doing the same thing. And the only reason he would have gotten away with it was because of *Zombie Pirate Caper.* The movie is going to be watched forever."

"Is it?" Amy asked.

"I had to stop him," said Tanya. "He was a monster."

"So, when you heard he was going to be on board tonight, you made your plan," said Heather. "You brought the weapon and costume on the guitar case before the guests boarded."

"Nobody noticed it," Tanya agreed.

"You put the black light X on him when you put on his sticker for entrance," Heather said.

"I added the paint to his jacket when I put the sticker on him. He had the gall to pretend he didn't recognize me," Tanya said. "Can you believe that? After all we've been through? He thought he could just treat me like a nobody. He thought I wouldn't make a scene because I was at work. Well, he made a list of all the women he was worried about. I should have been at the top of it."

"You're reaching the top of mine," Amy said. "I'm worried."

"Me too," said Lucrecia.
"You turned on the black lights for the dance and then changed into the costume that you knew countless others would be wearing," Heather continued.
"It was perfect," said Tanya. "I knew Lucrecia would be hiding when the spiders came on."

"You knew?" Lucrecia said.

"It was obvious," said Tanya. "You couldn't even be around when they were set up."

"Spiders are scary," Lucrecia said quietly.

"I turned on the black lights, changed into the costume and made my entrance onto the dance floor. Then I stabbed him and hurried away. I turned the lights back on to give myself an alibi and threw my mask and costume overboard," Tanya said. "I thought there would be enough people on board that loved and hated him that you would find a suspect who wanted to kill him. I thought I could slip through the cracks once we were on land."

"But when Captain Braxton told the musicians to pack up early, you became worried," said Heather.

"I thought that when you realized that the sword was kept in the guitar case, you'd realize it was an employee. I took the raft earlier, hoping that if you didn't find a guest you liked as a suspect that you might think that a stowaway murderer jumped ship," said Tanya. "But I kept it as a backup plan. And now I'm going to use it and get out of here."

"That's fine," Heather said. "But just let Lucrecia go."
"No," Tanya said. "She's coming with me."

"Please don't hurt me," Lucrecia said. "Wasn't I a good boss?"
"You love being scared for Halloween so much you'll love being a hostage," Tanya said.

"I said let her go." Heather yelled, "Now!"

Tanya didn't react, but something else happened. Suddenly the lights changed to the black lights. The spiders could be seen in the distance, dancing on their webs. Lucrecia fainted to the floor.

Tanya was momentarily confused, and Heather jumped on the opportunity. She pounced forward and grabbed Tanya's sword hand. With Amy's help, the two women were able to make Tanya drop the sword overboard.

Ryan and Captain Braxton arrived on the scene. Captain Braxton checked on Lucrecia, while Ryan helped the others with a struggling Tanya.

"Good news and bad news," Heather said.

"What's that?" asked Ryan.

"The bad news is that the murder weapon is in the water now," said Heather. "But the good news is that we caught the killer red-handed. She was willing to commit a second murder to make her getaway."

"What did she do to Lucrecia?" Captain Braxton asked.

"Actually, that was Jamie," said Heather. "I told him to turn on the dancing spiders when the time was right. It caused

Lucrecia to faint and gave us the chance to disarm her."

"Tanya, we're going to hold you in our custody until we reach the shore and you can be officially arrested by the police," said Ryan.

"It should only be about ten minutes from now," said Captain Braxton.

"Good," said Amy. "Now I've had enough of these tricks. I want more treats."

## Chapter 18 – Treats

After all the chaos of the cruise, Halloween day turned out to be relatively peaceful. Donut Delights sold plenty of Pumpkin Donuts, and Heather had prepared wrapped donut holes to hand out to trick-or-treaters, as well as some traditional candy.

That morning the friends had all gone to a Halloween parade and had enjoyed the sights. There had been floats and fanatical costumes. Heather was happy to lean back and enjoy the show with her friends and family.

Eva and Leila had even said the parade had given them some inspiration for their costumes. Combined with the advice Lilly had given them when they babysat, they were sure they would have one-of-a-kind costumes.

"Lilly, are you all ready?" Heather called. "Tada!" Lilly said, entering the living room. "Or should I say roar?"

"You look wonderful," Heather said. "Just like an Apatosaurus."

"Well, my mom helped me make it," said Lilly. "And she's pretty awesome."

Lilly started lumbering around the room in her dinosaur costume. Two dinosaur legs were connected to her waist, along with a tail. Her torso acted as the Apatosaurus long neck, and she had a special hat to give her the properly shaped head. They weren't sure what color a dinosaur should actually be, so they selected pink as the color.

Heather heard someone at the door and let Eva and Leila inside.
"Careful," Leila said. "There seems to be a dinosaur on the loose."

"You look just like a dinosaur, dear," Eva said. "It's the perfect costume for you."

"Thank you," said Lilly. "I like yours a lot too. But, um, what are you?"

Eva and Leila broke into giggles.

"We decided to be something silly like Amy and Jamie were," said Leila.

"And after seeing the parade with all their floats and you telling us to choose something important to us, we decided that maybe we should represent Texas," said Eva.

"So, we are Texas Tea," announced Leila.

Heather and Lilly joined in the laughter after they understood the costume. The two women wore dresses that were reminiscent of teacups and had attached handles to themselves.
"All we need is a giant spoon," said Eva.

"A giant spoon?" Amy asked, poking her head inside the door. She and Jamie joined the group, dressed up as the rainy cat and dog again. "I hope it's to go with some giant food. Maybe some giant donuts?"

"You don't want to ruin your appetite," Heather said. "We're about to gain a ton of candy from our trick or treating."

"I know," said Amy. "But I think I'd still prefer the Pumpkin Donuts."
"Me too," Eva confessed.

"Fine," Heather said. "We can have some donuts. But don't eat everything. I'm going to need some treats to give away."

Her friends didn't need the offer repeated. They all grabbed a donut snack. Dave and Cupcake joined them in the room, convinced that if those in the dog and cat costume could have a donut, then they were entitled to them too.

"After this snack, are we all set to go trick or treating?" Eva asked.

"We're just waiting for Ryan," said Heather. "He said he had to get something from the store. I'm guessing it's more candy. He was preparing for you all to come and converge on my donuts."

"Can you blame us?" Amy asked.

Heather laughed.

"I do have a question for you," Amy said after she had finished her sweet pumpkin pastry. "What's with you get up?"

"It's my new costume," Heather said.
"You're not Sherlock anymore?" Jamie asked.

"No," Heather said. "Today I'm the Watson to Ryan's Sherlock. I have my new suit and tie, and my cane and a doctor's bag."

"I like it," Amy said. "But to me, you're always the master detective."
"And you two decided to stick with your costumes?" Heather asked.

"We have to now that we're award-winning," Jamie said. "Captain Braxton still found time to award his favorite costume at the end of the night."

"To be fair, we were the only ones who weren't in a repeating costume," said Amy.

"No. I think he liked it for its own merit," said Jamie. "We're the cat's meow."

They heard the door opening and Dave's happy barks.

"Ryan must be home," Heather said. "Are we all ready to get our treats?"

"Yes," said Amy. "But no more tricks."

"I don't think you're going to get what you're asking for," Jamie said quietly as Ryan entered the room.

"Sorry if I'm late," Ryan said. "I know trick-or-treating is very important, but I wanted to make sure that my new costume was perfect. And now I have a doctor's bag for my Dr. Watson costume."

"You're Dr. Watson?" Heather asked.

"You're Dr. Watson too?" Ryan said. They both started laughing.

"We're going to have to improve our costume coordinating," Ryan said. "No shoot, Sherlock," Heather said.

They all laughed.

"Should one of us change?" Ryan asked.

"I think it's all right," said Heather. "We can both be Sherlocks and Watsons. And I wouldn't want Lilly to miss any candy time. Not when she has such a great costume."

"Roar," said Lilly.

"Let's get going then," said Ryan. "Follow the dinosaur."

The friends followed Lilly out, ready to help her collect her candy. It was a wonderful evening, and Amy's wish came true. It was only full of treats.

**The End**

# A letter from the Author

**To each and every one of my Amazing readers:** *I hope you enjoyed this story as much as I enjoyed writing it. Let me know what you think by leaving a review!*

*Stay Curious,*

*Susan Gillard*

74944202R00413

Made in the USA
Lexington, KY
18 December 2017